DALLAS

The Wildflower Series 2

BY RACHELLE MILLS

DALLAS

Limitless Publishing, LLC
Kailua, HI 96734
www.limitlesspublishing.com

Formatting: Limitless Publishing

ISBN-13: 978-1-64034-516-4
ISBN-10: 1-64034-516-7

Dedication

To Scott, my everything

CHAPTER 1

Training A Wolf

The eerie cries of the wind lasted all night, swallowing everything up in a shroud of white. The blinding sheets of snow just kept falling and falling. Mother Nature did what she wanted all night long.

This morning everything looks peaceful and calm. Tree branches are curling down with the weight they are holding, but the trunk doesn't bend; it's still as straight as yesterday.

As I walk outside with the Alpha, the air seems clean and fresh, yet very cold. It's still out here, a hot fire crackling in the middle of the yard as if it's been waiting just for us. Big logs in various stages of burning are melting the outer edges of the snow line, pushing the white back to expose the dirt underneath.

One single chair has been set out just outside the heat of the fire.

Alpha Clinton takes the chair, sitting down, legs spread, thick forearms resting on each of the armrests. He looks me up and down, eyes gleaming with sharp teeth showing. He's provoking the Nature of the Wild with the way he's staring deliberately at her.

"Shift." A one-word command not spoken again. He must be used to people following everything he says.

Leaning slightly forward, he watches as the Wild ascends slowly, not smoothly, but not as horribly as the first time.

Hips realigning into their sockets, fur still feeling like a million sharp needles puncturing from inside out. Knives pushing out from fingernails, a drop of blood pollutes the pristine ground.

Shaking out her fur, stretching her muscles lazily, attention focused on everything but what's in front of her.

"Shift."

She turns her head away from him, unwilling to listen. Instead, she takes a step toward the forest that's calling out to be explored.

Eyes off of the male sitting calmly in the chair, turning her back on him, taking another step toward the woods.

That's her first mistake to take her eyes off of something that can spring faster than sound.

Her nose is pushed hard into the ground. He holds her there by the scruff of her neck, knee on her back so she has to have her belly against the ground. A deep growl comes out her chest, which produces a deep chuckle from the Silverback.

"This is going to be hard on you, *Little Moon*. Your wolf thinks she has balls." He holds her in her place until her squirming ceases, the growls die down. Her fur is saturated with melting snow from the heat her body is giving off.

He gets off of her, and she rights herself, facing him again. A posture of intent says she's not happy with the way she is handled. Again he's on her, but this time, it's much more painful. Nails dig into the scruff of her neck, his teeth barely out, just the tip of those long canines descending.

He picks her up easily, slamming her down on the snow. Somehow she's turned on her side, and his knee is placed just underneath her ribcage, angling up in her abdomen, making it hard to expand her lungs fully. His hand is still on the scruff of her neck, pressing her cheek into the ground.

She's splayed out before him, a dominant easily toying around with his plaything.

"Shift." He says it into her raised ear.

Teeth coming out more, he's making sure she sees what he's holding back from her.

"Shift." His voice deepens with vocal cords that are starting to shift into his Wild form. She fights him now, trying to wiggle out of his hold, teeth snapping at him. She does not like this position of being dominated.

He lets her go. She thinks she's won until he pulls his sweater over his head, exposing a tight white shirt that stretches over his muscular frame. She starts to back pedal away from him slowly as that shirt comes off his body.

She still stands tall, but apprehension starts humming along her spine, tensing her muscles to the core when he kicks off his boots, his pants sliding down thick thighs.

He's not an underwear-loving male.

We just saw his father in all his naked glory. We will never un-see that.

"Shift." It's said one last time. Instead of waiting to see if she will follow, he's on her quick.

Wolf's teeth are shaking her neck back and forth before letting go. He rolls her on her back, biting to draw just a touch of blood to her exposed underbelly, teeth press into flesh in her tendons of her joints, making her muscles tingle slightly with the pressure. He could have ended her so easily. He keeps biting along her body enough to cause discomfort, but not true pain.

She can't right herself, unable to get up with his onslaught of teeth.

He comes to her neck, putting the whole thing in his strong jaws. Vibrating her body with his growls, she stills in his grip like a limp doll.

This is not a learned trait; this is the pure instinct of self-preservation to become docile at this moment.

The first law he is teaching her is about *hierarchy*: he's the top of the food chain, only listening to the will of the moon herself.

He holds her hard until her tail starts to curl under, crouching low on the ground, belly fur wet with the snow that's clinging to it, knotting it up on the underside.

With a snarling glare, he releases her from his death grip, only to come back again and attack her over and over and over again until she is crouched down as small as she can make herself, ears pressed flat against her head, whimpering, with a tail that curls around her body. Blood speckles the snow as if someone has flung a paintbrush out, polluting the white canvas that was so pristine just an hour ago.

Sitting on his haunches, he just stares into the Wild's eyes until she looks away at the snow, eyes going to his again. He's still staring; she looks away again. This continues with her unable to hold his glare.

Law number one: *He's the Alpha.*

Shifting, he starts to dress. With his back turned to her, he calmly instructs her to do what he wants.

"Shift."

Immediately, she shifts slowly into skin form, still not a pretty sight. Doing up his pants, he turns around as I'm shivering in the snow trying to turn my nakedness away from him.

"Shift." A long groan comes out my mouth as muscles realign, tearing, popping, fitting into place.

"Shift." He pulls his tight shirt down over his chest. Reaching for his sweater, he dusts the snow off of it before putting it on.

"Shift." Sitting in his chair, he just watches me.

"Shift." He starts to put his socks on along with his boots.

"Shift."

The Wild's head angles up with a loud whimper coming out her throat. Whining for this to stop.

She's splayed out before him, a dominant easily toying around with his play thing.

"Shift." He says it into her raised ear.

Teeth coming out more, he's making sure she

sees what he's holding back from her. His war of white teeth.

The Wild's head angles up with a loud whimper coming out her throat. Whining for this to stop.

"Shift."

It's as if he's sitting at the potter's wheel, throwing the clay down, releasing it, refining it into what his vision is of the final product. I just hope that I don't break in his hands before he's done with me.

"Shift."

The day is spent with one word in our ears, cracking the cocoon of skin to fur back to skin.

He doesn't let up, that one-word tempo becoming faster and faster.

Stunned with my loss of focus, colors shift in and out of eyes of the Wild and skin. I sigh as I grope the ground, trying to hold myself in place. I just can't as I shift over and over again until the night bleeds into the day, taking away all the light.

By the time Luna Grace yells out the door to come and eat, I can shift effortlessly, in shimmering smoothness that all full-grown wolves can do. I have no more awkwardness to my shift. I must have done it thousands of time throughout the day.

In the same breath, he says shift twice and I do before he can inhale another breath.

His eyebrows raise at what I have just done.

"You're the first female I have ever seen be able to do that." He's excited by this, as if this is what he has been waiting to see.

"Come, my Little Moon, let's eat." Walking behind him, my legs are shaking so much I have a hard time keeping upright. He hands me a colorful robe from the hook. My fingers feel numb trying to tie up the knot to secure the garment on me.

What must I look like to them as I take my place on the Luna's left? Kennedy remains in front of me. Her plates have been filled, stacked up high.

I notice the way her body slightly angles Cash's way. Her nose inhaling deeply, she tries to hide the way her eyes close slightly in pleasure. It's as if she's eating the roll I gave her the way his smell affects her with pleasure.

No one else's plate has food on it. My stomach clenches in hunger.

I can actually feel the saliva pooling at the back of my throat.

"Let's eat." He says it fast as hands start to grab platters, filling their plates high. The Luna gives a small growl at all her males as she takes her own portion. The Alpha doesn't need to growl as big paws swipe what he wants.

It's whirlwind fast how the food disappears; one piece of bread is left. I go to reach for it, but before I have time, it's snatched away by Crane, his grinning mouth bites into it fast, laughing silently at me.

Nothing is left.

"If you don't believe you should eat, you never will eat," Alpha Clinton says between bites of mashed potatoes. I look at Kennedy's overflowing plate and I hate her in this moment, yet I understand her need for it.

Yet she didn't take anything; it was all given to her. I wonder, if her body doesn't hold the future it's preparing for, will they always just give her food?

No one shares what they have with me. My plate lays untouched. Ready to be put back in the cupboard without being washed.

"Are you hungry, Rya?" The Luna is leaning toward me with compassion in her eyes.

"Yes."

"Well, maybe next time when you sit at our table, you'll be hungry enough to try and eat. You should go and try to get some sleep tonight. It's going to be an early morning for you." She dismisses me, yet I don't move right away. I can hear them eating, forks shoveling food that I didn't try for.

I realize I'm just sitting looking at my empty plate.

I don't want to go through the rest of my life clenching my jaw with gritted teeth. Lips in a straight line. I want to stop the pain in my lungs that repress the need to scream out. I don't want to feel crippled with my need to bend my tail constantly for others.

"You should just quit now, Rya." Cash's voice irritates my skin with the way he speaks to me.

"No female has ever lasted out there, let alone in the winter time. You're going to fail like you failed over and over again. It's like you were born to be a loser." Kennedy chokes on her food, looking at Cash in disbelief.

Everyone around the table puts their forks down as if waiting, watching for the next move.

What do I say back to him? He's right.

Standing up, I turn away from them all, making my way upstairs with my shoulders hunched.

"That's what I thought. You're wasting your time on her, Father." Harsh words tumble out of his mouth. I just hope one day his tongue tastes bad with the way he might have to eat them.

"We feel the exact same way about you, Cash." Big eyes all around look at Cash for his response. His mouth tries to move, but he has nothing to say.

"What?" I say it quietly, directing it at Cash, my body turning his way.

"I didn't say anything." That voice of his that held such a terrible tone has become a little shaky with what his father just said to him.

"I thought you said something. I was wrong." So much for his prideful effort.

"She has a tongue." It's Carson who blurts the words out before laughing at Cash. They look so much like each other, except one is growing his hair out and one has a shaved head.

"Don't pay him any mind, Rya. He's just upset that he's been saving himself for that." Carson's turn to hit him in the face with his words.

Cash tries to lunge for his brother across the table, but the Alpha stands up as his fists pound against the strong wood. How many blows has that table taken in its lifetime?

"How many times do I have to say it? Not in the house. Outside, all of you." He sits back down as the rest of the males get up, making their way outside to finish their conversation of fists.

"Rya, would you like to watch them, maybe learn something?" Luna Grace continues to eat her food, along with Kennedy, whose hair is now shielding the side of her face with how her new family feels about her.

I just walk away from them into the room I'm now calling home.

Picking up the paper that fell to the floor from last night, I place it on the pile of other crumpled papers. I look through the stack as if they have been crumpled up over and over again only to be smoothed out, never again coming back to their original form.

His acceptance letter to medical school, the contract of him coming to my pack. Legal terms that I can't understand. Money, he was paid a lot of money to come. More than I would make my entire life working as a midwife, and I get paid very well.

The terms of him finding a mate and how he gets to bring her back with him.

Another paper shows a house deed in his name and his mate's, Maysa. That's her name, and it's beautiful. She's the same age as him, birth dates only a month apart. He was born in the spring in the season of new beginnings. Clayton was born in the weaning month of March.

A black and white sketch of his face draws my attention to his eyes. They are sparkling even in the greyness of a charcoal pencil tip.

I wonder who drew this? I bet it was his true mate. She was very talented, an artist—that's hard to compete against. Natural talent. I bet she was able to eat at their table, unlike me.

The next image takes my breath away. It's a grainy black and white ultrasound picture. I can read it easily, a big healthy male. Nothing wrong at all with this pup, who looks to be growing perfectly in a little nest made just for him.

He must be around six months in gestation by the measurements on the side of the sheet.

A soft cry wants to bubble its way up my throat. It's his pup; I can feel it in my heart.

Picking up the phone, I call him again. He answers immediately, as if he's been waiting all day for this phone call.

"Hello." The deepness of his voice settles over my skin. It's amazing that the mark of his Wild allows me to feel him on my body.

I want to ask him, but my mouth refuses to open with its probing questions.

"Rya?"

Big breath in and out.

"I found the ultrasound picture."

Silence, except for his intake of breath.

"This is hard for me, Rya."

"I can't even imagine what you have been through, Dallas." The truth of what he has had to endure makes my life not as bad. So what if I got rejected by my mate? His has died with a pup inside her belly. How do you go on from that? I can understand now why he tried to give up on his life.

"It's not easy to move on from that." His voice cracks.

"Dallas, I'm so sorry."

"It happened. I had a mate, a pup on the way, and they died. I couldn't save them, so I decided to save others."

"You're a good doctor, Dallas."

11

"What did you do today?" His change of subject tells me the conversation needs to be changed.

"I shifted all day long."

"I remember he did that to me when I first had my shift. That hurt so bad. How do you feel?"

"Shaky, my legs feel like Jell-O."

"Mine were the same way, Rya." A slight laugh out from him with his memory that's not focused on his loss.

"Can I ask you something?"

"Anything, no matter what."

"Why does Cash hate me so much?"

"He's just upset at the wrong wolf, Rya. He thinks that you quit. We were raised never to give up on something we wanted. I think he feels like you just rolled over without a fight. I tried talking to him about it, but he's got it in his mind that you could have done more, that you gave up, and he told me that you will give up on me too. I think that's what he's scared of most—that you will give up on us."

"Dallas, I was whipped, shunned. I couldn't even eat with my parents for years."

"You don't need to tell me this, Rya. I can't even imagine how your life was like."

"Is it true he saved himself for Kennedy?"

A heavy sigh comes out his mouth.

"Yes, he had this image of a mate in his head, and he never strayed in his belief that when he found her, it would be worth not having anyone else underneath him."

"Did you save yourself for your mate?"

"No. I'd had a few females before her. She's not

my first, Rya." He sounds slightly disappointed in himself.

I'm slightly shocked by his revelation.

"Were you her first?" I wonder how she felt not being a first.

"No, I was not her first."

"Really?" I'm stunned; they were young when they met.

A knock at my door has my eyes looking into Kennedy's.

"I need to go. I'll call you tomorrow. Bye, Dallas."

"Bye, Rya."

"Why are you in my room?"

Leaning against the door frame, she looks at me with pleading eyes.

"I need you to help me. I need you to get me something so I can get rid of it if I become pregnant."

She's leaking an ocean of salt tears that I have no intention to provide comfort for.

"I can't have a pup, I can't." Her layers are peeling back like sheets of pastry dough. They look fragile and easy to tear, except I don't care.

"I can't help you. I have no access to their clinic. You need to ask Cash or the Luna about this. It's none of my business what you and your mate decide. Now get out." As she turns around, she comes face to face with Cash, who must have heard the whole conversation.

He has a bruise on his jaw but otherwise no other marks to say he was just fighting.

"How could you even think of doing something

like that?" His whole body posture tells me how hurt he is at hearing her words.

She says nothing back to him.

"Don't worry, if you get pregnant I'll raise that pup myself. You can go back to your pack, back to him. But I won't let you ruin this possible future I might have, my only chance to have something good." In this moment, I see his fight leave him; all the effort he was willing to put into her has gone away. There's no more light in his eyes. He's given up.

"Get out." Revulsion coils itself deep within me as I look at a female that I envied. I wanted to be like her, to mirror her so that I was wanted by him. She is someone I would never want to be like. An ugliness has settled over her once beautiful features in my mind.

It feels like I just closed my eyes before my name is called to wake up.

"Rya, get dressed. It's time to go." Alpha Clinton's voice is sliding up the steps to touch my ears.

I slip on something that I really don't like just in case I ruin it with a shift. My muscles are feeling so much better.

The Luna and Alpha are the only ones up this early in the morning, greeting me with heart smiles.

"Come on, Rya, it's a long way. I want to be back before dark today." He's giving me gloves and hat while he is in a snowsuit.

Before leaving, he picks up his Luna in his arms, pressing a lingering kiss to her mouth, which she enjoys. They have a strong bond, I can see this, and it makes my heart want that kind of love.

***

It was a long ride through giant snow drifts, with only a small path in the bush for the snowmobile to roar down. No four wheel drive could possibly get through this.

Holding onto the side of this male, I asked him where we were going, and he just replied that it's time for me to learn how to eat.

By the time we stop, my whole body is freezing. He takes away my hat and mitts.

I can hear some fighting in the distance between wolves; it sounds like they are attacking each other.

Walking toward the noise in the deep snow, my pants and shoes are wet up to my knees. A bitter cold is slowly letting me know that I have to get warm soon. The skin side could never survive too long in this weather.

Walking into the clearing, I see a fresh kill that the wolves are devouring. The site is stained in blood, muzzles dripping in the crimson life that the moose has provided them.

"You'll have to learn to fight for your place in the pack, or else you'll have no place. Just remember, if you believe you can eat, you will eat. If you don't believe in yourself, you will starve." He starts to walk away from me as I start to follow him.

"No, Rya, you're going to stay out here for a while. I'll come get you when they think you're ready."

"I can't live out here."

"You don't have to. Your Wild has to do all the work. When she has put her effort in and learns how to be part of the pack, then I'll come and get you so your skin side can start the work it needs."

The sharpness of authority in his tone leaves no room for argument.

"You should shift soon so you don't freeze out here. I'll see you soon. Just remember watch, listen, learn."

I can hear the start of the snowmobile, its engine roaring to life while I just stand in place contemplating what to do next.

The Wild inside me is excited by all of this, her dreams of the wild coming true. Except she isn't as wild as she thinks she is.

Shifting, the Wild slowly makes her way toward the pack, one brave step at a time.

She gives them her signs of peaceful friendship, tail wagging, tongue hanging out slightly. She's cautious but hopeful.

Grey fur bodies turn toward her as they lift their noses to take in the scent. Their muzzles are stained in blood that my wolf wants to taste.

They meet her signs of peace with their language of war. Large canines exposed with the curl of lip, noses scrunched tight. Ears flattened, not in submission. Shoulder muscles twitching excitedly to jump. Tails straight out. My Wild is watching all this posturing as she starts to give her own snarl back to them. If they want war, she can do exactly what they are doing. Stiff leg stance, her snarl of menace is just as fierce. This won't be an easy fight, she's telling them as she flashes her war of sharp white teeth.

She's taking all of them into her brain, trying to memorize who they are as she lifts a nose to smell scents in the air.

A large male approaches, more ferocious than the others. A female on his right, her head angling underneath his neck every so often. Paws turning up the snow, grey fur stained in blood. They both have eaten their fill with the way their stomachs are bloated out.

This is the most hostile environment we have ever been in.

She crouches down instead of holding her form high. The alpha has taught her that lesson of *hierarchy.* Do not challenge a wolf you can't beat.

The closer the pair gets, the more she starts to panic slightly. They smell wild, full of the savage nature they come from. I notice a few scents of others like me, but they pay the wolf no mind, concentrating on eating the fresh kill.

The leading pair approach cautiously, eyes regarding a new female that wants to enter the pack. The male putting his nose up against the fur, running it down the side until it's pressed firmly underneath the Wild's tail, taking her scent into his nose.

The female leader does the same thing, having a good sniff of the female parts. Both of them give another snarl but don't abuse us in any way.

The Wild takes it as a cue that it's okay to approach the kill sight. All heads turn her way in a wall of snarl and fang, which has her backing up, away from the threat. She's hungry and wants what they have. The only problem is they are also hungry, and they earned that right to eat.

The first wolf rushes us, biting into our shoulder once we get too close for their liking. They will not share, and their teeth hurt when they bite.

It's a long night of watching them eat pound after pound of flesh. Once all members of the pack have eaten, the Wild takes her chance, tearing into what remains, nothing but bone and a few pieces of meat clinging to the edges.

It's not enough to satisfy the hunger.

Another day turns to three and nothing has been eaten. The pads of the Wild's feet are bruised and bleeding with the way the snow freezes to it, cutting into the skin. The fur looks rough and mangled.

The Wild is welcomed in the pack but only on the edge, the *periphery*.

She spends the days watching the juveniles practice pouncing on the mice in the deep snow. The Wild puts her muzzle on the trail like they do, sniffing out their hiding places—finally figuring it out and relishing in the crunch of our first real kill.

It doesn't take long for the mouse population to suffer underneath her jaws. These little bites have sustained her throughout the long weeks.

The pack refuses to let her hunt the big game with them, only allowing her to watch on the sidelines.

Days and nights slowly go by as she learns from these wolves how to be a wolf. It's not all teeth and claws, it's licking, rubbing up against each other, it's family looking out for one another. It's companionship that makes her heart happy and mine.

Listening to their language, it's beautiful songs they sing at night to the moon. She even sings and no one is there to laugh at her. She is free to be who she is—a wild wolf.

Blizzards roll in, ice storms entombing the trees in clear sheets of crystal.

I'm really not sure how long I've been out here, but I know the way the moon was on the first night out here. The Wild has lost a lot of weight, but she's still surviving.

All the while she learns to start hunting with the pack. At first, they only let her observe, but today they are having her join them. No longer the juvenile that gets too excited by moving things, she understand that this is for survival.

She has to eat; it's not an option anymore.

The hunt takes her over miles of terrain, slowly wearing down the bull moose through deep snow. She watches as the wolves circle it, doing her part to close in, tightening around the moose until it faces the oncoming assault of teeth, nipping at its hooves and legs.

It has no chance now, its life just a memory as the alpha wolf grabs its throat, crushing it in its jaws.

Once it's dead, it's a viciously controlled order of things, hierarchy playing its role. The Wild isn't at the top, but she won't eat last either.

After some time, she gets the courage to approach the growls and snapping jaws, taking a few bites in the process, crawling belly low toward the goal. Sinking sharp teeth into the fresh blood-soaked meat, the Wild becomes drunk on its flavor. Her growls are just as furious as theirs. The Wild never tasted anything this good. Bite after bite she fills her stomach, and when she thinks nothing can be eaten anymore, she still continues to gorge until almost sick.

After the successful hunt, it's a lot of grooming each other, licking, smelling, and playing. They teach her how to play fight, nipping softly until she can hold her own against any one of them, including the Luna female. She is no match now for the Wild, who loves to sneak attack her.

Another phase of the moon passes, and that makes four months I have been left out here to be raised by the wild wolves of Valentine. Part of me doesn't want to go back. It wants to stay where everything is simple and easy.

That's why when my name is called, she deliberately runs away from the noise. Except the pack now tightens its noose around her, pushing her back toward the sound. Now it's the Wild's fangs they meet as she puts effort into not going back to a reality that has only brought pain and suffering to her. To me.

Those wolves return the bites until the pack's teeth are all against her. Whimpering, crying out to them, her wolf song pleads to stay with the pack, but they reject it, still pushing her toward the voices and heavy footsteps that crunch the snow loudly for ears to twitch against.

"Rya." That Silverback male is standing there with a collar in his hand. His males are flanking his side. It's as if they know that she's going to put up a fight.

"Rya, come. Let's go back home. This is not your home. You don't belong with them." His voice is strange against ears that have only had the animals to talk with.

Whimpering again, she backpedals, only to get teeth sunk into her haunches.

His sons start to spread out, trying to form a circle around the Wild, as if she's their prey getting caught in their web.

They close the noose tighter, hands spread out, looking bigger than they are. The hair lifts on the ridge of spine as she puffs herself out as best as she can.

"Dad, look at her eyes," Carson's voice raises. Looking around at the options, the Wild decides to take on the weakest male, try to drive through that line. They must have known that would happen, because the Alpha steps in front of Crane fast as she tries to knock him down.

With a grab to the scruff, he's holding her down, except he has to put his whole effort into not getting his fingers taken off.

The Wild has spent four months getting stronger, fighting with other wolves, running, hunting, using the body the way it should be used. She is powerful in her own way.

His jaw clenches with his effort to try to lock the collar into place. Once he does this, he attaches the steel chain. A muzzle goes over her mouth, leather straps binding tight to keep teeth from inflicting damage.

She cries the wild wolf cry while being dragged away from the pack that she has come to think of as family. They whimper and cry back but don't move to help.

A long rope is tied to the sled the Alpha is on. He runs her the whole way home. It's not as difficult as it seems...her stamina has greatly improved.

The Wild tries to break the binding, but it's just too strong, the sled too powerful for her to try and overtake.

The Wild cries the whole way back, her mournful song hurting even the males that are dragging her back.

Once back to the house, the collar is taken off. The muzzle is last, and all of them stand on the balls of their feet, ready if attacked.

Luna Grace comes out carrying a silk robe for me.

"If you attack her, I will end you," the Alpha states to the Wild.

"Rya, come inside. Dinner's ready." My ears perk up.

"Shift." Alpha Clinton's hard voice hurts my sensitive ears.

I do as I'm told, and the robe is wrapped around me, protecting my modesty.

It hurts to shift back, but I don't let on. I want to talk; it's just that I can't seem to find words.

Everything seems so strange walking upright on two legs.

"You are the first female to make it through a winter with the Wilds of Valentine. The whole pack is excited to meet you, Rya. We can't be prouder." She squeezes my shoulder with her hand. I push my face into hers, cheek against cheek, rubbing myself against her.

She has her fingers in my hair, pulling me against her chest. I can't stop showing her my love, with gentle bites and nibbles to her skin. If humans were to see this, they would think I am just not right. But to wolves, this is how we show we care about them, how we love them.

The food's laid out just like before. Looking toward Kennedy, she has nothing on her plate but a variety of fruits. She's pale and looking as if she has lost some weight. Taking a deep breath in, the future inside her is growing strong. Angling my head to the side, I can even faintly hear it's heartbeat.

Cash is sitting on his father's left; his head is shaved again. Not one stray hair on his head.

"You can have everything on the table except the fruit. It's for Kennedy. She can't stomach anything else," the Luna says gently.

"You should drink ginger tea." Words are thick in my mouth. "It will help your nausea." Luna Grace pats my hand.

"You're very kind, Rya. I will get her some in the morning."

"Let's eat," The Alpha calls out. This time, I take everything that is offered.

My growls are just as deep as the males sitting at the table. Gripping the platters of food, I take what I can. Fight for every bite. Kennedy looks at me as if she's seeing a stranger. I growl her way, lifting teeth that are meant to intimidate.

"Rya." A warning from the Alpha has me shoveling my meal into my mouth without dignity.

"Tomorrow is another early day for you. It's the skins' turn to start training, and I have the perfect sparring partner for you." I keep eating, elbows on the table, protecting my meal.

"Who?" I say between mouthfuls.

"Cash. He's going to help you train." Both Cash and I look at him like he's lost his mind.

"It's about time the two of you fought it out." Cash has a feral smile, and I give him mine back.

CHAPTER 2

Effort

Quiet indifference greets me when I walk into his room.

The ceiling fan blows cool air on my neck and somehow finds its way to my chest from the little gap in my robe. I don't hear the constant communication of the pack. The noise is humming, man-made. It's not true nature's music that I can understand.

I want to go back. Taking a step out of the room, I think if I make a run for it, they might not be able to catch me.

I'm very fast now.

I take the first step down, and Cash takes the first step up. Both of us stop and regard each other. I take another step down; he takes two steps up. I take two steps down, he takes another two up, neither of us giving way to the other.

Meeting in the middle, I'm just slightly taller than him because I'm on the upper step and he's standing below me. Does that irk him right now that I'm above him, looking down?

"You won't be able to get out, if that's what you're thinking." He says it like he knows what I'm about to do, a look shadowing his face.

"My oldest brother had to be dragged back at least three times before he finally stayed home. My father had his hands full with him. He even had to call my grandfather to help track him." I try to step around him; his hands go on both railings, blocking my path.

"Why don't you just turn around? I'm not in the mood right now," Cash says with tired eyes, as if he hasn't been sleeping well. He looks like he's bulked up slightly, hormones of his mate's heat and subsequent pregnancy making him more chiseled, with firmer muscle tone. His aggression level should be climbing more and more as Kennedy can't shift, unable to protect herself from any threats that might come her way. The moon provides a natural testosterone-induced bodyguard for her females at this vulnerable time.

I grab onto the railings with both of my hands blocking his way up.

He leans into me, touching his chest against mine. Lips close to my ears, he says, "Just because you made it out there doesn't mean—"

"Excuse me." Kennedy's standing behind Cash, wanting to pass by the both of us.

We both concede to her, letting the female pass by. It's as if our aggression dissipates as she carefully slips past.

I can see she accidentally brushes against Cash,

reminding me of the way the female leader wolf of the pack showed her affection for the leader male, but Kennedy somehow made it look like it was by accident. It wasn't; I can tell the difference. I watch her lean in slightly, smelling him. He angles away, looking everywhere else except her way.

When she goes by me, her shoulders slightly curl forward, the faintest of movements, but I can see now. I notice the language of wolves. No sound, but big bold statements are being made right now. Her scent is of life, motherhood.

"I'm taking a shower. You can have one after I'm done." He's talking to Kennedy as he follows the gap that Kennedy left from my hand being taken off the railing. His shoulder hits mine, shade thrown my way.

"Rya, I'll see you in the morning. Wear something that you don't mind getting your blood on." There is harmful intent in his tone, looking me in the eyes before he goes into the bathroom.

Walking back into the bedroom, I notice the way ice still clings to the windows. Winter's icy grip still hasn't broken its hold on the land yet, their winter lasting a few weeks longer than my birth pack's.

Everything is how I left it, except the bed is made, nice and tidy. A present sits on the desk by my phone. I smile slightly to myself as I look at it, giddy at getting a present.

I pull out a thick cookbook; the title is *The Carnivore's Guide to Meat*.

I open up the white envelope. Dallas's handwriting is scratchy, but it looks like he's trying to be legible.

I saw this and thought of you, my meat eater!

Congratulations.

I miss you

XO

Dallas

I feel like twirling again with a happy smile. I like his humor.

Opening the book, I like that the pictures are matte and not shiny and glossy. You get a better feel for the meal. Sometimes I think that instead of fairy tale books that little girls get about a princess meeting a prince and living happily ever after, they should get cookbooks.

Cookbooks can tell the history of the family, of regions, of culture, of religions, of how to get through the lean times. Not an illusion of make believe with a glass slipper that fits the right person and boom, your prince will love you forever, because that's not real.

Picking up the phone, I go into the bathroom and turn on the tap. The water sputters out just for a moment before it bursts out full of power. Someone has lined the counter with shampoos and conditioners, body wash, toothpaste, toothbrushes, everything a female needs.

Looking around, I see no towel, so I step out of my room, watching Cash leave the bathroom he was in with a towel wrapped around his waist. Little beads of water still cling to his bald head. As soon as his door closes, I watch Kennedy slink out quietly, going into the bathroom and quickly returning with the shirt Cash was wearing. She has it to her nose before shutting the door behind her.

She's probably feeling the extreme need to have her mate by her side while pregnant, her compulsions getting the better of her, stealing his dirty clothes to satisfy her internal needs.

Getting a few spare towels, I close my door, locking it behind me.

Steam starts to rise up, surrounding me like a warm blanket. Stepping in, I let the water pool over my ankles. It's slowly rising up, getting deeper. I sit down, pressing my back against the cold back of the tub. It's a conflicting feeling. I have hot water soaking into my bones, but the cold porcelain against my back has me gasping with cold.

It feels weird not having fur covering my body.

I must stink of wild musky wolves. How did they stand my offensive smell at dinner time?

The water is now up to my chest, relaxing me as I take a deep breath, the ends of my hair soaking wet, floating at my sides. Turning off the water, I turn my phone on. Noticing my messages are full, I place the call first before listening to them.

He picks up before the first ring ends.

"Rya." My skin shivers with the way he says my name. I feel a rush of nervousness, and I don't know why.

"Dallas." I watch as my toes peek out of the water, resting on the edge of the tub opposite me.

"My meat eater. I'm proud of you, Rya. I knew you could do it, and in the winter. First female to

29

ever do that!" Pride, that's the tone of his voice. It feels good to have someone have pride in me.

"Thanks, Dallas."

"How do you feel?" I can sense a smile in his voice.

"I feel weird. It feels different. Like I can see things clearer. I notice little things more. I can hear better without words. Does that even make sense?"

"I felt the same way when I came back. I had a hard time staying home. I kept running away from my house back with the wild wolves, drove my father crazy. He sent my grandfather the last time to get me, and I never ran away again. But I understand the pull to stay out there. After the accident, I thought I could go back out there and live out my life with them."

"I feel the same way. It was amazing. I was so scared at first, and I really didn't even know anything, but I watched them and studied and practiced. Finally, I was able to hunt with them and really feel as if I was part of a pack for the first time in my life." A hint of sadness that I didn't want to expose utters out with the last few words I say.

"That makes me angry, Rya. I just don't understand that. I can't comprehend how awful your juvenile years were. Trust me when I say this: you are part of the pack now. Never will you ever be treated that way again, ever!" A ferocity in his tone has a raw growl slipping out his chest. I understand that noise; it's one of warning to be afraid of what that wolf intends.

"Rya, I miss you. I just want you to know that." That makes me smile, that someone actually misses me. Not like last time, as everyone couldn't wait for me to be gone away from the pack. Out of sight, out of mind.

I miss him. That's the thought that grips me. I miss him.

"I miss you too. How long do you think I'm going to be staying here?" I'm really curious as how long my training might be.

"Who did my dad say was your trainer?"

"Cash." Dallas is laughing into the phone.

"My dad has Cash training you?"

"Yes."

"The training usually ends when you can beat your trainer." I take a deep breath in.

"What happens if I can't beat him?"

"My father would never put you against someone he doesn't think you can beat. It just takes time. Remember, he's third born, not first or second. He's strong, but you were made to be a Luna. You're naturally stronger than him. You have to believe in yourself. Remember to watch, listen, and learn. He has weaknesses. You have to find them and exploit them. I think once you're trained, you might even beat Caleb, or at least give him a good go."

"I wish I can believe that. He looks like he wants to eat me."

"Cash doesn't want to eat you. If he did, you would already be dead. He's just being a jerk right now, but I think once he gets to know you, he'll change his mind about you. I think once you get to know him, you might see him differently." His voice holds a conviction that I don't feel.

"Maybe." I'm not convinced at all.

A commotion in the background has his attention off of our conversation.

"Rya, I have to go. Call me tomorrow, okay?" I hear a hard groan of pain in the background from a female. It sounds like Kimberly's voice; I can hear a male's voice, asking for help. It's Clayton's voice, sounding panicked.

"Is that Kimberly's voice?"

"Yes, I have to go." He hangs the phone up, leaving me with a feeling of dread.

The water's becoming lukewarm as I play the sounds of her groan over and over in my mind while looking at my phone.

I have a full mailbox of voice messages. Putting the phone up to my ear, I hear Dallas on the other line.

"First day away, I can only imagine what you're thinking. I can tell you what I'm thinking about. It's you." The message finishes.

The next one is him saying, "It's the second day away and they tell me you made it the night without having to be dragged back to the pack. Good job. The first night with the wolves is the hardest."

"Third day away, Rya, heard you caught your first mouse by yourself. That's my female. Hard work, isn't it?" I laugh at how proud he is of me. How does he know all this?

I keep listening to his messages, day five going into twelve, turning into day twenty-five, to day forty-two. He's been leaving me messages every single day.

I'm lying in my bed now with the covers to my

chin, ready to fall asleep. He knows everything that I have been going through, all the little accomplishments and setbacks that I am having out there.

He told me in one of his messages that his father or mother is keeping him updated. They have spotters out there just in case I ran into trouble. I never saw anyone else out there, just the wolves. He said that there is a failsafe that if it looked like I really couldn't cut it, they would have rescued me before death took me. I feel kind of happy knowing at least I wouldn't have died out there.

The next message has me dropping the phone.

"Rya," It's one word that has my whole body responding to the tenor of it, my body's traitorous response to my mate.

"Don't delete this, but I understand if you do. I'd delete myself too, if I could." I can hear the way his lungs fill with air and the way he exhales it out.

"I had this whole speech written out." He takes a long sigh before I hear crumpling paper. I think he must have tossed it because I hear it hitting something, maybe the wall?

"Sorry—is that what you want to hear? It's not good enough. I can say sorry a thousand times and it's just not good enough for what I have done to you." His voice makes me cringe slightly; it's clenching my jaw, curling my shoulders in.

"I think I should start at the beginning when I figured out you were my mate, tell you my story. It's not going to be a good story, Rya. It's not going to be one of those fairy tales that you females like to read about. I've had a lot of time to think about

33

things, to think how I should have done things differently." Sitting up in bed, my hands are shaking, I'm shaking. I think I should delete his messages. I can't stand to hear his voice because it does things to me. Makes me long for him at the same time it makes me want to end him. The message ends; his time's up.

I click to the next message.

"Rya, heard you caught your first winter rabbit—who's the beast? You're the beast of the woods." Dallas is laughing in joy for me.

I click to the next message.

"Where was I, Rya? Oh yeah...how I found out you were my mate." Clayton's voice holds no tone. It's just him telling a story to someone who shouldn't be listening.

"Kennedy had a soccer game. She was a few years older than you. I was going to watch her play. While I was sitting there, your team was just finishing up. You scored the final goal, winning by one. This smile was on your face when you were celebrating with all your friends, jumping up and down, and our eyes connected for just a split second and I knew. It took my breath away. I couldn't stop watching you. Your parents were there, I think your sisters. You were really good for a pre-juvenile." I can tell he's smiling slightly with the way his voice now sounds happy with a memory.

"I watched as you ran to your parents, giving you hugs. I thought what a nice family you must have. I just sat there trying to breathe. Then Kennedy walked up to me with her beautiful smile, kissing me on the lips, asking what the matter was, and I told her *nothing*. I turned around and walked away from you and your celebration, knowing who you were to me. Thinking back on that scene, what sticks out in my mind is that your smile was even more beautiful than hers if only I would have looked closer at you." The message ends again; *his time's up*.

Clicking again on the next message, Dallas is excited about me learning to play fight, not sleeping at the edge of the pack anymore. Making friends on my own and them liking me. I can hear the slight emotion for a fraction of a second in his voice before he gives a little cough, saying how proud he is of me.

A few more messages from Dallas before Clayton's voice has my heart squeezing tight.

"I kept seeing you everywhere, Rya. You and your friends hanging out here and there. I had this fascination with looking at you, but you were this little thing with no hips, no chest, you weren't developed at all. You were a little pup, and I couldn't have thoughts about you like that. It just wasn't right. So I watched you. You started high school the next year; I knew you were getting close to shifting by the way your hips started to become rounder, the way you needed to start wearing a bra. I noticed every change in your body. I noticed the way you were growing into your face. I noticed how you were really good at all the sports you played, how you had many friends, how when you came into the room, you shined with confidence. You always walked with your shoulders straight and head up. That type of confidence you just have in you, it's not learned. Always a smile on your face. I noticed all the hair styles you went through. Do you know that I can't remember any of Kennedy's hairstyles, not one? I'm sure she had many, but thinking back, all I can remember is your style." He sounds sad about this.

More messages from Dallas, with such pride in his voice. Everything I'm going through documented in his messages to me.

"Rya, you're probably wondering how I got your number. Well, I stole it off my mother's desk a few years back. I never called you, but for some reason, I wanted your number." He hangs up this time, not allowing the time to run out.

Dallas's voice comes over the phone. "I delivered a male today, mom and pup doing good. I don't think I can do that again." His voice sounds slightly slurred as if he's been drinking.

Clayton's voice is in the next message. "Rya, where was I? Oh yes. I had to sit through assemblies at school and watch you up on stage because you're part of this play or doing something with the student council. Thinking back all this time, Kennedy never participated in anything like that, she never led, but you did. You organized, got involved. You were a naturally good leader, perfect Luna material." His voice sounds melancholy before he ends the call.

It's getting late, I should put the phone down and go to sleep, but I just can't. I tell myself just one more message and I'm going to go to bed.

"Clayton is up and walking around now, Rya. I thought you should know. I don't want to keep anything from you. Kimberly's pregnancy is going all right. She is still very low in her measurement, and her weight really isn't improving. I'm having Aurora talk with her. Maybe that's what she needs." Dallas sounds lost slightly on how to handle the pregnant female.

Another message has Clayton's deep voice coming over the speaker.

"When I told Kennedy about you, she was mad at the fact that I kept a secret from her for so long, then that I found my mate. I don't think she thought you were a real threat to us. You seemed weaker than her." His words are like acid that eats away at my skin as my heart tightens. Not a threat, I kicked her ass that day; if Clayton wasn't there, I would have ended her. I know it, deep down. I would have taken a life.

"I couldn't stop watching you, but I never did anything about it. I let you live your life and I lived mine. Until that day when you came up to me, with this face that had so much hope in it. I remember what you were wearing, jean shorts, a red tank top, flip-flops, your hair down. You must have just gotten it cut because it was just past your shoulders. I like it long on you. Looking back on that day, I can't remember what Kennedy was wearing. You wanted to talk with me alone. I think you really expected me to do that. *I didn't.*"

I'm crying now, big fat tears as my breath burns the back of my throat.

"It was hard for me to watch you beg like that, plead with me, grab onto my legs just asking for a chance. Your juvenile voice crying out in pain, my wolf was going nuts inside me. But I didn't give you that chance, did I? I didn't give you the only thing you have ever asked of me, just a chance. You never asked me to love you; all you asked for was a small chance. I didn't give you that!" His voice cracks and breaks along with mine.

The next message is Dallas and Caleb yelling into it with excitement…both happy males at the fact I actually ate with the pack, took my share of the moose. "Meat eater," they are screaming; I think they are slightly drunk in celebration.

The next one is Clayton's voice I hear.

"I watched your face when you were getting whipped. Your eyes never left mine until the pain became unbearable. I think we both looked away at the same time. I remember you put up a brave fight. You really tried not to cry out, but that whip makes even the biggest males cry like little pups. This will hurt, but I think you should know this. I screwed Kennedy that night just to prove that what we were doing was the right thing, that we loved each other. We did love each other, Rya, and to a certain extent we always will love each other." His time has run out again.

While I was lying in my bed, unable to move, he was inside her taking pleasure in my pain.

The next message is Dallas saying it won't be long for me to come back, maybe another month, and that he can't wait to talk to me.

Clayton's on the next message.

"The hardest part for me was when you came back. I was there in the cafeteria when you approached your friends with your food in your hands. I heard every word that they spoke to you. I watched as you walked away from them, a little curl to your shoulder that you never had before. I could tell you were still in pain with the grimace your face made with every step, yet you still came to school. I remember that you sat underneath that big tree eating by yourself, while I walked by you, hand in hand with Kennedy. I just left you there by yourself. I noticed that you stopped playing sports, were no longer on student council. You stopped trying different hairstyles. In fact, you just braided it, not cutting it, letting it grow long as if you stopped caring. I saw this juvenile female go from being so full of life to not wanting to be alive...still I did nothing to help you. I continued on with my life while I watched yours slowly erode away. I couldn't wait to get out of high school so I didn't have to look at you anymore and what I did to a soul. I'm supposed to be this leader, and I have destroyed something beautiful without a care in the world. I don't deserve to lead. I would go to the library sometimes at lunch in the winter time. I knew you were in the back corner in the cubicle pretending to study. I could hear your soft cries, and I did nothing to help you." His voice is so heavy with emotion he's having a hard time talking before he ends the call.

I can't continue anymore, so I put the phone down. It's just too hard on my soul.

Maybe it was two in the morning before I cried myself to sleep only to have Cash wake me up with a "get up" grunt.

I change into some workout clothes and running

shoes. I really have no idea what to expect from him.

Meeting him at the breakfast table, it's just us up in the early morning dawn. Both our eyes seem puffy and red. I wonder if we have been crying over the same wolves?

"We're going to run to the training facility." That's all he says as I follow him outside.

The high pines shiver in the freezing wind, and the world seems still asleep as I try to keep his pace. The sky blushes in the softest of pinks and blues as the sun cracks through the night. The moon slowly fades away. The air outside seems virgin young, pure and clean.

The briskness pushes itself inside my nose, stinging with its burning cold. The skin side is not used to running this fast for this long and is slowly lagging behind Cash.

I think he slows his pace slightly until I catch up with him. He doesn't say anything; we just run silently together, each in our own world of thought. A chipmunk scuttles around the base of a tree. If I were in Wild form, I could have had it between my jaws already.

Soon I think Mother Nature's winter cloak will be thrown away for spring's green dress.

The crunching sound of each step we take echoes in this soundless morning, even the wind seems to have a certain quietness about it.

My thighs are burning by the time we enter this grey-sided building, nothing fancy to it. Four walls and a high-pitched tin roof.

A group of very young juveniles are already

inside waiting, milling about, talking amongst themselves.

"Hi, Cash." All the juveniles are smiling up at him, revealing how much they like this male wolf. He smiles back at them, the only smile I have ever seen on his face since meeting him. It makes him look beautiful for a minute until I remember how ugly he can be.

Their curious eyes fall on me. I don't hide behind Cash; I stand tall, meeting everyone head on and looking them in the eyes.

These are baby wolves who don't pose any threat to me.

"Everyone, this is Rya. She's going to be training with you all for a while until she learns the basics." They have open mouths in shock.

"Is she her?" a male juvenile asks Cash.

"Yes, that's her." Now all eyes are on me, rolling over my body, assessing everything.

The males, all with their shaved heads, regard me, smelling deeply. They can't seem to stop staring as the females do the same. Lifting their noses high up, not being discreet. Taking my scent in and breathing it out. A low murmur of excitement is rippling through this crowd.

"That's her...look at her eyes, they freak me out...she's really pretty...why is she training with us?"

"All right, everyone, let's begin." Cash takes a step in the front, and everyone follows his instructions. I stand at the back watching everyone on what to do. He leads them in their morning stretch, getting their muscles ready.

Cash goes through the motions, guiding these young ones in routine after routine, sparring with them gently. His sinewy V-shaped body moves in fluid grace; he's sure-footed with every move he demonstrates.

I think he likes it. He has a lot of patience while working with these novice learners, giving them high fives when they do good, a gotta try harder next time if someone taps out. The sparring is rough and raw. No one holds anything back.

It's my turn to go against the youngest shifted juvenile here. He's skinny, without the fullness another few years will bring to his body. His voice even cracks as he says hello to me.

"What's the rules everyone?" Cash's voice booms over the noise.

"You either tap out or you get knocked out?" All the males and females chant as one voice. Cash smiles at this, pleased with the response of his minions.

"Rya, are you ready?" I'm not sure; I have never had a lesson in fighting before. I don't give him an answer, and he doesn't wait for one as he blows a whistle very lightly so it doesn't hurt our ears.

This male is on me before I have time to blink. He's got me one way, then the other, as he's trying to pin me against the mat in some kind of ninja move. I wiggle out of his hold only because I'm stronger, but he manages to catch me with an elbow to the lower jaw near my ear that makes me see stars.

He's quick as he assaults every inch of my body.

"Do you want to quit? All you need to do is tap

out." Cash has his eyes on me, looking, waiting for an answer.

"No." I face this little wolverine head on. He pounds on my body again and again. The Nature of my Wild is not happy about this little male hurting the skin side. She slowly starts to make an appearance. A growl rumbles out with our displeasure.

"Rya, no wolves here. Put her away." Cash takes a step toward me, and I try to rein her in, shaking with the effort.

This male seizes his opportunity and lays me out hard, falling to the ground. He's on me in an instant, no mercy. He has my arm, angling it up in such a way that if he continues, it's going to break. The pain is too much, and my hand goes to tap out. Before I do, I notice the way Cash is looking at me, as if he knew I would just tap out. Like he is expecting this. So I grit my teeth in my jaw and take this pain; I take it because I can. It's actually not as bad as the whip against my back.

"Tap out." The little male's voice is in my ear as more pressure is exerted on my arm. A groan tumbles out, and he pleads with me. I don't think that this male wants to do what he's been trained to do. I try to break the hold, I try to get out, to fight against this hold, but I don't know how. At least I am *trying*.

"Please tap out." There's a desperation in his voice now. I think only I can hear it, he's whispering to me so quietly. His face is red in concentration, and I'm red with the effort I'm putting up. I'm trying with all I have to break his hold, but I just can't, and the snap echoes inside the building as all eyes are on the fight, everyone cringing with the sound.

Cash is instantly on me.

"Why didn't you tap out?" He's shocked.

"I'm not a quitter." My voice travels between the spaces in my clenched teeth.

The small juvenile wolf rocks back and forth in dread. "I'm so sorry, I'm so sorry." He looks like he's going to get sick.

A trickling of older wolves starts to circle around us as they hear about what just happened, how I wouldn't submit, that I just kept on fighting until I couldn't anymore. Hushed whispers: *Is that her? What did she do? She never gave up?*

Their voices circle around me. The pain starts to set in, and I feel slightly nauseated with it.

"Can you get up?" I shake my head no. I can't move as I lay there holding my arm. I can feel the blood soaking into my shirt, onto the mat. I can't look; I know the bone is out of my skin.

Closing my eyes, I try to breathe through the pain the same way I tell my laboring females to do.

It's a concentration of wills, my will against the pain's will. I don't make a sound, just bear it.

"Rya, can you open your eyes for me?" I do, and it's a nice older wolf with silver hair. He's got kind, caring eyes.

"I need to take your shirt off and look at your arm. Is that okay with you?"

"Yes," I hiss out.

"Cash, come help me sit her up." It takes two of them, as I am stiff and just need to breathe.

He opens his black bag, and a needle plunges into my good arm. It stings slightly with the medication he's using. Next, he brings out scissors, cutting my shirt off from the back and down the side of my arms, so it easily peels off my head.

"What happened to you?" the kind doctor asks as my back is exposed for everyone's eyes. This is the first time more than a handful of wolves have seen my back. Voices grow stronger, disbelief of what they are seeing on a female's back.

Cash looks toward my back, eyes dilating slightly. I'm not sure what's worse in his mind: my arm bone sticking out of my flesh or the lasting kiss the whip's mark left on my pristine flesh.

"What happened?" Cash's voice sounds far away, the medication taking its hold on my system. It's making my vision fuzzy, my tongue thick; all the moisture has left my mouth.

"It was from the effort I put into my fight for what I thought was mine." The words come out thick, slightly slurred. The effects of the medication raging in my system.

He can't look in my eyes and I can't hold his as the pain medication takes its hold on me.

"Cash." That Silverback male's voice tone is harsh. It's the first time I have heard sound waves make the wolves freeze.

Cash squares up his shoulders to his father, like a male ready to receive his punishment.

"Father."

"You call him, tell him you allowed his female to fight before she was ready, and she got hurt on your watch." Cash nods his head to his father in agreement.

CHAPTER 3

We Get What We Deserve

Guilt pours off of him as if it were sweat.

"I did it on purpose. I thought you would just give up. I was wrong." It's just Cash and me in the clinic room. He asked if he could speak to me alone. His parents walked out, not very pleased with their third born.

He's sitting there in the orange plastic chair with his elbows on his thighs, hands gripped together, looking down at the floor.

"I'm sorry, Rya." His eyes lock with mine, no more menace left in them.

"It was easier to blame you than her. I just couldn't believe—" Unclasping his hands, he presses the palms into his eyes, as if trying to stop the tap that wants to open up.

"Everything she's said about me has come true. I'm a weak wolf. I knew exactly what I was doing. I let my family down, you down, and myself down. I acted without honor." This savagely beautiful wolf

47

is giving me a hard look at how horrible he feels in every way.

Love twists your soul, spiraling you into something different, something you thought you would never become.

"How old were you when you found out he was your mate?"

"I was sixteen."

"How long was it after you shifted?"

"I shifted that day, early in the morning. It was awful, but my family was there to support me."

"What happened to you?"

"I saw him. He was with her. It's as if they expected this. They stood shoulder to shoulder as I approached, and honestly, I thought I had a chance. The thing is my chance was gone before it ever began. I know that now. I wish I would have known this at the time. I think I would have done things differently. I would have been prepared, but I never was prepared to handle the rejection. I was on the A side of life back then, before him, before them. I was happy, and I think more than anything, looking back right now in this moment I did give up. I gave up on me. Not him, I just rolled over and gave up on me. I'm my biggest supporter, and I failed myself." It's as if a light bulb just turned on in my mind.

It's funny how if you talk about certain traumas in your life enough, it somehow gets just a little easier to come to grips with what was done. It's hard, but it's part of my history, like my own personal cookbook that makes me who I am. My past recipes, some good, some sour, some terrible, some burned and charred. My future recipes are still being written on the blank white pages; hopefully, they will be robust and full of a life I think I *deserve*.

"I didn't get that chance, so I turned on Kennedy. She was my easiest target, just like I am to you. I kicked her ass that day. Don't let anyone tell you differently, regardless of my fighting skills. I was the stronger wolf back then." It's true back then I was stronger than her.

"I was punished for going after her, then I became a ghost. I was really never there anymore. I checked out. No one cared, and I hate to say this, but neither did I. I stopped believing in myself. When I came back to the pack after my training, it was your brother that helped me. He saw something in me that I still don't see in myself. He saw a life that just needed a chance to breathe again." Cash's emotions are twisting and knotting around inside him. He nods his head, as if he understands what I am telling him.

"I was the one who found Dallas. He was almost dead. He could hardly even speak anymore. He couldn't move. I made a tourniquet for his arm, screaming the whole time for help, but we were all alone in that house we built for them and their future. Do you know what that did to me, seeing him like that? I have nightmares still to this day. I called my father. I had to wait for help. He looked into my eyes, told me he loved me, asked me if I loved him." Cash's voice breaks with hard emotions that he's trying to stop from seeping out.

"Of course I said yes. I was holding his head in my lap. He just looked at me, and with his soul, he asked me to *untie his arm*. He begged me and begged me until he passed out." Now I can't stop the tears from coming down, that burn coming up from the pit of my stomach to rest corrosively at the back of my throat.

"When he healed, he never came back the same. We referred to him as the ghost because he was around but not really there. So when you said you felt that way, I saw him be that way." I nod my head in agreement. I understand the feeling very well.

"He went away soon after. My parents pulled some strings, got him into a good university as soon as he told them what he wanted to do. After he left, he has only been home twice. We always went to him. It was just better that way. No pressure on him, no expectations put on his shoulders. He always promised he would come back. He just couldn't say when." Cash has a faraway look in eyes that can't keep the tears away.

"I was there when he called my dad saying he met someone, that he was thinking of letting his hair grow out again. There are only two times that my father has actually cried in front of us, and that was one of them." His truths are tumbling out his mouth as I feel slightly nauseated with all these feelings that are being caught and swallowed down my throat.

"My biggest fear is that you reject him and he does what he tried to do but succeeds. I just don't want him to get hurt because, in the end, you have a mate. I know what they say about you being moon blessed, but what happens if you chose him over my brother? What happens to my brother?" Those last words hang between us while Cash wipes away his own tears.

"Rya, Cash, time to go." The Silverback male looks at the both of us with our red puffy eyes, and something filters across his face, a slight smile.

"Your brothers should be arriving within minutes. Are you ready?" Cash stands up, back straight. He looks on with grim determination, as if he's going to take bitter medicine and swallow it down.

"Is someone with Kennedy?" His first concern is her, and I eye him suspiciously. A contradiction in how he's behaving, he acts as if he doesn't care, but deep down he does.

"Your mother has her." Alpha Clinton stares down this male who can't look his father in the eye.

"Can you walk, or do you need to be carried?" He's ready to scoop me up in those solid arms of his.

"I can walk." A chaos of fluttering butterfly wings tickles the inside of my stomach at seeing Dallas again. I actually give a little giggle of giddiness that has both males looking at me oddly.

"Sorry." I try to calm my face, but I can't. My smile is beyond control, beyond hiding. It's out there for everyone to see. I try to hide it behind my hand, but the Silverback pulls my fingers away.

"You have nothing to apologize for. Don't hide that; it's beautiful. I think this is the first time I have seen you smile. No shame in smiling. Come, let's greet your male." My heart is fluttering inside my chest, a slight shakiness in my gait. His big hand goes to my arm to steady me before he moves it quickly away.

"Rya, are you sure you can walk?'

"Yes, Alpha Clinton." He gives me a look, not believing a word I say, but he allows me to try and walk on my own.

"Little Moon, I want you to know that a lot of the pack is waiting for you outside. They couldn't stay away. They are very curious about you. Don't feel intimidated…shoulders back, hold your head high. Nothing can touch you with me beside you. Show them the female who ate with the wild wolves in winter, show them the female who didn't quit, fought to the very end, even though you had no hope of winning." Pride is now in his voice, the same pride that Dallas has in his.

A blanket is over my shoulders, arm in a blue sling with two pins sticking out of my skin holding the bone in place. I feel no pain because of the nerve block I was given. The doctor said it would last at least eighteen hours. Then the pain would start to come back with a punch; at least he told me what to expect, so I wouldn't be so shocked when the pain comes barreling in.

Walking out the door, instead of the faint blues and pinks of sunrise, the deep reds and purples meet me with sunset. Lots of wolves are milling about in the parking lot. Snowflake after snowflake drifts effortlessly down from the heavens, dusting the heads and shoulders of these people who came to see me, combatting the cold for just a glimpse.

Wolves begin to hush. Those juveniles who were there are in a small cluster together, huddled in their own little side pack. That wolverine in the middle of them as if they are protecting the weakest from something.

Taking the steps one at a time, a single clap rings out from the crowd, followed by another clap, then another until everyone is cheering for me. I stand a little straighter. A *good job* thrown out of male voices, *good effort*, repeated throughout the females.

The Silverback Alpha never leaves my side until I see his oldest. Standing there watching me, clapping his hands with the rest of the pack.

Arctic sea meets glacier blue as the crowd shifts away.

All I hear is the blood rushing in my ears, swooshing with the beat of my heart.

He doesn't take his eyes off mine, a little scruff on the side. I can't wait to feel that against my skin. I love the way his dark jeans are hanging so delicately off his hips; the stretch of his soft grey sweater across his chest has me wanting to inch it up to expose his muscled torso, run my fingers over his v-shaped lower abdomen.

With each step he brings himself closer to me, I can't help the tremors that are taking over. My eyes are for only him. My attention is captivated by *him*.

The single foot that separated our bodies is gone as soon as his arm wraps around my waist, pulling me up and into him. His scent seeps from underneath his skin. Did someone just pluck a guitar string? Because I am vibrating, humming, as his nose goes to the base of my neck, inhaling deeply. Teeth, I feel them at the base of my neck. I still, and so does he. He doesn't puncture skin, but he could easily. He places a soft kiss instead, another kiss on my jawline until his mouth finds mine.

He kisses me, long and slow. He is in no hurry to let me go; he doesn't care who is watching, who is present. He's making this moment the last chapter in those fairy tale books that I have always wanted but *never had*.

This is a special, one of a kind moment.

Pulling away, he sets me carefully on the ground.

"Why are you here?" I whisper, looking at him.

"You're my female. I needed to come. I wanted to see you, make sure you're all right." His words are soaking into every crack of my skin, and my happiness is shining out for everyone to see. Very carefully he brings me into his chest, hugging me close, making sure not to touch my bad arm.

"I missed you." His voice tickles my ear, yet it shivers my skin. The effect he has on me has grown, become more powerful. Potent.

Aching for another taste of his warm lips, I focus on them. Bending his head down, he gives me that compelling taste; his eyes are laced with his own obvious desire.

"If you weren't hurt, I would show you how much I've missed you." He nips my ear, whispering his words for only me to hear. "Are you in any pain?"

"No, I can't feel anything."

"Good." Another inhaled breath on my skin. He pulls the blanket tighter over my upper body as the ends slowly flutter open in the light wind.

Stepping away, he takes a stance as a predator

eyeing something that he is intent to have.

"Cassius." Turning my body, I face Cash. He's standing there, holding himself in position. The crowd that was slightly pressing in is now taking steps back, giving space to full-grown males that are about to use fists of war instead of teeth of death.

Cash keeps his body straight, taking a deep breath in. "I knew what I was doing." A twitch in his jaw, a brace in his stance.

"Then I'm going to give you the same chance you gave her. I expect a perfect effort from you, Cassius." He doesn't wait for an answer, attacking Cash with savage brutality.

Cash might have grace and edge on everyone here, but against his brother, he looks like he is no more than a juvenile fighting a fully trained fighter. The Silverback male's eyes do not leave the fight; it's as if he's taking some kind of notes. Eyes observing this, not as a spectator, more like an assessor of skill. A scout looking at a potential prospect for the team.

Once Dallas has Cash, he holds him pinned to the ground. Face pressed into the light layer of snow that has accumulated, both males breathing heavily. Cash is fighting to get him off him, red face straining with the effort. Cash does not give up as Dallas takes his arm in the same lock that small juvenile had mine in.

Dallas is merciless with his grip. "Tap out," he spits at his brother, but Cash continues on, trying with all he has to break the hold. Dallas continues bruising flesh and breaking bone. The snap is heard, the reaction the same, a sickening gasp in the crowd of watchers. The juveniles stand open mouthed while Cash still continues to try and fight. The bone does not break through flesh like mine did.

He catches Dallas with an elbow to the jaw. He has a merciless sneer, and I watch as his fist comes down as if it's going to drive through Cash's face. He is knocked out completely, body limp on the ground.

He gets off his brother, and his once-clean clothes are stained with dirt.

Now Dallas squares up to his father, who angles his head in interest. Dallas is on the balls of his feet, as if contemplating on springing.

"I blame you too." He points a finger at his father.

"If you come at me, I expect a perfect effort, son. Do you understand what you will be doing?" Dallas hesitates for a moment, trying to rein himself in. As if talking himself down from his own personal ledge, he realizes if he takes that step off, there is no leaping back up.

Turning slowly around, he faces the entire crowd. "Who was the juvenile that broke her arm?"

He looks toward that male, who's small compared to Dallas. He takes his step forward, meeting his fate, like a warrior.

"It was you who did that to my female?" He sounds surprised.

The male squares his shoulders, on shaking legs. His whole body is betraying him at this moment. He wants to seem tough, but he's completely scared out of his mind. Just watching his teacher get his ass handed to him, he's now having to face the same beast.

Dallas bends down to his level, except he purposely makes himself just a touch bigger than this small one.

"You did what you were trained to do. Good job. I know that it was hard for you, that you didn't want to do it; you made a hard choice. I expect good things from you." He grips this male by the back of his shaved head, pressing his cheek against his. Whispered words that make this male peacock out, his whole body puffed up, a proud smile on his face. Dallas releases him with a good job pat on his behind.

Cash is already being moved very carefully back inside the clinic.

Dallas comes back to me, a gentleness replacing the savageness as he cradles me into his body.

"I'm taking you back to the house." No other words, no saying hello to wolves he hasn't seen in years, all his focus is on me. I bask in the attention.

Caleb gets into the front seat while Dallas takes the back with me on his lap the entire drive back. His father is in the passenger seat. Cash has been left at the clinic so he can get fixed up.

Dallas insists on carrying me inside. It feels good to have someone who cares if I'm hurt, someone willing to ease my pain.

"Who's watching over the pack if you males are here?"

"Clayton is. He's much better. He's almost able to beat Caleb now. So we took a chance on him and left him in charge. I'll explain everything. I wanted to last night, but Kimberly came and I had to deliver another pup." A look of pure loathing crosses his face.

"It took all night. She didn't progress well. It was difficult for everyone. They're fine, mother and pup doing well. I was falling asleep when Cash called me, telling me what he did to you." Violent vibrations from his chest tumble out as he tells me the end of that sentence.

"He was supposed to train you the right way. I didn't expect this from him. He's changed for the worse since he met her." He looks saddened by this revelation.

I walk into the living room. Kennedy has her head on a pillow, body curled into a ball on the couch. She looks as if she physically hurts. A blanket covers her body. Her eyes go wide looking at Dallas, and I think I hear a whimper come out of her mouth.

"Mother, did you not give her what I told you?"

Luna Grace comes out of the kitchen with a cup of tea. "She wouldn't drink it, says that she deserves to feel everything he does."

It's in this minute that I smell it, the mingling scents inside her. The way the female and male smells coil around each other. Wolves will think she is having a female, but I know that scent. It's the smell of twins, one of each.

Very rare to have twins, very difficult on the mother to host two lives that are sucking away at all her resources so she can carry them to term. She will need to start to eat more soon because already she looks skinnier than when I went away. I contemplate telling her, but I don't.

"If that's what she wants, so be it." Dallas is acting like the Alpha of this house as the king slowly lumbers in and takes a seat, sinking into the cushion, regarding his son.

"I think that it's time I train you, my first born." The Alpha looks on at a son who is coming into what his nature has always demanded of him. Alpha.

Dallas gingerly places me on his lap, holding me close to his body. I melt into him. His heat feels good against my skin. I place my lips against his neck, a soft kiss that makes his body quiver. I can feel how I affect other parts of him as I'm adjusted slightly on his lap.

"I'm not sure yet." Dallas's voice feels far away as I close my eyes, the day's events and not getting to bed until late last night from listening to all those messages taking their toll on me. I feel secure with Dallas holding me. I like this feeling.

"Wake up. Time to eat." Dallas shifts me on his lap, still no pain from my arm. It's as if it's numb, without feelings.

Kennedy is already seated at the table; she is down in the middle. Dallas takes his father's left, while I sit beside him. He starts asking what I want before he fills his own plate. I don't feel like eating, just drinking some water, but I do eye Kennedy's fruit bowl that would be good to eat at this moment.

It's filled with yellow fleshy mangoes, halved green and red grapes, and pitted black cherries, and shaved almonds are on top of the medley along with a dash of sugar. Kennedy saw me eyeing what she has. Very subtly she pushes her bowl toward me, sharing what she has. I don't take it. Instead, I look away. I don't need what she has; I can do without.

Cash comes into the dining room, looking rough. Looking at Kennedy, he takes in her appearance with a hint of relief before sitting down beside her. He takes a drink from the bottle of water he's holding in his good hand. He's sporting the same blue sling I am. It's like we're *twinning*.

Kennedy goes to put her hand on his shoulder. He just angles himself away from her. That hand drops to her side.

Caleb's last to take his seat at the table, clothes looking wrinkled, as if he just put on something he was wearing from last night. He smells of many different females, his gluttony unmistakable.

"Next time you come to the table, wash yourself!" His mother is not pleased having to sit next to a son who smells of last night's pleasures.

He gives a dirty smirk, winking at me.

"Next time I will." He gives his mother a smile that probably works on all the pretty females, but not on her. She just huffs to herself.

"Carson, Crane, I'm having a small party tonight. You're welcome to join me in the basement." Both males look on with wicked, naughty eyes.

"Cash, how's the arm?" Caleb says between bites of food. He's instigating him for a response.

"Caleb," Dallas warns out.

"Just a joke." He puts his hands up in surrender.

"Kennedy." Her head picks up, as if she's not used to being talked to.

"You're having a female. Congrats." He raises his glass to her in a mock cheer.

"You're having twins." My words hang in the air as a smile makes its way along her always curved down lips. Could this be her first smile I'm witnessing since being in this pack? She glows with the news, her hands going over that small, round bulge. She looks beautiful when she shows her heart smile. She turns toward Cash, her eyes sparkling with the news. She looks at him as if she's expecting something from him. Instead, he keeps his face impassive, no emotion betrayed by his lips that are straight lined. Eyes that don't sparkle back at hers.

I watch as that beautiful smile fades on her lips, as her shoulders tuck in, as her head bends forward and her hair falls to the side of her face, shielding her from everyone's stare. I can see her tears dripping down one by one, landing on her thighs, soaking spots like random rain drops on the ground.

I can see her hands going underneath her thighs. For a moment, I see nails that are bitten down so badly they look like they bleed from being mauled constantly. Her shoulders shake as she quietly tries to cry without sound. Getting up slowly, I watch her not make eye contact with anyone. Instead she whispers, "Thank you for dinner." Her words come out painfully to Luna Grace before she turns around and walks very slowly toward the stairs to her sanctuary.

"I'm going to the basement." Cash pushes his chair away, getting up without finishing his food. Is his stomach as upset as hers?

Usually, when mates get the news they are expecting twins, it's a celebration, such a rare blessing they have been given by the moon herself.

I watch as Cash heads to a door that I can only imagine leads to the basement. We all finish our meal in silence until a chime of the doorbell rings.

Caleb gets up with liquid grace, voices of females and males getting louder, all carrying bags of drinks, all waving their hellos before being ushered downstairs. Carson looks sheepishly shy as a female touches his shaved head on the way down, letting her fingers linger across his temples, down his jawline before pulling away. He blushes and puts his hands in his pockets.

Crane looks on as if he's going to be helping himself to the dessert table.

Luna Grace grabs Caleb by the jaw hard, bringing her son toward her face.

"Behave, understand?"

"Yes." He gives her the answer she wants to hear.

"Rya, Dallas, come down later on."

"I don't think that Rya would want any part of your den of sin." The way she says it sounds like she's been putting up with it a long time. She's not surprised with anything anymore that her males can do. I wonder how hard it is to raise five males.

"Rya, let's go upstairs." Dallas rises, helping me up.

Walking up the steps, I smell fresh paint coming from Kennedy's room. Her door is open. I can't help but pretend to use the bathroom to see inside her room. Coming out of the bathroom, I see her sitting cross-legged on the floor. Her canvas is the wall, painting a mural masterpiece. Meticulous in detail, a scene of pack wolves playing, lying around in the depths of the forest. I never knew she was an artist.

It's paralyzingly beautiful.

"This is really good," I say outside her door. She doesn't turn around, only concentrating on every arch and sweep of her brush. It's amazing that she can make this out of a blank slate.

"When I was younger, I was accepted into the art program at the university. I never went. I should have." That's all she says to me, continuing on with her task.

I walk into my room, and Dallas is there sitting on the bed, looking at the crumpled papers in his hands. A look of melancholy on his face, his smile not as bright, but he's still smiling.

"Let's get you washed up first, then let me explain all this to you, all right?"

He places the papers on the desk, and I wonder if this is the first time he hasn't crumpled them back up into little balls.

"I'm going to wash you, Rya. Is that okay?" He's closed the bathroom door, water being turned on. I'm in front of the mirror, watching my reflection as a nail cuts easily through my sports bra. He takes it off of me. It lies ruined, on the floor.

The next are my yoga pants and underwear. He crouches down so when he does pull the material down, his nose is placed perfectly between my legs. He is smelling me. Inhaling, he gives a little growl of pleasure.

Standing behind me, I see him looking at me in the mirror, his eyes on every inch of me. He unzips, unbuttons his jeans. With just a slight pull, they fall to his feet. His sweater comes off next. Exposing those rounded shoulders, his bare chest pressed into my back.

Skin on skin is the most intimate of touches.

The bath is small, but he makes it work, positioning his body in such a way that I can lay between his legs. He removes my sling, putting it to the side, making sure the pins don't get wet.

"Dallas, can I ask you something?" He's kissing the back of my neck, pulling the flesh into his mouth.

"Ask me anything," he says while sliding his tongue along my collarbone.

"I want you to mark me." As soon as my words are out of my mouth, my phone starts ringing until it goes to voice mail.

CHAPTER 4

Revelations

The stillness of silence greets me, deafening my ears.

Both our heartbeats are dancing in our chests.

His fingers start drawing small circles on my knuckles, a small kiss placed on my neck. I think he's smiling into my skin.

Lazily he grabs the washcloth, dipping it into the water, lathering it soapy wet, before washing the sweat and blood from my skin.

"You want me to mark you, Rya?"

I press my back against his chest more, and he gives a slight moan. I grab his hand, kissing his knuckles that taste slightly soapy.

"I do." Words are spoken in conviction, no hesitation of thought.

"Then I will if that's what you really want." Gently he brings me even closer to him, the water threatening to slosh over the side of the porcelain rim.

"I'm going to finish washing you up, then I'm going to fill you up with my scent." Small vibrations from his chest ripple the water in the tub.

He takes his time, making sure to clean every single inch of skin. When his hand goes between my legs, he presses his cheek against mine, chin resting on my shoulder. I can feel his eyes watching his own fingers dipping inside me, disappearing from view. I bite my lower lip, but that doesn't stop the moan from echoing in the small room.

He knows exactly where to touch, his fingers sliding effortlessly inside, only to pull out for the briefest of seconds, stimulating another part of me that has my back arching slightly. Gently he pulls me up more on his body so I'm just barely out of the water. My thighs rest on his thighs, his excitement rocking gently up and down between my parted folds, the engorged head hitting my most sensitive feminine part.

A little sigh escapes out as his finger continues its circular motion with him very subtly rocking himself against me. My hips, anticipating his rhythm, move with him as if nature is guiding my movements.

Murmuring softly into my ear, he watches what he's doing to me, looking down between my legs. I can feel the heat from his stare. With my good hand, I grip him with his next upward thrust, a little hiss of pleasure from his lips that are kissing the base of my neck now, his eyes focused on how my hand is closed around him, watching himself be handled by me while his finger slips in teasingly slow.

Probing.

Rubbing.

Exploring.

A gasp, not a moan, comes out as he puts another one inside. It comes naturally to me to spread myself more for his exploration. My hand is still around his substantial male part, his hips rocking himself up and down just a fraction more, so the water starts to slip over the side of the tub.

Bliss.

Growing warmth spreads deep inside me until I become fevered with my own personal need.

Lovers' perfume mixes inside this steam-filled room. Both of us are breathing hard with flushed faces.

Slow, his movements so controlled as he rubs his length on the outside of me.

"I like this," he says into my skin.

He's driving me insane with some basic need that has to be satisfied. I can feel that tightening in my lower stomach, just a few minutes more.

He slows his pace, pulling his fingers out of me.

"Don't stop," a moaned plea trembles out of my mouth.

"I don't plan to. I'm just moving us to the bed." His words of promise quiver the inside of my thighs.

Getting out before me, he takes a towel and dries himself off. He has no shame, letting me covet his male flesh. I can't pull my eyes away from him. The way his muscles stretch and flex with movement has me licking my lips at this feast of flesh.

"I'll wash your hair tomorrow after the pins come out of your arm, all right?" He speaks to me as if I'm really paying attention to words. I can't pull my eyes away from what's standing at attention.

He's perfect.

"Rya, you're staring." His teasing snaps my eyes to his face.

"Sorry, I just—" I can actually feel my cheeks turning red.

"Don't be sorry. You can stare all you want. Do you need me to give you an anatomy lesson?" Walking toward me, he lifts me gently to a standing position. Taking another towel, he slowly dries me off.

"I wouldn't mind one." I can't believe I just said those words out loud. I don't recognize my own husky voice.

Looking down again, he's primal delicious.

He gives a slight growl of annoyance, eyes falling on my bad arm that I have cradled against my chest.

"I need to be careful with you." It's a statement to me, but I think he's reminding himself as well.

He steps into my space, bending his head, and the curves of our lips fit together perfectly.

He drags his teeth over my skin, starting with the length of my collarbone, toward my shoulder, giving gentle bites. The delicacy of his tongue dragging against flesh, into the hollow of my neck, stutters the breath in my lungs.

Reaching down, he picks up my sling, positioning my arm properly inside it. The Velcro straps are secured at the back of my neck.

Picking me up in his arms, he carries me to his

bed. The way he's so gentle and caring has my eyes almost water in happiness. "I don't remember my bed being so small," he says, a little shocked.

His turn again to look at my raw flesh that's exposed only for his eyes.

Climbing on the bed, he crawls on top of me, on hands and knees. Again he looks at my arm, shaking his head to himself.

"We can't, Rya. You're hurt." He slides himself against my side so his thigh is draped over my thigh, hooking his heel into my calf. Fingers trace my ribs, tickle my belly, glide over the flesh of my hip.

"I'm not that hurt." Disappointment shows on my face.

"Yes, you are. One shift the wrong way, your bone slides out of place. Trust me when I say this, I plan on shifting you all kinds of ways. Your body needs to fully heal before I put it through that." His hands are roaming around my inner thigh.

"I want to make this special for you, not just something that happens and it's over with. You waited this long; I think it's okay to wait until your body's ready for it." He pulls a loose throw blanket over the top of our legs, our upper bodies still exposed to air that has goosebumps on our skin, but it isn't from the cold.

"I've been doing some research on your eyes. There are a few consistent things that keep popping up. The first thing is, if I mark you, it will stay forever until death. Your bond with Clayton will fade, just like if he died. You will not feel that bond with him anymore. Clayton will always feel it, but not as strong; it's more of a longing instead of an intense need, the moon's justice. You have been wronged by many wolves, Rya, and the moon has seen this and blessed you with a choice of who you can have. If I mark you now, I'm going to send you into your heat. I don't want your training to stop. I want you to learn how to fight so you aren't afraid of any wolf or skin. You will have the skills to defend yourself against anything."

"I never had a heat, Dallas. I'm sterile." I don't look away as a flash of disbelief crosses his face.

"No way, there is no way. You don't smell moldy or sour. You smell as if you could get pregnant now. Everything seems ready for a pup. When I touch inside you, I can feel your body preparing for a future. You're not sterile, Rya. In fact, I've been thinking that you are in a constant state of heat to a certain degree. It's an anomaly, just like your eyes."

"Everyone says that they can smell it, but I'm not sure, Dallas. I'm too old. I should have had my first heat by now. I need you to be prepared if I can't have a pup. Would you still want me?"

"I would want you no matter what, no matter if you give me ten pups or none. I just want you, plain and simple." Lips find mine again, showing me how much he wants me.

The phone rings again, interrupting our make-out session.

Reaching over, he picks it up, handing it to me.

Looking into the screen, I stare up into his eyes, not wanting to answer it.

"It's Clayton. He's been calling me, leaving

70

messages." Dallas's lips form a straight line, showing his displeasure.

The ringing stops. I can only assume he's leaving another voice message.

"How long has he been doing this?" He's sitting up on the edge of the bed with his back facing me.

"Last night I was listening to all your messages and I found several from him." I don't lie; I can't have lies between us.

"Do you want to talk to him?" His back muscles flex with the tension in his body.

"I don't, but part of me is interested in what he has to say. Trust me when I tell you this. It's nothing nice. He has nothing nice to say to me." Clayton has ruined this moment for me.

"I can understand, and I think you should listen to what he has to say." His shoulders seem as if they are suddenly burdened with a heavy load.

"I can't mark you unless you're one hundred percent sure you don't want him anymore. I would be able to feel your longing for him. I would be able to feel your life's regret."

"He never gave me a chance. Why do you think that I should give him something that he never gave me?" I shout at him.

"Because I'm falling in love with you, Rya. I want the best for you. If that means that you need to give him a chance, then so be it. I'm the wolf for you, but you're the one who has to believe it." His whole body is facing me now, sea ice blue staring back at my own eyes.

"You can't have the both of us. It doesn't work that way. I need you to be honest with yourself about him. Even if it hurts me, he's your true mate. I would never be with you if my mate were still alive. You would not be a thought in my head." It hurts to hear those words. I know it's not meant to be cruel; it's to put things in perspective. He's alive, breathing, and I'm in his place. "My wolf's mark held. It never disappeared. I'm assuming if I marked you now, it would hold, but I can't do it until I know you're sure about me, about us." His fingers trace my jawline before he kisses me softly.

"I have Caleb training him. He's getting stronger and stronger every day. He's taking a lot of ass kicking, but I think soon he will beat Caleb. I want him to be the strongest wolf possible, so when I give him the pack, he can lead it the way it should be led. I'm training him on how to lead. He just needs some guidance. He's a good wolf. I know what he did to you was wrong, but as a leader of the pack, he is good. I think he's learned from everything that has happened in the months I've spent with him." His hands grip onto the bed sheets, scrunching the material in his hands.

"Why are you going to give him control of the pack you won?" I'm slightly confused why he would give up his Alpha position.

"If you don't choose me, then at least I know he will be everything he's supposed to be. I would be able to sleep at night knowing that you are taken care of. That the pack's strong. Also, I think it's time for me to take over my pack. I can't do both. I can't lead two different packs so far apart. I'm preparing him for my departure. It's the right thing to do, Rya. I always knew I'd come back here. I just didn't know when or how. But you made it possible for me. You helped me to start to live a life I was always meant to live." His throat is tight with his own feelings.

"I don't want to have to give you up, but I won't stop you from going to him. I understand completely. It's going to be hard for me, but I will be okay in the end. Trust me, I want you to choose me...not by default, not because you want to get back at him. I want you to choose me because you want me, love me. I can be everything you want, everything you need. I just want you to see this for yourself." He's holding me close to his body as if I might disappear from his grasp at any moment.

"Let's go downstairs for a while before I do something we might regret in this moment."

He gets up off the ground and goes to his bag, pulling clothes out, getting dressed. I watch him as he does the zipper up on his pants, then the button. He just throws on some random shirt that looks so good on him.

Going through drawers, he finds panties, a bra. Smiling, he holds up the material to ask if these are okay. They are my best pairs. I don't have many; I never had anyone to dress up for.

He gently dresses me, putting on my socks, pants, and carefully my shirt, before fixing the sling again.

"I'm going to take those pins out in the morning before I go." My eyes snap up to him.

"You're leaving tomorrow?"

"Yes, I have to. There are some more females that are due anytime, and I have to be there."

"I can understand, but I'm going to miss you." I think I pout it out. Is this my first pouty lip?

"Rya, have you noticed that there was an influx of females going into their heat after you arrived back into the pack?"

"Yes, they were just starting to come in about two months after I arrived."

"Did that happen in the pack you were training at? Did more females go into heat when you were there?" So he's caught on to what I have suspected.

"Yes, as soon as my eyes started to change color, so did the females' heat start to come more and more. Even the sterile females started to go into heat."

"I had a feeling that was the case. Another anomaly. I could see packs going to war over you." He kisses the side of my face.

"You look beautiful. Come, let's meet some wolves that I haven't seen in years."

When he opens the door to the basement, laughter, singing, and bottles clanging together meet my ears. He has hold of my hand, not letting it go. Is it for me, or is it for him?

All the talking stops once we are in the open room. Several couches have wolves sitting comfortably on all the cushions with drinks in their hands. A pool table at the opposite end of the room has gathered bodies watching the action.

A few wolves with guitars in hand are strumming tunes that other wolves are singing to. More wolves are huddled in private clusters talking and joking around.

It all stops once we arrive.

"Caleb, get Rya a water, and get me a beer." The king of the party gets up with a grumble but does what he's told.

"Rya." I think he must notice the way we are holding hands, because he twists the cap off before handing the cold drink to me, putting it in my hand that's in the sling.

"Brother." He opens the beer for him as well, because he's not letting my hand go.

I watch as the two brothers raise their beers in a silent salute, clanging them together, before tipping them into their mouths with a quick chug.

That's when I notice all the smiles, everyone starting to stand and come to him. Not enough to get in his personal space, but enough to press in slightly.

I can see Cash on a chair. His eyes already have that faded film look that alcohol brings. I wonder if he has his beer goggles on? Arms crossed over his chest with a beer dangling from his fingers, he takes another sip that I'm sure his body doesn't need.

Males start to come up to Dallas, each one giving him a quick hug, a pat or squeeze on the shoulder. He gives them back.

"Welcome home. You've been missed. How are you?" All words that are spoken to him are answered back with a smile. I notice the way the females don't come too close. Instead, they smile their happiness to him, but they don't touch him at all, and he doesn't touch them either.

The party starts back up, music picking up in volume. A female demands to hear a certain song from the guitar players. A few males linger around

Dallas, asking questions.

He places a kiss against my shoulder at random times while speaking with the wolves.

I notice the way Caleb is getting trash talked by a female with the deepest blue eyes I have ever seen. She has this swagger about her. They are playing pool against one another. She seems to be a foul-mouthed, whiskey-drinking, pool-shooting pro.

She leans over her stick, ass up in the air, a little wiggle of her hips before she shoots her next shot. Crane is behind her staring, along with what I presume are some of his buddies. This female just has it, the whole package wrapped up in a tight red dress that shows her cleavage to anyone looking. I think she's sexy, the way her hips sway from side to side when she walks. I have to practice that kind of walking. She's working the pool table, but I can see her working the males up, especially Caleb, who's giving her his filthy smile every time she meets his eyes. I like how they have their own private language between them, just with eyes and gestures.

Looking over at me, she gives a red-lipped smile, without teeth. I notice the way all these females have something red on, painted nails, lips, shirt, maybe it's a flash of red from the bra they have that's peeking out slightly.

The females love to touch these males' shaved heads, and the males love the attention.

I can tell Dallas is getting more comfortable with the wolves he hasn't seen in years. The way he's starting to laugh at the memories of his youth. They begin to tell tales of how he was, how they remember him being.

A hellion, that's what he was.

He must have driven his mom to drink with what kind of stories they are telling. How he got dressed up in the summer time in a full ski outfit complete with goggles and snowboarded off the roof into the pool. He would have these huge outside parties in the woods, no adults allowed; he would go cliff diving in the summer time, ski diving, always looking to push the envelope, a risk taker.

I can't help but laugh so hard, tears are coming out of my eyes, and my stomach hurts from it. He's looking at me while I'm laughing. I smile at him, and he smiles back. Another kiss to my neck before he tips back his beer, finishing it.

I notice Carson sitting next to another male, thighs almost touching, just a very small space separating them. Very subtly, I notice the hand of the male touch his shaved head. My breath slightly catches as I see Carson look at him before standing up and going to the bathroom.

The male sits there staring at the door, finishing his drink. He sets it down before getting up, looking around, seeing if anyone is watching. He opens the door, sliding inside. I look around the crowd to see if anyone is paying attention, and no one is. They are all lost in their own little conversations.

I wonder if anyone knows his fondness for males?

"Caleb, we leave early. Make sure you're ready!" By now, that red wolf is on Caleb's lap, whispering something that he must like because he's nibbling on her neck.

"I'll be ready." He holds his beer up to Dallas

before drinking it down and ordering Crane to get him another.

Before we leave, I watch as that male wolf exits the bathroom doing up his pants. He's flushed slightly, eyes shining.

Carson comes out, checking his pants, making sure they are done up. I watch him look around, seeing if eyes notice. His attention is on me; he knows I've seen. He stops mid-step before taking a big breath and turning away from my eyes.

Cash is still sitting in the same spot looking more glazed. His drink of choice now is whiskey. He's drinking it like it's water. A female comes over, trying to touch his head. He angles away from her hand. She grabs him by the jaw, pulling his face to hers.

"Grow your hair out then!" She spits out these words before pushing his face away from hers.

Cash drops his head, shoulders slightly bent. Carson, by his side, helps him up to stand. A little stumble from Cash has him almost falling on his face, but his brother is there to catch him before he falls.

He's taken away, half dragged, half walked. His whiskey voice slurs all his hurt out. Dallas lets my hand go to take his brother in his arms.

"It was nice to see everyone, but I think it's time for bed." He glances at Cash, who's now barely standing on his own. All the wolves have a look of sadness by Cash's behavior.

On the way upstairs, Cash keeps muttering to himself about twins, about her. That's what he calls Kennedy, *her*.

DALLAS

I think that Kennedy is Cash's beautiful poison.

Dallas encourages Cash, "That's right, lift your leg one more step and we're almost there. One more step, pick up your leg, Cash." He's bombed. I have never seen another wolf so drunk before. This was my first basement party, and I liked it.

Kennedy pulls her door open. Cash's head is down on his chest. She comes to stand on the opposite side of Dallas, helping to bring Cash to his room. She's taking some of the weight from Dallas. Their progress is easier with her help. Dallas puts him on his bed, then walks out. I watch as Kennedy starts to take his socks off quietly, unbuttoning his pants, rolling him this way and that so he's in his boxers. She curls up against him, murmuring softly in his skin. He's passed out, no hope of a memory of this.

I close the door as soon as Dallas walks out, not wanting to meet her eyes.

Dallas once again helps me out of my clothes as I watch him get out of his. He gives me a pill that was in the pocket of his jeans, saying that the pain should come in the middle of the night and he wants me to have a good sleep.

Pulling the bed sheets down, he gets in, and soon as I'm pressed tight against his side, my thigh now over his. He pulls the blankets up to my shoulders, making sure I'm held just right.

"This was nice, Rya, to see everyone again. I've been away too long." I'm smiling into his skin now.

"I'm happy for you, Dallas." The opiate he gave me before bed is working as it begins to eat my vision away, my body sinking further into his. His

79

fingers play with the ends of my hair.

"I want you here with me when I begin my training, Rya." That's the last I remember as I fall asleep in his arms.

***

Waking up by myself in bed, I dress awkwardly before going into the kitchen. The pain in my arm is biting into my bone.

I'm hurting.

Dallas is at the table with his parents having morning coffee. It's just him and his parents talking quietly in the soft light of morning.

"You're up. I didn't want to wake you." Dallas gets up, pulling a chair out for me to sit down and pushing it in slightly. He looks at the pins. With a quick yank, the first one is out, and the next is just as fast.

"The faster, the better, Rya," he says as the pins are laying on the wooden table. "If I did it slow, it would hurt a lot more. Think of it as waxing: the slower you pull the paper away, the worse it hurts. Same with these things."

His parents smile at me. His mother is on his father's right, with Dallas on his left.

"How are you feeling?" his mother greets me softly.

"It hurts, but I can deal with the pain."

Caleb walks up from downstairs, a mess. Bloodshot eyes, scratching his head, he's shirtless with just his boxers on. He has scratch marks all over him; I think maybe they were made by two different pairs of claws.

Opening the fridge, he takes the orange juice from the carton and drinks it all down in just a few big gulps. He tries to put it back into the fridge as his mother throws a spoon at his head. He barely moves in time as it catches the tip of his nose.

"If it's done, throw it out," she snaps at him. I think this is how they show their love for one another. It's a playful banter that they have.

"Mom, listen." He shakes the container with just barely a layer of juice left. "It's not empty yet."

"You suck the living soul out of my body, Caleb." But she smiles at him the way mothers do at their males who they love unconditionally.

The Silverback Alpha laughs at the exchange. I don't see Caleb playing any kind of games with his father. Maybe he knows better than to rile up the beast.

"Get dressed. We're leaving now." Dallas is firm with the way he talks with Caleb, no motherly love in his voice. A flash of annoyance crosses Caleb's face, but he does what his brother says without a word of displeasure.

Once Caleb comes back up in his wrinkled clothes that he was wearing yesterday, we walk the brothers out to the car.

"You're going to be great, Rya. I can't wait to visit you again." Dallas believes everything he says to me.

Dallas tells me that my arm will be better by the end of the week. We do what couples do, hug and kiss goodbye. I wave to him as he pulls away from the drive. I watch Alpha Clinton walk away with

Luna Grace, hand in hand, into the snow-covered morning. Their footsteps leave behind a trail to track them by as they walk away from the house.

I get back into my room. The phone is laying on the desk, innocently waiting for me to listen to Clayton's messages. I'm curious but feel guilty about wanting to hear them.

Taking a deep breath, I click to the next message. This is a slow pain that I will hear.

"Two years of watching you, Rya, I couldn't wait to graduate. I honestly felt as if I were cheating on Kennedy if I stared too long at you. I could smell you. I always knew when you were getting close. I would make it a point to leave before you came around the corner. You made it easy, though. I think you avoided me as much as I wanted to avoid you." He takes a long drink of something, ice clinking against the glass.

"I would catch you by the fence watching your old soccer team. Your braid was down your back. You were playing with the end while you were seeing them win the championship. You were supposed to be captain that year, weren't you? I never saw you against the soccer fence again. I did watch you leave with your head down, looking at your feet. The more I think about it, you stopped looking up. You started to walk with your eyes always downcast. Again I did nothing to help you. I could have said something. I could have been kinder. I wasn't." He's run out of time; the message ends.

"I remember you always used to laugh, even before I knew you were my mate. I remember hearing you laugh and thought what a cute sound. Unique. But as my last year of high school came to an end, I realized you never laughed anymore. In fact, I thought you forgot how to speak. Your sound died. Mine didn't. You had to endure my laugh, didn't you? I made sure you would hear how happy I was with Kennedy. I made sure that you understood there was never going to be any chance for you with me."

"I remember after I graduated I saw you a total of six times before you finally left. I wish it was for good back then. I prayed to the moon you didn't come back. It was easier for me. I didn't have to watch the way I ruined you. The first time I saw you after graduation was at a pack party. You hardly came to those functions unless attendance was mandatory. I think my mother did that on purpose just to see my reaction to you. I would purposely feed Kennedy in front of the entire pack because I loved her, while I knew you watched on. Sick, isn't it? I did it, though, and I watched you all alone at one of the back picnic tables by yourself with nothing to eat because by the time you were allowed to eat, nothing was ever left. You turned yourself away from the pack. I could see your shoulders trembling, your hands wiping at your eyes. I felt bad, but not bad enough to really care." The call ends with him taking another drink.

"I'm going to have Caleb train Clayton." Dallas's voice is such a contrast to Clayton's.

"I saw you again for the first time a year later, Rya. It was another pack barbecue. By then, your shoulders were permanently hunched over like that of an old person who had a hard life, except you were still in high school. You didn't even bother to face the pack. You just kept your back to everyone with nothing to eat. You sat there for just a few minutes, making an appearance before leaving. No one really cared, did they? Seeing you like that, but no one cared enough to do anything for you, help you in any way, that's including me. I could have said something, but I thought, no, it would encourage you in the wrong way about me." This is a slow pain from deep inside that just gets harder and harder to deal with.

Dallas is on the messages again. "I just want you to know that you are my first thought in the morning and my last thought before going to bed at night. I want you to know that I packed all my pictures up. She will always be in my heart, Rya, but you right now are my soul." I smile at his truths. He makes me feel good about who I am.

"The next few times I saw you, the exact same thing: you sat with your back to us, no one spoke to you, and you left. I never got to see your face those times. A part of me wanted to. I remember the last time I saw you, the same thing again. I was getting used to seeing your back, never your face. Your hair was really long, always braided. I loved the color of your hair; it suited you somehow. I felt guilty for thinking that back then, because I loved Kennedy's hair, but I liked your hair more, thinking back. I remember my mother congratulating your parents on how you got accepted into the midwife program at some college. You know what? Kennedy was accepted to university for this special art program. I remember when she got her acceptance letter in the mail. Jumping up and down, there was only two things she ever wanted to be in life: a mother and an artist. The first I could never give her, and the second I took away from her. I told her I would miss her too much. What I was really worried about was if she found her mate and never came back to me. I was scared that if she went away, she would never come back...but for you, I wished you would never come back." He hangs up. Maybe he's upset with his own revelation about himself.

"Rya, I just want to tell you that I am so proud of you again," Dallas whispers sleepily, as if he's drifting off to bed.

"I was doing some thinking. You should thank me for your education, because if you were with me, I don't think you would ever have become a midwife. You would have never gone past high school. So at least I can take some credit for that. You got yourself an education, not having to depend on anyone to support you except yourself. I'm trying really hard to look at the things differently now. If we were together, you would have never met Dallas. I like that wolf. Sure, we have some differences that need to get worked out, but all in all, he's not bad. I like certain things that his pack does. I like the way he's setting things up around here. I like that you get to fight with fists instead of getting whipped because of your nature." He's talking so long that his time ran out again.

"Another birth, Rya, another male. I'm doing things I never thought I could do." Dallas hangs up, not saying anything else.

"Kennedy knew you were coming back soon. The midwife just died. Our pack needed you. Funny, isn't it? No one cared about you all that time, and now you're going to be caring for all our future pups. Ironic, isn't it? I give you credit. I would never have come back." He inhales a long pull from something, holding it into his lungs before he exhales out with a small cough.

"I saw you in your car opening the door, closing it. I saw your white knuckles on top the steering wheel. Kennedy was beside me at the window. She was curious how you looked after all these years. I have to confess that for the last few months we really weren't getting along too good. We were fighting more and more. I wanted to break up with her, she wanted to break up with me, but we never really did because we still loved each other. But I think the end was near. My sister just got pregnant, and that was a common ground for us because we could take care of her together. Kennedy had this new sparkle in her eyes. I remember that we made love the night before you came back. She asked me to mark her; I think it was to show you that she was mine. I had to stop a long time ago from biting her neck, it hurt her too bad, but that night she begged me to do it. I did because I love biting when I'm inside her. I remember that when you got out of your car, I saw your face for the first time in six years. I had to lean against the wall, my legs started to shake so bad. Kennedy started to cry at how I was reacting to you. In that moment, my wolf gave its first growled threat out toward her. He's never done that before. I told her to leave our room so I could get under control. I kept looking out my window until I saw you leave. I couldn't take my eyes off you. You had the most perfect body I have ever seen on a female." His last words are spoken softly, as if reliving the moment.

Are his eyes closed with the picture of me walking away from him?

In this moment, all I want him to remember is my back.

CHAPTER 5

It Comes Full Circle

Kennedy

"Get out."

Electrified pain hurts my nerve endings, anguish, curling my shoulders with his spoken words.

"Get out!" His voice gets louder.

I uncurl my body away from his, my hatred for myself spreading inside like a malignant cancer that's eating away at my insides.

Without another word, I walk out of his room and into mine, making sure I close the door behind me.

It's hard to face him, his hate so vicious it leaves a thick coating that clogs my pores so my skin has a hard time breathing.

Getting dressed in clothes that no longer fit my expanding body is just the tip of my own humiliation.

I walk down the stairs. It's mid-morning.

Usually, I'm already up, starting on the mural I'm trying to finish before I go away.

The Luna is there talking with Rya. I keep my head down, unable to meet their eyes. My shame is too much to bear.

"How are feeling this morning, Kennedy?" The Luna is always pleasant with me, even though I know she can't stand me in her home. She loves her son very much.

"Good, thank you for asking." I still don't meet their eyes as I take a seat at the table, taking a piece of fruit. I don't make myself anything to eat. I don't go into their fridge or their cupboards. I only eat what is offered, and I think they are being too generous with someone like me.

The peach is sweet, the way Rya smells. She's always been sweeter; I just was too sour to notice it.

"I was just thinking that we could go into town, seeing as Rya can't train for a few days. I thought maybe us females could have a shopping day?"

"I'm not sure." Rya has hesitance in her voice. I know it's because I'm invited.

"It's okay, you females go. I have no money to go." A wash of shame hits me. I have no money of my own. I never had to work before, and I've no savings, nothing to fall back on.

"Kennedy, you need new clothes. You're going to grow out of those very fast, especially with twins. We haven't had twins in the pack for maybe fifty years. Besides, Cash has money. He has enough for you." I nod my head, keeping it down.

"Rya, come. It would be fun to get some new stuff. I don't get the chance to go shopping. Maybe we could get something to eat after?" I can hear the excitement in the Luna's voice while she speaks with Rya. There is never excitement in that voice when she speaks to me.

"If it's money—"

"No, it's not money. I have my own. It's just that I don't want to be around her." Rya's voice is hard to my ears, as it should be.

"I don't blame you, Rya. If I were you, I'd feel the same way about me. I don't know what to say to make things better for you. I don't know what I could even possibly say for what I have done to you. Sorry isn't good enough." I let my words hang in the air, except they fall down like bricks smashing on the floor as soon as Cash walks into the room.

I can't look at him either, so I just keep my head down, hands in my lap. Trying not to cry, I pick the edges of my nails. I use to have beautiful nails, colorful long nails.

"Rya, you can do and feel whatever you want. I can't even begin to understand how difficult this must be for you. I just thought that it would be nice to get out of the house. We all need to get stuff, so why not go together?"

"Where are you guys going?"

"Shopping," Luna Grace says to Cash.

I don't feel his eyes on me anymore. It's like I don't even exist to him. I don't blame him at all.

"She going with you?"

"Yes, Kennedy's coming. She needs money. Can you please give her some?" He huffs out a breath, heading upstairs before coming back to place his wallet in front of me.

I have to stop myself from bringing it to my nose, holding it there, and inhaling deeply from it. His scent is comforting. I can close my eyes and just pretend that things are different between us.

"Take what you need." That's the most he's spoken to me in a very long time. I just nod my head at him, unable to find my voice.

"Good, it's settled. Let's go. Rya, go get your purse. I'm driving!" She sounds slightly childish with her excitement.

Rya gets up, grumbling underneath her breath. I can't hear what she's saying, but I know it's some slur directed at me.

I wait until the two females are ready. I don't care what I look like; it's not like I'm going to run into anyone I know or who even gives me a second glance.

It's quiet on the car ride.

I stay a small distance away from them as they look at cute clothes that I have no hope of fitting into anymore. I just follow and listen to the way Luna Grace is encouraging Rya to try on these beautiful clothes that make her look like the moon herself. I notice the way Luna Grace is pulling outfits that really suit Rya's figure, skin tone. The colors make her eyes look eerily beautiful.

Rya, for her part, is smiling more. I can see the way her confidence is growing when looking at herself in the mirror and liking what she sees. She's not the little wolf that went away broken and defeated. No, this is a strong female wolf who is coming into her own.

A Luna in the making.

Passing by another maternity shop, I bite my tongue with the way I want to ask if I could just go in and look for something for myself. Looking in the window as we pass, I try not to look at the reflection staring back in the glass. She's not someone I want to see.

The shopping is winding down. They have gotten themselves lots of bags filled with things that I used to get for myself every week.

We pass the maternity shop on the way out. I keep my head down with the way they just forgot about me. I said nothing this whole trip. No one asked my opinion on anything, and I don't blame them.

I bump into the Luna's back as she stops in the middle of the mall.

"Kennedy, we just passed by another shop. Don't you want to go in and get some things you need?"

"It's okay, Luna Grace. I don't need anything."

"That's ridiculous. You should have asked to go in when we passed it twice. I'm not a mind reader. You need to ask for what you want," she scolds. She also turns on Rya. "That goes for you as well. If you need something, ask me." This little lesson done, she smiles to the both of us.

Walking into the store, I can't help but notice all the colorful dresses. If this were another situation, I would have all these cute outfits to buy. I would make myself look as beautiful as I could. Instead, I grab black shorts, black pants, and a few grey and white tops. Nothing fancy, nothing that catches the eyes. I get a plain summer dress that doesn't flatter me at all. I don't come out of the changing room to show off how I look. Instead, I take the pile of my new clothes to the counter to pay.

I open up his wallet, and a picture of his family greets my eyes that makes me smile slightly.

Looking down, I notice that popular book that goes through your pregnancy step by step, day by day.

"You should buy two of those books—one for you, one for Cash," Luna Grace advises.

I do as she says, buying two of those books.

We're running late, so we decide to eat at home instead of at the mall.

The driveway has cars in it that weren't there when we left.

When we walk into the house, Alpha Clinton is talking to a group of females with Carson and Crane hovering around them. They have their beautiful bodies on display, while the two brothers look on in appreciation. A flash of red on lips the color of blood wine. They have an invitation out for the males that they are available if they want them.

More males show up with shaved heads, letting the females know that they are ready whenever they are. I put all the pieces together early on. I just need to sit back and watch everything.

Cash comes down the stairs looking like he just got cleaned up for the arrival of all these guests. He makes no introductions of who I am to him. I stand there like a statue, looking at his shaved head. I watch a female touch his head, and he lets her. My first tear comes down my face when he walks her down the stairs, leading the way with her close behind.

I deserve this for everything I have put him through. I just hope he finds someone good, someone who will treat my young like their own. It's impossible to hide my tears from everyone else.

They don't look at me. It's easier if they don't.

The only one who really is looking is Rya. She's just staring. I understand now just a fraction of what she has had to endure at my hands.

CHAPTER 6

Goals

Rya

Packages drop to the floor. It's as if she can no longer hold anything but herself, and even that looks as if it's getting too much for Kennedy.

Slowly she turns away, shoulders hunched, trying so hard to hold her composure. Not a sound coming from her mouth, her body shakes with the effort she's putting forth to not let the sounds of her cry tumble out her mouth.

I want to be that leech that drinks this up in gluttonous waves of delight, but I can't find any joy in this.

The Silverback Alpha watches her slow ascent up the stairs. She's holding the banister for support, taking one slow step at a time. I notice that Luna Grace has tears in her eyes at what she's seeing.

The door is closed to the basement, but I can hear the faint laughter, the beat of the music softly

95

drifting up, wrapping around our bodies, but we are not laughing. We are all trying hard not to let our emotions out.

"Cash." The vibration of sound ripples through my body as if I'm standing right beside a speaker at a concert during the drum solo. One word spoke so effectively that not too long after, the door opens to the basement.

Eyes that hold whispering shame look to his parents, such gaping sadness in them. Didn't I hear laughter from down below? He doesn't look like he was laughing.

Alpha Clinton puts his hands on his son's shoulders. Cash can't meet his father's eyes. Luna Grace has her hand on her son's back before they lead him to another part of the house and shut the door behind them.

I pick up Kennedy's packages off the floor; my bad arm is able to hold the weight of a few bags filled with clothes. My good arm carries her books she bought. Walking up the steps, I set my own packages down on my bed before going to her room.

With a little knock on the door, I open it. The mural is outstanding perfection; it's as if she is pouring her soul into this masterpiece. I think she must be thinking of doing all the walls with the way there are faint lines of ideas on everything. Even the ceiling has traces of clouds and a moon looking down.

I can see Cash's wolf in most of the scenes. She's depicting him as the leader wolf, stronger than any of the wolves around him. She's created pictures of these pups' father as the ruler in this room. No weakness can be seen in his wolf's body, standing tall and erect, head held high, eyes that don't look down. I don't see a trace of her wolf in any of these pictures.

Her bed is made, and I don't think she has slept in it for a very long time, with the way the paints and brushes are scattered over the top. Looking around, I don't see her, but I can hear her muffled cries. The pillow she's using to hide her grief must be saturated in her feelings.

The only other place she can be is in her closet. Do I really want to open the door?

"Please leave." A choking sound comes out from behind the door.

The door creaks as I open it slowly. Cash's scent is mixed in with hers. I notice the way some of his shirts are hanging up without any of her clothes in here. I'm intruding in her den. It's dark and smells like her mate. She's curled up on the carpeted floor, head buried into her pillow, with her back facing me. A few of his clothes are placed around her small pregnant belly.

This is the most pitiful sight I have ever seen.

What do I say?

There is no joy in my heart in seeing this; it doesn't make me happy as I thought it would. It sickens me, because I see me on that floor, with my mouth buried in that pillow. I can't even enjoy her pain because it's my pain I'm seeing.

"I'm not sure what to say to you," I tell her the truth.

She cries harder into the pillow that muffles the

sound, trying to hold herself tight in her own arms; I don't think they are strong enough anymore.

I hear an intake of breath from behind me. Cash is standing at the entrance to her room, looking at the art on the wall.

It's as if he's seeing this for the first time. He looks at everything.

A wave of shame his eyes can't hide crosses his face as he looks at his wolf form so full of pride, yet he's not holding that pride in himself right now.

His eyes dart to the floor on the carpet. He's seeing his mate curled into herself.

A tremble on his lip, he inhales and exhales slowly.

"Please leave." Her plea comes out ragged.

She looks hollow, as if her bones have no more marrow left in them, empty and brittle, ready to snap without hope of repair.

Cash turns around and walks out the door into his room without saying a word to her.

"Cash," I call out to him.

"Don't, Rya. I deserve this. Please just leave."

"But—"

"Rya, I'm sorry for everything. I'm truly sorry for what I've done to you." She keeps her back to me, the words barely whispered out.

"I was so wrong. I'm wrong, everything about me is wrong. Just go, please." Her words are a begging plea. Closing the closet door per her request, I cast her in her own darkness.

This isn't justice. An eye for an eye doesn't free you from your past pains. You think that seeing another person suffer would ease the suffering you went through, but it doesn't.

The books that she bought are just barely peeking out of the bag. Taking one, walking out of her room, I open Cash's door. He's lying on his bed face down, muffling his own cries into the pillow. I place the book next to his head before turning and walking out, closing the door quietly behind me.

Walking into my room, I quietly call Dallas.

He picks up on the first ring. "Rya."

"Dallas."

"What's wrong?" he breathes out.

"I don't know. I just feel bad for Kennedy."

"What's going on?"

"She looks the way I looked. I used to think that I wanted that look on her face, but now that it's happening, I just can't stomach it."

"Rya, you have a good heart." I hear the smile in his voice.

"Thanks, Dallas."

A commotion has Dallas yelling at males to quiet down.

"Rya, I have to tell you something. Clayton is living with me at my house. He burned his down, and I don't think anyone will take him in. So he's going to be living here until he can find somewhere else to live."

"What?"

"He's going through some stuff at the moment. He'll be fine. He just needs to figure it out."

"Oh." I can't say anything else. I don't want to know anything else about him.

"Rya, Clayton said he was worried about Kennedy, said she didn't sound like herself." My chest tightens slightly, knowing that they have been talking together on the phone. I wonder if he calls her every day like he does me? Except he leaves me messages while he talks with her.

"She's not doing well, Dallas. Maybe you could call Cash and tell him he needs to be around her more. He doesn't have to love her or anything. He just needs to be close to her, to provide comfort to her."

"I'll do that. I'll have a talk with him."

"Thanks, Dallas."

"I should go. I'll call him now. Bye, my beautiful wolf." I smile with his praise.

"Bye, Dallas." Hanging up the phone, I contemplate listening to more voice mails. I don't.

As my training progresses, and the weeks start to usher one season out and welcome the new one, Cash and me walk into the house sipping on our slushies that stain our lips and teeth blue. I give a giggle out at how we look. Holding our celebration drinks filled with vodka, we laugh to ourselves. Cash has become a friend, and I haven't had one in a very long time. We can actually talk about things, he doesn't judge me, and I have been trying to encourage him to maybe give Kennedy another chance.

We discuss how the twins are growing inside her. Neither of us have seen her in a while; she's sneaky the way she avoids us.

"Dad, she just beat Carson," he calls into the house as we enter from the garage.

It took two months to do this. Once I was able to master the basic moves Cash showed me, it wasn't long to start climbing the ranks of the juveniles until it was the little wolverine against me. He was slightly pale, thinking he might have a repeat of what happened. I like how he's the littlest out of all the juveniles, but he acts as if he's the biggest rooster in the hen house.

He still struts around, all puffed out with what Dallas said to him that day. It's funny how all it takes is one person to say things to you that can affect your whole life for the better.

I noticed that a few of the juvenile females had to drop out from training because they started going through their first heats. It's hard on the juvenile males trying to spar with them. They can't help themselves, trying to rub up against them.

Cash had to break up the fights between the males trying to go after the same female. Instead of fists, wolves started to come out in teeth that wanted to kill. Friends became instant enemies with their basic instinct taking over to mate.

Next was the adult wolves. They proved much harder and fiercer. Most of the females had to drop out completely because they went into heat after the first month of sparring with me. I remember one of them crying and crying with happiness, disbelief on her face as she asked the other females if she could be going through her first heat. They all told her that she was starting it. They all held her close in happiness.

A celebration promised if successful.

The Luna commented on these strange findings. I just kept *quiet*.

Today I fought Carson and won. Next is Cash.

Usually, we are a lot later, missing dinner completely because of training, but today we're home earlier than expected.

Turning the corner into the kitchen, we appear, blue lips, blue teeth, and bruised faces.

We see Kennedy between Alpha Clinton and the Luna at the table. The Luna has her hand on Kennedy's back, rubbing gently, while the Alpha feeds her very small pieces of dry toast.

I can see her swallowing, but she's gagging on it. She has tears in her eyes with the effort to hold it down. She wants to eat; you can see the anguish on her face as her body just wants to heave it up.

"Keep it down, Kennedy, that's it." Alpha Clinton is using firm commands in his tone. Her stomach heaves again, but she is able to keep it down.

"Are you ready for another piece?" She nods her head at him, not looking our way. Cash tenses beside me, no longer happy.

"Kennedy, how's the mural coming?" The Luna looks at her in concern, trying to engage her in some kind of conversation to take her mind off of trying to swallow the food her body is rejecting.

Her lips are no longer soft and delicate. They're cracked in deep grooves that look like they bleed.

"It's going well." Her voice holds no moisture, dry and thick on a tongue that isn't used to talking to anyone anymore. She doesn't even look up from the table, keeping her head down.

"Is there anything you need? Anything you want to eat or have a craving for?" Luna Grace's voice is so soft.

"Yes, I need more paint, the same as last time, please." Her hands and arms are splattered with speckles of the colors that she's been using.

She's usually like a ghost, flittering in and out, staying locked away in her room, painting as if it's her only goal.

I've been looking in on her, opening her door. Always she is painting with her back to me or in her closet wrapped in his clothing that she keeps stealing with a pregnant wolf's compulsion to be close to her mate.

I've asked her if she wants to talk about anything. No answer comes out her mouth; all I hear is the brush stroking against the wall.

It's actually horrifying what I see in front of me. Her skin looks dry and drained, sunken eyes, ashen skin. Her heartbeat sounds erratic in her chest.

I watch as she tries to reach for her glass of water. The tremors that she is desperately trying to hide won't be hidden, as the water sloshes over the side of the glass, spilling out slightly.

A whipped dog doesn't shake so much. She must feel very vulnerable at the moment, no longer able to shift into wolf form. Her shoulders hunch forward so much she seems like a person beaten by life.

She stands on unsteady legs that now have a hard time bearing her weight.

"Thank you for dinner, Luna Grace." Her lips now have a bead of blood on them with the way they crack with too much movement of her mouth. She's not used to speaking so much.

She moves away from the dinner table, holding

onto the wall as she makes her way upstairs. One foot up the step, then the other, she rests halfway up before she begins the rest of her climb. I can see strands of hair falling out from her once glorious mane; it's brittle at the ends, full of knots.

She's not even brushing her hair anymore.

Cash cannot stop staring at her back. He looks shaken by what he's seeing—his mate is dying in front of his eyes.

She's in crisis; she looks just the way females get when their mates die when they are pregnant. I have only seen that look one time. That female never made it, but her pup survived. Kennedy will not survive this if she continues on this path. They all will die if someone doesn't do an intervention on her soon.

"She needs to go to the hospital now. She needs intravenous fluids, she needs medication, and she needs to eat. But what she needs the most is you, Cash, unless you're fine with her dying, because that's what happening now. She's dying, and the dead can't be brought back."

Cash's walking upstairs. I hear some yelling before he carries her fragile frame down the stairs. She looks so small and weak compared to him.

His body stills as he looks down at her belly, the side of it pressed against him. Can he feel the way his little ones are kicking instinctively with his presence? This would probably be the first time he has felt his young move.

"Please put me down. I have to finish." She's desperate to get back upstairs, putting up a fight that is laughable at how weak she is.

"No, you're not well, Kennedy. You need to get better," I say to her.

"It's all I have for them. It's the only beautiful thing I can give them." Her words choke in her throat.

Kennedy puts her nose in his neck, inhaling his scent.

"You smell like Rya." Her observations make her cry harder into his shoulder.

His hand rubs her back now, trying to comfort her.

"Do you mind driving us, Rya?"

He's just holding her like she's nothing but feathers in his arms.

At the clinic, the midwife is waiting for us, along with the doctor. I wonder if this is the same one who saved Dallas's life?

Concern is etched on the midwife's face as Kennedy's brought into the examining room. A nurse is there also, starting to put the intravenous in, with the doctor giving his orders on what to do. The midwife pulls up her shirt, revealing her bare stomach. The roundness of it is beautiful, harboring two futures that are very rare.

Cash is staring at her exposed baby bump, his hands going over it. Feeling over top her bare flesh makes her gasp out uncontrollably, her eyes rolling back inside her head slightly as if she hasn't experienced pleasure in a long time.

"Kennedy, the medicine that we've been giving you isn't working." Kennedy shakes her head no at them.

They look at each other, concern passing

between midwife and doctor over a patient that might be lost.

Kennedy is in heaven with the feel of Cash's hands on her. The way her body has stopped shaking, she seems more relaxed. I watch as her hands slowly come over his. She looks into his eyes, some kind of plea in them.

"Cash, she needs you."

"It's okay, I don't deserve him. He's better off without me. At least he can move on." The flatness of her voice gives me chills.

"Kennedy." Cash just gets to say one word before she speaks again.

"I want them to leave. I don't want them in here anymore."

"You heard her, out." The midwife takes a protective stance over her suffering female. The doctor squares his shoulders. He can't take Cash, I can see it clearly, but he will try.

The doctor is on the phone fast, calling in back up.

"Let's go. She doesn't want me here."

Walking outside with Cash, I bump his shoulder with mine.

I watch as his parents are pulling up in their car.

"Don't, Rya!"

"What will you do, Cash?" The Alpha and Luna look on at our exchange.

"She's dying, Cash. She needs her mate." I give him a slight shove with my hands that want to turn into fists. I feel this rage flowing through me. A power that I never knew I possessed.

"Put your teeth away, Rya." Cash takes an

offensive stance, squaring his shoulders, balancing on the balls of his feet.

"Make me. I don't think you have it in you, Cash. I think you've given up; I think you're the biggest quitter I have ever seen." He runs hard at me, catching me by the waist, lifting me high in the air before slamming my body on the ground.

It knocks my breath away, but I can take a hit now and get back up quickly.

"Stay down, Rya!"

My body is vibrating. I can feel the blood filling my muscles. I roll my shoulder and crack my neck.

"Weak little wolf," I taunt him now. I can get under his skin. This wolf I know well enough to know his weakness.

"Rya, stop it." He's pacing back and forth, snapping his displeasure.

I notice the way that Silverback is looking on, just watching.

"Quitter. I have never met a bigger quitter in all my life. What did you say to her? You told her that you would make her understand who you were to her. That you wouldn't give up on making her understand that you belong together. Are you also a liar, Cash? A weak little lying wolf." My slurs to him hurt his ears. Another running charge at me.

I've been taught well to deflect a charging bull. I can feel the dance we are about to engage in.

I'm going to win.

My turn to smash my elbow into his jaw, flip him with the momentum of his own body on the ground. Going down hard on his back, he recovers with graceful movement. I still believe in myself, that I can overcome him.

It's his turn to take the defensive.

He rubs his jaw. A flash of teeth my way. His father yelling, "Fists only, Cash."

It's a completeness that I feel as the wolf slightly ascends, helping guide my movements. In this minute, I am the strongest. I turn to the Silverback with a challenge in my eyes. I feel as if I can take him on.

"If I win, you have to go back into that clinic room and stay with her. You have to start treating her better. I'm not asking you to love her, Cash, just stay close to her while she's pregnant."

"You hate her. Why would you do this for her?"

"Because no one should feel the way she does. It's not right. You have to not give up anymore, Cash. Be the wolf that I heard about."

This time I run at him before he can comment on anything I say.

Everything I have been taught to do, I do.

Everything that I have *learned*, *watched*, and *listened* to is what I use to fight him. He's a stronger wolf, but I'm faster. He's more solid, but I am leaner. I have been fighting these last months to get to where I am now.

Taking blow after blow, I will not quit now.

I feel as if the moon, in this minute, is with me, lending me her strength.

Hitting him hard, folding him into himself, that's the moment that I need to get him into a submission hold. He has two choices: give up or get knocked out. I can do it.

He's squirming and fighting the way he was with

Dallas. I don't have the fluidity behind my moves like Dallas, but I have the moon inside me providing an inner drive.

Legs wrap around his body, squeezing the breath out of him, forearm wraps around his neck, and I squeeze with everything I have, not letting go while his elbow digs into my side, hitting it over and over again, cracking my ribs.

I put more pressure on his windpipe; there is no hope of him taking a breath. He keeps fighting until I feel him starting to go limp in my arms. I hold onto him tight until I know he's out.

Standing up, hands on my thighs, slightly bent over breathing hard, I spit blood on the now defrosting earth.

Spring is in the air.

"Little Moon, congratulations."

"Thank you, Alpha Clinton. What's next?" I say with curiosity.

"You go back home."

CHAPTER 7

Now I Know

Numbness spreads throughout my body, making me falter slightly on my feet.

"I don't want to go back." My shoulders suddenly feel burdened again.

"Little Moon, it's going to be okay. You aren't the same female that left. Show them who you always were." He smiles at me without teeth.

Luna Grace embraces me in her arms, pressing her cheek against mine.

"We'll miss you." She pulls herself away from me, looking into my eyes with tears in her own.

"I'm going to miss it here. It feels right, as if I've always belonged." There's a little wobble in my voice.

"Hopefully, you will come back with our first born. But if not, it was our great honor to have you among us." That Silverback Alpha stands close to his Luna as he talks to me, his hand wrapped into hers.

"Thank you." It's all I can say, because everything else seems too small.

"Do you need a ride home?" Luna Grace questions.

"No, I'm going to walk."

"We'll see you at home. We're going in to check on our Cash and Kennedy." Concern is etched in the fine lines around her face.

Walking away from them, I try with all my strength to keep it together, but I do shed a few tears. It's a slow walk back to the house, not the quick run that Cash and I have done every morning for the last two months. I get to take everything in without the rush of life.

I like the way the leaves are unfurling from the buds on the trees. Mother Nature looks as if she's slowly opening her eyes, her warm spring breath just starting to reach its way this far north.

A calm breeze whispers its breath in the trees, and the birds chirp, click, and clack as they make their nests in the great pines that line the edge of the road. The emerald guardians, standing virtuous, protective in all their splendor. Their height filters out the late afternoon sun, casting my path toward the house in shadows.

Passing by the house that nature has begun to take over, I get a shiver, making my hair stand on end.

It's tucked into the tree line, barely visible, hidden behind the dense overgrowth of forest life. It was a beautiful house at one time, now falling into decay. I take the driveway up. Cracks in the pavement are growing small stunted trees from the small space it has to live.

Trees have been knocked down by the wind but have not been cleaned up; dead branches litter the yard that no one has cared for in a very long time. I always had Cash with me on our runs, but I have always wanted to peek into what their home looked like.

A certain sadness calls out from the house, as if it were missing its occupants.

Spider webs cover the window panes, the buildup of grime on the glass making it difficult to see inside.

Going to the door, I turn the handle, and it clicks open. A dryness takes over my throat as my heart starts to race in my chest.

Everything is covered in a thick layer of dust. Nothing has disturbed the inside of this tomb until now.

Memories are encased in this house's womb, pictures still hanging on the wall. A few have dropped, cracking the glass, but their smiling faces still peer out.

Echoes of laughter can still probably be heard if you stood still long enough.

A gust of musty, stale air crinkles my nose up. I bet when they built this house, they never thought that it would be filled with air that hasn't moved in a long time…

Every corner holds memories of a time long past.

I can't bring myself to step into this memory of his. Their picture hangs directly in front of me…both smiling, looking into the camera. He's got his arm draped over her shoulder. Around the picture is writing on congratulations to the newly mated couple. Words of inspiration from pack members are written around their image.

I look at her eyes that have no idea that one day they would be looking into mine.

Why do I feel as if I'm snatching something away from her? She doesn't look back with condemnation; she's just bright eyed with what the future will bring to them.

Raven black hair that's cut short to frame her jawline. Bright green eyes that draw you into her. I can't stop comparing myself to her, and I don't see how Dallas could ever see me when he has had her.

Goosebumps prickle my skin. A chill travels down my spine as if someone is here with me.

I can feel eyes on me, prickling my skin. My hair stands on end, the cold shivering my skin.

The softest of breaths dances across my face, a featherlight kiss placed against my lips. In this moment, I feel as if she's here with me, standing right in front of me, except I can't see her, but I feel her before she fades away and the goosebumps are no longer there.

Closing the door fast, I run all the way back to the house as fast I can until I'm in the safety of my own room, and even then I still feel freaked out.

It takes a few minutes to calm down enough to call Dallas. I'm still slightly out of breath when he answers.

"Dallas." It comes out fast.

"Rya?" he questions.

"I beat Cash today."

"That's my female. So when are you coming

back? I miss you." His voice caresses my ears.

"I'm not sure when, but I think soon. I don't want to leave. I want to see you, but I want to stay here too." He's quiet as he lets me talk. In the background, I can hear a small pup crying out in rage. It's demanding something in the way the cries get more furious.

I hear a door close, the cries being muffled slightly.

"Who's that?"

"It's Kimberly's male. Clayton watches him every Monday for her while she's at school." That brings a smile on my face, a brother helping a sister. I never thought that something he did would ever turn my lips into a smile.

"What about Kimberly's mate or mother?"

"He's working. His mother works the weekend and Mondays, so that's the only day she needs someone to watch him until school is done."

"That's nice of him to do that."

"She's his sister, and he loves her very much. It's nice to watch them together."

"How's he doing with Caleb?"

"I think they secretly like each other." He laughs. "Not in that way, but I think that they could be great friends. He hasn't beaten him yet, but very close."

"When he beats him, are you coming back?"

"Yes, I've done everything I can here. I have a doctor starting next week. Clayton's taken almost all the day to day responsibilities of running the pack. Some of the wolves are coming around to trust in him again. He just needs to trust in himself."

"What about a midwife? Have you gotten him

one yet?"

"No, Rya, some things he has to do for himself."
It's my turn to be silent for a moment,
contemplating what his words really mean.

"I went to your house today, Dallas." Complete
silence on the other end.

"I went inside, not too far in, but far enough to
see the life you had."

"What did you think?"

"I think that you guys were happy, that you
loved her, that she loved you."

"We were happy, Rya, and I do love her." His
voice wobbles in his throat before he clears it.

"I felt her in there, Dallas. I just felt her love. I
felt as if she were giving me her blessing." I think
he's crying because the phone sounds muffled
against something.

"Could you ever love me the way you loved
her?"

Without hesitation in his voice, he answers. "I
could love you more." I believe him. "Rya, please
don't feel as if you will ever be second to her. She
was my past, but you're my future." It's my turn to
stifle the cries that want to seep out into the air.

"Thank you," I tell him in a choked whisper. "I
should go. Bye, Dallas."

"Bye, Rya." I hang up first because my emotions
are getting the better of me.

Turning the phone over in my hand, I
contemplate listening to my past so I can move
forward with my future.

He takes a breath. There's a slight pause before
he blows out slowly what he was holding in his

lungs.

"So after that first day I saw you drive away, I started stalking your house, trying to get glimpses of you. I saw you in that garden, poking around, pulling weeds. I tried not to stare at you so you wouldn't know I was around. Do you know I love to garden? It's kind of a hobby of mine. Kennedy had her art, and I had my garden. I always wanted her to come and help pull weeds, but she would rather sit underneath a shade tree and draw me pulling weeds." He laughs at the memory he's having. He wouldn't be laughing now if he could see her.

"I knew that you would be starting work on Monday. I just couldn't help myself; my Wild was pushing me to see you. I got up early that morning, sneaking around the house. It's funny, I was trying to be quiet so I wouldn't wake Kennedy to see you. I felt like I was cheating on her if I were to see you. I never told her, when I would leave the house, what I was doing. She trusted me." A sad laugh comes from his lips.

"I waited for you to open your door, just so I could get a glimpse. Our eyes connected, and I had a hard time pulling my wolf away from you that day. I remember going back to the house, crawling back into bed with Kennedy, and pretending that she was you, that I was fucking you. Not making love. I swear to the moon it was the most intense experience I have ever had with her. Nothing in my lifetime has ever come close to that. That was the last time we ever fucked. I couldn't anymore. I felt too guilty." The message ends with him taking another long inhaled breath from something he's smoking.

The next message is from him again.

"The next time I saw you was at the pack house. My mother made sure you were there. I watched you in your car. You looked pitiful the way you kept opening and closing your door, talking to yourself. I wanted to go over to you, but I didn't. A common theme with me. I didn't, but Dallas did. I watched how he opened your door, talked with you. I watched how he pried your hands off the steering wheel, getting you to get out of that car of yours. It wasn't me who was by your side but him as you walked into the party. No one really said anything to you, no hello's that you're back. Nothing. It's as if you still never existed. Isn't that right no one really cared that you were even back? Maybe they just forgot about you like the way I did." This hurts me so much that my pack doesn't even care. I bet when I get back, no one even notices.

"I saw you with him. You kept your back to me, but I couldn't stop looking at you. Kennedy was watching me like a hawk, getting more and more upset. I can tell when she's upset; she stops talking. Dallas was upset about something; he was talking to my father as if he were the Alpha. I have never seen him so dominant. I knew right then that he was Alpha born. I should have known better than try to fight him that night. My father put on a show for you, always the actor. To tell you the truth, Rya, I hated that male. We never saw eye to eye ever. I remember coming toward you and you freaked out. You couldn't even stand, falling to the ground. It

117

was hard to watch the pain I have caused you. For the first time, I felt the need to do something, to help you up. I tried to reach for you, but Kennedy wouldn't let me, and I allowed her to pull me back. I could have easily just brushed past her, to help you off the ground, but once again I didn't do anything but watch you come apart. The funny thing was you got up on your own; no one helped you but yourself. Our eyes connected for a split moment, and I knew that you were mine. You turned your back on me, and I let what was mine walk away." He takes a swallow of something that makes him hiss slightly with the way it must burn his throat.

There are no more messages from Dallas. I think I must be home from the being with the wild wolves. I check the date and, sure enough, I am back. So now all I have to listen to is Clayton and his side of the story.

"I waited for you to be done with work. I didn't know how to approach you. I should have just marked you that day. I should have just claimed you and said screw the consequences. I just couldn't do it to Kennedy. That was the only thing stopping me, what I had with her. I have loved that wolf my whole life, Rya. I don't think I could ever love someone that much again. My heart just won't let me. I'm sorry if that hurts, but it's the truth. She is my greatest love, and you're becoming my greatest regret." He inhales again from whatever he's smoking.

"I remember that day at Dallas's party that he decided to put together. He would sometimes invite people to his place, not usually, but when he did it was always a good time. I was a little upset when he called me, told us to stay home, that we weren't invited. I thought it was a joke at first. I laughed at him; he never laughed back. He said that if I was to go, you would probably leave, and he wanted you to stay. I knew then that he was going after you. He never had to say anything, but I knew that wolf wanted you. So, of course, I went with Kennedy. I had to. I just couldn't stay away from you, especially now you had some other wolf sniffing around you." He takes another drink, long swallows before he says another word.

"He walked right up to us. You know something? Kennedy always got looked at by other wolves, and it drove me crazy. He's probably the only one who never looked at her like that. To tell you the truth, he never looked at any female until you came along. Where was I again?" It's almost as if he's getting lost in his own thoughts, his words becoming slightly slurred.

"He came up to me at the party, told us that everything we said about you was a lie. He walked away only to come back, saying that since I don't want you, he was going to do Kennedy and me a favor and take you off my hands. I couldn't even say anything back to him because Kennedy was right beside me and I didn't want to hurt her feelings. I love her. " He hangs up the phone, slamming it down so my ear hurts with the sound.

Listening to the next one. "Rya, the night I went to Dallas's house, he just came back from yours...I smelled you all over that wolf. I couldn't stop myself. We shared some words, and then we fought with teeth over you, while Kennedy was waiting for me to get home. When I went into the house that night, everyone could smell Dallas all over me. Kennedy freaked out; I could tell in her eyes that she knew I just couldn't fight it anymore." His voice gets cut off as his time is up.

The next message he's sounds as if he's starting to slur; I can hear ice cubes against the glass. "Rya, when you came to our house the next day, you saw Kennedy and me by the apple tree talking. It was her favorite thing to draw, except this time she was painting a barren tree without the fruit on its branches, almost as if the tree itself was dying. I knew she was upset, so we had a real talk. Honest conversation. I was telling her that I didn't think we could go on like this anymore; the mate's pull was too much now for me to fight against. That my Wild was getting more and more agitated with her...that I was afraid he would hurt her, and trust me, I was trying to fight it with everything I had, because I loved Kennedy. I still do. I always will love her. I'm sorry it's not something you want to hear, but you need to hear it. While we were talking, you were watching us. I felt terrible for Kennedy. She's a good wolf, Rya. It's not our fault we loved each other. We loved each other, but in the end, without the moon's blessing, I just couldn't fight against the moon." He gets cut off again.

I get to the very last one. There are no more after this.

"Rya." He's really slurring his words now. He sounds very drunk; I've never been drunk before, but they always say that drunk words are your sober thoughts.

"You should let him mark you, because I never will." That's it. The call ends. He's left his last message for me to hear.

I need to sit on the edge of the bed. My phone falls to the carpet. I need to hold onto the fabric of the coverlet for a few moments as my breathing becomes difficult.

I can't pretend this doesn't hurt. It does.

CHAPTER 8

Forgiveness

Rya

Cash is at Kennedy's side as they enter the house. She doesn't look up, keeping her eyes to the ground. Her head is shaved; Cash said she didn't even cry when they did it.

Her hair was so knotted it couldn't be saved.

She hardly makes a sound, walking by as if she really isn't here at all. The faintest trace of silver hits my nose before it disappears, making me think I really never smelled it in the first place.

I thought that maybe she would look different now that Cash was with her constantly. Except the depths of her brokenness are a perversion to witness, vacant eyes staring at nothing. No joy on her face as she lets him guide her to the table. She's not as skinny as before; she's able to eat as long as he feeds her from his hand.

She looks like a funeral hymn all dressed in

black, slipping ever so slowly below the living.

"Kennedy, we were talking with one of the teachers at the school, and she asked if maybe you would like to help out with painting some of the back drops for the school play. They could use someone of your talent to help them if you're interested."

"I don't have the time. I need to get my painting finished." The voice holds such emptiness, as if no one is inside anymore.

"Oh, well, after you're done painting. The play isn't getting started for a while. We thought you would enjoy getting out of the house for a few hours a day. When you're feeling better." Luna Grace's trying to engage her in life.

"I need a tarp, Luna Grace." She dismisses the Luna's offer immediately.

"Why a tarp?" The Luna regards Kennedy up and down trying to see into her.

"I'm going to be working on the ceiling, and I don't want the paint to stain the carpet." I can see the way her lips are pressed together tight, eyes filling with tears before she swallows emotions down with the food she is eating.

"Okay, we can get you one." Luna Grace keeps looking at the Silverback, eyes meeting eyes in silent communication.

"I heard you're leaving us tomorrow, Rya." Cash has his hand on Kennedy's back, rubbing it soothingly as she continues to eat forkful after forkful.

"Luna Grace, I need that tarp tonight. Do you have one lying around?" Kennedy's voice holds an edge of panic.

"Yes, somewhere in the garage. I'll get it for you after dinner."

"Thank you." Kennedy almost gives a smile of relief.

Cash looks older somehow, his stubble on his beard showing a few days' worth of growth along with his and Kennedy's heads. They look like they're twinning with matching haircuts.

"How are the pups doing?" I ask Kennedy, but Cash answers for her.

"Better. They had to give her a shot to make their lungs mature faster. They thought that she was going to deliver a few days ago, but they were able to stop the contractions." Cash visibly is upset about the thought of almost losing his futures.

"Well, if you deliver now, then at least their lungs will be mature enough to breathe on their own." I try to ease Cash's worries.

"Rya, have you ever done a c-section before?" Kennedy asks me this odd question.

"No, I never have, but I have assisted with one. I can't perform that. I'm not a doctor." She doesn't say anything else as she finishes what's on her plate.

"Kennedy, c-sections for wolves are only done in emergencies. The mothers hardly make it. If that's done, it's done with the intent to save the pup only." A dark shadow passes over her face as the sun begins its descent, the moon to take its place in the sky.

Our watcher.

Standing, she looks at Cash's parents. "I just

want you both to know that I am so very thankful that my young will have grandparents like you." With that, she turns her back on us, making her way toward the stairs and up to her room.

"Cash, what's going on with her?" She still looks terrible.

I can't help but be soaked by the wave of her decaying grey misery.

"She won't talk to me. I've tried to talk to her. She only lets me feed her and touch her while she eats because she knows it's the only way to keep the food down. Other than that, she won't talk to me. All she says is everything will be okay soon." Cash has his hands on his head, elbows on the wood grain table.

"We got some clothes for the pups. Maybe Kennedy and you can go through them together. Also, we got the cribs Kennedy picked out. They're in her room. We took the bed out because she's going to start to sleep with you in your bed, right?" Luna Grace looks at her son with sharp eyes.

"Yes, it's comforting for her body if I'm close."

"Good." Her tone implies that she is pleased with his answer.

"Cash, something is very wrong with her." I can't help but blurt that out.

"I know, Rya. I just don't know how to fix it."

"I know this might not be what you want to hear, but you should call Clayton." Cash's fist crashes down on the table.

"He knows her the best. He could help you with her." Cash looks defeated.

"I was thinking the same thing, Rya. It's time to

ask him for help."

Alpha Clinton sits with his arms crossed, biceps peeking out his shirt. I can't help getting panicked for Dallas, having to take this great Silverback male on. I'm not sure how he's going to do that.

"Do you have his number?" Cash's voice interrupts my thoughts on how Dallas will have to train with his father when he comes back here.

"Yes, I do." Reaching into my pocket, I call him before Cash has time to think this through. I put the call on speakerphone for all of us to hear.

The phone rings and rings before he answers.

"Rya?" His voice seems to falter over the phone.

"It's Cash!" The sound that emanates from his throat is more of a low growl.

"Cash?"

I watch as Cash inhales a breath in. This must be hard for him to ask this wolf for help.

"Clayton, it's about Kennedy."

"Is she okay?" Now concern rings out. He would never feel that for me, because I was never a concern for him.

"No, she's not." A heaviness comes out his chest that is amplified in his voice.

"What's going on? What's she doing?" Clayton sounds as if he's sitting down, the chair in the background scraping against the tile.

"She's very depressed. She won't open up to anyone. I was wondering if you could talk with her. Maybe see if you can get her to talk to you? I need your help with her because no one knows what else to do." Silence on the other end of the line.

"Has she stopped talking?"

"Yes," Cash says immediately to him.

"That's not good. She loves to talk and talk. It will drive you crazy because she doesn't stop." I can just imagine all the late night conversations he has had with her in bed together.

"Is she painting?"

"Yes, all she does is paint."

"That's her way of coping with stress. She will just paint for days on end without saying a word to anyone when she's upset. Cash, let me talk to her." Clayton's voice is very soft on the phone.

Cash's jaw twitches slightly, teeth clenched together. He walks away upstairs with my phone in his hand.

It's just us three at the table until Carson and Crane join us.

"Are you all set, Carson?" Luna Grace looks at her son.

"Yes, everything's ready." He looks at his mother. He won't look at me; it's as if he is purposely avoiding me and my eyes.

This should be such a fun car ride home.

When we were training, he made it a point to never be alone with me and to surround himself with females.

I take a second plate of food because I'm starving at the moment. I think that run in the woods made me really hungry. I couldn't let my wolf kill the female animals it found; they were loaded with young in their bellies, and I couldn't have her kill them. We aren't that hungry; we aren't starving for that kind of eating, not like in the wild wolf pack.

Dallas said that he went to my house and put groceries in the fridge for me, cleaned everything up so it smells springtime fresh. He understands my thing with smells and how I like clean-smelling things.

He even got the garden ready for me. All we have to do is plant the seeds and watch them grow.

Monday I'll start back to work as if I never left. I guess there is an abundance of females ready to birth very soon. Dallas said I'm going to be very busy. It's going to feel good to get back to work and get a routine down.

By the time we're done with dinner, the dishes are cleaned and put away, and we have some cookies for dessert. I take more than usual because I can't stop eating, even though I am stuffed.

Cash comes back down red-eyed and puffy, as if he has cried a river of tears. He puts a silver scalpel on the table. That sharp-edged blade has the potential to end everyone's life here.

"Can you bring it back to the clinic? Kennedy stole it from the doctor. She was planning on using this on herself tonight. She needed the tarp so she wouldn't get blood on the carpet. I need to go back upstairs, but I just thought everyone should know what she's thinking now. Rya, tell Clayton thank you." He hands me back my phone.

Bricks of silence start to stack up on the table from those sitting around it. The weight we feel is enough to break its sturdy legs.

Her plight is sorrowful to my soul.

Before I go, I need to talk to her, make things right between us. I couldn't leave knowing that I haven't done my part to ease her suffering. Even though she never bothered to help ease mine, I can't sit back without doing something.

"Carson, what time do you want to leave?"

"I was thinking around seven."

"Okay, sounds good."

"We'll see you in the morning, Rya." Luna Grace with her hauntingly beautiful face sadly smiles toward me.

Making my way to Cash's room, I knock lightly on the door.

"Come in," he calls out to me.

Entering the room they now share, she's wrapped in his arms, cuddled into his side. Her nose is pressed against his chest, her eyes shut. Her shaved head makes her look so much younger than she really is.

Closing the door behind me, I take a seat at his desk. I can see the pregnancy book that Kennedy bought that day, all dog-eared throughout, as if someone has been studying it intently. The spine broken, I wonder if I would find coffee stains inside the pages?

The swivel chair allows me to swing from side to side. I'm not sure where to begin.

Back and forth my emotions go, contemplating how to start things off.

"First thing, Kennedy, is this…if you die, your twins die a slow death. They will not get enough to eat; they can't survive on human formula. One pup in the pack to feed is manageable. It could be done, but not two. It's a great strain on the nursing mothers to try and provide what is meant for their young to feed someone else. They would have to let their pups go without while yours feed. It wouldn't work. Cash would not only have your death to deal with but also the slow starvation deaths of his pups. Did you take that into consideration, Kennedy?"

I watch her shake her head no.

"You would be gone, but it's the living that would have to deal with the effects of what you have done. You need some help. Let them help you. Trust me, the first step is just saying you need help. There's nothing wrong with asking. There's nothing to be ashamed of. Sometimes we get so sick that we can't see clearly anymore. Ask for the help. You have a family around you now willing to give you what you need."

She has her head buried into his side, great heaving sobs coming out. Her body trembles with the grief pouring from her soul.

"I was jealous of you, Kennedy. I would pray to the moon to make me like you every night. I would lay in my bed, praying to have what you had so he would just give me a chance." One of her red-rimmed eyes opens up to look at me.

"I wanted this. I wanted you to suffer so much. I would daydream of the day I would see you suffer the way I did back then. I wanted everything I went through to happen to you. Now it's happening, and I want to take it all back. I thought that this would make me feel better, that somehow seeing you suffer would make me feel good. It doesn't, and now I'm going to pray to the moon for your suffering to stop. No one deserves this. Not even you."

"Rya—" A choked out sound comes from her throat. Her brown eyes look up at me; I used to think they weren't pretty, but they are in her own way.

"No, let me finish because once I say it, I won't say it again. Our history together will be done." Taking a deep breath, I let the weight that has been dragging me down for years fall off my shoulders, and I sigh with pleasure this feeling is causing me.

"I want to give you my forgiveness. I can't give you anything else I have, but I can forgive you." I get up. I don't want to say anything else. She needs to figure out the rest for herself. I just wanted to say what I had to say and ease her burden slightly.

"Cash, can you leave for a moment? I need to say something to Rya before she leaves." I watch as Cash untangles his body from hers. She sits up on the bed, covers pooling around her waist. She waits until the door closes before saying what she has to say.

"If you forgive me, then you need to forgive Clayton, Rya. Please just give him a chance. He's a good wolf." She can barely get the words out, emotions making her voice tight. I bet she never thought she would say something like that to me.

"Rya, he's going to try and push you away so you don't like him. He's going to say and do things to you that he doesn't really mean. Just try to look deeper at him because what you will find is someone you were made for." This is causing her pain to say, letting him go to someone else. Except I don't want what she had.

Getting out my phone, I play her his last voice

mail that I've saved. The only one I listen to over and over again.

Watching her face the whole time, she holds my eyes, not looking away, as if willing her whole body to do something incredibly hard.

"He's lying." That's all she says, nothing more, before she lays herself back down on the bed.

I say nothing back for a moment because my sound is caught in my throat.

"Goodbye, Kennedy."

"Goodbye, Rya." Her voice is muffled by the door being closed behind me.

***

Mist saturates the morning in a heavy silence.

Luna Grace and Alpha Clinton stand side by side, my bags tucked away in the trunk of the car.

"Come here." Luna Grace's arms open wide for me as I step into her warm embrace.

"We want to say that we have come to love you like our own. You will always have a place here if you want." Her kiss against my cheek is soft and comforting.

"Little Moon, shoulders back, head up, remember who you are." He has a light sheen to his eyes before he places a small kiss to the top of my head.

"Carson, we'll see you back soon. Be good." The Alpha's stern voice hits Carson in his chest.

The sound of the car door slamming shut echoes into the forest, startling the birds to take flight.

Tilting my head to the right, I watch as the land

goes by in a blur from the windshield of the car. My right leg tucked underneath me starts to cramp up slightly with the need to get out and stretch.

The warm wind tosses my hair around my head. Carson has to drive with the window down, mumbling something under his breath about needing the air.

"Carson, can we stop soon? I need to stretch for a minute, and I'm hungry. I skipped breakfast." He grumbles something under his breath. I think he's trying to break the record on how fast he can get me back home.

We stop at a roadside diner with a gas pump out front along the highway that snakes this way and that.

Walking into the place, it's an interesting cross-section of human society. Truck drivers sitting alone, giving their orders to the waitresses with a shrug, while reading the paper. Families with their kids who can't sit still from being cooped up for so long in a car. Some locals engaging in coffee conversations about last night's game, the short order cook putting his two cents in every now and then as he comes out from finishing an order.

Taking our seats opposite each other, I can smell a few wolves in the crowd, who have their noses slightly up in the air. Carson faces them, leaning back in his chair, looking hard into their eyes.

His father has taught him well.

We place our orders with the pretty female who can't stop fluttering her long lashes Carson's way. Her fingers fidget with the pen she's holding, staring at his lips, her cheeks turning red. I have to admit he is a very good-looking male wolf. He pays no attention to her. His concentration is eyeing down the wolves who have taken interest in us.

Turning around in my seat, I eye them myself. Three juveniles try to posture more than what they are. I turn my back to them; they pose no threat.

Our food arrives. Holding the burger in my hands, I shut my eyes before taking the first bite, moaning slightly with how good it tastes. I open my eyes only to see Carson slide his chair back, going to get up.

"Carson, what are you doing?"

"I don't like the way they're eyeing us."

"Carson, let's eat and leave, okay?" Taking another bite of my burger, I swear I can eat two of these at the moment, it's so good.

He begins to eat his meal quietly.

Picking up an olive from my salad, I pop one in my mouth.

"You like olives, Carson?"

"Yeah, I like olives," he says as he continues to eye those wolves, getting his fur more ruffled by the moment.

"I like olives too. We have something in common." I smile his way.

"My brothers don't like olives. It makes it hard in the house to like something that everyone else doesn't have a taste for." He takes an olive off my plate, placing it in his mouth. I watch as he slowly chews it before swallowing it down.

"Do your brothers know how much you love olives?" It's a question I'm wondering about.

"No, they don't." He looks shamed somehow,

and I feel for him. It must be hard to keep that part of himself hidden away in the closet.

"I would never tell them what you like. I promise." A sigh of relief comes out his mouth.

No more is said. We finish our meal in silence before Carson pays the bill that has the waitress's number on it.

Obviously, she didn't think we were together.

Getting back inside the car, we pull back on the road. The atmosphere is lighter, not so oppressive.

The landscape starts becoming more familiar as maple and willow trees start to replace the great pines of the north.

It's warmer here, spring singing her arrival weeks ago.

Everything's in bloom.

Pulling up to his house, my stomach is in knots.

He's waiting for me outside in the driveway.

Eyes that match my own now watch me get out of the car.

He's the first to move, advancing on me. My body tingles in anticipation of feeling him on me.

Slowly, my fairy tale picks me off my feet. Strong arms hold me against him. Pressing his nose in the soft spot just above my collarbone, he inhales deeply with a little growl of appreciation.

His teeth actually almost break skin before he pulls away, leaving a small indentation in my skin of his soon-to-be mark.

"I've missed you so much, Dallas." I nip at his neck.

Hands twine into my hair, pulling my head back so my neck is completely exposed to him. He's grown more into himself. He's becoming more than when I saw him last. An Alpha on the verge of taking everything he was born to take.

He places a soft kiss on lips that want to feel more of his strength.

"Rya, you smell different." A growl rumbles out his chest, vibrating into mine.

"What's this?" His eyes go to my exposed bra strap, fingers pulling my shirt to the side, exposing more of my intimate apparel to him. Fire red, no way to get the color confused.

"I just wanted you to know that I'm available." Understanding crosses his face.

"I'll take you back to your house. Carson, thanks for bringing her back. Caleb's inside."

I look toward the house. Green eyes like that of transparent emeralds stare hard at me, holding me in my place for a moment.

His head is shaved.

CHAPTER 9

Red

Rya

Warm sweet spring air tickles the inside of my nose, thick with the heaviness of pollen. Birdsong and breezes rustle the trees as if singing a lullaby for my ears to hear. This is not a barren winter wilderness; this is a flourish of fertility at how the land is coming alive again.

Dallas carries my bags to the door. Turning to the side, I see my garden ready to be planted with this year's harvest. It's cast in small shadows as cotton-like clouds drift lazily by.

"Dallas, thank you for doing all this work for me." He's staring at me, watching me take all his hard work in.

"I liked doing it for you." His face gives a little blush; I feel like licking his face. What is wrong with me?

Opening the door to my place, everything is the

137

same except the walls. They've been fixed and painted the same color they once were. On my large table are containers of small seedling plants. The aroma of parsley, thyme, and lemon balm saturates the inside of my house along with all the different varieties of herbs that will be planted. It feels as if mother earth is present inside my home. I take a deep inhale. Not a trace of the previous wolf is left inside my space. It's as if she has never been here.

"Did you fix the wall?" I call out to him.

"Yes," he says from my bedroom. I can hear the bags lightly dropping on my dresser. His hands are empty now, and I want them to be full again with me in them. I can't help these thoughts that grip me at the moment. I have this singular need at the moment to be consumed by him.

Trying to shove these thoughts to the side, I look into the fridge, noticing lots of different containers of food with little notes attached to them. Picking up the first small note, it's from Cora saying welcome home.

Looking at all the other notes, it's from the females who I helped birth their pups.

"This was nice of them to do this," I say, holding the small notes in my hands.

"They all got together and made you enough food to last a few weeks until you get settled back into the swing of things. They thought you would like it." Dallas is getting closer to me, and I can't take my eyes off of him.

His eyes become a darker blue as the Wild in him tries to stare out. That only spurs the Nature of the Wild to make her presence known. I have to hold the top of the chair; she wants to run with his Wild so bad.

"Rya." Voice dropping deeper, huskier, he takes a step into my space. I could moan out at how he affects me. A tremble of lust travels from the tip of my spine to the bottom of my stomach, resting heavily deep down inside me.

Our eyes lock together, neither one of us looking away. The feel of his hand on the curve of my hip has me inhaling sharply into his chest. A kiss to my shoulder, a nip at my ear. Closing my eyes, I have never felt so overwhelmingly needful in all my life.

Hand on my ass, he brings me against him.

Fingers go up the inside of my shirt before it's off completely. He takes a step back, taking in the sight that I hoped he would appreciate. He does with a growl that shakes his muscles and saturates my panties.

"This looks very nice on you, Rya." His finger lingers over the top of the material that's supporting my chest.

His other hand goes to my pants. The button is undone, zipper pulled down. A little hint of red hits his eyes that are dilating now. I can hear his heartbeat swishing in my own ears.

The feel of his overwhelming desire for me is intoxicating. His eyes burn a trail of need into flesh that's twitching with anticipation.

His finger hooks into the top of my underwear, pulling the delicate fabric away. He looks inside, and another growl consumes his entire being.

Males are visual; I'm aiming to satisfy his most basic sense of sight.

The kiss he gives me is soft, gentle, but as his hands start to travel over my backside, our kiss deepens, becomes more demanding. Arms tangling with arms, my leg tries to go over his hip to press him more against me.

Lifting me off my feet, he begins walking us to the bedroom. I rub myself on him, hands in his hair. He's bitten my lips slightly, the way his teeth are descending.

I'm trembling. So is he. He doesn't make it to the bed as he holds me against the wall, letting my body slide down him so his knee rests between my legs and I'm barely on tip toes. He leans into me, and my eyes almost roll in the back of my head.

Ravenous.

His palms collide with my inner wrists, raising my arms above my head, tongue and teeth beginning to nibble between the valley of my chest. His teeth leave red lines on flesh that is heated in the most basic desperation of want.

I need to feel him. I have to feel him.

His knee is pressing more firmly into my sex. I rock myself back and forth on him. His one hand keeps my arms suspended above me while his other hand goes inside the red bra, pulling the material away to expose myself to him. Head dips low, tongue twirls around my sensitive nipple, everything is so much more sensitive to touch.

This is everything…

Teeth gently bite down, tugging, taunting, to cause sighs of pleasure to ooze out in honey thick sounds.

"Rya, you smell good." His nose buries itself

into my neck. He's sucking the skin hard into his mouth, his body quivering along with mine.

Dallas wakes up some deep-rooted desire. It's starting to bloom to life.

I feel flushed. Hot.

My hands tangle in his hair, roam over his back, grab onto his bottom, trying to pull him closer to me. My body is on fire. I have one goal in front of me, and he's what I need. I gasp as he pulls my bottom lip with his teeth, letting his tongue sweep over my lip before letting go and claiming my mouth again.

Heavy breathing between the both of us...

"The things I want to do to you." His velvety whispers hit my ear, liquid warmth pooling between my legs.

I'm so wet.

His mouth kisses me until he is my mouth. I'm partly out of my bra; the swell of my breasts are heaving up and down, nipples standing out proud. Claws come out, ripping the material of his shirt from the back. I'll leave scratches on him. I need to feel his skin against mine. I need to leave my mark on his skin.

His back feels smooth. The way his muscles are flexing under my hand makes me moan. He's making senseless noises that are low and slow in his throat.

The wall has had its fun as he picks me up again in his arms, legs wrapping tightly around his waist. My hair falls all around us. Pulsing with such strong instinct, I latch onto his neck with my mouth the way he does, pulling on his skin as hard as I can without breaking it.

I want to break his skin.

He stills for a moment, angling his neck in such a way that if I want to claim him, there is no stopping me. I keep sucking on the spot above his collarbone, on the soft flesh of his neck. He lets out a long moan, one of his hands going to the wall to steady us. My inner thighs are quaking with the vibration of his wolf's low, pleasurable growls.

A little bead of sweat makes a path in the middle of my chest that he licks up.

"You taste sweet." He nips at my shoulder.

His hair tickles between my fingers.

Lips are everywhere, nose, cheeks, jaw, ears.

Somehow the mattress hits my back. He stands before me. His shirt now gone, I look to his pants that need to come off now.

I feel greedy with the way I want.

He reaches down with one hand, looking at me while undoing his top button. He waits as if asking for consent. I nod my head yes. There is no looking away as he pulls his zipper down with a purpose.

My eyes take in the picture he's showing me. A small gasp slips out.

A grin comes over his face when his pants hit the floor, this male standing in front of me with no inhibitions at all. He takes my pants off easily. I'm left in my little red garments that are meant for his eyes only.

He crawls over the top of me before laying his weight between my thighs, pushing me into the bed.

My legs go around his waist as if on a natural guided instinct.

His breath on my neck, rocking his hips into me, he moans right next to my ear. Almost on a primal level.

He's giving me the most dangerous kiss.

A finger slips to the edge of the flimsy material that is barely holding onto my body. It's more for show than a barrier to keep him out.

Desperate.

Feeling his finger slide along the inside of my folds, I moan out hard when it enters inside me as a second one follows, filling me up tight. But not enough. I want, no need, more than this. The pressure of them being buried inside me, stretching me, is moan-inducing. He's pushing them in as far as they can go, while I push back against him, getting them deeper, filling me more, stretching me more...I need more.

Vocalized pleasures are making him smile. My body squirms to his rhythm. Deep warmth is spreading, building up. His other finger strokes my sensitive spot over and over again, faster and faster. Another finger is added, and I bite my lip with the feeling of being stretched too much.

Stiffening slightly with the fullness, one's taken out, but just as soon as it's taken out, I wish it were back inside me, filling me completely up to the point of slight pain.

He groans as he watches what he's doing to me. Gripping the bedding in fists, arching myself, toes curling in bliss. He consumes my lips with his in a greedy embrace as I wither and start to come undone from his touch. Another groan is let out in my ear before his mouth starts to suck and pull on my left breast. He angles his head so he takes my right one inside his mouth, flicking his tongue over my hard nipple. It's so sensitive I think I almost jump from what a tongue can do.

Pulling his fingers out of me, I actually whimper, no...trying to direct his hand back to the place it just was...he starts to kiss my ribs, working his mouth downwards, biting and licking as he goes...

His hands on either side of my inner thighs, he spreads them just a little more so his head can fit nicely between them.

He inhales...

"I've had dreams about this," Dallas says, only to smell me once more. A long deep pull through his nose. His eyes close for more than a blink.

With the first touch of his tongue on me, I do jump, and he has to hold me down slightly. He begins to devour me from the inside out, licking, sucking, his finger back inside me while I arch my back, spreading myself more for him, his chest a non-stop growling rumble while my body vibrates its pleasure...

He holds me down by a hand. I want to rise to the ceiling; this feels too good.

So good.

My hips move while my hands are wrapped into his hair, trying to get him closer to the inside of me, not wanting this to stop. It's hard to control the shaking of my inner thighs.

"Please don't stop." Dallas only moans as he crawls up my body, trailing kissing all over.

Looking between our bodies, his maleness on full display, rubbing up against my wet entrance.

His blood engorged muscles rippling underneath tight flesh. I spread my legs for him as he fists himself to put just the very tip inside.

His eyes void of any color, teeth fully descended, the Wild in him tries to break out. He holds himself above me for my approval, silently asking for my okay. The tiny nod of my head is enough for him.

His hand goes to my hip, holding me while in one powerful stroke he pushes himself inside me. I try to wiggle away, but he's holding me in my spot. It's too much to accommodate what he's giving me, and I whimper. I'm too full.

He doesn't pull himself out, just lets me get used to the intrusion of something so filling inside me, stretching me to beyond I thought was possible.

"Do you want me to stop?" It's an agony of words that are breathed out.

"No."

"You can tell me to stop, anytime."

"I don't want you to stop." My voice is so deep, it's hard to recognize.

He stays inside of me until my hips move very slightly. That's all he needs, thinking that he's pulling out of me. I wrap my legs tighter around his waist, trying to push him in deeper.

My hips grind into his.

"Rya, you feel so good." His voice, by the moon, his voice is so sexy the way he says my name all deep and husky has me wanting more of him. He gently rocks inside, very slow and controlled.

A whimpered breath in my ear, nails digging into the soft curve of my hip. Pulling out slightly, he goes back in deeper, and my back arches with another rock of his hips. The scent between us is strong, heady, driving us forward.

A slow side in and even slower slide almost completely out. Almost.

We're connecting.

Another slower slide in. I can't breathe. He's all the way inside. Filling me.

The heat from his body penetrates into my flesh.

"Rya," he says while pushing back inside my entrance. Almost slipping back out to push in a fraction faster than the last time. There is power behind his thrusts.

I feel him everywhere.

His breath on my neck, the rhythm increases faster and faster, and I hold onto him. My nails plunge into his back, the feeling electrifying my senses.

Pleasure and pain mix as one.

I surrender to him in this moment, this male who owns every inch of me. His mouth on mine, our moans slip between us with our tongues.

This is scarlet passion.

Trembling lips say his name out loud for his ears to hear.

He's diving further into my core, my whole body moving with his.

The only thing I feel is us connecting, becoming of one body, no other thoughts. Just this moment we are sharing now. Here. In the present.

I can't get enough of him.

Shifting, pulling me with a primal force.

Warmth pulses, infiltrates all of me.

Dallas moans, and so do I.

My hips rise off the bed, and he pushes me back down, demanding I take every inch of his shaft to the base.

Core. Muscles. Tighten.

Nothing matters. Only him, only this, only *us*.

He pulls now almost deliberately out to push deeper inside. The pace becoming fevered, harder. Hotter.

Everything is building up. I'm not sure I can handle it. A whimper from the back of his throat.

He holds me closer. I've dreamed about this.

My body lets go, and for a moment, all I can feel is the clenching deep inside before everything stills, then plunging down as it lets go in wave after wave of powerful rhythmic contractions that grip him firmly inside me.

He pushes himself deeper and deeper, rocking himself at a furious pace.

His body tenses, an inhaled breath before he buries himself as deep as he possibly can, coating my insides with his seed. He makes a low sound deep in his chest while saying my name. I can feel him pulsing inside my core. He has so much that it's dripping out between my legs. I think even his toes are curling along with mine.

A glistening sheen of sweat coats our bodies, our breathing coming back down. Opening my eyes, his are there watching me.

A kiss placed on my eyelids, he pushes away some of my hair from my face. He rolls me over, so I'm resting on top of his body. He smiles up at me. He looks boyish slightly in this moment. My hair creates a curtain, so even though we're by ourselves, it's acting more as an intimate screen to hide behind.

He pulls my face toward his and kisses me again before letting my lips go.

"I wasn't expecting this, Rya. I'm not sure what came over me."

My heart drops to my stomach slightly. "Do you regret this?" I think my eyes are starting to water slightly with anxiety.

"Rya, never would I regret this." His fingers entangle with mine as he brings them to his lips, placing gentle kisses on each fingertip. "I wish I could calm all your fears. I wish that you could see yourself the way I see you." He's holding me close, and I want to cry with the way he makes me feel.

"I just get this fear that I'm still not good enough, that I don't compare. I'm sorry." It's my sad truth. "My own mate didn't want me. Something has to be wrong with me." Dallas shows his teeth in displeasure.

"Rya, please, please try to get this out of your mind. You are my future now. You're everything I need and want. Nothing is wrong with you. You're my meat eater."

My stomach rumbles at this moment.

"Are you hungry?" He's looking at me as if trying to figure a puzzle out.

"Starving, I need to be fed. We didn't stop for dinner."

"Do you want to hunt up some food, let the wolves out?" That's all he needs to say as I'm up and off him in a flash. The wolf inside me wants to show him how she can eat.

Running hard, I feel fingertips trying to grab onto flesh before I'm out the door, shifting in a giant leap. Skidding to a halt, she turns to face him.

He's standing naked in the doorway, looking at the wolf who is standing proud and fierce. She is nothing but sinew and muscle under of fur. She's not the inexperienced wolf that left; she's in league with the wild.

The Wild stares into his before she takes off fast, paws pounding into the rain-soaked soil, leaving her paw impressions behind, dirt kicking up behind in grit behind her.

Dusk slowly creeps in, the moon starting to ascend in the sky.

She runs hard and fast until hot breath is felt. Giving a sideways look, she stretches out her body to the fullest, nose pointing forward, tail stretched out. She runs as he takes the lead easily, his body still not stretched out completely.

The Wild bumps into his shoulder, trying to roll him onto his back. He gives a slight playful growl, bumping into her shoulder, stumbling her sure steps. Again she bumps into him, trying to gauge his strength, nipping at his ears.

He nips back before actually rolling her, exposing the soft underbelly. He playfully bites into it, biting into her neck. She tries to stand, but he's quicker, and she can't react as fast as he can.

He allows the Wild to get up off the ground. She leaps at him, trying to pin him down, but every time she tries, his head goes against hers as she's tossed sideways. A huff of annoyance as he decides to lick our muzzle.

149

Nose to the ground, she stalks toward the trail for food.

A shift in wind alerts her to a deer. Running toward the prize, he pulls ahead. She could lose him in the shadows of the setting sun, his fur blending in with the night.

The Wild rubs herself against his side, letting her smell saturate him. Her tail curls underneath his chin. She's acting slightly off, starting to roll on the ground on her back, pressing her scent into the earth. She does it against a tree next, then she's on him again. This time instead of nipping, she's licking inside his muzzle before getting behind him, trying to mount him, rubbing the inside of her legs on him.

He gives a low growl out, biting her neck. She wiggles her bottom toward his, getting underneath him, her tail angling away. His wolf starts to rub against her. With a swiftness, he bites into our neck so there is no escape. Front paws going around her chest, he mounts her quickly. Pushing into her, she gives a low rumble in her chest. They are locked into place once he's spent. Our wolves looking into each other's eyes, cheek pressed against cheek until he's able to slip out.

Running once again, they find the meat trail. It's a two year old. It's fast, but not faster than Dallas's wolf, who kills it easily.

A ravenous gluttony takes over as she tears into the fleshy underside of this welcome prize. Crimson drips off the muzzles, saturating the forest floor.

Chunks of meat start to expand her stomach in a fullness of misery, yet she still continues gorge on this feast fit for kings. The pregnant moon looks on at her children underneath the darkening sky.

After the carcass is almost cleaned bare, her stomach is so engorged it's hard to trot home. I want to throw up with this feeling, yet it's deeply satisfying to eat so much.

Coming into the house, my stomach is distended, protruding out almost like the soft curve of a newly pregnant female. I touch it, letting my hand go over the roundness of it before my shoulders hunch slightly with the fact I could never produce offspring of my own.

Dallas goes to my room, picking his clothes off the ground, going to get dressed.

"Do you want to have a sleepover with me? We could go out for a good breakfast in the morning. Maybe go to that cool place you brought me before?" I give him my eyes, flashing my lashes his way.

"You want me to stay the night with you?"

"Yes, I do. I missed you and I want to lay next to you." This is easy to say. I have needs and I make them known to him.

"All right, but I have to get up early in the morning to train. I'll be back once I'm done." He drops his clothes and runs into bed, bouncing off the mattress before getting into the blankets and pulling them back for me to step into. I drop my robe to the floor getting in.

"Could I come with you in the morning? I'd like to watch you, if that's okay?"

"Sure, if you want. I just have to stop at the house to change my clothes."

151

Getting into bed with him, I press my ass into his hips, wiggling myself slightly into his ever expanding manhood.

Turning me on hands and knees, he positions himself like a wolf taking their mate. He holds me with his teeth, not enough to break the skin, but enough to know that a male is taking me hard.

Throughout the night, he takes me in all kinds of ways, over and over again until we can no longer stay awake. Falling asleep wrapped up in each other's arms makes me feel loved and cared for by this male.

CHAPTER 10

Symptoms Undetected

Rya

Peaceful.

The way early morning hangs in the air, with its barely there breeze.

Individual drops of dew cling to the blades of grass, sparkling, before lazily sliding down to moisten the dirt. Dallas is inside his house, getting changed.

Clayton is settled down deep into the chair, his head resting on his shoulder. Arms hanging down off the chair, his fingertips almost touch the empty bottle that's been dropped once finished. He feel asleep outside. The fire is no more; nothing but ash remains. Cold and grey.

I wait for Dallas to get changed so we can go on an early morning run, just as Cash and I did.

Leaning against the hood of the car, I don't look

away from the sight in front of me.

I can tell exactly the moment he startles awake, his fingertips twitching, body stiffening.

I watch him straighten up in the chair. He doesn't turn around. Instead, I see his hands grip onto the armrests, squeezing them as if trying to hold himself in his spot.

I don't look away.

He continues to stare straight ahead; I continue to stare at his head. Until he turns around, getting off his chair.

Glacier blue meets forest green.

The way our eyes connect, wind chimes tingle my spine.

Tingling.

Vibrating.

Strumming.

His lips turn up in a smile. I can't return it because I'm focusing too hard on maintaining my composure.

Magnetic, the way this bond tries to pull me. Whispering the deep desires into my marrow.

He moves forward, one step, then the next, the space between us growing smaller.

"How are you?" My skin shivers with the mirage of his voice.

"Good." Looking away, I hope Dallas comes out soon.

Arms go around my chest, and I hold myself against the waves of desire crashing against me, threatening to drown me in a tidal wave of indecent wants.

Why?

I don't want him. How come I'm reacting to him this way?

"Rya." His silver-tongued voice lashes against my internal bindings, trying to free my self-imposed restraint.

Looking at him blankly, I ask him the question I want to know the answer to.

Think.

Watch.

Listen.

"Your last voice mail, did you mean it?" I watch his answer.

Eyes looking away for a fraction of a second, heart rate increasing, a hesitation. He licks his lips that still hold the smell of the whiskey he was drinking the night before.

"Yes, I meant it."

He looks away again.

Liar.

Pushing off the hood of the car, I can't help my shoulder hitting him. It should be my fist. I can't help the way my wolf wants to surface and take the competition away from her mate.

Her anger tries to completely take over. She has a mate already, and this male in front of us is not hers.

The eyes of my wolf stare at him, assessing the threat in great detail. He needs to be taken out in her simple mind.

Barely able to turn us around, I need to go into the house and find Dallas to calm her down.

I pull the door open and stand just barely on the inside looking in. Scents mingling together, a small pup mixes in with every other wolf's.

"Excuse me." As if trying to gently move me out of his way, Clayton's slight flicker of his hand, the pad of his thumb runs along the side of my hip.

Flesh against flesh, a jolt of electricity has my heart fluttering, eyes widening. His nose is so close, I feel the tip of it against my head.

This is all done is mere seconds, but to me, it's slow motion.

Deep, grumbling vibration shakes my body, the wolf not pleased he touched us.

Watching him, he fills a glass with water, drinking it down greedily. He looks parched. A few drops escape his mouth, landing on his shirt. Pulling out a jar of peanut butter, he takes a spoon, dipping it in. Taking a giant scoop, he puts it in his mouth and swallows it down.

The silence between us is blank static.

He continues to eat out of the peanut butter jar, one spoonful at a time. His eyes stay on me. I feel the burn heating my body, reddening my cheeks.

Can he tell what his eyes do to me?

I let my eyes travel the rest of the room. Carson is belly down on the couch. He's trying not to wake up, putting the pillow over his head. He's just in boxers that are tight against his thighs.

One arm dangles over the cushions as his fingertips touch the floor. One leg is bent, the other leg in the crack of the couch.

A frantic morning cry of a pup has my eyes traveling down the hallway. It sounds like it's hungry. The cry grows more demanding until it's replaced by soft sucking, mewing sounds.

Caleb opens a door and comes out into the kitchen.

"That's sick. Put some in a bowl if you're going to eat out of the jar." I watch as this wolf goes into the fridge, opening the milk carton, drinking it all down before putting the empty container where he found it.

"Rya." Caleb gives me a giant welcoming smile. "How are you?"

He approaches closer, eyes trailing up and down my body, nose taking in my scent. He takes a step backward, looking slightly off.

"Good, how are you, Caleb?"

"Never better." He gives a stretch, his shirt rising to show off his tight abdomen.

"How's Cash doing?" His voice sounds slightly strained. Caleb sits down on his brother's back, bouncing up and down until he wakes up.

"He's managing. It's hard for him." Looking toward Clayton, I see the spoon deep in the jar. His knuckles have a smudge of peanut butter on them.

He pulls out the spoon, licking the spots where it's dirty. He catches me staring at him as his tongue is tasting the last of the peanut butter. I need to look away.

"Get off me." Carson elbows Caleb in his side before shoving him off. Sitting up, he sways slightly, rubbing his eyes. He looks like he had a rough night.

Dallas comes out of his room, just a pair of shorts on. I actually lick my lips at the feast of flesh. The wolf's fur settles down with his presence.

She relaxes slightly.

Going up to him, I run my bare arm against his, my cheek pressing into his chest for just a fraction of a second before pulling away.

His head dipping low, he kisses the top of my head before squeezing me close to him.

"Are you ready?" There's a gleam in his eye.

"Where are you going?" Caleb tilts his head slightly.

"Rya wants to train with me today."

Both brothers are up off the couch. "We're coming." Before Dallas can say anything, both of them are running into Caleb's room to get changed.

Dallas is laughing at his brothers, and in this moment, I realize how much I adore this wolf.

The heat of his eyes are burrowing into my back. When I look at Clayton, he can't look away.

Dallas looks toward Clayton. Eye contact like this between males is very dangerous. A rumble from Dallas lets Clayton know he is not appreciative of him looking at me.

Clayton does not look away, instead glaring right back at Dallas.

Kimberly comes out of her room carrying her small male.

She looks exhausted, eyes puffy as if she's been crying all night long.

She hands her brother this joy, taking him easily as if he's comfortable with holding a tiny form. Bringing him to his shoulder, I watch as he lifts his head, looking around wide-eyed.

"Kimberly, he's beautiful." I go to take a step so I can see him better. She stands in front of them, looking at me.

She's posturing toward me, riled up for some reason.

"Is something wrong?" My head angles her way. Clayton puts a hand on her shoulder, squeezing it slightly.

"No, nothing's wrong." Her eyes are taking in the length of me. A male walks into the kitchen with black messy hair and presses a small kiss to Kimberley's forehead. Taking the pup from Clayton, he kisses the young one's mouth before tucking the pup into his arm. He stands beside Kimberly, looking at her.

The way her eyes look at this male holds a depth of sadness that hurts my chest.

She looks away, only for her eyes to turn on Carson as he and Caleb come out of the bedroom dressed in workout wear.

I can see her fists clenched, a snarl showing her small juvenile canines.

Carson tenses at the sight, looking at the male with his bed head hair.

"I told her," this male says, who must be her mate.

"You had no right." Carson's finger points toward the male.

"She's my mate. It would come out anyway when I mark her." He gives Clayton the pup, squaring his shoulders toward Carson, who looks completely broken. He almost looks as if he could cry.

Carson walks out the door, heading down to the lake. Dallas follows him out, trying to figure out what's wrong.

Caleb shrugs his shoulders, not knowing what's going on.

"What's going on, Kimberly?" Clayton's voice is hard against his sister, who wilts by the force.

"Jake—" The words strangle in her throat.

"When I was away at college, Carson and I were together." Laughter of disbelief comes out of Caleb's mouth. "Not possible." Caleb wiping his eyes of tears.

"Carson?" Confusion etches in the lines of Clayton's face.

Jake doesn't hang his head; he meets his eyes. "You cheated on my sister with a male?"

"Yes." Jake's voice is trying not to shake. Caleb's mouth is hanging open with the confession of words.

"Carson never knew I had a mate. I never told anyone. It wasn't his fault. It's all mine."

The quiet intensity of Clayton's rage seeps slowly out. The little one in his arms starts to scream, throwing its head back, fists raised, actual tears coming out of its reddened, toothless face.

Kimberly takes her male out of her brother's arms, trying to calm him down with a rub of his back, a coo in his ear.

"How could you do that to my sister, your own mate?" There's a lethal edge to Clayton's voice.

"I'm no different than you. My tastes are just different," Jake fires back at his mate's brother.

"That was different."

"How?" Jake's arms cross over his chest as he waits for an answer.

Clayton can't answer back. It's true. He had a

mate, but he continued to screw someone else.

I give a little huff of breath.

Kimberly points a finger at me. "You're no different than them, coming into this house with him all over you, so my brother can smell that. How do you think that affects him? So huff all you want, but you're no better." I see it now, the absolute contempt she has for me.

Looking out the window, I see Carson wiping away the tears that can't stop falling. Dallas pulls him into a hug, whispering words in his ear that make his head nod up and down.

Walking away from Kimberly's judging eyes, I'm not going to justify my actions to a juvenile female who knows nothing about what I've been through.

Before I go out the door, Clayton tries to hold my eyes in some form of communication that I don't understand. Maybe if I were Kennedy I would know his look better, but I'll never be Kennedy...that will never be.

Dallas makes his way toward me, one long step at a time.

"I've got to cancel this morning. How about I take you out for dinner tonight? Just me and you, on a date. If that's okay with you? Carson needs me right now, and I want to be there for him."

"No problem, I completely understand. Besides, I have so much to do at home anyway. I'm just going to run home. You don't need to drive me. I'll see you around what time?"

"I'll pick you up at five thirty. Thanks for understanding." He kisses my forehead before walking back to Carson, who's facing the lake. The wind has picked up slightly, rippling the once-tranquil surface.

Running back to the house, I'm touching every tree branch that's close to the road. I have this compulsion to leave my scent everywhere.

Walking up the driveway, I'm flushed with the exertion. My body has heated up so much I contemplate running into the lake to cool off.

Sweat saturates the fabric I have on. Usually, I don't get so sweaty, but it's getting hotter outside.

Drinking down glass after glass of water, I can't seem to quench my thirst.

Looking into the fridge, pulling one of those containers out, without even warming it up, I take a spoon and fill my face with the delicious casserole. I eat the whole thing over the sink looking out the window toward the lake.

Kimberly's words play over in my mind. I just don't see it the same way. For me, it's different, and that's what I tell myself. I'm not cheating on my mate because he was never my mate in the first place.

Looking at the plants on the table, I should put them in the ground before they wilt and die.

Not bothering to change, I dig up the soft earth, placing each plant where I want it to be.

Halfway through planting, I feel the back of my hair raise as if eyes are on me.

I turn around. A few males wolves are sitting at the forest edge, eyes of wolves looking out. I don't really recognize them. My dealing with males from this pack was non-existent.

"What do you want?" Standing, I wipe off the dirt from my knees.

I wonder how long I have been watched? They tilt up their noses as the breeze catches my hair, blowing it toward them. A growl breaks out and they're on each other, fighting with teeth that want to tear throats. They all fight one another before tumbling back into the woods, unable to be seen but heard.

I'm slightly shaken with the sight of that.

Heading into the house, I start to get ready for my date, locking the door behind me.

This is a first real date. Stepping out of the shower, I take my time preparing myself. Looking over every outfit I have, I decide on something that shows off who I am, a female who's trying to impress her date.

The cut of the dress reveals a touch of lace if I lean over just slightly. My arms are bare, but the back is covered. My hair is worn down. I go to do my makeup, but my cheeks are already blushed, lips slightly redder, and I make a mental note to wear a hat outside because the sun is strong even this time of year.

Pacing inside the house, waiting for five thirty, I'm hungry again. I nip at another dish inside the fridge and finish the whole thing before I hear a knock. I open the locked door for him, and his eyes go down the length of me, and before I can even say a word, he tugs me toward him, kissing me hard on the mouth.

Hands go up my thighs, bringing the fabric of my dress up with it. I'm drowning with this kiss, only focusing on this warm sensation of our mouths clashing together.

"Sorry, Rya." He pulls himself away with a little gasp, ending the kiss. "You make it incredibly hard to have self-control." His fingertip traces the tip of my nose before he places a quick kiss on it.

He stands tall before me, letting my eyes trail over him. My cheeks are hot again with the thoughts of what I want to do in this moment. Such crippling single-minded desire pumps through my veins.

Is this how it is to fall in love? The need to be around someone so much all you can think about is him and what you want to do with him?

He's tantalizingly good looking, all male, with such a hard surface.

Taking my hand, he leads me out to his car, opening the door for me. He waits till I'm buckled in before closing the door. He holds my hand the whole way there, kissing my knuckles every now and then.

Walking into the tiny place, the dimness balances between perfect, not too bright, not too dark. Candlelight reflects off the faces of the humans that surround us.

We take our seats, and the waiter leaves us with menus.

Dallas doesn't look at his. Instead, he's just watching me. "You look very beautiful, Rya." I blush from his words.

After ordering our meal, Dallas takes my hand in his, entwining our fingers.

"I have a question to ask you." He seems

nervous to ask this question. "I was wondering, Rya, if—" He takes a deep breath. "I would like to have a mating ceremony with you in front of my entire pack. I want to say the vows with the moon looking down at us."

"Yes." I have to try to keep my voice low, but I want to jump up and down in happiness.

"Good, I'll have my mother start working on everything. She'll call you with all the details. Are you sure about this, Rya?"

"I've never been surer of anything in my whole entire life, Dallas." He leans over the table, kissing my lips.

The food is not enough as we both finish our plates, but at these fancy places, they really never give you enough, so I'm told. Talking throughout the meal, he even shares his cake with me because mine wasn't enough.

The drive back, I let my senses indulge in the male sitting beside me. His spicy smell—my tiny receptors of pleasure are on overdrive. Embers spark with excitement as his hand rests on my inner thigh, moving upward slightly. A sigh escapes, and I widen my legs for him. I clench the inside of me with the feeling of a deep hunger for him.

Needful scents rise off my wanting body.

He parks the car. Before I get out, he tugs me over top him, moving his seat as far back as he can. His fingers slide through my hair before pulling my face toward his.

Kissing him deeply, our feast of flesh is just beginning, our night alone just starting…

CHAPTER 11

11 Hourglass

Rya

Lazy Sunday morning.

Every crevice and curve of my skin is saturated in his smell. It's the sort of scent that's subtle yet very powerful.

His mouth is gloriously captivating as he kisses me slowly.

His hand running in my hair, I feel sensations of fingers touching my skin everywhere. Laying side by side as close as we can get to each other, no space remains.

Toes playing with toes.

"You make me so happy, Rya." Gentle kisses between thoughts, our tired eyes look at each other. We stayed up most of the night, talking about bits and pieces of our lives. Our words turned to moans then back to words, until we could no longer keep our eyes open.

Running my fingers over his body, exploring every inch, leaving none without my scent.

"I don't want to get up." I nip at his neck.

"Me either." His thick arms pull me closer to him, while the words make me smile.

"How's Carson? Is he okay?"

"Carson's upset. He thinks we won't love him anymore, that Mom and Dad won't love him anymore." The constant state of anxiety he must have felt growing up must have been soul-consuming. His fears and worries must have been like fighting Goliath.

"It must have been very hard to keep such a secret from everyone for so long." My fingers play in his hair as we talk eye to eye.

"He'll be fine. At first, he was so upset, but as the day went on, he felt relief. You could see it in him; the tension inside him was disappearing. Looking back, I missed the signs. He left clues, but I just never really took the time to look. Some things can be right in front of your nose and you miss the clues." He kisses my lips again softly before pulling away.

"My parents will understand. It's just hard because he will never have pups." My body tenses, muscles tightening underneath his soft grip.

"That's important to your parents?" I still underneath the pressure that I can never produce offspring for this male, for this family.

"Yes, it was important to them, but after the accident, they just want all of us to be happy."

"Are you sure that it's okay that we'll never have pups, Dallas?" My whole body stills, waiting,

167

watching his face for an answer.

His reply comes instantly. "Yes, I'm sure. I want you, Rya. It's okay if we don't have pups. I still think you can because you don't smell like you can't. And the inside of you feels as if you are preparing for a future. But if we can't, we can't. I never expected to find you. I'm so thankful just for that." Watching him, I believe every word he says.

"Do you have anything else to ask me?" His face makes it easy to ask him anything without fear of being laughed at.

"I was wondering when we go back to your pack."

"Our pack, Rya, it's our pack." Another kiss is placed on the tip of my nose.

"When we go back to our pack." I kiss the tip of his nose now.

"Where will we live?" I can't live in that home he and his mate built. There is no way; it creeps me out.

"Not there, Rya. I was thinking that we could build our own home together. I have this little spot that I always loved. It's by the water. It would be a good place to live if you liked the area. It's close to my mom and dad's home, not too far away. I was going to give Cash and Kennedy that house. It's still a good house. I think that it would be good for them as a starter home. Then when they get too big for the home, my other brothers could use it." His eyes look far away at the moment. Squeezing him close, it must be so hard for him at times.

"I love the water, Dallas. If I could be anywhere, it would be close to the water. I always wanted to live by the water. I like the sounds of the waves hitting the shore, the way the storms look crossing the lake. I have this dream of having a big deck, just like the one you have at your house now." My turn to have a faraway look.

"When we go back to our pack," his eyes look at me before he continues, "I'll show you the spot, but for now we'll have to live with my parents." He laughs. "I'm a grown ass male and I'm going to be bringing you back to live with Mom and Dad." I even giggle at that.

"Dallas, I can help pay for the house. I have a lot of money saved up from working the last couple of years. I never had to pay for really anything, and I own my car." He stretches himself, the length of his body tightening, muscles flexing easily.

He's my glimpse of morning bliss.

"I appreciate your offer Rya, but I want to pay for it. How about you buy what you want for the inside. Is that fair?"

"Yes, it is." He grabs my ass, twisting my body on top of his.

"We should get up." That's the third time he's told me this, but every time we try to get off the mattress, it turns into…

Grasping.

Grinding.

Groaning.

This time he means it. He sits on the edge, looking through his overnight bag. He laughed when he pulled it out from his backseat; he came prepared.

Up on my elbows, chin resting on my hand, I

169

ogle him without the least bit of restraint.

"You make a male feel good about themselves, Rya." His eyebrow arches, slapping my bare ass before pulling his gym clothes out.

"Let's run to the gym after I'll make us some food." Flopping down on the mattress, I don't want to go anywhere but here in this room. It's private, closed off from the rest of the house. It's even cooler as a big shade tree blocks out the sun's rays all day long over the top of this spot. I feel the need to stay in this place all day.

"Let's go. Caleb will be there. You can school me in some of the moves you've learned." Now he's got my wolf's ears perked up.

"I really don't want to go anywhere today," I protest as he takes my hand and helps me off the bed.

"How about this: we go train for just an hour, come back, eat, then go out on the lake? I'll take you to that little island, but this time I'm going to do things to you that I wanted to the first time I brought you there." His proposition is tempting me.

"Let's shower, then we'll go and come right back." He leads me into the shower where he scrubs me clean and I scrub him, not missing any inch of his skin.

The shower was a lot longer than expected, startling us when the hot water ran out.

"Do we have to go?" I try to do a pouty lip like I've seen girls on TV do.

"I need to get a workout in. I missed yesterday. Beating my father is not going to be easy. I need to get stronger to even stand a chance with him."

"Have you ever fought him before?"

"Once, he destroyed me completely, but that was a long time ago when I thought I was a king. He had to humble me for my own good." His brows furrow with some unknown thoughts. When we mark each other, I'll be able to tell what he's thinking all the time instead of just feeling his strongest emotions.

"How long do you think it will take you to beat him?" As quick as a flash, his emotions change from some long lost memory to hard determination.

"A long time. It took him five years to beat his father, so I'm thinking I have a long road ahead of me. It's not just fighting, Rya, it how to deal with wolves, how to solve conflicts. How to manage money, support and defend the pack. There is so much learning to do, things I never really thought about, things I took for granted. It's more of an apprenticeship I'm going through. Yet in the end, I'm going to have to beat that wolf somehow. And if he thinks I can't lead well, he'll open it up to someone he thinks can lead the pack. Because only the strongest mentally and physically can lead." He's in the fridge taking out a dish, opening the lid, giving it a sniff before getting a fork and eating it down.

"Hey, I thought you said you're going to make me breakfast."

"Sorry, Rya. I just need a little bite." Except his bites are huge. I open my own mouth so he can give me a fork full as well. We stand by the fridge eating the cold food from the container, only stopping once it's finished. I never realized how being intimate is so taxing on the body and how your

171

body needs replenishment often.

We let the meal settle slightly before our run. It feels good running with him. I know that I'm slowing him down, but he doesn't seem to mind.

Going to the gym, there are multiple male wolves in various stages of working out or sparring with one another. It sets my senses off slightly. I inhale deeply, giving a shiver of delight, that makes me feel sick with myself.

Dallas takes my hand, which is much bigger than mine. I love the feeling of it. A squeeze, reassuring me that everything is good.

Seeing Clayton sparring with Caleb, he's going blow for blow with him until he notices me. That's when Caleb takes the advantage and puts him in a submission choke hold. I can't help feeling slightly sorry for Clayton, but at least he's trying.

All these males have their shirts off except Clayton. He's kept his on. It's saturated in sweat and sticks close to his body. His whole body is drenched with his effort.

I can smell Clayton so distinctly that it's hard to focus, just like the way I smell Dallas, both their smells combining into ecstasy.

I wish I never agreed to the mating ceremony. I need to mark Dallas so the bond's pull is broken with Clayton. Everything I have read about being moon blessed, the thing that stands out the most with all the other things is that my bond with Clayton will go away. I will never feel anything for him anymore.

Clayton will be an hourglass thought whose sand has run out.

CHAPTER 12

Catalyst

Clayton

Sweat trickles down my forehead, burning my eyes.

"All you have to do is beat me and I go away." Caleb's irritating voice taunts. Circling around, I have no choice but to follow his movements.

The wolves around us are watching, expectations in their eyes. They know the struggle I'm facing day after day.

I feel stronger, bigger, better.

"If you beat me, I'll stop treating you like a willing female." He leans in close, his words low, for my ears only. He's huffing hard himself, wiping away the blood from his split lip with the back of his hand.

"You're always saying the sweetest stuff, darling." I knee him in the side, and he almost goes down with a long groan.

"Hey easy, this is a learning experience. No need to get full out violent." This male is something else. It's hard to fight him when he makes me laugh all the time now.

We've been at it a good thirty minutes before Rya and Dallas walk into the training center. He's holding her hand, saying things in her ear. Her eyes look at me, and I have to hold myself still for just a second. That's all he needs to pin me to the ground hard, forearm coming around my neck, choking my air off.

"What have I told you about looking away from me? This is what happens when you don't pay attention to the prettiest one in the room." His words are whispered to me. No one else can hear his taunts. He only lets Dallas hear them, saying he doesn't want to shame me too bad in front of these males that I need to lead.

Her eyes don't leave mine as I tap Caleb on the arm. He lets go and I choke on the air that's trying to rush into my lungs too fast.

Shame washes inside, and I feel like I will drown, having Rya here to witness this.

I can smell her, that nectar that's made just for me. I should be tasting what was made for me. Her smell sends tremors into my very fiber. His sick scent saturates into her like a thick cloud. It's encasing her, permeating out. This must be how she felt, smelling Kennedy all over me. I want to scream, throw my fists through his face. Her eyes just look at me, tingling my skin. My breath quickens in my sore chest.

I would do anything to have just one minute with

her, a chance to talk.

Getting off the ground, my hand rubs my sore neck. I try not to let it show how bad it hurts. I walk away slightly, just trying to get away from her presence. It's easier if she isn't around, standing too close, looking so good.

"Rya, you want to go a round? He was just keeping me warm for you." I have never wanted to destroy him so bad as I do right now.

Watching, Dallas puts a hand on Rya's shoulder. He turns away from us, whispering words in her ear. I can see her head nodding up and down with the things he's telling her.

A slyness in the way Dallas looks at Caleb, who's not smiling anymore.

"I don't think I can, Dallas." He takes a little step away from her, breathing through his mouth as if a smell is offending him for some reason. All I can smell is her; that's all that surrounds me at the moment.

"Caleb, she beat Cash, and his mate is pregnant. It's almost like she was fighting you." Caleb doesn't like that too much with his irritated look. The mention of Kennedy hurts my heart. I know we can't be together, but she is still a big part of me, and I want her to be happy. That's all I want for her is to be happy.

"Cash is not me." Caleb is now physically annoyed with Dallas's words.

"You're going to be able to handle this, right?" Caleb points his finger at Dallas, his voice rising slightly, waiting for a response.

"I think so?" That does not sit well in my

stomach. How could he let her in there with him?

Rya rolls her shoulders out, giving a few little jumps, trying to shake out her extra energy the way fighters do just before they start a fight.

Except she isn't a fighter.

"Are you for real?" No hiding the shock that's in my voice. "Dallas, really? You're really going to let her fight him?" I'm starting to pace the length of the floor as she approaches Caleb.

No one answers my words.

"I'm not Cash." Caleb laughs out to her, yet his eyes are not laughing; they are totally focused on her movements.

"I'm not him." Her eyes go toward me, and Caleb's eyes look where she's looking. Instantly, she attacks, while his attention is on me. Smart female. She's fast, striking hard, bending down, shoulder in his gut. She lifts him off his feet, slamming him down on his back belly up before she backs away as if she is toying with a juvenile wolf.

"You need to pay attention, number two." Rya's voice is antagonizing Caleb, ruffling up his fur.

Dallas laughs hard. "Good job, my meat eater." His words puff her up.

Caleb goes to grab onto her, and she moves as if she doesn't have bones.

Flexing.

Twisting.

Bending out of his way.

They start a dance of steps, the whole time her mouth running over Caleb's ego.

Taunting him, she lands another blow to his side before side stepping a near-hit to the face with his elbow.

Her knuckles mold into his flesh, landing another punch to his stomach. She's really fast, but she doesn't have the strength of a male wolf.

He growls, showing teeth towards her. Dallas takes a step toward his brother.

"No teeth, Caleb." A harsh command that Caleb shakes his head out from.

The rest of the male wolves are staring, really looking at her now. Their noses flare, taking in her smell. I don't like the way male eyes are devouring her. A few of them start to shove each other to get in the front row of this show.

Taking her smell in, sweet nectar and sunshine, it's always the same since she's been back, except maybe just a touch sweeter. I can see how it affects these males.

Striking his ribs, she makes him groan. She's quicker, faster than him. She doesn't have his strength. If he pins her, it's over.

He lands a few hard punches to her back, catching her before she spins out of his way. Dallas growls out, pacing the floor now, watching with eyes of his wolf. He looks as if he's having as much trouble as I am when she gets hit. My need to protect her is running high, instincts kicking in. I need to restrain myself, saying she really won't get hurt. He won't really hurt her, will he?

He connects a fist to her face, and Dallas rages on the sidelines, a growl of warning so powerful it quakes the rest of the wolves.

Caleb stops, looking at Dallas. "I think we should stop."

"Why?" Rya has her hand on her hips. She's bent forward slightly, chest heaving up and down. A small trickle of blood comes out her mouth that she spits on the ground, as if she's a male.

"Because number one can't handle this." Caleb looks relieved in a way.

"Go on, I'll be fine." Dallas grits his teeth along with me.

Caleb looks like he's trying to wear her down with kidney shots. I grimace every time he lands one. Dallas is pacing up and down, his eyes completely white, scary as crap. I read that her mate's eyes will turn her color as the bond between them gets stronger. In a way, I'm happy for her, but at the same time, I want what he has.

She's my fighting rejected desire.

Her skin reddens in exertion, flushing her cheeks. I try to buffer my defenses against her.

Rya's smell seems to be getting stronger the harder she's exerting herself. Caleb catches her in his arms and slams her down on the ground belly up. He's quick to try for a hold, except she squirms her body to the side. He's on top of her, trying to pin her down on her stomach. He has her by the hands, putting all his weight on her body, pressing her further into the mat. He's using his entire body weight now to pin her in place.

Her ass presses into his groin, trying to flip him off her. This is breaking my resolve. I take a step toward this scene, unable to control myself. Another step, my hands clenching into fists. Caleb's eyes glaze over as he grabs onto her hips, pulling her into him. His canines are descending, angling toward her neck. The wolves in the crowd start to shove, showing their own teeth.

Combustible.

Growls tumbling out of throats, Dallas runs toward Rya, who's desperately trying to get out of a grip that's hooked into her flesh, keeping her in position.

"Dallas." It's a cry for help. It's his name she uses, not mine. Her nails are now coming out, clawing at the ground, trying to get away from this aggressive male wolf. Taking a running leap toward Caleb, both Dallas and I hit him from both sides. We knock him off, probably harder than he has ever been hit in his life.

She scrambles away, into the arms of her chosen.

"Caleb, what was that?" Dallas is in his brother's face.

Before he can answer, I'm on Caleb. I can't control the way I want to destroy him, punish him for touching her in such a dirty way.

I can actually see myself breaking him in half, tearing his head from his body, and that's what I try to do.

He's on the defensive, trying to evade my punches, kicks. The old me is surfacing, before the whipping.

Powerful.

The feeling of my muscles filling with blood is powerful, the need to teach this second born what a true first born can fight like.

A hush falls over us, the wolves all gathering around. I think they can sense that this is different. Caleb has no smile, no stupid words being flung from his mouth; he's really paying attention to me.

His eyes are not leaving mine.

Both of us charge at the same time. He will get my perfect effort.

Crunching.

Breaking.

Bleeding.

That's what we do as our bodies collide. He's not faster anymore; he's not able to maintain the upper hand because I believe that I can overcome him.

Blood sprays the surface of the floor, while our footprints smear it everywhere.

Getting him on the ground, in the same hold he often uses on me, I wrap my arm around his neck, my thighs wrapping around his middle, and I squeeze with everything I have. My jaw clenches so tight with the effort I'm producing, I'm afraid my teeth will snap.

Applying more pressure on his neck, I can feel his throat crushing against my forearm.

It's just a matter of minutes before he passes out if he doesn't tap out.

I find Dallas's eyes looking at me, watching. Applying more pressure on Caleb's neck, I wish this were Dallas in my arms.

His eyes dilate at how I'm staring at him. He must understand the language I'm using without words.

Feeling the tap on my head, it's light, but it's a tap. Letting go, I get myself off the ground and face Dallas. I'm puffed up from all the testosterone flowing in my system. Flying high off this win that took me months and months to do.

My pack males start to clap. It's soft at first, but it starts growing louder and louder.

Paying it no mind, I can't look away from Dallas, who's slowly putting Rya behind him.

"Time for you to go." That's all I say to him as I try to compose myself, try to control all the urges I feel toward Rya.

"You need to take her with you. She can't stay in this pack. She's not wanted." I've dug our grave with my own hands. This is just the last nails in our coffin.

I've failed her in every single way. This is my only redemption. May the moon forgive me.

A single tear makes a trail down her cheek before dropping on the ground, and I have to fight mine from coming out.

CHAPTER 13

Deconstruction

Rya

Liar.

He's lying. Everything he's saying is a lie. I watch his face all bloodied and bruised, the strain of the fight blooming in dark bruises along his jaw, neck. I can even tell he's fighting not to cry with what he's saying.

He's an artist of lies.

"How could you be so cruel to her?" Dallas just looks at Clayton with ears that don't believe what he's been told.

"She needs to hear it." That's what Clayton says, that I need to hear it.

"I will never understand how you can just give her away like this without even a fight. Is she not worth your fight?" Dallas challenges.

"She isn't worth my fight." Another stray tear comes down my face. He watches it with eyes that try to hold his own tears in.

Repressing emotions is not good. They have a way of coming out eventually.

"You're a good wolf, Dallas. I can't thank you enough for what you have done for this pack, for me, for her. But I want you out now. I want her out and away from me. I need her to leave because I don't want to have to fight you for her."

"You wouldn't win, Clayton. You can't beat me. I know it, you know it. But I would welcome the fight with teeth. I would honor her in a real fight. Give me a real fight, Clayton." Dallas is posturing. The smell of male testosterone is sending my electrical pulses to every nerve ending I have.

"I won't fight you for her. You can have her." I'm just a throwaway. Dallas shakes his head in disgust.

"We'll be gone by the end of tomorrow. We just have to pack our stuff."

"Good." That's all Clayton says as he turns his back on us, going into the male changing room.

"Rya, I'm so sorry. I didn't mean to do that," Caleb says with his head hanging low, shoulders hunched over. He delicately steps toward me.

"I'm not sure what happened. I just couldn't control the wolf for a second. Please forgive me." Caleb is now at my feet, kneeling in front of me, his head down low in great shame for what he was going to do.

"I got too close to you. When you started to press yourself against me, I just couldn't stop." He's barely able to say these words his throat is so tight; the sounds are barely cracking out.

"I would never do that to a female, ever, especially one that belongs to my brother." It's hard to stay mad at this creature. Males always react somewhat different around me. My smell, they say, is tantalizing to their senses, along with my eyes. Even Dallas says I smell as if I am in a constant state of heat. It must be hard for Caleb because he loves all types of females.

Putting a hand on his head, I forgive him, but I won't ever fight him again.

Dallas is looking at his brother as if he could eat him.

Grabbing Dallas's hand, I pull him away and out of the training center. I don't stop walking until we are far down the road. Every now and then, Dallas turns toward where we came from to growl or start walking toward it, only for me to pull him back toward the way home.

"I need to go home and pack, Rya. I don't have very much left here. I started shipping it home a few weeks ago. You should start packing. Maybe tonight you and I could go visit your parents to say goodbye." I laugh slightly. I don't even think they know I'm home or even left at all. Not a word from them, but then again, I never called either.

"All right, Dallas, we can go together." This feels somewhat rushed, as if we're being thrown out and not just leaving of our own accord.

"I won't be long, okay? Just a few hours. Then we can just leave." I give him a quick kiss, and he leaves to get his stuff. No need lingering where I'm not wanted.

Taking my suitcases from out of the closet, I

start packing everything I own, which really isn't very much. Going into the fridge, I heat up my meal, pouring myself the last of the white wine that was in the back, pushed to the side.

No use wasting food or wine.

While eating my meal, the wine is hard to swallow for some reason. The food that I'm eating tastes kind of funny as well. I sniff at it, poking my fork around. I throw it away because I think maybe it's gone bad. I rinse my mouth out with water, throwing the rest of the wine away. I just can't stomach it right now.

A knock at the door startles me. The way the wolf approached was quiet, a shadow in the doorway. Another knock comes, almost urgent this time.

Opening the door, I smell him before I see him.

"What do you want, Clayton?" I cross my arms over my chest against him.

He looks guilty, as if he knows he's doing something wrong.

"I just needed to see you one last time. I wanted to say that I'm sorry for everything that I have put you through. That I only want you to be happy. You deserve to be happy, Rya." The way my name falls off that mouth of his makes my legs shake slightly.

It's with the greatest of effort I hold onto the open door frame for balance. This will all go away once Dallas and I mark each other. I can't wait.

I block the entrance of my door so he knows he's not welcomed in.

"I just don't understand why I wasn't good enough for you." If he wants to say goodbye, I just need my questions answered.

"You have always been good enough. I just was in love with someone else. I loved her, I loved her so much I refused to give you a chance. I can't help the way I felt—feel about her. How was I supposed to turn it off? How could I stop loving her? She will always have my heart in some way." I hit my palm against the door frame. He's hurting me all over again, as if I'm back to being that young juvenile.

"So you came here for what, Clayton? To rub my nose in your love, to press me down in it, to make me relive it? Why come here now? Why bother saying goodbye? You have said everything that needs to be said." I try to keep my quaking voice as even as possible, but it's hard.

He takes a step closer to me, and I step back slightly, so I have nothing to hold onto. He looks around inside my house, not much to see. I haven't even put pictures up.

There is a feeling of deep heat coming off his body, the smell of him snaking up my legs, slithering slowly around my torso, before it hits the tip of my tongue so I can almost taste his flesh. My mouth starts to water with the thirst for him.

Trying to shake this feeling off, it's hard to fight the closer he gets to me.

"Don't come any closer, Clayton." Putting my hand out to stop his approach, his eyes are dilated slightly, nose flaring. A moan that's deeply based in the back of his throat makes the insides of my thighs tremor.

My hand actually touches his chest, and the both of us freeze. I can't remove my hand, and he stills.

His whole body shakes, goosebumps ascending. He licks his lips, and I watch the way his tongue moves over his mouth.

Clayton takes another step closer. "I should leave." He says this to himself because I already thought the same thing.

Instead of turning around and walking away, he comes closer.

"You need to leave," I say as he steps completely into my space.

"I know." His hand goes around my waist, his breath hitting my neck. I can feel the vibration of him.

"What are you doing?" I'm breathless, my voice dropping slightly.

"I'm not sure." His nose goes into my neck. I need to stop him.

"You have to stop." My eyes feel as if they are rolling back into my head with how close he is to the place that holds wolves' marks.

"I know," he says yet pulls me into him, no space between bodies. The earth shifts underneath my feet. I sway, yet he's holding me.

"This is wrong."

His mouth comes closer to mine.

"Is it?" His question is asked just a feather's breath away from my lips.

"Yes, it is." I don't think he believes me.

Touch.

Our lips sink into each other.

His lips are fire, a glorious torture that I can't pull myself away from. His hands caress my face as I kiss him the way I have always dreamed about. I am living my juvenile fantasy in this moment.

Warmth slides through my body. It's energizing on a cellular level.

Hands begin to roam down my back, cupping my bottom, my chest crushed against his.

"Rya?" Instantly I back away from Clayton while I look at Dallas. He can't hide his devastation from my eyes.

"Dallas, I can explain."

"What can you explain, Rya? Tell me. How can you explain this?" I can taste his hurt. His emotions wash over me as if I am a break wall.

"I believed you, Rya. I believed everything you said to me. Now." He shakes his head to himself.

Clayton steps away from me, sliding past Dallas.

"You're a liar, Rya." He turns his back on me, walking away.

Running after him, I beg him to wait and listen to me. He doesn't. He just keeps walking away, growling low in his throat.

"Wait, don't leave, Dallas." I beg and plead, trying to grab onto his shirt for him to stop.

"No, Rya, it wasn't a mistake. The mistake was in me thinking somehow I had a chance with you."

"Dallas, stop. Just listen to me for a minute." I'm shaking because I know how much I just screwed up. I've ruined everything.

"Dallas, wait, don't go." My heart pounds so hard that I think it will explode.

"I'm an idiot," he says to himself, shaking his head.

Watching him drive away from me leaves me with an emptiness that shakes me to my core.

CHAPTER 14

Reconstruction

Dallas

She's outside the car Carson and I have been packing as soon as I got home from her house. I need to leave now.

"Rya, you need to stop." I pry her hands off the car door. This is killing me inside.

"Please don't go without me. I'm so sorry. It was a mistake. I don't know why I did that. Please, just listen to me." I have to pry her fingers to let go of my door. Still, she tries to hang on.

"Carson, let's go." He needs to drive me home because I can't drive at the moment. He's got tears in his eyes as he starts the car.

"Rya, you need to stop this. You're making it worse than it has to be." She's crying so hard, I can hardly understand what she's saying.

"Please just listen to me. I just need a chance to explain what happened." Desperate pleas tumble out of a desperate mouth.

"I thought you said that you didn't know what happened. How can you explain it to me then?" She stumbles for words, to find the right things to say.

"You can't have the both of us, so I'm making it easier for you. Stay here and try to work it out with your mate. Give him a chance. Obviously, you two have some things that need to be worked out, and I'm glad that this happened, because if I were to mark you, I would be forever tormented by this unfinished business with him. The what if's would kill me inside. I have no what if's. I only can see you now. My path is clear, unlike yours." She's trying with all her might to keep the door open between us.

"Please, Dallas, please don't do this. It was a mistake; I realize this now." Her voice is shaking like her entire body.

"Oh, you just realize this now. What about the times I asked you if you were sure with what you wanted? I believed you, but now I don't believe anything you have to say to me." She stills, her eyes looking at me with tears that won't stop.

"I never lied to you Dallas, ever."

"Then you were lying to yourself, Rya. I think that's even worse."

"Please don't do this, not like this. I love you, Dallas. I love you so much. I need you."

"Stop it, Rya, stop. You're making this hard." She tries to pull the car door open fully, but I won't let her. I'm prying her fingers away that are anchored onto the steel frame. Giving her a shove, so she falls on the ground, I close and lock the door.

She scrambles up, pounding her fists against the window. Her words are muffled, but her eyes hold nothing but despair.

My gut is all twisted up and turning sideways inside myself. I feel as if I could throw up with what I'm seeing.

"Go, Carson." I can hardly say the words.

Feeling the car lurch forward, we pull away from this pack, from her, and go toward my home. Looking back, she's on her knees holding the ground in her hands, head pressed against the earth.

"Are you okay, brother?" Carson's hand goes to my shoulder, giving it a squeeze.

"I'll be okay." I have been through worse. This is hard, but I will recover.

"What did Mom and Dad say?" Carson's voice holds sadness.

"They understand that this was the best decision to be made." I look out the window because I can't bear Carson's pitying eyes.

When I called my father telling him I'm coming home alone, he was quiet for a few seconds before asking if I was going to be all right. I told him yes. He was quiet again before telling me that I had to try, to take that chance. I knew what I was up against, the bond. I know what that is all about. I was just lying to myself that she could beat it, that I could beat it. But in the end, it just beat me.

I owe Rya a lot. I owe her for giving me my life back. For waking me from sleepwalking through life. She made me realize I didn't want to be alone anymore, that I wanted more from life. I can't help the way my own tears now come. My throat burns with emotions. I try to angle away from Carson so he can't see me. I try to refocus, but I just can't control my hurt.

From the moment I saw that female, I knew she was special, the way she smiled when I was showing her around the clinic, the way she dealt with all those females. Even when she was at her most vulnerable, she tried to hold herself up on her own. She has such strength inside herself. She made me laugh. She made me believe that I could become what everyone wants me to be. She made me believe in me. I'll always love her for that.

My shoulders start shaking with the way I'm trying not to sob in front of my brother, my weakness showing through my armor that I have built up through the years.

She was mine for a moment, and I loved every single moment we had together.

"I love you, Clayton." Carson uses my first name. I have a hard time hearing it. It reminds me too much of who I was, not who I am now.

I was to irresponsible back then, taking chances, never really thinking about consequences.

Rya will be happy with Clayton. They just need a chance to be what the moon wanted them to be in the first place. I need to keep telling myself that or else I might have Carson turn the car around and go back to her. Give her a chance, like she gave me, except her chance is with her mate and not a fraud like me.

Stopping only for gas and drive thru, we make it to the pack in record time. Caleb will drive my car home once he decides to leave. He's become slightly attached to those wolves.

Pulling into the driveway, the pack is there waiting for me. Every single member is here to welcome me back. Getting out, I straighten out my shoulders, meeting everyone's eyes.

"Welcome home," the pack murmurs as one. They reach out, touching my shoulders, my arms, my shaved head.

Making my way to my parents, my mother kisses my cheek in welcome. My father embraces me into his arms, and it takes everything I have not to break down in front of my pack.

No words can leave my mouth at the moment. It's too difficult. We hug each other for a long time until I can let go.

Making our way into the house after I thank every single wolf for coming to welcome me back, my mother has cooked a feast for me.

"You look bigger." Cash squeezes my bicep, trying to make me smile. Kennedy is beside him looking down at the ground, picking at her nails. I can smell her nervousness. It's like everything that used to be her is gone and replaced with something new.

"How's everything going, Cash?"

"Better." One word answer, but at least it's a good word.

My phone starts to ring. Taking it out of my pocket, I see it's Rya. I turn it off. I can't talk with her anymore, and it's not good for either of us. She has a mate, and I have a pack that needs me.

Dinner is quiet, hushed with our mood. In time, this won't be so bad. It will be like she never happened to me.

Carson gets up from his chair, facing our parents. "I'd like to talk with the both of you in your office, Father."

My dad's looking at him in question. I don't think he's ever asked this of both my parents at the same time.

"All right, are you okay?" my mother asks.

"I am, I'm okay." Those are his words, and I believe them.

"Your training starts now, my son. You need to make your own way to the wild wolves and come back on your own. You need to get back to basics before you can move forward with me."

"How will I know when it's time to come back?" I'm not sure that I'll want to come back.

"You'll just know, trust me. Now go." My father's deep voice urges me to follow what he's saying.

Giving my goodbyes to my family, I head out toward the wild, and hopefully, I'll come back ready to face what I have been putting off for so long.

The wolf ascends from cocoon of skin turning to fur. He run full out, noses pointed forward, tail straight, stretching our body out completely.

The Wild runs the way the wind can blow, fast and furious to greet his nature head on.

CHAPTER 15

Forgiving

Rya

Motionless.

The inability to move, fingers gripping into the earth as its axis tilts underneath my body. Trying so hard to just hang on so I can't fall off the world.

My tears stopped hours ago, yet somehow I just can't seem to pick myself off the ground. I want to decompose into the earth, like all things that have died.

I *can't* get up.

This is what love does. This is always what love does.

It ruins you in the end.

Floods of emotions in, only to flow out once again in great sobs of distress.

The ground is damp with all the tears I've shed. Muddy face, I can feel the grit in my teeth, up my nose, irritating my eyes.

"Rya, it's time to get up." Clayton is behind me, urging me to pick myself up. I wish somehow I could.

"I'm going to help you get up, but that's all I'm going to do. I'll take you back to your house. You can't stay like this." I can tell when he gets closer to me. I hate him, but I hate myself more.

I open my mouth to scream, but no sounds come out.

My body is shaking its betrayal when his hands make contact with my arms, electric energy pulsing inside me into a soothing relief that I don't want to feel.

"Rya, I'm not sure what to say." He picks me up off the ground, setting me down on my own two feet that want to crumple underneath me.

Somehow it's impossible to support my own weight. So he now has no choice but to support me.

Tremors ripple my flesh from within, skin on skin contact that my flesh craves, but my mind loathes.

Words refuse to answer him back.

I have done this to myself. I have no one to blame but me. I should have been stronger. I should have stopped it, fought harder against it.

I was weak.

"Take a step for me, Rya, one foot in front of the other." Clayton sounds like his voice is cracking inside his throat.

Trying to take a breath in, I suffocate on the rush of pain so deep, it feels as if my bones are cracking, except it's my heart that's peeling away.

How long does a heart take to disappear?

In this moment, I need for mine to be gone.

The only male that has ever seen me worthy of love, and I ruined it. I threw it all away with a kiss.

All I have left are memories now. That's all I will ever have of him…memories.

Hopeless, the word doesn't mean enough.

Dallas saw me kissing him. He will never unsee that; he will have that with him forever. How could I even convince him I'm not a cheater, because I am?

"Another step, Rya. Walk for me." I can hear him, but my eyes refuse to focus on anything. The puppeteer working the puppet, he's stringing me along where he wants me to go.

"Rya, take a big breath in. Breathe for me, Rya." The panic vibrates in the wobble of his voice.

"He'll come back for you. He was just upset. He'll be back. Take another step, Rya. You need to keep walking. That's it." My legs start shaking again with the image of Dallas's eyes, how they looked at me.

"Don't you fall down, do you understand! One foot in front of the other." Burning heat saturates into my skin where he's holding me up. Most of my weight is in his hands, my feet only dusting the ground. Sometimes I miss a step, but he won't let me fall.

"It was wrong of me to come to you. It was so wrong, but I couldn't stay away. I had to be selfish one last time. I had to just see you one last time. I didn't mean for that to happen. I just thought I could let you go." His words sound so far away from my ear, but I know that his lips are close. The way his breath hits my neck sends drumming fingers down my spine that pools deep inside my core.

Clayton opens a car door for me. Was it my car that I drove here with? I try to think about how I got here, not expecting Dallas to be leaving as soon as I came.

He had time to shave his head.

Before he can put me in the car, I vomit on the ground with the disgust I have for myself. He holds my hair away from my face, letting me empty the contents of my self-hate for the earth to soak up. It's not fair for the dirt to have to hold all that vileness.

I'm an old brittle paper that's crumbling.

I let my head rest against the glass window, watching nothing as we drive.

"Rya, time to get out of the car. You can do this, one leg, then the other. Now walk toward the door." I can't see anymore, I can't talk anymore, I can't anymore.

Love destroys.

***

Week one

Heartbeat flat lines…

Anxiety waking me in the middle of the night, clutching my chest, sweat trickling down my skin. It's so hard to breathe, but I do.

Statue still, it's easier if I don't move, don't talk, don't think.

Clayton is here along with my parents and

sisters; it's gone supernova. Hatred over so many years bubbles out of mouths that have been silent for so long. My family says things to him that can never be unsaid, but I think it makes them feel better. I'm a silent spectator watching the gladiators compete, flinging insults at one another, accusations on both sides falling on ears that burn with truths. It's a domino effect. He says, they say, the fury of words are like blocks falling one right after the other.

My father flings out words like useless, weak, disgusting, not a male of worth in this sanctuary where there are no eyes to witness a member of the pack raising their voice at the Alpha. All done behind closed doors as families do, no need to air the dirty laundry out in the open.

Clayton flinging out his own words to them, saying they weren't really there for me, not a true support when I needed them most. How does he know all this?

Viciously they verbally attack each other, both holding their own ground from one another. My family is a group of mongooses going after the cobra.

My once-peaceful space is gone, replaced with anger.

I stay paralyzed on the couch, not reacting, not looking, barely trying to listen. Is this how it is to be in a coma, everyone talking over you thinking you can't hear?

I'm lost in my own madness.

They come to some form of a compromise once the rage has been burned out.

No one will leave me alone. Someone's always here with me. I still can't talk, I can't eat, I can't.

It's funny, no matter how bad you feel, the world still keeps going on with or without you; the world keeps moving regardless if you can't.

This is what love does. It builds you up, then it quickly destroys you.

***

Week two

Fingers twitching, eyes start to focus in and out.
Soft energy surrounds me, hands running through my hair when I wake up.

"Why are you here?" His fingers stop. My head's resting on his lap. It's comforting in a sick way.

"I just couldn't walk away again. I couldn't do nothing. I have to do something for you." A tear rolls down my cheek, darkening a spot on his shorts. He's a little too late.

"I don't want you here."

"I know." Getting up, he puts my head on a pillow, covers me with a blanket. I remain cold once his heat is taken away.

"It's going to be really simple, Rya. All you have to do is start living again and I'll go away. I'll leave you alone." He sounds like the Valentines, the way he's using their words against me. Putting my mouth against the pillow, it holds my cries. Fists pound against the couch that do not damage the fabric.

***

Week three

It's starting to become easier to talk, easier to breathe. The weight that's pressing on my chest is lifting slightly. It's not as suffocating.

I can walk on my own, but I still cry.

The world keeps going, and so do I.

Limping progress.

"Did you brush your teeth today? I see you never combed your hair. It's a good look for you." Clayton's taunts aggravate me.

"You smell like old underwear. Change your clothes." Clayton acts like he's my friend, as if we don't have a history together.

He comes in the morning, never staying for long, then he comes before bed just to make sure I'm still alive. My family comes as well, each one rotating a shift in this acute crisis.

I catch Clayton by surprise one morning. He's trying to get me to eat some toast, and I hit him as hard as I can. Harder than I have hit anyone in my life. I think I broke his jaw. He takes the hit and the next ones I give him until I can't hit him anymore. It's not making me feel better. In fact, it's making it worse. He hugs me to him. He holds me as I cry into his chest, while he pats my back, saying it's going to be okay, that it gets easier, I just need time. Dallas will come back for me.

Backing away from him, I go into the cupboard and pull out a whiskey bottle, pouring him and me a drink. He takes it from me, pouring it down the sink, both the glasses and the bottle.

"It won't help, trust me." He talks like he knows what he's saying.

So now comes my verbal insults, the lashing of silver tongues on one another. All those years of rage pent up inside me comes out. Screams, accusations, blaming. Both of us screaming at the other, both of us blaming the other because things didn't go our way.

He blames me for being his mate when all he ever wanted was her. I blamed him for everything.

He slams the front door shut. I slam my bedroom door shut over and over again, screaming until I fall asleep still in the clothes I wore all day long.

Caleb is sitting on the couch when I come out of the bedroom with Max in his arms. It must be Monday. I've lost track of days, one running into another, but I know when Mondays come. It's their day together to watch this little pup. What's going to happen when Kimberly is out of school and those males won't have their Mondays with him anymore? Caleb is going to make a good father when his time comes. That makes me cry because I won't get to be involved with any of them. Maybe if I'm lucky I might catch a word here or there about the lives of the Valentines.

"Rya, it's going to be okay." Caleb hates when I cry. I just can't stop.

"Is he back yet?" Always the same question for him.

"No, not yet." Max is snuggled in this male's arms, safe and secure. Not a care in the world except when his next meal is. What a lucky male.

"How long do you think he'll be out there?" In a way, I'm envious of Dallas, able to just move on like I never existed. For me, he's always walking in my mind, always there; he's always a thought that I can't escape from. I can't turn him off, but it's getting easier to let life in again.

"I'm not sure. It's when he feels it's time to come back. No one is going to drag him back. He's getting back to basics." I look out the window. Clayton is watering the garden. He's been taking care of it because I refuse to do anything to help it grow. If it was up to me, I'd let it all die.

"Do you hate me, Caleb?"

"No, Rya. I don't hate you. Disappointed in you, maybe a little, but hey, I've made some bad decisions in my life. Who am I to judge you?" Max starts stretching in his arms, waking up from a big sleep. Caleb smiles down at the little pup.

"Do you think Dallas can ever forgive me?" I can't look at Caleb when I ask the question. Instead, I pick at the cushion on the seat.

"Maybe." One words answers are really not good. Burning pain in my throat makes me gag slightly. I just can't stomach myself these days.

Clayton enters the house, and I give him the side eye of hate. I'm not affected by him so greatly; the desire for him is fading. I still can tell when his eyes are on me—my skin shivers with his voice—but the intensity I felt with his presence has faded.

I can control myself now. I can focus on his words instead of his lips.

"Ready, Caleb? We should get him back. Kimberly will be home shortly."

The first time she came here to pick her male up, she had something so smart to say. Something that scraped along my spine. The wolf inside ascended to look in her eyes. She went to move to get her male, but I blocked her path, asking, "What did you just say?"

Her posture changes as well, becoming more rigid, more dominant. "I said it's not the end of the world." She takes a threatening step toward her, a rumbling growl warning her to stand down, to bend her neck or else I'm going to make her.

She doesn't. Instead, she shifts from foot to foot, testing me. A small growl rumbles from her chest, challenging me to do something, and I do.

We are on each other fast, fists hurting flesh. She's a juvenile without any training, and I feel as if I'm the wolverine, and she's me on my first day of training with the Valentine Pack.

Getting her pinned down so her nose is rubbing into the floor board, her pup is screaming, but I don't let up. Taking her arm, twisting it back, I'm applying pressure. Still, she doesn't concede to a higher power, so I apply more power to her arm. It's going to snap. I come close to her face, letting my teeth out. She's screaming when she looks into my eyes. Her neck bends to me, a submission earned, yet I don't let go. I keep exerting pressure. It takes the combined effort of Clayton and Caleb to pull me off that female who needed to be schooled in the art of keeping her mouth shut!

***

Week four

"Rya, you should try to go back to work." Clayton comes into my home like he owns it, always at unpredictable times. He only comes once a day now. My family comes around less often because I don't need them constantly around me anymore. The crisis is passing somewhat.

"You should knock before you come in." Irritation drips heavily off my voice.

"How was your day? What did you do? I can tell you showered, brushed your teeth. Are those fresh clothes you have on?" His eyebrow arches up in question.

"Yes."

"Progress!" He pats me on the head like a young juvenile learning something new for the first time.

"Rya, it gets better. Trust me on this."

"If it wasn't for you, I wouldn't be in this mess." Lashing words meant to hurt him.

"You kissed me back." His response always.

I can't fight those words because it's true.

"You went outside today, Rya." I just came in from sitting by the water for a few hours. Mother Nature's healing beauty surrounds me. I forgot to look at her for so long that I just need to sit and reflect on what I have, not what I don't have.

He's carrying a bag of groceries for me, everything in my fridge gone because he and Caleb ate everything. I only can stomach certain things; heartbreak does that, makes you have no appetite, makes you crave things that aren't good for you.

Taking the bag out of his hands, I grab the cold

container.

All you need is a spoon and a tub of chocolate ice cream to make you feel better. Reaching back into the bag, I pull the Oreos out. This is what I have been dreaming about all day long. The crunch of the cookie along with the cold melting ice cream going down my throat has me almost moaning in pleasure.

Clayton's staring at me funny but knows better than to say anything as long as I'm eating. His presences makes it easier for me to eat; it's as if he has a calming effect on me.

Caleb comes into my home looking like he's going out for the night. All dressed up and smelling like a male trolling for something to pass the time with.

"Rya, really. Where's the bowl? That's just gross. Use a spoon."

"Caleb, you don't live here. I can do what I want to do in my own house." He grabs a spoon, taking a big scoop and a row of Oreos for himself.

"Those are mine." I try to take them back, but he holds them above his head out of reach.

"I could fight you for them, number two."

"Rya, why do you have to be that way? I thought we were friends." Holding his heart, he makes his face look sad with downward lips.

"Stop coming here and eating my food, Caleb." Before the words come out my mouth, he's going to the fridge, pulling out the milk, putting two Oreos in his mouth, and sucking back milk from the container.

He's insane.

DALLAS

*****

Week five

Looking in the mirror, I still avoid my eyes, but I brush my teeth, comb my hair, get dressed. I still can't eat very good, but it's the little steps that are important. My breath hits the mirror, tainting it with my regret.

Decisions.

I've been contemplating my life, what I want, what I need.

I've decided that I need to leave, get out on my own for a while. Live my life.

Clayton has been hanging out by the lake waiting for me to get home. His hands are in his pockets, as if holding himself away from me.

"Where have you been, Rya?"

"I was at my parents' house saying goodbye."

"Goodbye?" Clayton's body visibly stiffens, a tension in his shoulders starting to build up.

"I always wanted to travel. I have things I want to do. Places I want to see. I've got some money saved up. Why not waste it on me?"

"Will you be back?" He rubs his chest as if it hurts.

"I'm not sure. I don't know." It's my truth. I'm not sure, but for now, I know I want to go. Not because anyone is forcing me to leave, but because I want to leave. Start to live my life that I am going to start living. I can't wait on Dallas to come back here. What happens if he never comes back? I would have wasted my life waiting for a dream that never will happen.

"When are you going?"

"I'm leaving in the morning."

"So soon. I thought maybe that—"

"Clayton, I need to tell you something." Taking a breath in, I square my shoulders to him. He does the same. Ready to meet what my words have to say.

"I've been doing a lot of thinking, and I just want you to know that I forgive you. I won't forget, but I can forgive you. I can't move on unless I do this." I grit my teeth together.

"I just want you to know that I only want you to be happy in the future. Thank you for helping me through my time of need. I think in time you'll be happy. It's hard to get over someone you've loved." Both of us just look at one another, deep orbs of pine looking at a glacier blue.

A sadness spreads inside me for a lost past, but excitement is starting to build up for a hopeful future.

Letting go is okay. It hurts, but it will be okay in the end.

If you let them go, will they come back?

CHAPTER 16

Scenic Route

The sun filters through the window of the car, its path switching directions on the dashboard with every turn and change in direction. The light flickers and fades before glaring into my eyes, depending on the path I take.

I'm not sure where I'm going, just that I want to end up with my feet in the ocean. I've never seen the ocean before. I thought that's a good place to start. It's going to take a week to get there. Instead of taking the highways to my destination, I'm taking the slow scenic route. The road snakes and twists as the tires roll over the blacktop through the little communities I pass through.

I only stop for gas. I'm trying to put as much road and distance behind me as I can. Southeast is the direction that is calling to me; I'm not sure why.

Following instinct, I go with my gut.

I stop for the night at a cheap motel and go to bed early. Closing my eyes as I lay my head on the overstuffed pillow, I can still picture the curve of Dallas's face. The way his mouth tastes, the way his skin feels underneath my hands that were so greedy to take what his body offered me. The wolf inside me gives a whimper with my thoughts. She's been so quiet, not wanting to do anything. She's content to just lie around with her tail over her eyes in stillness. She's hurting just like me, and all she wants to do is sleep.

The early morning comes, and I'm back on the road, driving, looking for interesting places to stop. Little curiosity shops in these towns hold the neatest things. I like how some of these communities have angled parking. It has such a small town feel to it.

I pull off at all the scenic signs along the way, taking in the view that no picture can give justice to.

Mother Nature is so powerful, her art is magnificent.

The next gas station has postcards of the last scenic place I took pictures of. Buying two, I scribble out a little note for my parents and leave the other one blank for Clayton. Looking for a place to mail them, I pass by a salon. The glass window holds my silhouette, not a crisp image, more just the outline of features.

Glancing at my reflection, I notice the braid that goes over my shoulder, the same braid I have always worn. I used to change my style so much when I was younger, never afraid to try new things. With a big breath, I push the door open, and little chimes to go off above my head.

"Hi, can I help you?" the lady behind the counter says with a soft smile.

"I was wondering if anyone has time to cut my hair." I feel awkward, unsure of the proper wording. It's been so long since I had a real haircut, not just a trim to cut the dead ends.

She looks at the braid that's over my shoulder. "Do you know what you want?"

"I just need a change. I'm looking for something different." Now her eyes light up with ideas.

"Well, you've come to the right place. Let's get you in the chair and talk about what you want to be done." Leading me to her chair, she puts a black cape over my shoulders. She takes the tie out of my hair, running her fingers through the strands.

"Is this your real color?"

"Yes." Humans are always shocked at the white blonde.

"You have beautiful thick hair." Her hands make my head tingle in delight. "Your eyes are very unusual." I can tell they creep her out slightly with the way she needs to look away from them. It's always the same; humans have a hard time holding a conversation while gazing into my eyes. They look away as if I'm just not right in a certain way...an instinct born in them that says this person is just off slightly, but they can't put their finger on it. The next thing I need are contacts. It will make it easier on everyone, especially if I bump into any wolves along the way.

Watching my hair fall to the floor, laying in little clumps, has my stomach rolling on itself slightly. Another worker sweeps the mess away. By the time the clippers hit the back of my neck, my head feels lighter, less heavy. Putting down her scissors, she's

211

giddy with her work. You can tell the pride in her eyes when she's looking at the completed masterpiece.

She swivels me around in the chair, and my gaze fall on my head. Gone, all of it. A short pixie cut greets my happy eyes. It suits me in a very simple way in a risk-taking way. It's just hair, but for me, it feels as if I'm cleaning the old me off and starting the new me.

My beginning.

I touch the back of my head, turning left to right and back again. She holds a mirror up to me so I can see the back.

"Perfect!" When saying the word, she breathes a sigh of relief. "Thank you, it's just perfect." I mean it; this is what I needed.

Walking out of the shop, I have a lighter step. It's weird how just a haircut can make you feel.

Every so often, my hand goes to the end of the braid that's no longer there. I'll get used to it. Finding an eyeglass store in the next town, I purchase my first set of non-prescription contacts. The eye doctor asked me several questions, if I can see color, if he could examine my eyes for free, no charge—he's never seen color like that before. He's been a doctor for over thirty years, and this is a first for him. I decline his offer, paying for the contacts that are the color of a perfect blue sky.

A few days later, I stop for the night in a town bustling with excitement. The fair has come, and I was lucky to get the room. Some last minute cancellation has me snagging the last room available before the no vacancy sign comes on.

The clerk said I should go check it out; food trucks will be there, that's new this year. I remember Caleb watching the Food Network, groaning over the pictures on the screen.

Looking into the mirror, I smile at myself; hair that's super cute, eyes of the sky. Lips have a tint of pink to them. My outfit is eccentric, a mismatch of contrasting colors that I loved to wear when I was younger. I'm going back to my roots, what I always wanted to wear but had no ambition to pull those looks off. I stop every so often at unique places to buy a certain item of clothing that just calls to me, knowing if I let the opportunity pass me by, I might not ever see that style again.

I'm buying things for me.

The long skirt drags slightly on the ground while I walk toward the sounds of this festival. Music and laughter hit my ears. The gears of the rides grind with the screams of the adventurous. My nose catches the scents of many different food items. The one that hits me the most are the deep fried funnel cakes. My mouth waters with the need to consume that particular item.

Adults laugh while their children explore the rides. High school girls in halter tops, boys chasing after them. It makes me smile. This is the first real fair I have ever been to, and I can't help but take it all in.

I see a tent set up with a fortune teller, and it's an internal debate whether to go in and get a reading. Stopping at the sign, I contemplate hard. Do I want to know my future?

No, my future is up to me. No one can predict it.

213

The funnel cake truck has a long line. I read all the items they offer until my eyes focus on a deep fried peanut butter and jelly sandwich that I have seen on TV with Caleb. He groaned at the thing.

Placing my order, I get that funnel cake, but I also get that deep fried bliss it seems most people are ordering.

Sitting down at the picnic table just outside kiddie rides, I watch the crowd going by.

I'm a people watcher now.

Opening up the middle of the sandwich that is surrounded by a sweet, deep fried crust, the contents ooze out warm and sticky. Licking the ends of my fingers, I snap a picture, sending it to Caleb with the caption,

Don't hate.

Instantly, he sends me a text back.

Caleb: What's that?

Rya: Deep fried peanut butter and jelly sandwich with a side of funnel cake. The cake has a dusting of powdered sugar that gets all over my face with the first bite. One napkin won't be enough.

Caleb: Where are you at?

Rya: Some town.

I don't want to get too specific. I snap a picture

of the food truck for him to see. I'm living what he's been only able to watch on TV, smiling to myself at that thought.

Caleb: I'm jealous.

Rya: I know, that's why I sent you the pic. Have a good day.

Caleb: You too.

Our conversation ends. Filling my face with sugar and dough, I can't seem to get enough. I'm actually contemplating going up to get two more.

The smell circles around me, a slightly sour smell. A she-wolf is in the area. Looking around, I spot her looking at the toddler rides. Her eyes hold a certain longing in them. I watch the way she's gazing at the little ones. The desire to have something she will never have. My heart goes to her because I've always looked at them the same way.

A male comes up from behind her, holding her close to his chest. He whispers in her ear before giving her cheek a quick kiss. I watch this intimate moment between mates.

He tucks a stray hair behind her ear. "Are you okay?" His words can only be heard faintly above the carnival noise.

"Yes." She tries to smile at him, but it's just lost in longing.

"I love you." It's hard not to get a little emotional with the way he says it.

As if they can tell someone is peeping on them,

the eyes of the wolves regard me. I don't look away. I could help them; I could give them what they desire the most if I wanted to stay for a little while.

The big male approaches my table, hands going on the wood.

"Female, this is my territory. You're intruding." He shows a flash of fang, not happy with me.

"I'm just passing through, taking in the scenery. I'll be gone in the morning." I don't bend my shoulders but keep them straight.

"Where are you staying at?" His mate comes up beside him, looking at me with eyes that hold years of misery in them. Sadness ages you. It has a way of leaving its mark on your soul, and I can see it inside her.

Looking her in the eyes, I say, "I could help you if you want. I could give you what you want most." Her eyes dilate, and she breathes in.

The alpha grabs my chin hard in his hands, barely able to control his rage.

"You need to leave now!" He flings my head back as he releases my jaw.

"I'll leave now." Getting up, I quickly move away from the beast that is barely able to control his shift. His mate rubs his chest, kissing his mark.

"Don't leave, wait," she calls out to me, halting my progress.

"How can you help me?" I need to think fast…I don't want them to know what I am. Looking at the fortune teller's sign again, an idea comes to mind.

"I've got special tea. It helps females with your problem."

"Liar." The Alpha pounds his fist on the table.

"We have been to healer after healer—nothing has worked."

He looks so upset, and she looks so hopeful, as if maybe this time something might work. He seems as if he's had his heart broken one too many times, believing in something that just can't happen.

"I've helped a few females in your condition, and I'm offering my services to you if you want them. If not, I'll be on my way." A few weeks' delay is just a detour. Maybe I could use my gift for others. Maybe this was my path the whole time and I was just too blinded by my personal grief to not really look and see how I can help others with a gift that was blessed to me by the moon herself.

"If you're lying in any kind of way, I will eat you alive, consume you slowly, feet first. We've been through too much." He's looking at his mate with a fierce protectiveness.

"I'll have to stay with you for a few weeks. My tea needs to be made fresh every day. It's a special combination of herbs that I use, a family secret." I'm trying to sound mystical, but I want to laugh at myself. I know that lots of wolves would be interested in the gifts I possess. I'm not a fool.

"What do you want from me?" Keen eyes peer at me, waiting for my request.

"I get to move freely on your land. I need a place to stay, preferably by myself. Keep all other females away unless they are sterile, then they can come and have tea with us. No one is to know that I'm here. You can't talk about me or else I'll never come again." He looks amused; I think maybe he thought I was going to ask him for large quantities of money.

"Is that it?"

"That's it. You either take my offer or leave it. Your choice."

She pulls him away, taking a few steps off to the side. I can hear the way her voice pleads, the way desperation is noted in each word she uses. "We have to try."

"I can't watch you go through that again. I can't."

They argue back and forth, one point made, another uttered until a conclusion is made.

"Welcome to our pack." She greets me cheek to cheek, taking my smell in as I take her sourness in. Only a male deep in love can tolerate a smell like that.

The next day has me driving to a tiny house that they assigned to me. It's old and somewhat rundown but filled with character. It's how you have to look at things. Old and rundown doesn't mean that there is not character to be found; it just needs help shining again.

They left me brochures of places to go while I'm here, the big sights of the town and the surrounding areas. There are old mines to explore, a national park that belongs to the pack territory. Lots of things to go have a day adventure and I have a home base to do all this. Cuts down on the expense of hotels, so I take advantage of all that there is to do. All I have to do is have tea in the morning and evening with the three female wolves. There is a male in the group who is sterile; he holds himself like a male, but at the same time, he has hunched shoulders. I bet as a juvenile he was teased constantly for this by the male wolves in the pack.

I couldn't promise that the tea would work for him because I have never had a sterile male around me before. I made sure to have his mate at our teas, saying that she needed to drink as well. No one questions me, thinking that I know what I'm talking about, hoping the magic will work, and it does. The second week I'm with them, I can smell their scents changing, a sweetness gradually replacing the souring nose-curling smell.

During my visits with these females, I get to learn about them. Their culture, how they met their mates, that not everything is perfect all the time, that things can be a struggle.

That things are hard.

The Luna of this pack tells me that she refused her mate for many years, knowing she could never provide him with an heir, that he would be better off without her. She was mean to him, and for a few years, they ended up hating each other, doing things to each other that were hard to forgive. But as time went by, slowly they became friends and somehow trusted in the moon that their path was supposed to be together instead of apart. I cried while she was telling me this along with the rest of our little group.

I'm so emotional these days.

Waking up, rushing to the toilet, I heave my stomach contents out into the porcelain bowl. Violent waves of gastric contents rush up and out from deep inside with such force my eyes are tearing up, and I dribble a little urine out from it.

Sitting on the floor after I'm done, I feel slightly

better. An odd feeling comes over me, a little nipping thought in my mind that's trying to whisper to me. Taking deep breaths in through my nose, I smell of vomit, but something else…that's when I start to shake. My whole body tenses up with what I'm smelling on myself.

No.

Impossible.

No.

There's no way that's possible.

No.

I'm pregnant.

CHAPTER 17

A Wanderer's Home

Rya

First light of the day filters in through the blinds, its beam unhurried while it travels across the wooden floor in a show of time crawling slowly forward.

Fingers probing low, I feel for that hardness that's just below the surface of the skin. The telltale sign of a lining that's building a nest for my future inside me. Feeling it, just the slightest, barely there swell. Not noticeable if I wasn't trained to look.

How could I have been so blind about myself?

How did I miss all the signs that were in front of my nose?

Looking back, I put each piece together. The big neon sign in my mind going off. I've been an idiot not to recognize what my own body was telling me. Everything made sense: the increased appetite for food, then seeing Dallas, how my appetite grew for much more than food. How he fed my body over and over again with his nutrients.

Sometimes the most educated wolves are the most blinded when it comes to themselves.

Part of me wants to keep this little secret safe and secure for just a few more weeks. There's time to tell, but do I really want to tell?

Do I want Dallas to forgive me because I'm carrying his future? Maybe he will only take me back out of obligation, staying with me because of our young. I don't want that for him or for me. I want him to want me without knowing this. But then I shouldn't keep this from him either.

Decisions.

Picking up the phone, I dial Luna Grace. I hold my breath. *Please be home.*

There are a few rings before a tired voice answers the other end.

"Hello."

"Hello, Luna Grace, this is Rya."

"Rya." A little crack of her throat. "Thank you for calling." It's as if her voice is on autopilot, as if someone else is guiding her to say the right words for the occasion.

"Luna Grace, are you all right?" I've never heard this side of her before.

"Rya, you haven't heard?" My heart starts to tick just a little faster, apprehension prickling the back of my neck.

"Heard what, Luna Grace?" I can't control the rise of panic coming through in words. The wobble of anxiety, the small tremor in fingers that holds the phone.

A pause.

Muffled cry.

"Rya. I'm so sorry to tell you this, but…" I could picture her sitting down with what she needs to say, the heaviness so great in her voice it actually weighs me down into a sitting position.

"Rya, Kennedy had the pups late last night—" Luna Grace begins to paint the picture in words of grief.

"The pregnancy was hard on her body, weakening it. The labor was long. She just wasn't strong enough with the demands of having twins." Another pause, trying to get tight emotions under control.

Bracing myself for the next sentence is like trying to stand against a sledgehammer aiming at the center of my chest.

"She just couldn't push the first out. The twins were in distress. She started to hemorrhage. They couldn't stop the bleeding." It's as if she's reliving it again. Cries so deep, short intakes of breath. Her words become unclear, my vision blurring and unfocused, words slipping into one another with the strangulation of breath.

"A decision was made to use silver. She couldn't push them out. We had to take them." She stops to gather herself, sniffling into the phone.

"She already lost a lot of blood. She understood what was happening almost to the very end, until she couldn't keep her eyes open. She put her best effort to stay with us, with them, with Cash." It takes Luna Grace time to rein in the storm of emotions. "She was able to see her beauties before—"

Wiping away my own tears, it's hard to swallow with the constriction I feel in my throat. Luna Grace takes a few minutes to regain her composure just enough to say the next line.

"She passed away in Cash's arms last night."

Crumpling, the sledgehammer strikes true, dead center.

"Cash, my poor Cassius." Luna Grace's pain is a horror to my ears.

"We don't have enough nursing mothers in the pack to support two pups. I don't think we can even support one." Hearts know pain, and mine is now experiencing pain on a whole new level.

The realization of life hitting me in the face, how life easily begins to quickly end.

Mothers have a hard time sharing what is meant for their young. Survival of the fittest. If you can't provide, then yours die. Every feeding is needed to a growing pup. To take one away is not noticed, but to take several feedings away, then the growth and development are affected. No mother will endanger her pup for someone else's, no matter whose it is.

Instinct.

"They're beautiful, Rya. They look like Kennedy. They have her eyes." Another muffled cry and I cry along with her.

She has now become that funeral hymn that they will sing about.

"What can I do, Luna Grace?" I feel helpless, useless.

"Pray to the moon for them." That's all she can say, knowing what the future will bring to her grandchildren who has no one to feed them.

"I'm coming." I need to be there for Cash. We had a rough start, but our ending was what mattered.

"Don't. There's nothing you can do for the dead. Cash won't even notice you're here. Continue on with what you're doing. Caleb told us you left the pack, that you are wandering. There's no need to come back. My oldest won't be back for a long time. Live that life you need to live. It's too short, Rya. Do all the things you want to do before it's too late. You just never know when it can end." Another fresh rack of sobs renders her speech garbled and hard to follow.

"Little Moon." That Silverback Alpha's voice is steady, sturdy.

"Alpha Clinton." I can hear Luna Grace's cries that are muffled sobs; he's probably holding her against his chest.

"Little Moon, you're on your wandering journey. Stay on course. You need this just like my male needs his journey. We're proud of you, Rya. If you need anything, please ask. Otherwise, we will know you're doing okay." I contemplate telling him the future I hold inside me, but for some reason, I don't.

"Can you tell Cash how sorry I am for him?"

"We'll tell him."

"Can you tell Dallas when he comes home to call me? I need to talk to him." I try to stress the importance of my words, but I think it's lost in the events of grief.

"We'll tell our oldest, but it's his decision whether to call you or not. We hope he does call you. Sometimes things just need time to get over."

"I understand."

"If there's anything I can do for Cash, call me." I really mean it. I will drop anything to be there for that male who's probably completely ruined.

"We will, Rya, thank you." His voice is deep and comforting, a rock in turbulent waves that you can hold onto.

"Goodbye. May the moon be good to you, Rya."

"You as well, Alpha Clinton."

Hanging up the phone, I'm a mess. Even though I don't like that female, even though she was the thorn that pricked deeply into my heel, I can't bear what her death means for everyone, especially those pups.

They don't deserve a hunger that can never be satisfied. Not only does Cash have to burn his dead mate, he has to listen to those pups cry and cry from the hunger. Their cries will get weaker and weaker till they are only whimpers.

Looking at my phone, I send Clayton a text.

Rya: Are you okay?

Clayton: No.

His reply comes a few minutes later.

Rya: I'm sorry.

What more can I say? His everything forever gone, her happy ending never finished in that fairy tale book of hers. Did it ever really have a chance to

226

begin in the first place? He doesn't say anything else. No more replies from him.

I contact Caleb next.

Rya: How is he?

Caleb: Taking it bad, both are. I'm heading back in the morning. Cash needs me at home.

Rya: Tell Cash I'm going to help him somehow. I'm going to find a way to help him.

Caleb: Rya, you should come back here. Clayton needs someone.

Rya: I can't Caleb, I can't go backward. He's going to be fine he just needs some time to handle things himself. I can't hold him while he cries for her. I don't have that in me.

Caleb: I understand.

Rya: Safe trip.

Caleb: You too.

His final words to me as we end our conversation.

I'm glad I made peace with her, at least that part of her and me I won't regret. I said what I needed to say, and I won't have that regret over my head.

A knock on the door brings me out of my own thoughts.

"Rya, it's past our meeting time and—" The Luna of this pack looks me up and down, taking in my appearance.

"Your eyes!" Surprised, she takes a step back from me. I forgot to put my contacts in before answering the door.

"You swore to secrecy. You can't say a word. I will never come back here, and I can take away what I brought. I can end the future inside of you. I have the power," I lie. She doesn't know that I hold no power of destruction, only the power of creation.

"You're moon blessed." Instantly kneeling down, she touches her forehead to my bare feet.

Awkward.

"You can't tell anyone, not even your mate. Do you understand?" I try to make my voice sound deeper, more menacing, flash fang.

"Now stand up." She's looking at me as if she's looking at a god. Her whole stance changes, nervous energy pulsing off her body. I think she's frightened in a way. Leery movements, not walking fully into this house. Standing on the outside of the door, refusing to be cornered inside with me.

Again she assesses with cunning eyes. The keenness in them dilates the irises black.

"Are you all right, Rya?"

"I just got some bad news from a pack that I was with for a while." A tear that I don't want to show trails down my cheek. Strong arms pull me into her. Hands rub my back. She just holds me until I can let go of her.

"What can we do for you?" She pulls herself away from me. Her beautiful sweet scent fills the room. Her lips are a shade darker, her cheeks flushed, her heat coming in hard.

I know now what I can do for Cash, for that family who has given me so much. I will provide for them in their time of need. I'm going to be the bringer of food.

"I need your help."

"Ask anything." Her debt to me knows no bounds.

"This pack that I have spent time with just lost a mother of twins." A sad intake of breath from the Luna's throat, she understands the dire need of those pups.

"They don't have enough nursing females to handle the strain of two more mouths to feed. In a few months, they will have plenty of females to help provide for those twins, but in the meantime, they need help. Can you provide them with what they need even if it's only a little bit? Anything will help."

"Do you know what you're asking of the mothers?"

"I do. I'm just asking for one feeding, that's all. One feeding to go toward the twins' needs. I need you to freeze the milk, then have someone drive straight through and deliver it before it thaws. Can you do that? Can you help?" Wisps of sound come out as soft desperate pleas from my mouth.

"I have favors owed to me, not only in this pack, but the surrounding packs. I will call in every single one of them. I will have my mate call in all his favors with different packs. He will do whatever you ask of him. I will arrange a shipment by tomorrow morning. Then I will arrange one every week after that. You can count on me. I just owe you so much more than this."

"No, this is enough. Any help you give them is more than what they have. Thank you."

"Rya, I have a favor to ask you." She looks slightly nervous.

"Ask."

"I know of two females three hours away. One is the Alpha's youngest daughter. I was wondering if you could go and see her. Do what you did for us?"

"Make the arrangements, tell them my demands, and also about needing the milk. I won't go unless that demand is met. Also, you need to tell them the importance of secrecy. No one is to know about me. Can you keep my secret?"

"I will die with your secret. I will make the call. Thank you, Rya, for everything."

"This is my last day with your pack. I need to leave. My job is done. You're starting your heat, all of you. I hope you have a successful outcome. Tell them that I said goodbye, that I wish them the best. I'll start packing. I expect an answer from that pack within the hour. If not, I'm going my own way." I try to sound as if I couldn't care either way, but in reality, I'm bluffing. I need the milk for those pups.

The Luna leaves, but not before hugging me one last time.

Packing my belongings, I know I can do this, make the connections I need to help with something that is bigger than me. I might not have liked Kennedy, but I will fight for her pups' survival. I will do everything I can to help them survive.

Within the hour, the Luna's back with directions to the next pack that takes me slightly closer to the ocean. I give her the address to the Valentines' pack. Again she assures me that everything that can be done for them will be.

Later the next night, my phone rings. Smiling to myself, I answer.

"Thank you, Rya," Luna's Grace says even before I can say hello.

"I'm not sure what you mean." Trying to play dumb with her is beyond my skill level.

"How did you manage this? We asked them how they knew. They remained tight-lipped, just saying when the delivery date is each week. They wouldn't give us any more information. They said that they would take nothing in return. I found it odd that the female who was driving such a long way was going into her heat. For some reason, I thought of you." She persists with her questioning.

"Odd you thought of me." I wonder what couple delivered the milk. Who took all the time to drive that distance only to drop off what was needed and turn around again?

"Rya, now listen to me. I know it's you. Tell me how?" She pronounced each word clearly, with an edge to it, leaving me no choice but to tell her something.

"They owed me a favor." That's all I say, no need revealing too much of my activities.

"A favor? Rya, you're sounding and acting like a true Luna." I need to change the subject.

"How's Cash doing?"

"He's still in shock, but he's surviving."

"Tell him everything I do is for him and them." It's hard to get the words out.

"I will, Rya."

Taking a few days to myself to grieve, I pull into this new pack house with a fresh supply of tea and magic pixie dust. That thought gives me a little laugh. All these wolves believing in magic and I'm the one to bring it in a special tea. It's really ginger tea infused with vitamins. My morning sickness is just starting to grip me, and I need every trick and knowledge I have obtained with my training to be used on myself now. This is the beginning of the second month and I know I have a few hard months ahead of me.

Opening the door to this pack house stands an older looking couple, the Alpha with white hair, his mate's skin translucent, showing her blue veins all wrinkled with age. They are older than what I'm used to in a ruling pair. They are well past their prime but continue to rule anyway. Different cultures have different ways to go about things. I once heard that mates paired for a long time even die around the same time, one from natural causes, the other from heartache.

That's what love does: it leads to death from heartache.

The Luna places her cheek against mine, inhaling deeply before pulling away.

"Sorry for your loss." At first, I'm not sure what she means, then realization set in: she can smell I'm pregnant without a mate's mark. She must think my mate has died and my mark faded.

"Thank you." That's all I say. Let them believe

what they want to believe. I'm not here to tell my life story. I'm on the trail of meat, except its milk that I'm after.

This gives me a purpose to continue on, to go from pack to pack. It's as if I'm a wanderer but with a set goal. The ocean is just within reach, yet my path detours off course constantly.

Month three has me starting to lose some weight, just a little. The craving for Dallas is beyond what's normal. My body feels unsettled, in a state of constant worry that we are not safe without his presence. All the Alphas of the packs that I visit pledge their protection to me. Nothing will touch me as long as I am in their territory. I am safe with them.

That eases my mind slightly, yet I do ask for a silver knife that I keep hidden and on me at all times. A little reminder for anyone who challenges me I will not go down easily. Teeth and claw against silver, not a fair fight, but I would do permanent damage before I'm taken out.

From this pack, I learn that age is valued, that the elders of the pack are the leaders, warriors are the up and coming, but it's the elders who govern and make pack decisions with the Alpha having the final say. I'm taught to make perogies from scratch from the old mamas. They use it as an excuse to get together and drink. It's funny watching old female wolves getting together laughing, drinking, and talking with the filthiest mouths that I have ever heard. The stories about their youth have me blushing. They get out their phones that some have a hard time working, showing me pictures of their grandchildren.

One older wolf, who looks wobbly on skinny legs, has a devious smirk to her. Pulling out her phone, she passes it around to the other wolves, saying, "Look at the picture I had the neighbor take. I put it as my profile picture on Facebook."

It's her with a beer in her hand, smoke hanging out her mouth while driving a riding lawnmower. "It drove my son crazy as soon as I put it up." She snickers to the rest of her friends, and they all howl with laughter. They try to one-up each other who can get the best reaction out of their young. She won the twenty bucks this month with that picture. She pockets the twenty in her bra, winking at the rest of the mamas.

I love watching the interaction of these loving females. Friend love is good love.

Cash's twins are surviving. Caleb tells me that everyone is taking shifts, helping raise those pups as if they belonged to everyone and not just Cash. Everyone has claimed them as their own. It feels good that the pack bands together in times of need, helping someone who is in need.

Community, that's how it's supposed to be.

Rya: How are you?

My message to Cash every week is the same, yet he hasn't answered me back. I hope he sees my effort.

Month four has my pants just barely doing up. I can't button them anymore. I resort to skirts and sundresses. The heat is oppressive this far south.

My hair's growing out slightly in its own messy style that's all mine.

This is the month I feel his fishtail kicks, as he flops and twists inside me. At first, I thought it was gas bubbles, but as I really sat still, I could feel him running around in there, happy and content.

He will be a strong male.

I feel as if the moon herself is cradling me in her hands. This pregnancy is going so easy for me.

I'm so lucky.

Giggling, never would I use those words to describe myself, but now they are my everyday words. How lucky I am, I constantly think this as I feel my love inside me. I can't stop the way my hands find that they love to rest on top of the small forming bump. The way he kicks when I put the phone to my stomach and Dallas's voice comes over saying he's unavailable to take the message.

Just that short message has the pup reacting in bursts of energy. I have never left a message, preferring just to hear his voice tickle my skin.

It soothes me to hear his voice even if it's in a message of "please leave a message."

I had a dream about Dallas the other night, about our twisting bodies, naked, coming together hard and satisfying. This dream only left an ache between my thighs that's not satisfied. I have to prepare myself that I might not see him for a very long time. That makes me whimper inside. I have to be prepared he will never forgive me.

Can I share my male with Dallas if he doesn't want me? A very little whisper mists up my back, tentacles anchoring into my spine, pulling dark thoughts into my mind.

He could take him away from you.

He wouldn't do that, I always say back, but there is a little fear, if I'm honest with myself.

Whenever I bump into wolves, it's always the same "sorry for your loss." Their eyes always fall to my unmarked neck, then looking away quickly, like I have a birth defect of some kind. I always respond with a thank you and go about with what I'm doing.

Month five has me needing to buy my first pregnancy clothes—nothing but bright colors. Everything flowing from the pretty blouses, skirts all floral and layered, providing me warmth while fall is starting to roll in with cool winds from the north.

Eccentric. That's what some of the wolves say about me now.

I look as if I'm a gypsy and feel like a nomad, not tied down to one place. Doing things I only dreamed of doing. The postcards to my parents telling them of my adventures, never a return address on them, and in a way I feel guilty for not telling them I'm expecting, but the more I let my secret stay a secret, the harder it's getting to actually tell them.

No other packs are needed for the supply line of milk. It's time for me to touch the ocean with my bare feet.

Month six, no hiding my belly—it's growing more and more with each day. I make it to the ocean's edge, driving along the coast.

It's big sky and blue water, the waves white tipped in the gusting wind.

236

I've been looking for just the perfect house to den up in. I need something small, secure, and private. The off-season for beach rentals is winding down, and I have a few that I googled that will rent me the home for six months. All I have to do is decide on the right location.

My hunt is not a successful one. This is the last stop before I have to research my options again.

I pull up to a private drive made with a mixture of small rock and sand that the tires crunch on. The homes are hidden behind thick layers of trees and bushes.

Following the curved road, I smile to myself with the way these little shore houses are lined up. All bright colored and well-maintained on the outside.

Getting out of the car, I hear the waves crashing against the shore. The sea breeze moistens the air I breathe in. A chorus of screaming seagulls talk to each other from up above.

The owner of this property wants to meet me before she will rent anything to me.

The house itself is perfect. It's light blue, matching the sky. White window trim with storm shutters. If I was to guess, it might only hold two bedrooms...perfect.

No one is around to meet me yet, so I go to the beach side of the home. A large deck looking out toward the sea, the sand brushing against the steps. I can picture myself sitting on the porch having tea, watching the sunrise in the early morning hours. The constant crashing of the tide will lull me to sleep at night.

I found my place.

I walk toward the ocean. The water laps at my ankles, and my feet sink into the sand as every wave flows in and ebbs out.

Snapping a picture of my feet with the foaming water swirling around my toes, I send it to Caleb.

Caleb: You made it!

His reply to me instant.

Rya: I did!

Caleb: I'm happy for you, Rya.

Rya: Thanks, is he back yet?

Can't help but ask every time I talk to him. I get no instant reply this time. I wait for his reply before I text him again.

Rya: ?

Caleb: He's been back for two weeks now.

He's been home for two weeks and hasn't called me, no contact, no text...nothing. All the hope that I have been clinging to is slowly slipping away as each wave goes back into the sea.

Rya: oh.

That's the last thing I text to him as I throw my

phone as far as I can into the water. The splash it makes is barely heard over the music of the great big blue.

My hope is gone.

"Hello," a female's voice calls out from around front.

"Hi, just looking at the view," I call out to her above the pulse of the water.

We both round the house at the same time, almost bumping into each other. She takes a fighting stance instantly, and I go for my knife. Her fur ruffled up, my need to flee shaking my legs.

The both of us back up, giving space between the wolves who don't know each other. She half circles me, while I follow her body.

"She-wolf, this is my land. Why are you here?" A growl rumbles out her chest that would make Alpha Clinton take notice of this Female Alpha.

"I never knew this was wolf territory. I apologize." Another step backward toward the safety of my car. The knife's handle digs into my closed palm.

Coffee brown eyes regard the knife in my hand. Her eyes travel up my rounded form, taking in my neck where I bear no mark. Her posture changes from balancing on the balls of her feet to skittish wariness.

I relax barely. My heart thumps hard in my chest. My pup inside me stills, not moving with the threat of danger.

"Be calm, she-wolf. I won't hurt you." The voice of truth hits my ears. She holds my eyes while she says this; they take on a topaz look now.

Regarding her, she's the color of warm caramel, and her cheeks have a touch of cinnamon with being out in the sun. Her full lips start to angle upwards in a honeyed smile. Locks cascade down her back in tiny braids that have been woven by nimble fingers.

Shoulders of strong muscles that angle down into a slim waist and ample backside, lean smooth legs that are toned from someone who runs. She's a fantasy that males would have a hard time walking away from.

"Sorry for your loss." Those are her words as once again her eyes fall to my neck.

"Thank you." It's a cautious start of words.

"Is it just you and your male?" She looks at my stomach.

"Yes, that's it. I need somewhere to stay. I have money to pay you. I won't be any trouble." I try to cover the desperation in my voice.

"Why are you not with your own wolves?"

"I need some time away." I keep my answers short. I'm not giving anything away. She's looking like she's trying to put the pieces of me together. They won't fit, but I will let her believe she knows me.

"I don't want any trouble." Arms cross over her chest, fingers tapping along her forearms.

"You won't get any. It's just us." I touch my belly, giving it a rub of reassurance.

"All right, I tend to keep to myself, so don't expect me to socialize with you. You're on your own, understand. I'm not someone you can count on."

"I understand." My words hold a smile because I don't want to socialize either.

"Come, I'll show you the inside. My name's Belac." She holds her hand out like humans do.

"Rya." Putting my own hand out, we shake before pulling away quickly.

The way she leads me toward the house has me marveling at how she owns her own swagger. A female in complete control of her body.

Pausing at the door, looking out into the expanse of water that goes on more than the eye can see. This will be the place I birth my pup. I'll do this without him. When I'm ready, I'll call and tell him about his male.

Hopefully, Dallas will forgive me for this.

CHAPTER 18

Trail Of A Wolf Part One

Dallas

Howls long and soft fade with the distance I'm putting behind me. The trees fly by in a hazy blur. The wolf has grown since being away, giant paws crushing leaves, snapping twigs every time one touches the ground, only to lift up again in a run that pushes its limits.

He has pushed every physical limit there is to push.

I'm more than what I was when I went away.

Making it back in record time, he prowls the perimeter of the house. The wolf marks the building as its own over top of his father's strong wolf scent.

My father sits on a chair as if he's been waiting for me. He tosses a robe at me to put on as I shift for the first time in I don't know how long.

"Welcome back, my male." His voice is deep and thick, the way I remember it.

"How long?"

"You've been gone for six months."

"Six." I knew I was gone a long time, but it felt as if it were only a month.

"You've grown." His eyes take me in. I even feel taller, wider. I feel as if I put on twenty-five pounds of pure muscle.

"We have some things to discuss before you go inside." His tone doesn't sit well with me.

"First off, I want you to know that this was my decision to keep you where you were. There was nothing you could do." My eyes don't leave him. I can hold his eyes now.

"Kennedy died giving birth to the pups, and Rya has left her home pack. We aren't sure where she is." The news falling from his mouth slams into my chest. My vision sways slightly.

"What?" It comes out quieter than I want it to.

He's trying to explain the situation to me, but my heartbeat is rushing too hard in my ears to hear everything he's saying.

It's too much.

"It was the best choice to leave you out there."

"Alpha, you thought that was the best choice!" I flash my father my sharpened fang that's been feasting on nothing but raw flesh and bone for months. The Alpha doesn't take too kindly to it.

"It was a decision I made, so yes, at the time I felt it was for the best. What would have happened if we came for you? Would you have listened to us? We wouldn't have even been able to get into range of you to pull you back. You had to come back on your own. You knew that when you went out there that you needed to come back on your own." He gets up from his chair in a smooth motion. A step toward me, I don't like how he took that step. My wolf doesn't like it either. He's used to being a leader wolf, all puffed up with the strength he's built over the last six months.

"You had no right, Father." Pointing my finger at his face, I make sure my eyes don't leave him. I take my own threatening step toward the Alpha.

"I should have been brought back. He's my brother." The wolf in me growls viciously toward its Alpha. He's not afraid. In fact, he's starting to pace, wearing down that dirt path back and forth inside my head. A growl of warning from my father's own wolf has his eyes flashing for a brief moment of the danger we will face if skin turns to fur.

A flash of teeth toward my father again. "You made the wrong decision, Alpha." I say it with a snap of jaw, blood pumping fast through my heart that's beating faster and faster.

I take the next threatening step forward, not hiding my posturing. I balance on the balls of my feet; the cold wind tries to cool off my body that's inflamed with a feral rage. Its darkness travels inside me, growing darker and darker with what he has taken from me. I should have been here holding my brother the way he held me so long ago.

Another growl of menace, the wolf's ascension is forcefully coming to the surface.

"Control yourself. You're not ready yet for teeth, my son." As my father is saying this, he starts to unbutton the cuffs on his shirt before taking it off completely, throwing it on the chair he was just sitting on.

He's a big wolf, but I'm just as big *now*. Battle scars of old line his chest while mine are still fresh.

"Control myself? How did you think that I would react? You tell me my brother's mate has been dead for six months, that Rya's gone, she went away on her own, and nobody knows where she's at!" Trying to maintain skin on top of fur, it's impossible to work down the convulsions of the flesh.

Another step toward my father, a flock of crows gather in the treetops, cawing and clicking their beaks to one another as if they're having betting wagers about the outcome of this inevitable challenge.

His body is firmly planted into the hardened ground that's slowly been freezing with the drop in temperature.

"Understand if you do this what it means, my son. I will not go easy on you. I will show you why I'm the Alpha. You are not ready yet, so I suggest you get some control over yourself before I control you." That comment earns him a primitive growl that pounds out my chest. My animal instincts are kicking in hard from being out there for too long.

My tongue drags on incisors that are edging out with the need to challenge something I feel is mine to take.

"Do you even know what he must have gone through? What he's probably going through still? No, you don't!" Words fly in barely controlled anger.

"I should have been here for him. You took that away from me." I hit my own chest hard, and fur starts to sprout out from pores that are giving way to my *true nature*, stretching my jaw out with teeth and muzzle that elongates with my change. I want him to see me and what I've become while away, my own beast.

I don't take my eyes off him.

"You need to stop now. I don't want to do this. It solves nothing, my son." His words are becoming muffled slightly with my threat that, as Alpha, he has no choice but to answer.

My mother makes her way toward us. She's as much to blame as him. She could have sent one of my brothers to me. She could have done something as well. The eyes of the Wild turn on her, showing her my full set of teeth. A paw takes a step toward her in threat. I have never threatened her before. Always with her, I've had control, but now I have descended into my own wild.

My father springs toward me, leaving the wind in his wake.

He's ripping into me like a ravenous hyena, all teeth and jaw as he tears flesh from bone. He doesn't like his mate being threatened, no matter who it is.

Fight or flight.

Shaking him off, the Wilds circle each other. Eyes never leaving eyes, always at attention. Muscles contracting, vibrating fur with the need to lunge. Hind legs sinking down slightly as he springs.

A full-on assault. His wolf has no problem

showing why he's the Alpha. Instead of taking the offensive, the Wild is reduced to taking defensive tactics in a need for self-preservation.

Again and again, he eats away at flesh slowly, making it hurt. The trail of blood saturates the ground, unable to be absorbed by the frozen earth. Paws drip, painting the mosaic of red abstract art on the canvas of life.

He doesn't relent. He shows that the wrong decision was made. Sometimes you just have to learn the hard way in order for things to sink in. I had no chance. I wasn't ready for this fight yet.

He severs the muscle that attaches the shoulder to front right leg, crumpling the Wild's body down. Still, the wolf inside me tries standing on three legs, facing him head on. He pauses, head tilting to the side before severing that ligament in the back leg that's needed for movement. Next is the base of my spine; legs cannot move anymore. He feels no pain now, just a heavy numbness.

Paralyzed.

He stands before the Wild with my blood dripping from his muzzle. He brings his teeth slowly to his neck. Holding him in his mouth, he bites down hard, not hard enough to end, but hard enough to show who he is and how much of a mountain I have to climb.

Whimpering in submission, I would have my tail tucked into myself, but I can't move anymore.

Letting go, he edges back. Growls still tumble out of his body. My mother makes a move to come toward me, and he gives her a look. My mother doesn't move a muscle. She just stares at my father, eye to eye. Until my father stretches out his body slowly, shaking his fur out, splatters of blood flinging off him like water in a rainstorm.

He comes up to the Wild, licking his jaw, nuzzling his cheek in a show of no hard feelings. We're friends again.

It's my mother that he slowly approaches, caution in his steps as if he's been a bad wolf. He presses himself on her leg, making her step back slightly.

Her anger is screaming in silence.

A whimper from the wolf who is crouched slightly, ears pulled back in a humbling stance. A lick to her hand, he grabs her flesh, giving it a little nibble before he licks her again. She has no love for him back, putting her hands in her jacket pocket.

"Go." That's what she tells him. I have never seen my parents argue until now. I know they have fought, but I have never seen it with my eyes. His tail looks like it wants to curl underneath him. His wolf whimpers slightly before his nose nudges her thigh. All she does is angle her eyebrow up, jaw clenched tight, her eyes saying everything to him in a silent dialect that they have mastered over the years.

He paws her leg without ripping the material of her pants. He nudges her again, forehead pressed against her thigh. She gives him a quick flick of her hand to his head before he ambles away into the tree line.

Crouching down, she has her hard eyes on me.

"You're a very stupid wolf, do you know that?" It's just her and me. The wolf snaps jaws close to her face that she doesn't flinch from. Instead, she grabs his jaw, muzzling it with a steel-like grip.

"I see you still have a little fight in you, pup." Her hands squeeze the muzzle so hard it makes teeth crush together. If she doesn't stop, the back molars will explode with her force.

I'm not sure who to be scared of more at this moment: the Alpha or his Luna.

"You need to think about what you're doing, my son. This is going to hurt me more than you." Walking away, she comes out with the collar. The Wild can't even crawl away; his limbs are useless. My brothers are behind her.

"If you bite them, I will show you a mother's love." Her teeth descend, and it's not pretty. She's lethal if provoked enough. She hardly rages her anger toward us, only when necessary.

Only to prove a point.

"Pick him up. Put him behind the shed." A wooden pole made of oak stands thick and tall, that's been dug deep into the ground. My mother attaches the collar to a neck before my brothers lay me down near the chain that attaches at the base of the beam. I hear the click of the lock that attaches to the loop in the silver collar.

"Now, let's begin, shall we?" My brothers take a seat on the picnic table, watching my mother.

"I think that it's too much information for you to process at one time. Too much all at once makes you do crazy things, like trying to take your father on when you have no business trying to challenge him. So you will remain out here until you have control over yourself, and we will fill you in very slowly on what you've missed out on. When you are caught up, I'll let you out." The wolf is laying on its side, the bleeding stopped on its own. I will have new scars. I wonder if those scars on my father came from his father?

Looking into my brothers' eyes, I can see that they are slightly unsettled by this turn of events.

Fingers dig into the scruff of the Wild's neck, angling my muzzle toward her nose.

"Do you understand?" She waits for an answer from me. We give her cheek a fast lick before she lets go, making my head fall hard into the dirt.

She walks away from us before coming back, pointing a finger in my brothers' faces. "You will not release him until I say so." Each one of them nod their heads quickly with her unspoken threat.

Once she's gone, Caleb is the first to speak. "Got your ass handed to you. Not so tough now, are we, number one?"

Cash says nothing, no response from him; he's all I can look at. I want to wrap my arms around that male. A low whimper from a throat tells him my sorrow for him.

He's lost so much weight, sunken in cheeks. He looks only like a fragment of himself. Eyes haunted, does he see the nightmare when he tries to sleep like I did? I know this look; he looks just like me so long ago.

He gets up and walks away from our group, hands in pockets, head bent down. His gait is slow, walking to his own saddened song.

Crane follows him, talking to him, but Cash doesn't answer back. I should have been here. Rage once again growls out. I must look a sight, unable to move, just a mess of wolf, but still making my displeasure known.

I guess my mother is right. I can't handle what's about to come in words. I need time to process all of this without posing a danger to everyone and myself.

"We have a lot to talk about, number one, but I think for today you've had more information than you can handle. See you in the morning. I'll bring breakfast!" He and Carson both get up at the same time, leaving me to chew on everything that I've been told so far. I'm not sure I can handle any more of what's been going on in my absence.

What I know at this moment is that Kennedy died in childbirth. That Rya left her pack, but why? She has gone off by herself without Clayton by her side. A new hope infuses into me that maybe there still is a chance for us, if she didn't choose to stay with him, maybe. I cut that thought out completely.

All that's been slamming into my mind when I let it is their bodies molded together, his hands gripping her, while hers were traveling his lines. Their tongues exploring each other, my gut clenches with the sight of it. The way he pulled her into him as if he's done it before. It was natural, no awkwardness. She made no protest; she only wanted more from him. The ways her hand was slowly creeping up inside his shirt…I try to make the image disappear, but it's hard to not see what I did. I just thought that with me out of the way, they would eventually be what they were made to be. I guess she proved my theory wrong.

The next day has Caleb eating a plate of food and throwing me bites every now and then. "Here, catch." He tosses a piece of meat my way that lands beside my wobbly legs, whose feeling has come back, but not enough to work properly.

"That sucks, hate when dirt gets on my food." He casually stabs a piece of pancake with his fork, placing it in his mouth, making a show of how good it tastes.

That earns him a low, rumbling growl.

Pointing his fork my way, while he chews with his mouth open, he does it on purpose. He knows how much I hate when he does that. "Now, brother, no need to growl, we're friends. Look at you. It's shameful, really." He shakes his head in mock displeasure.

"So Mom said to tell you about Rya. Shall I begin?" He tosses me another piece of meat, just shy of my jaws so it's covered in a coating of dirt that I swallow down. He's doing it on purpose.

"Once you left, she was heartbroken, you know that? You broke her heart. I can understand you caught her kissing her MATE!" He yells the last word out to me. For my part, I snap jaws his way, letting my teeth hit together hard.

"No need for violence, just stating facts. Mom was right. It's good you're collared, always flying off the handle." The pole groans slightly as I pull with all my effort to try and break free of my hold. The chain's not giving up any extra inches. He smirks at me.

"You knew what you were up against when you pursue someone who has a living mate. You of all

252

wolves should know what kind of connection they have." Those words hit me hard. I was her fraud.

"It took a long time for her to come out of her funk. She cried a lot. I think she might still be crying. Do you know that every time we text each other, she always asks about you, if you're home yet? Not a conversation goes by that she doesn't ask about you." The wolf's ears perk up, head angling to the side, listening to him closely.

"Don't worry, Clayton was there every step of the way to help her through it. He was everything that a mate should be, yet in the end, she chose to leave him behind." My shoulders hunch slightly with this.

"Don't like that? Hey, well, it's the truth. You left too fast, you should have stayed around, but you didn't, and now she's off on some great adventure while you're tied to a pole eating food covered in dirt." He laughs to himself while I glare.

"All I'm saying is that she made a mistake that she wishes she could take back. What's done is done. I'm sure there are mistakes that you wish you could take back, aren't there?" He tosses me another piece of meat, but this time I catch it in the air, not allowing it to drop to the ground.

"Sometimes I feel as if I'm the smartest one in this family. It's a heavy burden to carry." He places another piece of pancake into his mouth that's dripping maple syrup on his shirt. Tossing me the last piece of meat, he leaves me alone to chew on everything I learned in the morning sun.

The following morning has Carson coming to give me breakfast. "I told Mom and Dad about me."

His shoulders back, head held high.

"I did it myself. I feel good about it. I couldn't live a lie anymore." He gets close to me, putting a bowl filled with steaming meat in front of my nose.

He takes a seat on the frosted picnic table that looks like it has a crisp white tablecloth on it. The crisp air has our breath hanging in front of our faces for the gusts of wind to carry away as soon as our words are said.

"You were right about Mom and Dad. They still love me even if they don't understand my choice. Rya knew, you know. She kept my secret from everyone. She could have told you, but she didn't. She had my back. I wish I would have stopped the car, helped her up. It must have been hard for her that day. I wonder what she thought when she saw you with a shaved head? I can't even imagine what her poor mind was going through. She's a tough female. She rallied, didn't she? And now she's off on her own, not needing anyone to hold her up." My shoulders sink into themselves, the weight of guilt so heavy I feel as if I could be pressed into the ground by it.

"Don't worry, Caleb gave us a play by play of everything that's been going on. I just can't believe a female as good as her keeps getting rejected, first by her mate, then by someone who I thought was putting in some kind of effort. I guess effort to some is mediocre to others." He just looks at me, not looking away.

"I'm kind of disappointed in you, always talking about watching and listening, try to get the whole story. I heard you didn't even give her a chance to explain. I guess with you, it's do as I say, not as I do." He gets up off the table and walks away. I think he's come to love her in his own special way. My ears hurt from what he says to me. I can't stomach the food, but I'm starving.

A few more days pass with my mother clicking her tongue at me, bringing me breakfast before muttering to herself about trying to teach me what's right. How I'm not ready to take control of this pack, that she and my father won't even be able to enjoy retirement together because I can't get my act together.

The seventh night, it's Cash who comes. Sitting on the picnic table, he looks at me silently before the palms of his hands press into his eyes. He shakes his head before walking away without saying a word. I try barking and pulling on the chain with everything I have in me. The pole groans with the strain but doesn't budge with my effort.

It's impossible to move something so rooted into the earth.

Crane comes sauntering the next morning toward me. "My turn to feed you." He seems put out by this.

Watching him, he looks angry in a way, body tense slightly, jaw tight. A frown on his face.

"I don't even know who you are. Who are you?" He gives me his back, walking away. His words surround me with ice. It has more of an effect than last night's storm that has entombed everything in a thick layer of ice. At least with ice, it will melt when the sun comes out; with those words they stick inside my head, playing over and over again…who am I?

Cash comes the next morning, both of us somber, not really wanting to move. He places the bowl in front of me, then scratches my head before he takes a seat.

"I screwed up with her. I thought that I could just claim her and make her mine. I was so wrong. Maybe if I were nicer or maybe if I just waited for her to work her own issues out, things could have been different. I did some bad things to her, to my mate. I can make excuses saying how hard it was to lay next to her while she dreamed of him. Do you know how that feels? What kind of way it gets you twisted up? Knowing your mate preferred someone else." He looks to the tree line. He smells of pups and milk, the way mothers smell.

"I didn't know what to do. I still don't." He pounds the table with his open palm.

"I don't know what to do." He screams it out, and the birds take flight from their perches in the naked trees. The echoing of his voice crashes against the still morning silence. I want to get close to him; I want to hold him in my arms the way he held me. I want to do what he did for me so long ago. The way he hand fed me, he never gave up on me when I gave up on myself. I try to speak, whimpering, barking, trying to communicate with him. He's still looking away in his own world.

He gets up, pausing before leaving. "I'll bring them to see you. They look like her." His shoulders are shaking while he walks away.

It's lonely out here without my family, without the ones I love. I miss Rya. Out in the wild, I only thought of how to get my next meal, about surviving. It was nice to take a mental break from the skin side, but now all I can do is think in terms of skin.

Cash and my mother bring me breakfast the next day holding both pups in their arms. They stretch their fingers out toward the Wild that holds completely still. They grab onto ears roughly, pulling and tugging, yet the Wild doesn't make a move. It puts a nose against them; they smell as if they are being raised by many wolves instead of a mated pair. The Wild gives them each a playful lick before one grabs onto a lip, pulling roughly, making me take a step back from tiny pinching hands.

We play for a little while before they pull them away from me. I want to tell Cash that he's right, they do look like her, except they're smiling and happy.

My father comes the next day, crouching down, testing us. We are no threat to him. We aren't naïve now to the nature inside of him.

"You remind me so much of me when I was your age, it's scary. One day you will have it all, but do you really want it? Do you really know what all this means?" He stands to his full height, arms outstretched, doing a small circle around until he faces me again.

"You were just a small pup when I beat my father. Just so small you fit in the palm of my hand." His lips turn up in a smile that makes his face seem less lethal, but I know better.

"I knew a day would come when we would have to spar. It's inevitable. That's the way packs work, but when I tell you you're not ready, listen to me. I will never lead you astray. I'm going to teach you everything I know, everything my father taught me, and his father has taught him, but you have to be prepared to listen and take advice." His hand goes behind my ears, scratching them roughly as if to say, *No hard feelings. I handed your ass to you.*

Cash comes again the next day. "I understand how you could have done it. I never could understand what would make someone try to take their own lives, but I understand it now. It's such an empty feeling you have inside. It hurts right here." He points to where his heart beats in his chest.

"Thank the moon for my pups. It's funny how bad you can hurt but at the same exact time feel so much joy. It's hard for me. Do you know what Rya did for them?" I shake my head while stretching my limbs that are in need of a good run.

"We didn't have enough to feed them. I knew they were going to die. I knew it. Everyone knew it. I could see it in their eyes. Part of me was contemplating putting them out of their misery quickly than letting them die that way." He stops to take in big breaths of air, pushing them out as if they are emotions he's trying to release.

"The next day, someone was at our borders saying they needed to see the Luna, that they had a gift. It was enough milk to last a week. They wouldn't tell us where they were from or why or anything, just that they brought us a gift. They wanted nothing in return, just dropping off the coolers that were filled with ice, and they left promising to come back the next week with more.

As the weeks kept coming and the pups needed more and more, the supply increased with their needs. Never a week was missed, the couples that delivered them either in heat or already pregnant. They just said it's a gift, not revealing anything. It's as if they were scared to give out any information." A single tear slips out of eyes that must have cried rivers.

"It was Rya who did this. She is the one who feeds the twins. She hated Kennedy, yet she took it upon herself to save her young like they were her own. She texts me all the time. I just don't know how to thank her properly. What do I say, thank you? I just feel it's not enough. I can't repay her for what she's done for me. I have nothing to offer her that she would even take from me because she isn't that kind of wolf, is she?" He knows her well. She is the least selfish wolf I have ever met, and I let her slip through my fingers.

Caleb is here in the morning, a little later than usual, smelling of old whiskey and dirty crotch. My brothers should thank me for having the basement; I was the reason why they finished it in the first place. Those days are over with. Never again will I do that.

He looks tired, like he hasn't slept all night. No bowl in hand. My stomach has gotten used to this time of feeding; even my mouth is dripping with anticipation of being fed. He's carrying a flowered silk robe instead.

"Mom said to untie you." He looks a little put off by this. His phone chimes. Before releasing me, he takes it out of his pocket, and a wicked smile comes across his face as he throws the material at my face.

He's laughing to himself, texting something into the phone.

"Look at her." He holds up the phone for me to see feet in the sand with water lapping at her ankles.

He reads the screen before typing again.

"Wait for it," he says to me. "There it is, she's asking if you're back yet. Hold still. I want a good picture of you for her. She's going to have a lot of questions why you're collared and tied to a pole." He's laughing while taking my picture, and the wolf in me crumples with what she's about to see.

He texts something back to her.

"I can't wait for her to see this." He's staring at the screen, waiting for her response. He unlocks the clip, that's attached to the collar. He frowns slightly.

"She must have thought your picture was pretty ugly. She couldn't even comment on it." He places the phone in his pocket.

He takes the collar off, and the Wild contemplates biting his hand, but my mother would end me if I did that. So I shake out my fur until I feel the cool wind on my skin. I wrap up in this robe that hardly covers my ass, and he's trying to take my picture again.

I get into his space quickly before he apologizes. "Sorry, it was a joke. Why can't anyone take a joke around here?" he mutters while walking beside me.

Walking into the house, my father yells to me, "Call Rya. She needs to talk to you."

Up in my bedroom, I change into clothes that my mom must have put away for me. The phone's on my bedside table. I call Rya, letting it ring and ring until it goes to voice mail.

"Hi, Rya." I pause, not knowing what to say.

"I heard you wanted me to call you. I'm back, so if you want to give me a call…" I end it awkwardly, where before there was never any kind of awkwardness once I got to know her.

Later on that day, I try to call her again, but she doesn't answer before bed. I leave another message, but she doesn't reply. I don't blame her.

Waking up early, I try to call her again. Still no answer. I check my phone for any messages. Clayton is the first message I listen to. It's from the day I left her crying on the ground.

"You are a worthless male." His accusations fling at me like blades.

"Do you even know what you have done to her? She doesn't deserve this, not again. That kiss was a mistake. It was wrong. I don't know what happened, but it did, and it will never happen again. You better come back for her. She needs you." The phone slams down, hurting my ears.

"You're a cruel bastard. She's better off without you and me." Another bitter message from Clayton. I think if I were there, he would have given me the fight that I wanted, then walked away.

Message after message of him seething strong words into the phone.

"She left. She left and won't be back, and I'm glad. I'm also glad you won't be in her life, either. She's better off without you. I can only hope she finds someone who makes her soul happy." Again he hangs up. I contemplate calling him.

The week flies by, and still, she doesn't answer my calls. I keep calling and calling. She must have rethought what she wanted to say to me. Maybe she has nothing more to say.

"Caleb, have you talked to her lately?"

"Who?" he says with a straight face. I just look at him until he pulls out his phone to text her.

"She must be busy." He shrugs it off but texts her again.

A few more days pass until a delivery of milk comes our way. The wolves who are carrying the coolers are a mated pair. The female is pregnant. She holds her hands crossed over her chest as she looks around.

"Where are you guys from?"

"We brought you a gift." She smiles sweetly at me.

"I asked you a question. Where are you from?"

"We brought you a gift," she says more firmly, mouth forming a straight line. Her eyes look at my eyes, surprise on her face taking in the glacier blue irises that freak all wolves out, except me because I know she hasn't marked anyone else yet. They will change back to my normal color once she takes a mate.

Her mate comes back, carrying a cooler that they must exchange every visit. I block his way to the driver's side door.

"What pack are you from?" Again I ask the question.

"We're here to deliver a gift. We want nothing in return." It's as if that's the only thing these two can say.

"Do you know where Rya is?" Both postures pause a fraction of a second too long.

"We need to leave now." The female's hands go over her belly protectively while she scurries to get inside the vehicle.

"You're not leaving until you tell me where you're from." Leaning against the driver's side door, I make a show of crossing my legs, getting comfortable. I have all the time in the world.

"Get away from the car." Cash comes out carrying both the pups. They wiggle and try to angle their bodies toward the ground. Almost seven months now.

Stepping away, the frightened male yells out to Cash. "Keep him away from us next time." There is an undercurrent of a threat in the tone he uses. I eye him up and down, ready to make him tell me.

"Step away from the car." Now it's my mother's icy voice hitting the back of my spine. It's dripping in malice.

"We apologize for this." She's trying to smooth over their ruffled fur. Taking me by the arm, she leads me away like a bad juvenile. I'm just thankful she didn't pinch my ear in front of these wolves.

"Stay away from them until the twins are weaned." She walks away, and I take the little female in my arms. Giving her a little cuddle helps calm me down. She smells slightly like me now; they both do. I make it a point to take my turn with them. Getting up in the middle of the night to do a feeding. They still don't sleep through the night. I thought they would by now. They're greedy with the way they demand food. Always someone jumping to meet their demands.

It's hard to go into their room. It reminds of Kennedy, the way she painted the walls with her love for them. She could have been a great artist. A single picture of her is on the wall; it's her holding her giant belly with a smile on her face. It even reaches her eyes. She looks excited in the picture. Her hair is long enough to tuck underneath her ears. She looks as if she's glowing.

"Cash, have you talked to Rya yet?"

"No, not yet. I was thinking of calling her soon."

"Could you call her for me? I need to talk to her. She won't answer my calls." He looks at me hard.

"I'm not your back and forth guy." He smiles at me instead of scowls with his little joke.

He lets the phone ring and ring, but she doesn't pick up.

"Maybe she's busy?"

"Maybe." It barely comes out of my mouth as I walk away from him. I can hear the phone ringing again until her voice mail comes back on. He makes another call, only for her messages to keep playing again.

The twins pass their seventh month, and Rya has not made any kind of contact with any of us.

"I think I want to go find her. I want to hunt her up just to make sure she's all right." I say this to everyone at the dinner table.

"I'm going to need some help. I want you to come with me, Dad. I want to take the lead, but I need you with me when we go to other packs asking questions. Can I count on you to take my left?" A glimmer reaches his eyes.

"It won't be easy to find a she-wolf who doesn't want to be found," he challenges me.

"There is always a trail. You just have to know where to look." I'm confident I'll be able to hunt her up.

"Then I think we should try to see what our Little Moon has been up to." His voice is steady and calm.

"I'm coming," Caleb begs to the both of us.

"You can take my right, Caleb, but I swear to the moon, if you screw this up for me, I will not be easy on you."

"I'll be good, I promise." Both my father and I give him suspect looks.

The wolf is excited about the chase. I'm excited to try and get my *female back*.

CHAPTER 19

Trail Of A Wolf Part Two

Dallas

Leaving in the early morning, my mother has been up leaving messages for Rya to just call her. Cash, Caleb, Carson all call Rya leaving messages, but she's not answering any of our calls.

This leaves us all unsettled. It isn't like her not to answer her phone.

The ride is full of laughs along the way. My father is a funny wolf when he wants to be. I love when he tells his stories before he met my mother. He always starts off the story, "I really shouldn't be telling you this," or "don't tell your mother, but…"

He's telling us stories we never heard before as he looks out the window, laughing to himself. It's quality time spent with my father that I haven't had in a long time.

The snow now changes to rain that batters and whips against the windshield, making the highway look washed in a tide of water. The windshield wipers swish fast and furious, back and forth, working to keep up with the deluge.

The lightning is so close all our hair stands on end. It's as if nature is having a great big temper tantrum at the moment.

Stopping along the way for food and gas has any wolves keeping their distance that we bump into. Not one approaches us. They leave us alone, we leave them alone; it's a written rule to highway driving.

No wolves' land.

Pulling off the highway now has us in territory that we aren't familiar with.

The time crawls by as the rain still beats down against wipers that are furiously trying to keep up. Flooding, turning fields into small lakes, the weather warming slightly. I should be able to taste it in the air, but all I smell is Caleb's ass. He had three burritos that didn't agree with his stomach, and we had no choice but to roll the windows down as he kept apologizing for how rotten he smells.

"It's not like I can hold that in. I'll get cramps," Caleb says as he lets another one rumble out of him that pollutes the air with a gagging quality.

"Sorry." He's waving his hand in front of him. "I think I can taste the burrito in it." Smacking his lips together, he scrunches his nose, but I know secretly he likes to smell himself.

My father turns around in his seat, reaching a giant hand toward Caleb's neck, pulling him by his shirt so their eyes meet. My father says no words, but Caleb understands he's not to let us taste what his ass is serving up.

A little longer in the trip, he's now holding his stomach, looking pale, begging for me to stop so he can defile a toilet beyond cleaning.

"Please stop. I don't think I can hold it any longer." He's sweating. My father's trying not to laugh, but every now and then he lets a little chuckle out as we pass by a gas station. That one looked too clean for me; I'm trying to find one that's old, worn down, where even the soap container looks too dirty to wash your hands after.

"We'll stop at the next one, I promise." I can hear his stomach gurgling loudly as he groans to himself.

He's deep in a mind's concentration not to fill his underwear.

Finally finding the perfect spot, we stop to stretch, get gas, and have Caleb expel those burritos. The bathroom that he's using is not clean. I can even smell it before he enters it. My father and I laugh at his expense.

"I feel dirty." That's all Caleb says before slamming the door shut.

A car pulls up for gas that's the same car that was at our pack house. The wolf gets out, going to the gas pump before stopping to look around. I'm still pumping my gas as I wave hello to him. With a speed that surprises me, he gets back into his car, driving away quickly. I guess we'll have a "welcome to our territory" party at the packhouse.

Pulling up to the pack house, we're met with their warriors. A lot of males line the driveway, watching us come to a stop in front of the doors.

"This is my hunt. I'll take the lead. I just need you on my right for the intimidation factor." My father says nothing to me, his whole body changing from relaxed and carefree to one that's on guard and dangerous.

"Caleb, you keep your mouth shut." He gives me a hurt look but says nothing. I like when he follows orders.

We get out as one body, closing the doors together. Walking slightly in front of my father, he's on my right, brother on my left. I wonder what kind of picture we make as we approach the Alpha, who's trying to puff himself up the best he can.

His pregnant mate is slightly behind him.

His eyes take in Caleb, flickering over him, unconcerned. The Alpha's eyes land on me longer, staring at my eyes, but it's my father who keeps his attention. The warriors around us bristle, posturing skittishly as Caleb holds each one of their gazes until they look away.

Posturing, preliminaries at their finest.

All my father does is watch me, paying none of these wolves any kind of second thoughts.

No threat, no attention needed in his view.

"What are you doing here?" The Alpha male tries to sound intimidating, but it's not working.

"We're looking for a she-wolf, thought she might have come this way about seven, eight months ago?"

"What does she look like? Around that time, the fair was in town, had a lot of wolves visiting." He crosses his arms over his chest.

"She has long hair, white blond, usually kept in a

braid. She is about five feet six inches tall, medium build. Likes to wear pants, mostly dark colors. Her eyes match mine. Have you seen someone like her?"

All of these wolves shakes their heads while staring at my eyes.

"Nope, nothing that fits that description." He's not lying, nothing in the way he holds himself that says he's not telling the truth. Watching his mate, she tucks her head behind his shoulder, not meeting my eyes.

"Have you seen this moon-blessed female?" My words try to go through his mate's body.

She shakes her head no, but her body tells me otherwise. Her mate has a surprised look on his face that he quickly hides.

"I think your mate might know this female."

"No, I've never met or saw a female wolf by that description during that time." The female is cradling her pregnant belly; a scent of fear is starting to saturate the air. Her mate growls heavily now at us. The warriors start to balance on the balls of their feet, just waiting for something from their leader to say it's okay to attack.

"Get off our land before we have no choice but to make you leave. But you won't be leaving the same way you came." His threat is laughable.

"We think she's in some trouble. She's not answering her phone anymore, and that's not like her."

"How do we know she isn't running from you?" I wasn't expecting that question.

"She's not running from me." My father

continues to watch me, not saying a word.

"We have never seen that female. Now get off our land. If you don't, we'll stop the shipment of milk. Those pups aren't ready to weaned yet, are they?" Clever male.

"We just need some information about her, that's all. She's my female. Look at my eyes. I don't lie about this." The Luna's gaze doesn't leave mine, but her hand is on her developing future inside her belly.

"We have never seen that female, and if we have, I don't think I would tell you anyway. If a female is running from her mate, there is a good reason, isn't there?" Her eyebrow goes up in question.

"Now leave. We won't say it again. We will stop our shipment and I will call everyone else to stop what they're doing as well." The Luna isn't bluffing. A hardness has set into her features that cannot be swayed. There is no going forward with them, and the twins need what they have to offer.

"Thank you for your time. We'll be leaving now." My father is the first to turn his back on these wolves, followed by me. Caleb takes the back, giving each one a good staring at, with a threatening smirk. He might not say one word, but he's saying a million with the way he's swaggering back to the vehicle.

"They must think she's running away from me." I say it more to myself than anyone in particular.

"Why would they think this?" My father doesn't have the answer for me. Neither does Caleb, who always has something to say.

We stop at a motel for the night, and my mother

texts me the directions to the next pack where their license plate is from. It's only a three-hour ride.

Getting settled into the room, my father has his own bed, but Caleb and I have to share ours. Finishing the bag of chips and pop before I lay down, I have to think of a plan on how to greet the next pack. If they think that Rya is running from me, then they will never tell me what I need to know.

Late into the night, I keep trying to work out ways to approach this pack that won't have me seem too aggressive, but not have me seem weak either. There's a fine line that needs to be walked.

Trying to close my eyes is impossible. My thoughts are just too big for my mind to shut down.

She's my insomnia.

The morning comes quicker than I would have liked, but it's a hunt we're on, and the mornings are always the best times to start the chase.

I shake off the sleep with coffee and a big breakfast that has me finishing even my father's plate. I smile to myself, remembering the first breakfast Rya and I shared. I could hardly eat, I was so nervous watching her. The delicate way she held herself. The way she was so happy with the place I brought her to. I did make her happy. I just need to take things slow when I see her. I'm not sure what I even should say, but I have to do something.

The shirt that I have on is stretched uncomfortably tight across my chest. If I flex my back too much, I think I could tear it down the middle. I think I need to ask my dad if I can borrow one of his t-shirts.

After breakfast, we're greeted by a welcoming party before entering the territory of this pack. It's as if they have been warned beforehand of our arrival.

Stopping outside the pack house, we all get out once again. This time greeting me is an Alpha way past his time. He's using a walking stick to keep his balance on feeble legs that are withering with age and wear.

His mate is just as elderly, but both have sharp, keen eyes that take all of us in. They don't dismiss any of us because of position. With a welcoming sharp smile, he leads us to his table.

Their warriors flank us but keep their distance standing against the walls. None are posturing toward us in threat. Not even an eye is flicked our way; nothing but statues stand at attention. They have been trained well.

The table is old, worn, with many cracks and grooves dug into it. I don't think it's ever been refinished, because the quality has held up through the generations. Taking his seat, the Alpha has a slight grimace while he sits, hips no longer the same, degenerating with age.

This Alpha holds his warriors with a current of absolute controlled strength, and my father is taking notice of him. My father must see something I don't, so I pay attention. Arthritic fingers gnarled with age curl around the spoon he's using to stir the tea with. Blowing on the steaming liquid before he puts it to his mouth, he's starting to lose the ability to hold a tea cup without fine tremors vibrating the liquid. He sips it slightly before putting it back down. He's not in any rush; it's as if he has all the time in the world.

Nature will eventually take him, sooner rather than later.

Around the table already sits a group of maturing wolves, male and females. All of them sip their own tea.

His voice is quiet, yet the strength he throws around is unbending iron. In this moment, I know I will get nothing out of him or this pack.

The eyes and ears do as I was trained: watch and listen. I'll try to learn what he wants me to.

My father is even leaning in slightly, all attention on this wolf who he's impressed by.

"We understand you're looking for a she-wolf who might have been traveling in our territory a few months past. Is this correct?" He waits for my answer.

"Correct."

"It seems that no she-wolf fitting your description has entered our territory around that time." No twitch of his face, no eye moment, no flinch of body alerts to any lie he might be hiding.

"Now, if a she-wolf did come into my territory…" A pause of breath, his eyes looking around the table, they nod their heads toward him as a group. In this moment of clarity, I know that he is entrenched deeply; he will not be moved by me to divulge any information about Rya.

"We wouldn't tell you. There must be a reason why a young female wolf would leave a pack." Every single syllable he speaks hangs in front of him for me to understand clearly. He takes another sip of his tea while looking at me intently.

"She left because of me. I said and did some things to her that were not honorable. I didn't think things through, I was rash, and it cost me a great deal of time that we could have been together. All I want is to be able to find her and try to make things right between us again. I let her slip through my fingers." The older female wolves give each other side eyes and send me nothing but disgusted looks.

"We all have to learn from our mistakes. That's how the moon teaches us. Maybe when you meet up with this she-wolf of yours, you will have become a better wolf." Another sip of tea that he drinks slowly.

"The moon is teaching me very well." I take my own sip, and it's infused with ginger and mint. I know this tea. This is what Rya uses for her females who are pregnant that are having a hard time with nausea.

"I like this tea. Where did you acquire it from?" Another sip for show.

His eyes change slightly, dilating blacker into themselves. That's his only giveaway about her.

"It's a gift from a friend." He pushes the cup to the side while clasping his hands together.

"I think that it's time for you to go." The old Alpha smiles politely before dismissing us.

Caleb is the first to stand. I follow behind, but my father sits for a minute longer, showing the elder Alpha he's in no rush to leave. A few minutes go by without my father's movement; he just sits and finishes his tea with all the time in the world. With my father's point being made, he stands to his full height, backing away from the table very slowly.

His steps hit the wooden floor, assaulting the stillness in the quiet room. The noise thunders, wanting an answer back for his rudeness.

No one in the room moves, no twitch or blink of an eye. Nothing that can be mistaken for aggression, so my father leaves them with his peace.

Making our way south along the highway, our plan needs to change. There is no use continuing on with these packs.

Picking up the phone, I call him.

"Hello." The voice on the other line sounds annoyed.

"Clayton, I need your help finding Rya." I hear a laugh on the other end, turning into another full belly laugh.

"I'm sorry, did you just say you needed my help?"

"I did."

"Didn't you get my messages I left you?"

"I've got them."

"I'm not going to help you find her. She's better off without you. You aren't what she needs in her life. Otherwise you would be in it right now. She made a decision to leave because of you, because of me, because of everything. I think that you should respect her decision. You owe her that much. You're always talking about honor to me. Why don't you live what you preach and do the honorable thing and walk away from her?" His words are laced with cutting edge silver. They slice at my flesh.

"She had no choice but to accept your decision

when you left. She grieved for you, mourned your loss. Guess what?" I don't reply back because I don't really want to know what he's going to say next.

"I watched her recover from you." That was the home run he was looking for, because I have nothing to say back to him.

"I made a mistake, Clayton." Regret is heavy in my voice as my body sinks deeply into the seat with the weight I feel from truths I was blinding myself from.

"I made mistakes, Dallas, but I'm respecting her choices. I might not like her choices, but it's hers to make." Melancholy resonates from his voice.

"Don't like what I'm saying? I know it's not what you wanted to hear. Hurts, doesn't it?" He's right, it does hurt, right in the center of my chest.

"I just need a chance to make thing right between us."

"A chance!" His voice grows harsher. "You had your chance and you blew it. She's happy now; let her be happy. She deserves to be happy." It's hard to swallow everything he's saying.

"She does deserve to be happy." This is said more to myself than him. It's as if the wind has left my sail and nothing but a deflated sagging remains.

"Good, we agree."

"I agree, you're right. I just want to know if she's okay. She hasn't made contact with any one of us for weeks now. Have you heard anything from her?"

"Yes, she sends postcards. She started to text me when Kennedy—" That's when his voice wobbles.

A deep breath taken in.

Silence. It's as if he's trying to get control of himself. I give him his minute before asking the next question.

"Has she texted you recently?"

"Yes, just yesterday." It's as if they are becoming friends.

"Can you text her? Can you ask her to call me?"

"No." His reply is instant before the line goes dead.

Calling her mother is my next step. Self-awareness of all my mistakes makes me gulp down my pride. I'm sure this is the stake that will be buried deep in my heart.

"Hello." Her mother's voice sounds so similar to Rya's.

"Hello, this is Dallas."

"Dallas, this is a surprise. How are you doing?"

"Not good. I was wondering if you could have Rya call me. I just need to talk to her, but she won't answer her phone."

"She hasn't talked to you yet, Dallas?" She sounds surprised.

"I've been away for six months, didn't get back until several weeks ago. She's left messages with my family to call her, but when I do, she doesn't answer. I've left messages, but she's never called me back. Even my family tries to contact her and she doesn't reply back. It's as if she wants nothing to do with any of us, and I know that she likes my family. Just not me at the moment."

"Dallas—" A slight pause

"Can you just tell me if she's okay? Is she

happy? I won't bother you again." She lets out a deep breath.

"She called a week ago. She's fine. She threw her phone in the ocean. She's mad at you. She found out you were home for two weeks and you never called her."

"I couldn't call her back right away. I was physically unable to." It's really embarrassing to think back on it and how Rya must have seen my wolf collared to that pole.

"Well, she thinks that you don't want to speak to her anymore, that you don't want anything to do with her, and it makes it hard for her to tell you things that you should be aware of."

"What things?" The way she's saying this, it's as if she has something life changing to tell me.

"I can't tell you that." Her resolve adds a sharpness to her voice; she will not be swayed.

"Can you give me her new number or anything that might lead me to her whereabouts? I need to see her." A pause of breath, and I'm holding mine as well.

"Yes, I'll give you her new number. We also received a postcard from her three days ago." I should have just started with her mother; it would have made this so much simpler.

"Can you send me a picture of the card, front and back? I just want to see her for just a minute, explain that I was an idiot. That I just wasn't thinking things through."

"I can do that. If she hadn't called me last week, I would never share this information with you— know this! All I can ask is that when you see her, let her explain. She's frightened right now. She doesn't know how to approach you with what she needs to tell you."

"You're scaring me…what does she have to tell me?"

"I can't say. What I can say is that she thinks that you have moved on from her, and she doesn't want to be a burden to you." The look on her face slams into my eyes with the memory of how broken she looked when she saw my shaved head. I'm responsible for that look on her face. I was mad at her, mad at myself. I wanted to make a big statement of how hurt I was. I always have a way of hurting the ones I love the most. She knew the statement I was trying to make when she wouldn't stop staring at my head.

"I haven't moved on. I can't move on from her. I just want to make sure she's all right. That she's happier without me. If she is, I will respect her choice and leave her alone. Is she happier without me?"

"I'll send you the pictures and her phone number, Dallas." She doesn't answer my questions as she ends the call.

The pictures coming through a few minutes later has the view of soft summer sand and a burning sunset overlooking the ocean with the town's name scrawled across it. On the back is Rya's writing.

My view.

That's the only message she writes, but in the top left hand corner is her return address. The picture has a little happy face drawn after the words.

She has her view that she's always wanted of the water.

The number is staring back at me, and her address is in hand.

"Caleb, put this address into the GPS." He does what he's told, and that makes me happy for once.

Fluttering anticipation is quivering my insides, almost to the point I feel slightly nauseated with the anxiety I'm feeling about seeing her after all this time. The closer we get, the more my thoughts race with how I will approach her.

Driving down the coast, it's a beautiful sight in the descending sunset. The mist in the air is slightly salty on my tongue as I breathe in the warmer weather.

We pull off the main road toward this small seaside town. It doesn't take long to find the house. It's nestled off a private drive with a few other beach houses around it.

Opening the car door, I can hear music and laughter coming through the walls of her house.

We make our way toward the back entrance. The windows are open. The wind starts rustling up all the scents of the wolves inside. Walking on the back deck, it creaks with our combined weight. The glass door lets me see inside. It looks like a party, lots of food out, lots of wolves playing different instruments. I see Rya with a giant smile plastered across her slightly flushed face.

The scent of her hits my nose; the scent of my female drops me hard on the wooden planks. I try to stand, but my legs buckle underneath me. It's as if my whole body is rebelling against what my brain is telling it.

A pattern is forming, as if I'm trying to solve a Rubik's cube. It's turning and sliding inside, shifting everything into place. My eyes and mind are working out what was right in front of me. I just hadn't paid attention.

I can't move, only stare.

It's a supernova explosion inside me, once all the colors matching up. I try to crawl on hands and knees toward the door with outstretched hands. I can see the way her smile fades instantly, her whole body stiffening as my eyes meet hers.

I've become useless.

Caleb's taking great lungfuls of air through his nose; it's as if he's going on tippy toe, slowly twirling himself hypnotically around, in his own trance. His eyes are blown-out black, teeth have started to descend, and the rippling of skin is starting to transform his body to more fur than skin.

He's losing complete control of himself as he falls down on both knees that can't hold his weight.

"She's here." Muffled words come through his extending jaw as it shifts into a muzzle.

My father's voice is just whispers, my mind so completely overwhelmed at the moment nothing else registers.

I try to stand again, and tears blind my vision. I can't pull my breath into my body. Rya's eyes don't leave mine, until my eyes fall on her heavily pregnant belly. Gripping my chest, I raise myself up, only to have a blur of fur rush past me head first, crashing into the glass patio door, shattering it as if a bomb just went off.

Mass chaos erupts as my father's massive wolf follows his son inside.

CHAPTER 20

A Father's Love

Rya

Sometimes loneliness can be overwhelming.

At night, laying in my bed just thinking about things, my mind is unable to calm down. I've dug a deep hole for myself, and I'm not sure how to really climb out of it.

With each passing day, my pit is getting deeper, sides steeper with no hope of escaping.

I thought that away would mean freedom from thoughts of Dallas, but no matter where I go, it's impossible to escape him. It's as if now that I'm not busy with things to do, I have the time to think.

Dallas haunts my nights and ghosts through my days as an apparition. Sometimes if I'm really still, I think I can get a side glimpse of him. When I turn my head, I realize it was just my imagination playing tricks on me, again and again. Walking through a busy store, my side view shows a silhouette of him at times, and I stop completely until realization hits. That's not him.

Sleep is the hardest. Closing my eyes at night, my rapidly moving eyelids see the dreams of him and what could be. Mornings have me crying into my pillow that it was only a dream.

That it wasn't real.

Waking up from my dream late one night, I reach for the phone, needing to call Dallas, but it's Clayton my fingers dial without direction, as if it is the most natural thing to do.

Someone who won't judge me, who will just let me talk and listen.

"Hello," his tired voice mutters.

"Clayton, it's Rya." There is hesitation in each word I say as I shift slightly on the unfamiliar mattress. I'm sure I'll get used to its hardness eventually.

"Rya, are you all right?" He sounds like he is waking up a bit.

"Yeah, I'm all right. Is it too late? Did I wake you up?" I hold in my breath. Maybe I shouldn't have called.

"No, it's fine." He sighs. I can hear him shift his position in bed. "I'm up now. What's going on?" Just hearing his voice naturally calms all my anxiety.

"I'm not sure."

"Not sure?"

"Screwed up, isn't it?"

"No, not screwed up. Why are you calling me from this number?"

"I threw my phone in the ocean." I give a sad

laugh out. "This is my new one."

"You threw your phone into the ocean? What did it ever do to you?" He chuckles lazily, poking fun at me.

"It was a real jerk, so I threw it away." Smiling into the darkness, I close my eyes, listening to his breath. It's a perfect rhythm. Even the heart inside my chest syncs to his rhythm.

"Whoa, a little aggressive, don't you think?"

"That's me, Miss Aggressive." The flush his voice gives me spreads throughout the length of me, growing warmer and warmer as we continue to talk.

"How's your trip going?" His voice sounds sleepy, a touch deeper than usual.

"Good, I rented a beach house. I'm going to stay here for a while. Is this okay? Me calling you?"

"Call me anytime, Rya. Anytime you need me, I'll be here." He's trying to sound so serious as if he means it.

"How are you doing, Clayton?" Do I want to know? If I can't handle the answer, why do I ask the questions? Because this wolf will tell me like it is, no matter if it hurts my feelings.

"It's hard, Rya. I won't lie. Everything is almost gone from my life. It's a daily struggle to continue. Some days are better than others. Today was a good day." My heart does hurt for him; I'm not insensitive for what he must be going through.

"I can't believe she's dead. I made up a story in my head that she was happy there with her mate, that she had pups on the way. She was getting everything she always wanted. Somehow it made it easier for me. She always wanted pups. When her heat came, we always thought maybe we were the special ones, and we could have a pup of our own. It never worked." It's hard to listen to their dreams, while mine were never given a chance.

"Then when the call came that night." A crack in that deep voice of his. A pause in breath, the moment turns to minutes before he continues to talk. She was his everything, and she died. I can't even imagine the loss he's felt and still feeling.

Death is final; you don't come back from it.

"I'm sorry, Clayton. I'm sorry for your loss."

"It's getting easier; it's still hard, but it's getting easier for me. How's Cash doing?" My stomach tightens up.

"I'm not sure. I've left messages for him, but he hasn't called me back. I don't think he wants to talk to me. Maybe I did something wrong." I wish I could have talked with Cash one last time before cutting ties with all the Valentines. It's for the best; their brother has moved on, and I shouldn't keep calling them anymore. It's like I'm just trying to keep contact to hold on to just a thread of him in some way. It's wrong no matter how good friends we are, plus I don't want to hear that he's with another she-wolf. Not while I'm carrying his pup inside me.

That I will not be able to handle.

"I'm sure Cash has a lot of things to sort out. He'll call you when he's ready. Don't think for one moment that you did something wrong. He understood the situation was not your fault even though he blamed you for it in the beginning for not fighting for what was yours."

287

"How do you know that?" I'm surprised he knows so much about what happened between Cash and me.

"Caleb and Dallas…they kept me informed while I was healing. They said if I was to get everything all at once, I would go nuts."

"True, I guess it's better for one brick to hit you at a time than the whole wall." He laughs with my wording.

"Something like that." He yawns.

"I heard what you did for him and those pups. We sent them milk too."

"I couldn't let them die no matter what I thought of Kennedy; they deserved a chance to live. She wasn't that bad; I just couldn't be her friend." The taste of bitterness that I have for those two has left me entirely, replaced with a growing sadness for them.

"Understandable." He's quick with the response. "You're a good wolf, Rya. You're smart to put that all together. I don't know how you were able to manage it."

"I called in some favors." That's all I'm going to tell him, no need to get into great detail.

"Rya, I wish things were different." I can taste his regret over the line. Its deep, heavy flavor lingers in the back of my throat, almost painfully.

"Me too, Clayton. I should go. Thanks for talking with me."

"No problem. Anytime you need to talk, call me."

"Bye, Clayton."

"Bye, Rya." The line goes quiet. His voice acted

as a muscle relaxer to my tight fibers, loosening me up.

The moon's natural pill for a pregnant female.

Before drifting off in a slumber bliss, another thought enters my mind: I need to call my mother. I need to talk with her, just not yet.

A slate grey morning greets me. I take my tea out on the deck, curling up on a deep chair the best I can. I wrap the blanket around my shoulders, the breeze gently lifting the edges up. The waves are rolling in one after the other in a sea of never-ending movement. I've been doing this every morning for the past three days since my arrival here; I will never get tired of watching the water.

"Rya." I didn't ever hear her approach; she knows how to walk in silence.

"Belac." I straighten myself out until I'm standing to greet her.

"I just was making the rounds and thought that I would make sure you haven't birthed that beast yet." She points her finger at my belly that's bulging out front and center. Rubbing my hand over the male that's nesting inside me has the smile on my face widening.

"No, he's not ready yet, but soon." I hear someone else approach loudly, as if they want to be heard.

A she-wolf rounds the corner wearing glasses, which is odd for a wolf. She's smaller than a female should be, warily sniffing around until she's standing just behind Belac but looking at me. I can see Belac's hand on this timid she-wolf's shoulders. It's as if she's trying not to shake too much.

Putting up a good front.

"See, not so hard, was it?" Belac whispers in her frightened ear. The smell of heavy silver is on this wolf; she's saturated in it, making me sneeze with the noxious fumes.

"This is Treajure." She pulls her out from behind her back. "This is Rya; she's going to be staying with us for a while. Go ahead and greet her like I showed you." This poor female is so full of self-doubt that I think at any moment she will either pee herself or vomit. She takes a step toward me, looking at Belac, who gives me the hardest stare I have ever received.

Play nice, it says, or at least I think that's what her eyes are telling me.

Letting my shoulders relax, smiling without teeth, I still myself as she approaches. A hand goes to her waistband, fingers grazing what's hidden underneath the material. I hold my position until this scared wolf is in front of me, breathing hard. It took a lot of her effort to do this.

"Treajure, it's nice to meet you." Looking at her closely, I can see very fine scars lining her face, thicker ones descending underneath her shirt. Arms covered in fine lines that crisscross, overlapping one another; these could only be made with silver.

This is an abused wolf beyond the degree my mind can register.

Holding my cheek out to her, I let her come forward at her pace. She places her cheek on mine before pulling away in a sweat, quickly making her way back to Belac. She tucks herself into the folds of Belac's coat.

"Good job." Belac lets her stay close for a moment before making her stand on her own.

"Would you like some tea or juice?"

"No thanks, we were just passing through. I needed her to meet you since you plan on staying through the winter. She tends to get a little twitchy. I didn't want her to knife you if you ran into her by accident."

At first glance, this female looks nothing to be afraid of, except the amount of silver she's carrying makes her a deadly threat that you would think twice about messing with.

They leave as quickly, refusing my offers of tea, coffee, and muffins. A little sadness spreads. It would be nice to share a meal with someone at my new place.

Weeks and weeks are flying as if time is in fast forward. Belac is always dropping by with visitors, introductions made. Now she's staying for tea and juice; we've progressed to food as well. I always keep the kitchen stocked with homemade cookies or pies, the stuff that sits well on my stomach. I can't stand meat.

I've learned that Belac is a second-born twin, and her brother is the Alpha to the neighboring pack. Belac bought this piece of land and claimed it for herself; it's a small piece. Her brother leaves her alone, not wanting to fight with his sister. This is how she earns her living, renting out beach homes in the peak season, then she has the off season to do as she pleases. These wolves that she keeps bringing by are part of the smallest pack I have ever heard of.

Looking at my phone, trepidation creeps inside me as I dial my mother's phone number. She is my mother, but not every parent is perfect. They make mistakes just like their children.

"Hello."

"Mom, it's Rya."

"Rya, I know your voice. You don't have to tell me who it is." A pause, and I take a deep breath before I begin.

"I have something to tell you." This is harder than I thought; even my palms are sweaty. It shouldn't be this hard.

"Tell me." Her voice changes with those two words, as if she's bracing for the impact of nothing good.

"I'm—" I can't say the words, I'm a grown female, and this is difficult.

"I'm pregnant." As I exhale those words out of my lungs, a lightness enters me. It feels good actually as I wait for her reply.

"You're pregnant." Each word is spoken clearly with a hint of disbelief.

"Correct."

"How did this happen?" I'm dying internally.

"How do you think?" Her turn to be quiet again.

"This is shocking news, Rya, but happy news at the same time. Congratulations." Suddenly I feel so silly for being nervous to tell her.

"Thanks, Mom."

"Who is this wolf? Where's he from?"

"It's Dallas."

"Dallas, but I thought he left—" Her voice trails off from that thought. "How far along are you?"

"I'm just over eight months along." I wait for it, pulling my phone from my ear.

"Eight months! You kept this from us for eight months?" The need to hang up is strong, but I don't.

"I got scared, Mom. The longer I didn't say anything, the worse it became. I have no idea how to tell him."

"He doesn't know? How could you keep that from him? That's his too." She's not pleased with my decisions at all.

"I was going to tell him. I was waiting for him to get home. He was away for a while. I asked them to have him call me when he got back. He never did call. When I found out he was back for two weeks and never called me, I threw my phone in the ocean. I just cut off contact with all of them."

"That was stupid, Rya, but at the same time I can see myself doing something like that when I was your age."

"I just don't know how to tell him. He's shaved his head; he left, he's moved on. I would just be a burden to him. I don't want to be anyone's burden. At the same time, I need to tell him. It's his pup. I'm afraid he could take him away from me. What happens if he tries to take him away from me?" Hysteria is starting to build up inside my mind, a panic that makes the pup inside me still, as if danger is around.

"Do you think he would do that to you?" My mother's the voice of reason.

"I'm not sure anymore. I don't know." My voice is filled with doubt.

"You need to tell him, Rya."

"I know, I will, soon. Very soon." I need to change the subject.

"I mailed you a postcard. You should get it in a few days."

"Rya, I'm happy for you. Things have a way of working themselves out. I'm glad you told me before the pup is born. Is it female or male?"

"Male, and he's a big one." I'm already boasting about my pup.

"Male. I cannot wait to meet this little one. Can I come see you?"

"When I have him, yes. You can come for a visit. I just need some time to get everything ready first. I don't want you telling anyone yet because Dallas doesn't know, and I think I need to be the one to tell him."

"I promise, Rya, I won't even tell your father until you give me the okay." I believe what she says.

"I'm going to go now, but I just wanted you to know."

"Rya, thanks for telling me. I can't wait to see you and him."

"Bye, Mom. Thanks for understanding."

"Bye, Rya." I end the call feeling way better than when I started the conversation.

A symphony plays outside, seagulls squawking and crying as they dip and glide effortlessly on the murmuring breeze. The tide rolls in with unstoppable force, waves rising and falling in a babbling tune. The crystalline blue waves look sharp and clear even with the coming of winter.

The salty sea has already embedded firmly into

my pores. I smell almost like a local wolf now. The salt has stripped away the last of my homeland scent. No pines, no maples, no oaks—nothing but wind-swept ocean and gritty sand remains on me.

Walking the picturesque town, signs are up in most of the stores reading **"Closed for the Season, See you in the Spring"** scribbled on white sheets of paper taped to the inside of the cute window fronts.

It's a ghost town with only a few shops remaining open for the community that lives here all winter long.

Ambling into the only restaurant that remains open, the little bell chimes, announcing my arrival.

It took one month before I could sit with the wolves at their round table. It started out slow, the group of six sniffing at me the first time I entered their claimed breakfast joint. They were skittish, wary, on high alert. I sat on the sidelines, at the back, with no view of the water, ordering breakfast for one. Quietly watching them, I listened and learned all I could. I came the next day and every day after that, slowly edging my way to sit at the table just behind them. By then they used to my smell and understood I wasn't going away, but the most important thing, I was no threat.

The day finally came where I was invited to sit with them as if I always was a part of their pack.

They remind me of wildflowers, mismatched, unassuming, yet put together they're a beautiful bouquet. They are of the hardy variety, all transplants from different areas. These wolves are the runts, omegas, lesser wolves of the packs they've come from. Somehow they found a place here with Belac, and underneath her rule they've flourished. The once-beaten and neglected have grown into highly skilled prized winning wolves. Any pack would be proud to have them.

Belac has a way of turning the defeated into the undefeated.

This is how new packs are formed. Little by little, wolves gather, becoming a bigger and bigger group.

Stepping inside the diner, an easiness is in the air without any more forced smiles greeting me. This is no hipster heaven; this is grease and coffee-stained tables with banter and teasing. Foul-mouthed beasts with quick-witted tongues. Highly intelligent minds, but lacking the bodies to match, that's why they all carry silver.

I take my spot at the table. They've welcomed me without judgment. All have stated sorry for my loss; all my response is to say thank you.

Belac sits in her usual spot, facing the door so she can see everyone entering her little gathering. Her long braids are piled in a top knot bun that makes her look delicate in her own fierce way. She carries her own silver, but she doesn't need to bluff with it. She has sharp teeth that I'm sure have been used several times. Treajure is tucked into her side.

The wolf never speaks, doe eyes looking around. Belac found her at a dump six months ago in Wild form, scrawny, unhealthy. Not one word she utters, Belac even had to name her.

"So let's see it." She holds out her hand for me to give them the first picture of my male. The grainy picture has him curled up inside me, nice and snug where he belongs for now. All of the wolves pass the picture around. You can see his tiny little head, nose, lips, fat belly. Small arms and legs that he was constantly kicking for the camera as if showing off his strength as males do.

"He's beautiful. You can tell he comes from good genes," Belac states, certainty in her voice. A mother's smile spreads on my face being told how strong their pup is.

Already I'm proud of the little pup.

"So how did you like the midwife?"

"I liked her, but she's really old." The midwife had laugh lines dug deep into her eyes; she's a wolf who has laughed often and smiled more. It's a face I hope to carry when I'm as old as her. The only thing that creeped me out about her is she's very superstitious, lots of small charms all over her birthing rooms, some of those things look dark, almost evil to me. It was hard to suppress the uneasy feeling that came from some of those rooms. She was surprised that I didn't miscarry. She assumes my mate died. With the death of a mate, it's hard to keep what's inside you from spilling out, especially so early on in the pregnancy. She said that he is going to be a big male to birth. That gives me just a little shiver of fear for what I'm going to have to go through my first time.

"My brother's been looking for a new one but hasn't come across anyone yet." I could be what they need, but I choose to keep my mouth shut. I'm not committing to anything here yet. No long-term plans. This will be my den for a few months after the birth, then I'll tell Dallas.

The longer I put it off, the worse it's getting for me.

"What are you doing today, Rya?" Belac's sultry voice caresses my skin. If I were to play for that team, she would be my queen.

"I'm putting together the crib; I need to get everything set up and ready." I feel as if I don't have a lot of time anymore. His arrival will be within the next few weeks, and I have nothing prepared yet. My instincts are driving me hard to get my home ready for the pup's arrival.

"I can come over and help you. Nothing going on today." She's trying to take more food off the others' plates, but they hold their forks like spears, ready to puncture skin if necessary. All these females are sitting here starting their heat; they smell mango sweet, ripening with each passing day. Belac's lips look like blood wine that are full with her approaching heat.

"I'd appreciate that." For someone who didn't want to socialize with me and says she keeps to herself, I can't get her out of my space. Constantly over, bringing all her strays with her. She is someone I can count on. It's ingrained into the fiber of who she is, no matter what she thinks of herself.

Second best.

"You want a ride home?" the only male at the table asks. He's deliciously sexy in an understated way. He doesn't have to try, and I know why Belac has chosen him to ride out her heat. He's not full of himself; he's a quiet cool. Not saying much, but when he does, it's of substance and you can't help lean your ear into his words so you catch everything he says.

"No, but thank you for the offer."

Belac leans in close, her top slightly dipping down, giving this male a peek at what's underneath the material. "Can you drive me home?" The slyness of her smile has the male wolf almost dropping his keys. She owns her rhythm, the natural way she moves to a music that only she hears, and we have no choice but to follow.

This female holds this piece of territory like she's an Alpha. It's just six wolves in this pack. But it's their pack, and they make it work somehow. If I chose to stay, their numbers would increase by two.

"How about you all come over tonight? I'll cook and I'll have drinks. You just bring yourselves and anyone else you want. Belac, you can put together the crib for me. We can have a crib-building party." I can't help the anxiousness I feel inviting wolves over for my first real party.

"I'm in!" Belac is the first to respond as the others follow.

"Come over around six. Don't bring a thing. I'll take care of it all." After finishing our meal, I walk with a bigger bounce, probably jostling the pup inside me.

My body's deep with the pregnancy sway, hips side to side, back arched slightly with the redistribution of weight.

I'm starting to waddle now.

My eyes feel as if cement is gluing them shut. I need to take the contacts out when I get home. They are becoming an enormous burden to wear.

Stopping at the butcher before going home, I buy

a feast fit for wolves who are becoming my true friends. I feel as if I can be part of them.

The Wildflower Gang.

Maybe I could stay here; maybe this might be a place for me…maybe.

Choices that I need to think hard over.

The first guests start arriving with presents. Big gifts wrapped in bright colors for me.

"What's going on?" I'm slightly confused.

"We decided to bring some gifts for the pup. Things we think you'll need." I can't hide my emotions as the tears come to my eyes.

Happy, joyful tears.

A hand goes to my shoulder. It's Belac squeezing it before taking a seat on the couch, looking over the directions I left her for the crib she's going to put together.

She shoots the paper the middle finger as if it can understand what she's meaning.

"It says ten easy steps. I call bull crap!" Her voice rises toward the white pages of clearly written directions. Treajure takes the instructions from her, her eyes skimming over words before she gets up and proceeds to start on the project herself with a confidence she rarely shows.

The male wolf enters my home, slowly on guard, looking around. His soft blond curls fall into his eyes. He has long hair that goes past his ears, making him look as if he's a carefree surfer. Belac's scent is all over him. She's washed, only a lingering trace of this male on her skin remaining.

As the rest of the group comes in, I put the presents to the side to open up later. I want to feed my group of friends with everything I have to offer them.

Some of the talented wolves have brought instruments with them. The music gets louder as the wolves around my table start to sway after the alcohol makes them more relaxed.

They're riding those waves that liquor can bring. Belac is up, swaying her hips to the beat of the tambourine. Everyone is enraptured by this creature.

She's velveteen, hard as a male on the outside, soft and feminine on the inside.

When the music switches beat, her hips shake and move as if they have their own brain. I try to copy her, and everyone starts to laugh at the pregnant she-wolf moving her bum that way.

Laughing at myself, it's when I feel it.

Eyes on me.

I can never forget that feeling those eyes give me. The pup inside me can feel his gaze the way he squirms and wiggles in great trembling motions.

"Rya, is something wrong?" I drop my water, spilling it on the floor.

I look out the sliding glass door. Dallas is on the ground, crawling toward the door, his face contorted in anguished distress. He tries to stand, tears spilling over in steady streams that he doesn't wipe away. The music stops abruptly. He's struggling with his breath while a warm feeling descends on my belly.

His eyes hit where my words should have spoken.

The wolves at the table stand just as the glass door implodes, sending flying missiles our way. A giant wolf making a grand entrance, it's the wolf that follows him in that has everyone reaching for knives to kill this monster of nightmares.

It plays out slow motion.

With the glass still raining down on us, the Silverback goes for his son's throat, bringing him down at Belac's feet, but not before knives are thrown, trying to stop the charging of the first wolf. The Silverback takes the knives willingly that were supposed to be for his son.

The great wolf took down by the weakest.

Blood. The metallic taste starts to swirl in the air.

Caleb shifts as the Silverback pulls in labored breaths. He holds his father's head in his hands, rocking back and forth. Dallas comes in looking at me, looking at his father laying on the floor.

"Don't touch him," he says calmly in the chaos. Dallas is on his knees assessing the situation calmly, except hands used to handling deadly situations have a fine tremble in his fingers as he touches where each knife has struck. A bubble of blood starts coming out the wolf's nose. A lung has been punctured.

"Where's the nearest facility? We need to get him there now." Caleb doesn't look anywhere but to his father now. His legs are red with blood that just keeps flowing out with an unstoppable force. Dallas takes his shirt off, ripping it into rags, placing it around the knives that he's not taking out, trying desperately to stop the flow of blood with hand-held pressure.

"Hold this," his commanding voice rings out to the nearest wolf that quickly obeys him.

Belac is giving me the eye to explain myself, but I don't have it in me to say anything.

"This is my pup's father." Dallas's eyes quickly shift my way before being consumed once again by his father's need.

"Pick him up gently." All the wolves follow his direction, including Belac.

It's quick progress as everyone helps out to carry his great weight, putting him into the back seat. Belac drives the vehicle while Dallas takes the back, along with Caleb, holding pressure as best they can.

It's a fast drive, racing against the clock. He doesn't have much time.

"Caleb, when we get there, call Mom. Tell her she has to come. Tell her to bring our brothers—all of them." I don't like the little panic that's creeping into his words.

Caleb is throwing on some clothes from a bag in the backseat. Through tears, Caleb tells his father that he loves him, that he couldn't help himself. Belac is cringing into herself.

They're waiting there at the open door for us. A stretcher is already outside. Dallas is the first to get out, screaming orders that take the doctor by surprise. It takes all of us to pick him up. His eyes aren't as sharp anymore.

Before going inside with his father, Dallas's hand tries to touch my stomach. I angle away. His eyes meet mine with so many emotions that it staggers me backward. How could I have kept this from him? This is all my fault if his father dies.

"I might be a while, Rya. Please go back to your

place, rest. When I'm done here, we'll talk about this calmly." He tries to hug me, but I step out of his grasp, which doesn't seem to surprise him.

He's taking in my whole appearance. "You've changed so much, it's like I'm looking at a different wolf." Turning, he walks inside, leaving me outside in the darkness.

Caleb is a mess coming outside. His face is crumpled in self-persecution.

"I shouldn't have done that, Rya. I just couldn't help myself. I just smelled her and lost my reason. He knew what he was doing. He took all those knives for me." Caleb starts crying on my shoulder while Belac is watching from a distance, not approaching. I rub his back for him.

"It's my fault, Caleb. If I would have just told Dallas in the first place, this would have never happened." Now both of us are messes of snot and tears while we hold each other for comfort. Except the belly is in the way of a full hug.

He places a hand on my stomach. "Why didn't you say something?"

"I was afraid. The more time I let it go on, the harder it was to say something. Then, when you said that he was back for two weeks, he never called me. He moved on with his life, and I would just be a burden to him."

"What are you talking about, Rya?"

He stands away from me. "He couldn't call you. He was collared to the pole. Didn't you get the picture I sent you?"

"What picture?" He pulls out his phone, scrolling through messages until he finds mine.

"This. Look." He shows me a picture of Dallas's wolf looking embarrassed, tied to a pole, wearing a collar.

I read our message. It dawns on me that I threw my phone into the ocean before I received the picture. If I didn't act with such emotion, this might have been avoided.

"We kept calling and calling you. He called you as soon as he was released, but you never answered any of us." He sounds hurt.

"I thought Dallas never wanted to talk to me again when you told me he has been home for two weeks, so I threw my phone away. I never got your picture of him. I thought that since he didn't want me anymore, I should break up with his family too."

He's looking guilty too. "I shouldn't have worded it that way," he says as he scrolls the message again. "This doesn't read well, does it? I can see how you got upset." His head turns toward Belac.

For a wolf who has something to say all the time, he can't form words. It's as if he's tongue-tied, nothing intelligible coming out. He looks foolish in a way.

She doesn't look impressed by her mate as she walks away.

His eyes never leave her hips, the sway is hypnotic to any wolf, but his brain must be entranced by his mate.

"Dallas wants me to bring you to your place. I need to come back here after I drop you off. We need to do what the good doctor says." He tries making a joke, but I don't laugh.

"You stay. It's not a long walk, and I need the air." He gives me a side eye.

"I'll be fine. Stay with your father. Keep your family updated." Turning from him, I begin the slow walk back, stopping every ten minutes for little breaks, because of the dull pain that's spreading in my lower back from the exertion of walking. The day's been too long.

Taking my contacts out, I wash my face. I get a blanket and pillow, wrapping myself up on a chair waiting for him to come. I don't want to go back inside. The stench of blood is making me gag. It looks like a bomb went off inside the house with mass casualties. Bloody footprints stain the wooden deck.

Opening my eyes, I see him approach me like the great tides of the ocean. He flows toward me, unstoppable in his path. It feels as if nature has gone silent. It's an uncomfortable stillness. The ocean waves have ceased rolling on the shore as the moon stops breathing, wanting to listen to every word.

"Rya." Kneeling in front of me, his hands go to my outer thighs, his forehead touching my knee. He postures in front of me a moment before he lifts his head, his glacier eyes regarding me.

He just looks at me, defeated, while his hands go underneath the blanket, then underneath my shirt. He's feeling his male, skin on skin. The little one inside me is going insane. It's almost borderline painful with the full strength of him showing off for his father.

I can tell Dallas is taking in the positioning of him, the way his hand goes around every curve of his young. He feels his head, shoulders, bum. He pushes back on feet that poke at his hand. He places his nose against my bare skin, kissing my belly. He pulls great lungfuls of scent through his nose, imprinting his smell.

He places his ear against the skin, eyes closed and listening. We sit like this calmly without words to muddle the moment.

My hand goes into his hair that he's letting grow out again.

"I'm sorry, Rya."

"So am I, Dallas."

He cries into my stomach, tears dripping down, soaking into the waistband of my skirt. His arms wrap around my lower back, just holding me close.

CHAPTER 21

What's Really Important

Trepidation creeps inside me on tiptoe.

"Your father?" Barely a whisper comes out of my mouth.

"Alive." The sound is muffled; his lips are pressed against the exposed skin of my abdomen. The male inside me finally quiets down, exhausting himself to sleep with all the showing off he was doing for his father.

Exhaling the breath I was holding in, I give silent thanks to the moon for her mercy.

"I'm so sorry that this happened to him. I feel that this is my fault. If I just would have told you in the first place..." Guilt threatens to restrict my vocal cords with each word I say. I love that Silverback Alpha; he's a good wolf. One of the few males I have ever met that I completely trust.

"It wasn't your fault, Rya. He made a choice. He knew what he was doing when he took those knives that female was throwing my brother's way. I'll have to go back in a little while to check on him. We need to talk first." He's looking at me, glacier blue eyes that bind me to him, his hands never leaving his male.

"I've missed so much." He says this quietly to himself, shaking his head in disbelief. Great waves of despair roll off of him, crashing into me.

Quicksand sets in. I'm sinking in my own emotions that are gripping me firmly by the ankles, slowly climbing up my calves as I sink deeper and deeper inside myself.

"You're right, we need to talk." I'm holding his eyes now with mine. He can't look away either.

"Rya, I was so wrong. I should have stayed that day. I shouldn't have left like that. I wasn't thinking properly. I was mad and only thinking of myself. I wanted to hurt you the way I was hurting. It was the wrong decision."

"Actually, Dallas, looking back, I'm glad you left. It forced me to do things I never thought I'd get a chance to do on my own. I feel I've changed." Even on his knees, he's taller than me. He's physically grown so much. Leaning into him, inhaling his scent, it's so naturally calming to my nature. I could get drunk on it.

"It looks like you've changed so much." His fingers touch my hair that's just barely able to tuck behind my ears.

"I have." I believe what I just said. I still have issues, but I know that I can survive in this world without anyone holding me up anymore. I can hold myself up. I've learned from my heartaches; it's made me more rugged, a survivor with a calloused heart.

"I was wrong to keep this from you for so long, but you were gone, and I had no way of contacting you. I was hoping once you returned home that the first thing that you would have done was call." I hold my eyes to his. He's paying complete attention to every word I'm saying.

"Then I found out that you'd been home for two weeks without calling me. I didn't want to be a burden to you. I didn't want to be that female who can't let a male go. You shaved your head; that was telling me enough that we were through, that you were moving on from me. Even though I didn't want to move on from you. I made a mistake, Dallas, when I kissed Clayton, but in a way, I'm glad it happened. I always had this unfinished business with him. The what if's, even though he's hurt me so bad. I still always wondered what it would be like to kiss him. The kiss was incredible, it was everything that I dreamed it would be, but here's the thing…it wasn't you. It was just the bond pulling me to him, nothing more." He's not saying a word, just watching and letting me talk, absorbing everything in.

"I have no regrets with him. That part of my life I can say is completely over. I have moved on from the mirage of him. He's a wolf who's my friend, nothing more. I wish him well in the future, but my future will not involve him. I will never go back to that pack, ever. I don't feel as if it's my home anymore. I don't belong there. I haven't belonged for a very long time." Letting go of my past is the most important step in creating the best future possible. I've learned from it, it made me a stronger wolf, but I will not let it weigh me down any longer.

"It was getting to the point that I just couldn't tell you. I was afraid that maybe you would try to take him away from me. I can't have you do that. I won't survive it." An edge of panic trembles out of my voice. He grips onto my hands that have clenched at the sides of my thighs. He's unraveling them before entwining them with his fingers.

"I would never take him away from you." His words blow away the fear that's been clinging inside my mind as heavy, grey-misted paranoia.

"I couldn't call you because—"

"I know why. Caleb showed me the message. Before I could see the picture he sent, I threw my phone away. I didn't wait. I just presumed I knew why you didn't call me. Now I know why." He's leaning into me very slowly, inching toward my body, so my legs have to spread a little more as he tries to create no space between us. The belly is hindering his progress.

With his arms around me, I feel completely safe for the first time in a long time. His warmth engulfs all my nerve endings, tingling up my spine.

"Where does this leave you and me?" His question to me is spoken with his own building anxiety. I can feel it coming off of him. His heart rate picks up with the each minute I let pass without answering him.

"I'm not sure anymore, Dallas. At first, I was heartbroken that you left. I understood why, but I was still heartbroken. I had a lot of guilt built up inside me because of what I did to you." Taking a deep breath, I must continue on with the truthful way I'm feeling.

"I'm lonely without you, but at the same time, I'm continuing on. One foot in front of the other. I have bad days and good days. The good days are outnumbering the bad now. I don't think that I can go through that again, Dallas. What happens if I do something that you don't like? Will you just leave me, leave us? Shave your head again?"

"No, never again, Rya."

"I have my doubts now. I'm just not sure I can trust you not to leave me again." A single tear sheds out of my eyes that have cried too much.

"Rya, listen to me. I will never leave you again." He's trying to convey the importance of his words. His voice never raises, but his words are heavy, trying to sink into my chest.

"I realized when I came back from the wild, I just couldn't get you out of my mind. You consumed me fully. I just thought I was giving you a real chance to be happy with him. I was wrong once again. Caleb told me you left the pack. He told me a lot of things." I arch my back slightly with the uncomfortable pressure of sitting in this position for so long. He stands up slowly, brushing his knees off.

"Scoot up." Dallas sits directly behind me, so I'm between his legs. He raises my shirt up so the skin of my back is touching the skin of his chest and stomach. He leans me back into him, taking the pressure off my lower back. His hands bring the covers over us as he reclines us back in the deck chair.

"Better?"

"Yes." I'm looking out at the darkening sky, the ocean once again starting to roll, ebbing and flowing as the tide starts to go out, only to return once again tomorrow. The breeze is cool against my cheeks, but my body is cocooned in warmth he's creating.

"Lay all the way back. That's it, Rya. I promise I won't do any more than touch my male. Nothing more." My cramping muscles are relaxing. The heat from his body acts like a warm compress saturating into my tissues.

Closing my eyes, this is what I've been missing the whole pregnancy. This feeling of real safety, of warmth, of protection, of love.

"I like it here, Dallas. For the first time since being in your home pack, I feel as if I belong. That this could be my home if I give it a chance. I could have a job here if I want it. I could have a good life here with my pup. I could provide him with everything he needs except you." His hands have stopped feeling my stomach. A stillness has overtaken him. Even his breath sounds quiet.

"I don't want to be a weekend and holiday father, Rya. I never thought that I would have a pup after what happened. All those dreams were gone for me. But now you've given me a miracle. I have no intention to let that slip through my fingers. Even if I have to leave my pack behind, I will. It's not the two of us anymore. It's the three of us now."

"You would give up your pack for me?"

"In a second. This is the most important thing in the world to me. You and this male, nothing else

313

matters, Rya. Everything else is a distant second. Understand this. I have made mistakes, and I might make more mistakes in the future, but leaving you again will never be one of them." His chin is resting on my shoulder, cheek pressed against mine. His scent is pressing into me. I'll smell like him soon.

"I'm just scared, Dallas. I don't want to go through this again."

"We can take things very slow, at your pace," he pleads.

"I'm just not sure, Dallas."

"Well, that wasn't a no." A faint flicker of hope is lighting up inside him.

"What about your parents? They'll be devastated."

"It's not their life to live. This is between us and no one else." His voice caresses my skin. His words mean so much to me.

"But—"

"No, Rya, this is my life. Without you, it means nothing. I would just be going through the motions, empty again. You have awakened me. You have brought me back to life. I'm yours and you're mine. It's that simple." He does place a small little kiss to my shoulder very quickly. His lips feel electric against flesh that hasn't felt touch in a long time.

"Let's just take it slow, no pressure." His mind races with strong thoughts of hope now the longer I let him talk to me.

"No pressure?"

"No pressure, Rya. Just me and you figuring things out." I sink into him, letting my body really relax against his. His hand comes up, running his fingers through my hair.

"I love your look, Rya, my beautiful female." His fingers massage my head. My eyes roll back. The wolf in me who's taken a sabbatical inside whimpers to him slightly. It's a barely there noise, but his wolf answers instantly back with his own whimper of longing.

I can feel myself drifting off to sleep. His words are a lullaby to my body. His body is a natural sleeping pill, letting my mind shut down enough to just take a moment to drift off to sleep securely in his arms. I know no one will be able to hurt me when he's this close. My first real sleep in months overtakes me completely.

Mother Nature slowly opens her eyelids as the morning is bathed in tinted tones of sepia. The seaside air is heavy with salt as the rushing tide comes in.

November wind blows in strong and full; the dog days of summer are scampering out like an unwanted pest.

Caleb is walking up the stairs looking at us before pulling out his phone and taking a picture.

"Cute, I'll send you the picture." He gives us a fake smile.

"The doctor wanted me to tell you Dad's stable, holding his own." Relief is etched on his face.

"Carson called. Mom's wearing her war colors, just so you know what's coming for me. She blames me completely. I found my mate's house last night, and I almost killed a male wolf that had her scent all over him. Before I could rip his throat out, I got shanked in the back by that female with the glasses." He turns around, lifting up his shirt where lots of stitches are holding the damaged skin together. Deep bruising surrounds the area where the blood leaked underneath his skin.

"Belac and her brother should be here soon. It seems in this pack, once you find your mate, it's expected that the male wolf marks her instantly. No mating ceremony, nothing. I guess all her family is coming to make sure this is done the right way." He touches his fingers to his temples, rubbing them slightly.

"Oh, I also found out my mate's an Alpha to her own six wolf pack, perfect. The icing on the cake is she has to give up her territory to her brother, because it's customary for the female wolf to move away to her mate's family pack. She's blaming me for ruining her life, so I've had a great twenty-four hours. I can tell you that much." He takes a seat next to us on the chair, looking crushed. This male who usually is so happy looks like he has the weight of the world on his shoulders.

My hand goes out to his thigh, patting him.

"Sorry, Caleb."

"Will you mark her, Caleb?"

"She's my mate. Of course I'll mark her. I just wish it was different somehow." He just looks at the ocean, watching the waves touch the shore. The seagulls are out diving around like fighter jets. I feel as if something bad is coming in the air.

CHAPTER 22

A Mate's Rescue

Dark clouds seem to be hovering over the deep water. Grey skies take over the blue; the air feels charged, full of menace, as Mother Nature's pent-up power will be released soon. The wind turns the waves to whitecaps, the temperature dropping slightly.

Unease.

Nervousness.

An overflow of energy is vibrating out of Caleb while he sits at the edge of the chair. His whole body is in constant motion, the way his fingertips tap along the armrest. A knee that won't stop trembling. Quick breaths. He keeps glancing in all directions, not knowing what way they will come from.

Standing.

Pacing.

Sitting.

Repeat.

He looks tortured at the moment as he waits for the in-laws.

"Rya, congratulations, by the way. He seems to be a strong male. I can already smell the power he carries." Dallas smiles, a father who's already proud of his male.

"Thanks, Caleb." Dallas's hands are on my belly again. The male inside me frantically kicks, making his presence known to his father. His lips are taking more opportunities at tasting my flesh, as his mouth hovers just a hair's breadth over the back of my neck. He doesn't kiss it but puts his nose against my spine, inhaling deeply. He squirms in his position a fraction, trying to adjust himself as I lay against him.

Dallas hasn't moved, and neither have I. My body hasn't felt this good in such a long time. I'm rooted into the chair with no ambition to leave my spot. The very fibers in my muscles have all been relaxed; he's medicinal without the cough.

Slow, deliberate fingertip pressure traces along my collarbone. His lips press against the back of my head. A desirable warmth spreads all over my body with the way his touch affects me. He keeps repeating this calming motion as Caleb is unraveling before my eyes.

"Caleb, try to take some deep breaths." Dallas speaks at a volume only his brother can hear. He doesn't want the wind to carry his words.

"It's hard, Dallas." His eyes are scanning back and forth, sometimes stopping their sweep as if he has seen something, but it was only the wind.

"I know. How do you want this to play out? Do

you want me standing on your left when they come, or do you want me to take the lead?" A few minutes go by before Caleb answers back.

"If I start acting like a fool, I want you just to thunder punch me in the throat, drop me hard. Put me out of my misery." Somehow his words cut the tension, and we all start to laugh. Belac and the Wildflower Gang round the corner with her in the lead, head held high. She's walking with a hard purpose.

Her topaz eyes hold such great sorrow at this moment. Her world is unraveling around her.

Grim faces greet us, tear-stained cheeks of the females. All in a single line behind their leader, with heads bowed down. They look as if they are in a funeral procession, slow, shuffling along, quiet as if already in mourning for their fate.

All wear black on black, armed with silver.

Caleb's face is no longer holding the usual smile.

Standing with a smooth grace, he puffs himself up to his full height. Dallas gets up from behind me, a hand gripping my hand helping me up. Dallas angles his body slightly in front of me.

The group halts their progress, looking at me sideways, contempt in their stare as eyes meet mine that is no longer hidden behind the burden of fake lenses.

"We trusted you. I trusted you." Belac's voice rises as she steps forward. Dallas takes his own step toward her, with a low warning growl.

"Look at the destruction you brought to us." Her Wildflowers look cut down. No longer the happy group that has found their place in a special community, now unease is spread among them.

The male is missing; that was the only real soldier of the group. Is he a deserter?

Treajure remains hidden behind Belac. The only reason I know she's there is because I can smell a deep-seated fear that slithers out from behind Belac. It leaves a lingering taste at the back of my throat of her ruination.

"Who are you really?" Belac's eyes fall to mine, each syllable said slowly, lingering in the air for me to swallow.

I can't answer her back.

"What? I can't hear you." Arms crossing over her chest, she looks me up and down. Her eyes never once fall on Caleb. It's as if he's unimportant in this minute.

"I never lied to you."

"You omitted the truth." Her stronger comeback, her voice rising just barely. The wind picks up, the material of my skirt tickling my ankles as it sways back and forth.

"Is Rya even your name?" She tilts her head, eyes cunning and strong. This she-wolf is tuned up; vibrations are pulsing out of her as if a tuning fork has been struck. Her aggression is not silent. I see a flash of canines my way, and a shiver of fear pulses out of me.

"Watch yourself, female. Think before you act." Dallas is like the tide rising up to his full height, threatening to engulf everyone in his presence. They take a collective step backward, even Belac.

"We have no problem with you, wolf." She points her finger his way. "Step aside." He says nothing back, instead looking at Caleb, who's just watching her, taking everything in. Nose flaring slightly, shivers running down his body. I can see the slight tremble of her body as well with his closeness.

She conceals it much better.

"My name's Rya. I didn't lie to you. I just didn't tell you everything." This is my battle to fight, not Dallas's, as I try to stand in front of him. They all turn to me.

A betrayal, that's what I see staring back at me. Their trust in me broken. This is a group of hardy survivors that have been the bottom of the bottoms, the outcasts, rejects of packs. They have never held true friendship until coming under Belac's reign.

"I'm sorry I didn't tell you more about me. I just didn't want to spoil what I had with all of you." Looking each one in the eyes, I try to convey the mistake I made not telling them my story.

"You should have told us. You could have trusted us with your secret." Her topaz eyes are luminous, reflecting the dimming light with golden hues. It's fascinating what you can see when you really pay attention to the details.

The sound of many shuffling feet in the sand reminds me of slippers that really don't fit well: you can't pick up your feet, so you drag them on the floor. That's how numerous shoes sound against the grainy beach. A screech of sound from the ancient skin has Belac stiffening up.

"Grandmother." She bows to the older female whose congregation comes sliding behind her. A big male who looks just like Belac looms over this weathered female, hunched over from the many years she's lived. All the wolves wait for her sermon to start.

"Belac, you know why we're here?"

"I understand why. You all must be so relieved." Her voice is angled her brother's way. He's a big, broad-shouldered male, with strong, rigid features. His skin is a shade darker than burnt caramel. He's a male in every sense of the term. A first-born wolf who knows where his place is meant to be with the way he holds himself confidently.

"We don't make the rules, Belac. We just live by them." A gentle hardness of dialect is present in the old female's voice.

"You knew this day would come. We tried to prepare you. You just never listened to us, always wanting to have your own side hustle. Never really understanding your place." Twins have a special bond, they say, but this pair looks as if they could sever it at any minute. No love lost between them.

"Oh, I know my place. I've been told hundreds and hundreds of times, haven't I, brother?" She's starting to take a stance her brother's way. He's not backing down from her.

"Don't do this again, Belac. You can't beat me." He heaves a frustrated sigh, as if they have been down this route before. Several spectators stand just behind the grandmother, taking in the show, talking low among themselves. A murmuring of a group that covers their words with hands over their mouths, pointing their fingers at me.

Witch.

Demon.

Monster.

Words that escape on the wind that are directed at me. Dallas gives his growl of terror toward the superstitious wolves. The grandmother whispers words to her grandson while staring at me. He nods his head in understanding.

"I'm not part of your pack anymore. You can't force me to do anything I don't want to do." Hard lines are etched on her face. She plants her feet firmly into the ground. Now Belac rises to her full height, just a few inches smaller than her brother.

"That's where you're wrong. I have allowed you to hold that land just to keep the peace between us. Who do you call when you need help? Whose territory do you use to run on? Who loaned you the money for the property? Who has defended your borders? I did. The pack did. You are part of this pack even though you refused to be in it. You were always tied tight to it. It's time for you to go. It's better this way, Belac. You are a female. You can't lead a pack of substance. These will be the only wolves who will ever want to follow you." Her brother is just throwing out insults to her. No wonder she wanted to get out from under the thumb of this pack. They must have told her continuously that she could never lead, never be better than what she already is.

Family sometimes has a way of breaking your dreams.

"Belac, we will force you if we have to. We don't want to do that to you. Don't make us use force." The Alpha now takes a step toward his sister.

323

Caleb's long lengths have him reaching the siblings in a few strides until he's standing side by side with Belac. She eyes him sideways but says nothing to him.

"She'll do as she pleases. I won't mark her if she doesn't want me to. If she wants to stay and hold her territory, then I will fight by her side." Caleb lets his eyes hold this Alpha wolf, both large males sizing the other up. Caleb smiles with his teeth, showing this stranger wolf what he might have to deal with if it comes to a fight. The Alpha pays him the same respect back.

A first born facing a well-trained second. I have to give Caleb credit for his display.

"It's our custom to mark on sight." The grandmother's voice hits Caleb dead center in his chest, raising a crooked finger his way. She's wearing a necklace made of teeth, wolves' teeth. It is on full display. They look old and yellow. Made many, many years ago.

"We have our own customs that we follow." Caleb directs his words toward the gathered group. Each pack always thinks that their customs are right; that's how wars can start, each pack thinking they are the right ones and the others are wrong. That they know the moon better than the other packs.

"Then it's force. Your choice will be gone soon. We have ways of making that happen." Belac now takes a defensive stance toward her family. The only male soldier in her army stalks slowly forward from the back of the house, each step soft without any sound. He's bringing up the rear, knives drawn.

This small pack will fight with the captain, but their ship will sink against a whole pack.

Caleb snarls his way but holds his ground toward her brother.

"No need for this, Belac. We don't want to put your little wolves down. It's time for you to leave, marked by your mate. If you don't do this, then we start to take away what you love the most." With a series of high-pitched whistles, her brother calls out over the pounding surf. Instead of hearing shuffling feet, I feel the ground vibrate with many running pairs of feet. In the distance, I can see pack warriors coming with the speed of swiftness, urgency. He's threatening her where he knows it will hurt her. She is loyal to these wolves who probably have never had loyalty in their lives.

"So this is how it's gonna be. This is how it plays out between us? You taking what I have built up. You're a leech, sucking up everything good that I have." Her finger pokes him in the chest, pushing him back slightly. Caleb takes a step in front of Belac; he cracks his neck to the side. His eyes are black as night.

The Warriors now half crescent around us. All posturing great intent to hurt.

"I'll challenge you for your title." Caleb steps up to this Alpha-born male; Belac gives Caleb a once over. From the tip of his head to the soles of his feet. It's a slow assessment. I wonder if she thinks he can do it?

"It looks like my sister has the perfect match. Both of you think you're more than what you were born to be." Belac places her hand on Caleb's chest, stopping him from flying at her brother. It holds him in his place. The Alpha wolf turns his fangs toward Dallas, a cunning smirk spreading wide across his face as if he has already won this battle.

"We'll do a trade with you. We'll give you back your father…in return, we want the witch. You leave, taking Belac with you." A crack of lightning flashes above our heads, humming its current.

"No deal. I never knew that my father was being held hostage?" Dallas snarls to this wolf who can't hold his eyes.

"A change in plans. If you don't give her to us, your father dies. It's very simple. You can't hold us all." Caleb's skin is rippling.

"Rya." Dallas places keys in my hands without anyone noticing. Taking his first step on the deck, he makes it loud, so the cracking of wood echoes out. His teeth are descending down for all to see. Hands are stretching out slightly, claws descending, eyes the shade of deep black staring out into the crowd. Another heavy step on old wood that makes the whole deck groan with the pressure. He looks at each wolf, holding their eyes with his progression toward the steps. He's taking his time, putting on a great show of dominance.

Leaning into my ear, he whispers, "I'm going to get you to my car. You need to drive away from here as fast as you can. Don't look back. You keep driving to our pack. I love you, Rya." He kisses my forehead before he tucks me into his side in protection. The Warriors growl as one body, snapping teeth that want to bite as we step down the stairs.

"I come for you first, you have no chance of living." The lethal promise Dallas makes has all the warrior wolves taking a step toward him. He takes a backward step off the deck, angling me behind him. These wolves will have to go through his wall to get to me.

"Caleb!" Luna Grace's voice is tearing through the scene. All the wolves stop for just a second, including Dallas.

"Who's that?" Belac's question has Caleb smiling.

"My mother." Rounding the corner of the house, Luna Grace is terrifyingly beautiful. Wrapped up in a shield of woven silver armor, she is the lightning that has come. No wolves' teeth could ever puncture through.

She's a weapon of destruction.

Leading warriors behind her, flanked by her sons, it's architecture of movement. They are one body that moves with graceful fluidity.

High animalistic aggression churns out of this she-wolf as she sets her sights on Caleb.

Carson and Cash are to the right, and left of her, Crane follows closely behind. All these males have their hackles up.

Power has descended on this land, and it's brought by a female.

"What's going on here?" she asks Dallas.

"We have no fight with you," the Alpha announces as he takes in her warriors. Dallas takes this opportunity to direct me behind his three brothers, who all look at my belly in shock. Luna Grace's eyes linger on the male that's inside me. I don't think Caleb gave up that information to them.

Now Dallas takes a position on his mother's left, having Carson and Crane flank my sides. The warriors in the back are waiting for the sign to launch themselves.

From this view, I see Treajure gripping Belac's shirt. The tremors of fright are so strong that I'm surprised her legs haven't given out yet. Her glasses keep sliding down the bridge of her nose that is saturated in sweat. She keeps pushing them up, but every time her head bows down, they try to fall off her face. I wonder if Belac did that on purpose? Having her glasses fit loosely, so she has no choice but to keep her head up instead of always bowed down?

"A disagreement, it's family business. Nothing that concerns you." The Alpha male's confidence has taken a slight shift. It's barely detectable in sound, but the quiver of tone is there.

"I think this concerns me. My family is surrounded by your warriors. Usually when families have matters to discuss, it's only with family present. Isn't that right, Caleb?" Her son's head bows down slightly.

"Or am I wrong on this?" Her question riles the big male up. She stands much shorter than the Alpha male, but at this moment, she is the fiercest wolf here.

"Watch your mouth, female. We have your mate." With Luna Grace, the only clue that something is about to happen is when it happens.

With wolves, there are always preliminaries, posturing intent, bluffing, showing off, displaying canines.

Not her, she just does.

She brings her storm. High voltage descends on the unsuspecting Alpha. Grabbing his jaw, she picks him up with the ease of a practiced weightlifter, slamming his head into the ground. His body follows slightly after. A knife is held to his throat. So fast is her reaction to his words that he has no time to react.

"What did you say, male?" Her canines have come out. Fingers clench his jaw until the familiar crack of bone is heard. He doesn't move because the blade is drawing blood from his throat of life.

"It's not nice to keep a female waiting on a question she's asked." Another crack of his jaw, that just made it impossible for him to answer her back.

She just broke the bones at the hinges.

"If your warriors so much as move, I will destroy everyone in this pack. Nothing will live...do you understand me? Nod your head yes." Her words are spoken loudly, so every wolf hears her. She does not bluff. This is not an idle threat.

She's the real deal.

His eyes are unblinking, a slight nod to his head in deep understanding.

Belac is wide eyed at this female who has just taken down the wolf she has probably been fighting against her whole life in less than a few seconds. Extreme reverence filters across her face at this Luna who wears armor of silver.

The color of war has never looked so good.

"Dallas, take Carson and a few others. Bring me

your father. It's time for everyone to go home. Rya, you need to leave with us. It won't be safe here anymore for you." I understand her words completely but mourn the loss of a life that I was just beginning to live.

Belac faces Caleb. "I can't leave without them."

"You won't have to. They all come with us."

"All?" She looks suspicious, as if she doesn't believe his words.

"Every single one of them." She looks toward Luna Grace, who gives her a smile before a new line of blood trickles down her brother's throat. The rest of that pack is immobile with the threat of death that this warrior wrapped in silver has promised with any of their movement.

Looking over at the Wildflower Gang, I see them huddled close in a great discussion about their future.

Caleb is standing to the side, watching them with eagle eyes. All nod their heads in agreement. Dallas takes his keys out of my hand, unhooking a single key from the ring.

"They can all stay at your house." He tosses the key to Caleb, who looks at it, turning it over in his fingers. A flash of sadness crosses his face. "Are you sure?"

"It's all yours, Caleb. It just needs to be cleaned out first."

Cash comes to stand beside me. So does Crane. The little wolverine that I fist fought with flanks behind me. He must have grown five inches since I've seen him. He's still lean but filling out the way young male wolves do.

330

"Rya, I need to talk with you." Cash keeps his eyes forward. Belac leads Treajure over to me, putting her behind my back. I can feel her fingers dig into the waistband of my skirt, her head leaning into the curve of my back. I can smell that she has peed her pants. The poor wolf is nothing but a giant ball of fur, struggling to keep her glasses on. Cash takes a quick glance at the female before looking away, as if she really isn't even there.

"Could you just watch her for me until I get back here?" Belac is entrusting me with her most precious.

"She's safe with me." I can't smell any knives on the female. Belac must have taken them away from her. I think that was a smart decision on her part.

It doesn't take that long for the caravan of vehicles to pull away from this place by the ocean. The van holding the Silverback leads the way with everyone else following. All the Wildflower Gang has agreed to give this new place we are heading to a chance. I think they can tell by the way Luna Grace greeted them all that this pack's leadership is unique. Things might be different for them and they're willing to take a chance on it.

CHAPTER 23

Lessons

Our group of cars arrived much later than the main caravan that pulled away from the oceanfront house did. I think it was a combination of two things: me being heavily pregnant and needing to get out every few hours to pee and stretch and Caleb not wanting to face the female wrapped up in silver.

Before we left, the Luna grabbed her son by his chin, bringing his face down to hers very slowly. No words were exchanged, just eye contact. Letting him go, she leaned into him.

"We'll talk when we get home, privately." Luna Grace walked away.

Caleb paled.

Belac looked on in such reverence to the Luna who's dressed in the color of war.

"It's going to be okay, Rya. We'll figure everything out together." I like the way Dallas's voice changes when he talks to me; he's no longer putting on a show for anyone. It's just him and me.

Hours and hours of driving do things to me while pregnant. The pressure on my sciatic nerve is constant, making shooting pain descend down my legs. No position in the car is comfortable, and at one point when it's time to get back into the car from a bathroom break, I refuse, planting my feet, rooting them in their place, making myself unmovable. Everyone in our little group mills around, pacing back and forth while watching Dallas try to talk some sort of reason to a heavily pregnant female who's refusing to move.

Hysteria bubbles with the thought of getting back inside that vehicle. "I'm not going back in there. I can't do it." I shake my head at Dallas while rubbing just to the left of the base of my spine, trying desperately to take the pain away. Dallas walks back into the gas station, gets a bag of ice, and applies it to the worst spot.

"Just leave me here, Dallas. I'll be fine." Dallas laughs as soon as my words come out.

"Let's see if the ice helps." He holds the bag there. My clothes become wet, and his hand must be freezing, but the pain shifts enough to a tolerable level that I climb back inside with a low grumble instead of on the verge of tears.

Dallas has to drive with one hand on the wheel while his other hand massages my lower back. My head rests on the dashboard facing the passenger side window, watching the winter becoming more and more. The snow drifts get deeper and deeper the closer we get to his territory.

Branches of the pine trees bow, pulling toward the ground with their heavy burden. Ice and snow cling to the landscape. It's glistening, as if fairies were here and sprinkled the north in magic pixie dust, making it sparkle and shine.

Pulling up to the main house, it looks the way a picture perfect postcard would look, undisturbed snow covering the roof of the house, the chimney billowing out thick smoke that curls up toward the darkening sky. The snow banks are high along the window ledges, as if cocooning the house in its embrace. The porch swing gently sways on its own with the gentle wind. I wonder how many generations it has rocked?

"Let's go inside. I'll get the stuff out later." Dallas shuts off the engine, gets out, and walks toward my side of the car. He opens the door, giving me his hand to help me to a standing position. I can't help the way I stretch my back then lean over, trying to take the pressure off of it.

"Are you all right?" He's looking at me funny.

"Yes, I'm fine." More car doors start to close behind us. The Wildflowers are all congregated behind Belac. Unease cuts through the crispness of the cold.

The door to the house opens wide, Luna Grace stepping outside dressed in a warm, long, deep grey sweater and black yoga pants. She seems so unassuming, but all of us know better than to make that presumption of her.

"Just don't stand there. Come inside. It's freezing out." She smiles at every single one, without teeth, trying to put fears at ease.

"Come, it's okay." She ushers all of us inside with the wave of her hand. A delightful squeal rings from the inside of a pup's voice, followed by laughter.

Still, no one moves yet. The amber light pouring out from the open door casts a warm reflection on the white snow.

"I made dinner. We want to share in your first meal here with us." She watches the way they all eye each other, with apprehension chiseled hard on faces that hold their worry and fear. Looks of disbelief cross their faces until they all look toward Belac for guidance. She takes a breath before taking that first step toward the house, leading the way like a general. The others fall in tight formation behind her, crunching the frozen snow underneath their feet.

All their heads scan the landscape, taking in the northern nature. It's very different than the smell of salt. It's wild, fresh, laden heavily with the smell of many different kinds of trees.

Caleb walks beside Belac, not touching in any kind of way, but just there, side by side. Belac takes just a side step away from Caleb, creating a small distance between them.

We bring up the back. The male with his curly blond hair walks cautiously inside, making sure he's as far away from Caleb as he can get. He smells heavily of large quantities of soap, no other smell, as if he's dipped himself in bleach, coming out squeaky clean.

Smart male.

Stopping at the entrance, everyone takes off shoes. No coats were brought. I don't think they own anything too heavy and thick. No need with their milder winters on the ocean.

The smell of fresh bread starts creeping up my nose. It's inviting and warm.

Homey.

Luna Grace and the Silverback are standing side by side to greet their guests. He has a small bead of sweat on his brow, looking extremely pale, but still an overwhelming presence. All the gang, once seeing him, take a step back, almost knocking us back outside into the cold.

"Be at ease. Nothing will hurt you here." The way he says this smooths down their anxieties. They take a collective sigh of relief.

Belac is the first to step forward to be greeted. Both parents are impressed by this strong female standing in front of them with shoulders back, head held high.

"Welcome, it's an honor to have someone of your strength joining our pack. I can't wait for your training to begin." Alpha Clinton offers a compliment of praise, giving her a head nod but not touching. Luna Grace embraces her, pressing her cheek to hers, smells exchanged.

"We are so blessed to have you and your pack here with us. The moon exceeds our imaginations sometimes. She brings us the most wonderful gifts." Belac has tears trying to escape out of eyes that I don't think cry very often, but at this moment words escape her as she struggles to rein in emotions that are pouring out in salty lines down her face.

"Caleb, after dinner, I need to have a chat with you behind the shed." Caleb nods his head, while his body slumps slightly with what's ahead of him.

Belac gives Caleb no reassuring smile. She holds her face neutral.

Luna Grace touches her cheek to each one of the Wildflowers, whispering words for their ears only. It's as if she is trying to make them feel special in a certain way with the time she's spending on each one as an individual.

Treajure is the last to be greeted only because she keeps stepping backward, letting the next wolf take a turn before her. Anxiety threatens to consume this female as Alpha Clinton pays special attention to her. He's seeing what fury can do to flesh, the way it can be marked up, leaving razor-sharp lasting impressions. Her glasses keep sliding off the bridge of her nose. The lenses are thick, making her hazel eyes seem much bigger than what they really are. Without her glasses, she is almost blind. Silver has a way of ruining sight. Her fingers are feeling for knives that are no longer there.

Skittishly, she holds herself still for them, crouched shoulders, head bowed. She's making herself even smaller.

"So this is the female that almost ended me." He doesn't take a step toward her, but Luna Grace does. Treajure whimpers. It's the only noise I have ever heard her make. She knows how to whimper and whine.

With exaggerated snail slow movements, the Luna approaches with extreme caution. Calm, so not to spook the scared animal, Luna Grace wraps her up in strong arms. A kiss is placed on each cheek, and she rubs her scent into her, as if claiming this frightened female as her own. Her hand brushes over the top of her hair that is kept tightly French braided to her scalp.

"Nothing will hurt you here. You have my personal protection now. We have lots of work ahead of us." That's some of the words I hear from the Luna's mouth that is pressed against her ear. A soothing hand to her back, rubbing it up and down. I think I see Treajure melting into this female who holds godly powers.

"Little Moon, you look so different." He's taking in my whole wandering look. "This is a surprise. We never expected this." Alpha Clinton reaches out, touching my belly. His hand is firm, pressing into my flesh. The little male inside me stills suddenly, as if shocked scared. The hand remains there until an explosive kick takes my breath away with the pain. We both look down at the same time, this little one making his presence known to the Silverback, who's smiling with pride.

"It was a surprise to me too. I didn't realize I was expecting until I could smell him." He looks at me sideways, not believing what I'm saying.

Luna Grace embraces me the best she can, the belly not giving an inch, no sucking it in. Both her hands feel the male. He's kicking up a storm once again.

"He's going to be a handful, just like his father. You should have told me, Rya. When should we expect him?"

"I wanted to tell Dallas first." A look of understanding passes over her face.

"He should be here in about three weeks, give or take a week." Her hands are really feeling my belly.

"We have a lot of preparing to do. You need to have somewhere that's your own space." Wheels are turning in her head as she thinks.

"We'll figure something out."

Her hand comes to Dallas's face, giving it a pat and a kiss on his cheek.

"We're happy for you." He leans into her hand. It's as if they are having a special moment between mother and young. No matter how old you get, to your mother, you will always be her little one. It brings thoughts of my mother to my head. I need to call her again, let her know where I'm at. I need her to come and visit me.

"Let's eat." Luna Grace has her arm around Treajure, guiding her to the table. Cash is already sitting down. His hair is ruffled and shaggy, as if he hasn't cut it in a long time; his beard is not trimmed. It's a homeless look he's mastered. Looking at his neck, no longer is there a mate's mark. It's completely gone, as if it never existed in the first place.

A pup sits on each side of him in highchairs. Both have messy faces that tell they couldn't wait for the guests to arrive. The female and male look to be a mixture of both parents, except the eyes. They're all Kennedy, encased in long lashes, deep amber staring out at me.

Magnificently beautiful.

They spot Caleb, and both their chubby arms reach his way. They start to laugh and kick their legs, hands hitting the plastic table, squealing as they send particles of pureed food everywhere. With quick strides, Caleb reaches the twins, picking up the female while the male cries out, wanting his turn. With them secured in both his arms, he gives them kisses, getting baby food in his mouth.

Cash just shakes his head to himself.

"Missed me?" They give him their toothy laughter, as if he's the funniest one in the room.

"Everyone, this is Ken, and this is Dee. Just so everyone knows, I'm their favorite." Caleb is dead serious while nuzzling them with his nose. "For being so young, they have incredible taste," he tells the group boastfully as he kisses them again, making them laugh out loud. Everyone around the table sports smiles, even Treajure. It's just a half smile that can barely pass as a real one.

"You need to put them back. They aren't done eating." Cash sounds as if he's a mother instead of a sidelined father. "You can play with them after." Grumpy faces pout as they are set back in their seats.

The Wildflowers take seats at the empty spots. Carson, Crane, even Cash sniff the air. All these females present are in their heat. It's a distraction for any unmated male. They take in the females that are at the side of them. The only one that doesn't attract any attention is Treajure. I think in the eyes of a male, she's not what you would call beautiful. Caleb takes a seat right next to Belac. I can see he brushes his arm against hers. They both look at each other before pretending it didn't happen. A smile creeps on her face as she looks at the smudge of baby food above Caleb's jawline. I wonder what she thinks of that wolf?

Watching her, she takes a drink of water, looking

at Caleb. I bet money her thirst is real for that male. That bond is going to play all sorts of twisted games with those two.

The strong sturdy table has been extended by many leaves placed inside it to accommodate the extra bodies that now sit around it. The table is already set up; large pieces of fresh bread are in front of empty bowls. Giant pots of soup are steaming up in the air. Luna Grace serves her male first before anyone else. She gives him a kiss to the temple, and he pats her on the ass, giving it a tiny squeeze that makes her blush. His deep low growl makes us all look away, uncomfortable.

"We're right here. We're sitting right here." Crane's voice breaks the uncomfortable silence.

She doesn't even look his way as if he's just talking to talk.

"I have beds made up for all of you downstairs until the house is ready. After dinner, you all can get your stuff and make yourselves at home. Caleb, you might want to give Belac your room upstairs. We tried to clean everything up downstairs the best we could with the little time we had. It's still a little bit dirty." She gives him a hard stare. His face shadows in understanding. Belac turns her head his way in silent regard.

"It's okay, I don't mind it being a little dirty. My house might just be as dirty." Her face watches Caleb as he chokes on his soup. His eyes start to water slightly as he's trying to pull in breaths of air. Everyone puts some more soup in their mouths so no one has to reply to that.

The Silverback laughs hard, gripping his side,

trying to splint the area that the knife did the *most* damage to. A mixture of pain and happiness filters across his face. He's trying to gain control of himself, but he's having a hard time. Luna Grace gives him a look, and he settles down completely to put another spoon of soup in his mouth.

"In the next week, we will gradually introduce you to the pack. Depending on your skill levels, we'll find you jobs so you can eventually get out on your own. Hopefully, you will like it here and decide to stay. I think you will all find your place." She's talking to the group, but at the same time, I feel as if she's talking to me.

Cash clears his throat slightly, wiping his mouth with a napkin as he gives the twins a baby cookie each to chew on.

"Rya, I just want you to know—" He stops his words, clearing his throat again. "I'm not sure thank you is enough for what you did for them or for me. Without you, they would have died a terrible death. We are forever in your debt." Belac and the rest of the Wildflowers are listening with ears turned our way.

"I couldn't let them die, Cash. I'm just thankful how everything happened for a reason. If I hadn't left my old pack, this would not have the ending it has now." Sometimes bad things happen for good things to come out of it. It's just how you have to look at it.

"I've started a site where packs can donate extra milk for young in need. It's evolving into a nationwide help center for packs unable to feed their own. We have already saved three pups from death." He's turning his tragedy into hope for others. That has a way of helping your soul heal sometimes.

"What did you do, Rya?" Belac asks.

"She was able to secure milk for the twins when their mother—" Again he stops his words, clearing his throat.

"Sorry for your loss. My mom died as well. My brother and I were raised by our granny. My father died shortly after her. We were lucky that we had a nursing aunt who just lost her pup and was able to feed us both, or else we would have died as well." Belac holds sympathetic eyes his way.

"How were you taken out? Were you birthed or cut out?" Odd question to ask by Luna Grace.

"My mother died before we were born. They had to cut us out."

"Interesting," Luna Grace comments but doesn't say anything else. Her eyes find the Silverback, who smiles to himself.

"Can I ask a question?" Belac is so interested in the Luna. Her eyes are trained on her.

"Ask."

"How did you do that, and where did you get that outfit?" Her voice can't hide her worship of this female.

"I was taught well by his father." She squeezes Alpha Clinton's hand, and he brings her fingers to his mouth and kisses the tips gently.

"The outfit was a mating present from my mate. I was surprised it still fit." Her tone holds a sense of pride that something so old still fits as if it were bought yesterday.

"Just like a glove." The Silverback is giving his mate a smile that conveys more than I want to know about them. A look of hard lust crosses his face. In this moment, she is the only thing he sees. He nips at her fingertips before she pulls her hand away, mouthing the word "later" to her male.

All her males are looking away, anywhere else but them; the ceiling holds such interest in their eyes. The rest of us are open mouthed staring at the display of affection from an Alpha couple.

Standing, I need to stretch my back again. Gripping the back of the chair, I arch my back up, trying to take the pressure off of it. My skin feels tight and itchy, as if it's stretching again to accommodate the growing male inside me.

"Are you all right?" Dallas stands, pressing the palm of his hand into my lower back, rubbing the sore area.

"I just need to lay down for a few minutes or take a bath." His fingers start to rub away the ache.

"You can have my room." He grips my hand in his, leading me away from the table.

"Goodnight, everyone." I give everyone a tired wave as I allow Dallas to lead me away.

"A nice bath would relax your muscles, and after you get out, I'm going to give you a massage. How does that sound?" He's standing right behind me as we enter his room. It smells like him. The bed is still messy, as if he just got out of it in a rush.

"That actually sounds so good. I just need my stuff out of the car."

His mouth is close to my ear. "I'll go get your stuff. You get in that bath." He doesn't touch me, but my body wants him to.

Left on my own, I try to stretch out the ache that's not going away. A small contraction tightens my stomach. It's fleeting, just barely there, but it does make me pause for a minute. I've been having them now on and off for the last few days. It's nothing to concern myself over.

This is normal, I tell myself while starting to run the bath water.

Taking my clothes off, I step into the hot bath and breathe the warm air that carries only his scent. Beads of sweat run down the side of my face after only a few minutes of being immersed in the water. It's peaceful inside this room. Leaning my head back, this is the first tub bath I have taken in months; the beach house only had a shower. The steam rises up, casting the room in a thick cloud of haze. The warmth seeps into my flesh, soothing sore muscles. My toes rise above the water. I just take this moment to enjoy the experience.

Losing all sense of self in blissful relaxation, I could fall asleep.

"Are you all right in there?" The door cracks open slightly, letting the steam out.

"This feels so good. I haven't had a bath in such a long time." Dallas is standing just outside the cracked door.

"Can I come in?" I don't reply instantly, which leaves a hesitation in the conversation flow. "I just want to put your stuff on the counter. I brought your robe, and your hair stuff. I thought you might want it." He's hesitant, but the crack in the door opens more.

"You can put it on the counter." Sitting up in the water, I pull the glass door closed to hide my body from him. It's changed a lot since the last time he saw me without clothes. I'm not ashamed of myself, but I am uncomfortable with him seeing me completely this far along in my pregnancy.

Sliding the glass door a crack, he hands me the shampoo and conditioner.

"Thank you." He doesn't close it. Instead, he sits on the floor right beside me.

"Do you want any help? I could wash your back for you." He sounds hopeful.

"No, I'm fine. You can go. I'll be out soon." He gets up off the tile floor, leaving the door open behind him. I make quick work of washing my hair before letting the water drain away. While drying off, he enters the bathroom again, as if this is the most normal thing to do. He closes the door behind him.

In the mirror, his reflection is obscured by the fog, yet I can see his outline as he strips his body of clothes. He's completely bare. I take a long peek at his backside. My breath pulls in slowly while I dry my hair and wipe away my makeup that has been on for two days.

As I wrap the robe around myself, he gets out of the shower. Drops of water are slowly making irregular paths down his form. It's intoxicating to my eyes. I want to take in everything he's showing me.

He lets me, not covering himself.

Slowly Dallas walks toward me. Stopping just in front, he reaches behind my body, grabbing a clean towel. My heart tremors as he dries off his head, his chest, the lower body, only to wrap it low on his hips. He smiles innocently at me. "Are you ready for that massage? The thirst needs to be swallowed down; my throat is dry.

Opening the door, the soft flickering candle casts shadows on the walls. The light is low in the darkened room.

Taking my hand, he leads me to the bed. "I need to take this off if I'm going to massage you properly." His strong fingers are slow as he looks into my eyes, untying my robe so it opens in the front. He keeps his eyes on mine. Fingertips run along my collarbone until they are on my shoulders, underneath material that is being eased off my body. The robe falls to the floor and I'm completely bare to him.

He keeps his focus above my head.

"Lay down." He holds the covers open for me to climb into. I can only lay on my side with my leg slightly bent over the other. He covers me up so only my back is exposed to him. I can hear lotion being put on his hand. He rubs them together before skin touches skin. I give a small moan as his breath quickens.

His palms slide slowly down my spine before coming back up. Strong hands mold me, pressing into my pressure points. "Close your eyes, enjoy it." I hadn't realized that his lips were so close to my ear.

Dallas's upper body hovers over the top, just a fraction away from my skin. The heat from him warms outside as well as deep inside.

Slowly.

Gently.

Fingers gliding over flesh that has goose bumped, while his breathing has shifted to become deeper. Slowly his fingers inch down the arch of my back. My breath grows shorter and faster.

Another moan escapes my mouth.

His fingers are gifted with the way they are making my muscles feel.

Dallas traces all the lined scars the whip has made.

Love's hard lessons will always be etched into my back.

He kisses those lessons learned long ago, replacing them with his own lessons in love.

Sliding his hands up the side of my body, it tickles slightly. He turns me easily in bed so I'm facing him.

"Do you feel better?" His lips move closer to mine.

"Yes."

"Good." His breath is on my mouth, he's so close to me. Anticipation builds as he lingers just over my lips with his.

"Goodnight, Rya." Pulling himself away, he walks toward the dresser, putting on a pair of joggers.

"I'll see you in the morning." He shuts the door quietly behind him. He leaves me with an unsatisfied ache for him.

Putting my nose in the pillow where his shoulder was pressed, I inhale deeply. It takes all my willpower not to go and drag him from wherever his bed will be tonight.

A few minutes later is when the first contraction hits me. It's more powerful than anything I have had so far. Frozen, unable to think about anything else, I wait to see if there will be a next one, and sure enough ten minutes later another one lets me know that maybe this male inside me might make his grand entrance earlier than planned.

CHAPTER 24

My Love

I curve into the pull of his voice. "Rya, wake up." His nose is nuzzling the back of my neck. Turning slightly toward the sound, it takes me a minute to recognize where I'm at. The contractions last night ended up stopping within that hour. A normal part of being this far along in pregnancy.

It was a false alarm.

Feeling Dallas's palm on my lower thigh makes me think he has big hands the way a male should. They are strong when they have to be, yet soft when he wants them to be. His fingers wide and long, with a broad palm. They are the kind of hands that can keep me safe or hold me to keep me warm.

"Did you sleep well?" His palm, with his fingers trailing behind, slides up my thigh. The higher that hand climbs, it leaves a trail of hot flesh. He lingers, slowly feeling my navel to ribs, a soft growl of pleasure from his chest radiating into my bare back. His nose presses into my neck. A small kiss is placed. He's in no hurry to pull his lips away.

Fingertips feel between each rib, and higher still they climb. A scrape of teeth against my collarbone. Just the faintest touch of sharpen tooth before he pulls his teeth away to be replaced with lips that trail up to my neck, inching closer inside the covers with me. I feel the first touch of his bare thigh against mine.

My speech waivers when he shifts again to press himself behind me.

Skin on skin.

His toe runs along the arch of my foot, making my toes curl inwards.

A lick to my ear. "Did you sleep well?" The faintest of whispers, barely audible above the rushing of my pulse. I feel my skin flushing, while his hand traces the lines of my chest. Another gentle shift of his body has no space between us; I can tell he's just as affected as me with our closeness.

"I would have slept better if you were with me."

His mouth not leaving from behind my ear. "Tonight you won't sleep alone." There is deepness to his voice, ringing with something else. A little tinge of anticipation for what tonight might bring.

His fingertips become just a fraction rougher with the way he's gripping my waist. He starts to kiss the base of my neck. The tiny hairs start to stand on end. His head dips lower, following my vertebrae down, licking and kissing each one. When his nails dig into my flesh, my body ripples, and I gasp at the sensation. Pleasure courses up and down the inside of me. He raises himself again, following the trail he was just on.

Hands gently ease my whole body to turn his way.

Face to face.

I'm still sleepy as I look at him and smile.

He smiles only when our noses touch gently. His hand caresses my face, a single fingertip tracing the outline of my lips. I give it a small little kiss before he pulls it away from me.

"I want to look at you." A voice that's husky, eyes shining with deep want. A hesitation on my part, the blankets pulling slightly off my shoulder. Taking a deep breath, while holding the covers up. "I'm not the same. I've changed." Can he tell I'm slightly embarrassed?

"Only for the better." His reply is soft, the blankets coming down a fraction of an inch because I won't let go of the cover. His lips on my shoulder, he keeps his eyes on mine.

"What happens if you don't like what you see?" I let go of the covers.

"Impossible." The blanket rests just above the top of my chest before he brings it down some more. Revealing my upper body to him, yet he still doesn't look; he keeps our eyes connected. His pupils are dilating, the faintest traces of blue remaining in his irises that are exactly the same as mine. Still, the blankets pull off my hips, only to stop mid-thigh. He pulls me up and on top of him, so I straddle his lower thighs, my legs spread wide. Still, he maintains eye contact with me, his vision never wavering lower.

"You can look." I close my eyes so I don't have to see his reaction.

"Open your eyes, Rya. Watch me look at the most beautiful thing I have ever seen." When I open my eyes, his are still on mine.

His palms are on my shoulders, fingers massaging into flesh. His eyes travel to my lips; I can feel the warmth from his stare. I can feel his gaze travel the length of my neck, stopping briefly where his mark should go.

Reverence is all I can see as he takes me in, vibrations of want traveling up my inner thighs.

I give him a nervous smile, but his eyes are no longer on my lips to notice. He's taking in my chest, his skin rippling underneath his own skin.

"Beautiful." His fingers brush ever so lightly against my goose bump flesh. Hands resting on either side of my abdomen. Taking in all of it.

"Look what we've done together." He entwines his hands in mine, bringing them up to my belly as the both of us feel him inside me.

"Look what we've created. How could I not find this beautiful?" I watch him regarding me, knowing deep down his words are his truth.

Leaning into him, touching my lips to his. With that first touch, he takes control of the kiss. No slowness now, it's fierce and hot. I'm not sure where his mouth begins and mine ends. Seconds or minutes go by as I become lost in his kiss.

Whimpering when he pulls himself away from me.

He's breathing just as hard as me.

The contraction that tightens the flesh on my belly has me grunting, closing my eyes.

"Rya?" His voice is a question.

"It's nothing. I've been getting them throughout the night, and they eased up. I thought that I was going into labor last night, but then they just stopped. False alarm."

"Why didn't you get me?" Deeply etched hurt drips from his voice.

"Because it wasn't the real thing. I waited a good hour. They weren't regular contractions, they were all over the place, and then they just went away till now."

"I want to check you." He flips me with ease on my back. His hands are slightly shaky, as he feels the position of his pup.

"He's head down, his shoulders are here, and his bum up here. Rya, you can go at any time. Do you want me to check inside you, see if you're dilating?" I close my legs instantly so he doesn't have access to the inside.

"No, I should go to the midwife today. Just for a checkup."

"We should go now." I laugh at the anxiety that's bubbling up his throat. He's no longer calm; a nervousness is creeping out of him. I've never seen him so shaken up.

I touch his shoulder, rubbing his fur down in a calming manner.

"I'm fine, Dallas. Everything is going to be just fine. I'm hungry. Let's eat some breakfast first, then go to the clinic, see if the midwife has time to see me. All right?" He nods his head, getting up quickly, dressing quicker than I have ever seen him.

"She has time to see you. Make no mistake, she's going to see you today."

I get dressed slowly. Another contraction ripples the flesh of my stomach, and I bite my lower lip, stifling any sounds that want to come out. Dallas's hard eyes are on me.

"Rya?"

"Dallas, it's all right. They aren't regular." I pull my shirt over my belly. The male inside me has grown so much since I bought this.

Watching Dallas taking a calming breath through his nose, blowing it out his mouth, makes me think he's trying to practice the art of patience.

We go down the stairs together, taking them one at a time. The pup's sitting lower inside me. I can tell he's dropped into the birthing position.

"Rya, come and sit down." Luna Grace takes a pillow that's on the counter, puts it on the chair for me to sit on.

Sitting on the cushion, it feels good against my butt. Treajure is at the table without her glasses. She's feeling at her food before putting her fork into the cut-up piece of meat. It's slow progress as she lifts it up to her face, sniffing it before her mouth goes to the fork. It hits her cheek first; she looks defeated before it goes into her mouth. Cash is feeding his twins blueberries as he sneaks them peas between bites. Their little faces scrunch up with the taste of them, tongues sticking out trying to spit the taste out.

"What happened to her glasses?" Treajure stops eating, puts her head down, and wilts like a flower on a hot summer day.

"Well, it seems that Caleb got her drunk last night, and she ended up throwing up all over Cash."

Treajure's shoulders sink lower, along with her body, as she stops chewing the food in her mouth.

"Cash brought her to the bathroom, she got sick again, and her glasses fell off her face and smashed against the tile floor. The lenses are ruined. We're getting them fixed, but she has to go without them for a week. That's when the new glasses will be here." Luna Grace's voice is a controlled fury. She rubs Treajure's head before walking away from the table.

"Where's the rest of the gang?"

"Belac is out for a run with my mate. He's showing her some of the territory so she can show the rest of them when they get up. Also, he thought that it would be a good idea for their wolves to meet by themselves, just in case she has delusions about herself." Cash gives a little laugh out, putting a spoonful of blueberries in Dee's mouth. She's smacking her lips together, smiling. Ken has his mouth open waiting for another bite.

"Where's Caleb?"

"Out back." That's the only thing Luna Grace says before she shows her teeth that have my heart stopping for a brief second.

"I fed him this morning, Mom. We had a really nice talk. It's refreshing when he can't talk back," Dallas says with a smile on his face. He pulls out his phone, showing me a picture of Caleb's wolf with his back turned to the camera.

"I'm getting this blown up, framed actually. It's going to be a real nice home warming gift for them." He has such an evil smile on his face.

"I owe him more than this. It's just beginning for

him." Cash laughs with Dallas at Caleb's expense.

Another contraction grips me so I have to hold on to the table to steady myself. It's then I feel the gush of liquid come out of me.

I freeze up from the shock of it, the time of it. I'm going to have my pup very soon.

Dallas's head lifts up, sniffing the air, his eyes going wide. Not long after, Cash and Luna Grace even Treajure's heads lift, sniffing the air. Cash drops the spoon that he was feeding the twins with; it clangs on the floor loudly.

Another contraction grips my breath in a tight vise until it gradually loosens enough for me to take a lungful of air.

"We're going now!" Dallas gets off his chair, pulling mine away from the table.

"Dallas, I have time. I need go get cleaned up and changed. I need to pack a bag. I don't have anything ready." I'm starting to panic slightly now at how unprepared I am for his arrival.

Dallas is by my side helping me up off the cushion that's saturated in fluids of birth.

Cash is looking at me as if he's seeing death walking. His fears are saturating the air thick and heavy.

"Cash, I'm going to be fine. No need to worry. This is all normal." I try to soothe his nerves down. The twins start to cry because they have to wait on being fed, their bellies demanding food.

Treajure is motionless.

"Don't worry about a thing. I'll have everything ready when you come back here. Now go clean yourself up. I'll drive both of you to the clinic." She

357

gives me a kiss on the cheek before turning around and taking the soiled cushion away.

Walking toward the bedroom, Dallas has already beaten me to his room; the shower is turned on.

He's pacing back and forth. Another contraction has me gripping the dresser. I can breathe through it, but I have this fear that the longer the labor continues, the harder it will be to focus on breathing.

It's one thing to read about labor, teach about labor, it's another thing to experience it yourself for the first time, and I am just beginning to learn what pain is about as another contraction grips me hard. Dallas runs his fingers through his hair as he's talking into the phone.

"We're coming. I want everyone there and waiting. Will be there in ten." He's giving orders as if he's a general.

Taking my time in the shower, I let the warmth soak into my skin. "Rya, are you almost done?"

"Almost," I call out to him. First-time mothers usually have anywhere from six to twenty-four hours of labor. I have time.

Getting out, I dry off. It looks like he packed my bag for me. I search through it, getting different outfits than what he picked out. I can see him breathing in deep, trying to show great restraint with me. The art of patience never looked so hard.

"Rya, are you ready now?" His voice is strained slightly but calm.

"Let's go." He takes my hand in his as he leads me out of the bedroom. Luna Grace is waiting for me by the door; Dallas is carrying the bags on his shoulder.

"Cash, release Caleb for me, please. Also, you need to call your grandfather. Have him on standby just in case number one needs a handler before your father gets back. Can you make sure Treajure is taken care of until Belac comes back?" Cash looks at Treajure before looking at his mother with big eyes.

Luna Grace mouths the word, please.

I'm just happy that Treajure can't see this exchange; it would make her feel bad.

"Specs, it looks like it's me and you today. Just no throwing up on me and we should get along fine." Her shoulders slouch even more, so it's almost as if she's half under the table now.

Before I get into the car, another contraction makes its presence known. Holding onto Dallas's shoulders until it eases up, I can still breathe through these contractions.

He kisses the top of my head. "We can do this." He says this to me, but I can tell the faint shake in his voice.

Once the door closes, he takes a seat in the back as his mother drives away slowly, taking her time. She turns the music on. There is no nervousness with her, just a calmness that's nice to have around me.

Turning in Luna Grace's direction, I ask, "Would you like to stay for the birth?" Her head turns to me before focusing back on the road.

"I wanted to ask you, but I didn't want to intrude." Her smile is ear to ear.

She squeezes my hand, and I squeeze hers back.

It's comforting.

A team is waiting for us as we pull up to the clinic; it's not every day the next Alpha is born. Dallas gets out and comes around the car. He helps me get out. I have to stop midway; another tightening of my skin has me breathing the way I teach about. I can't move from my spot for just a minute, needing time to catch my breath.

Once inside, Dallas starts to bark orders as if he's in charge. "I want an IV 18 gauge started stat, 0.9NS at 125ml/hr," he calls out to a nurse. She looks toward the doctor, who has to square his shoulders back.

"Let's check her first, then I will decide what she needs." The doctor steps up to Dallas. As soon as his words leave his mouth, Dallas has him up against the wall. Dallas shows his teeth.

Luna Grace goes over to him. "Don't do this, my son. Let's just have you be the father and not the doctor."

"Where's his father just in case he needs to be handled?" the doctor questions the Luna.

"I can handle him for now until the Alpha arrives." Dallas tries to settle himself down, pacing up and down the room.

"Dallas, you need to behave, you know what happens to mates—" Dallas stops mid-stride, coming over to me.

"Did you just call me your mate?"

Smiling to him, I reply, "Yes, I did." He gives me a quick kiss.

"Do you know how happy that just made me? Do you know how happy you make me?" Another kiss to my lips before he pulls away.

"Dallas, you need to just settle down. You're not the doctor here. You're not in charge. They will throw you out if you become difficult." He looks ashamed of himself. He knows better; he must have seen this countless times when he was the one to deliver all those pups. Except it's different when you're the one to go through it.

"Rya, let's have a look, all right? See what's going on." This midwife has a softness about her. She's in her mid-fifties. Her hands have caught more pups than Dallas and me put together. She is an expert in her field.

Well seasoned.

Another contraction grips me, holding me in my spot until it fades away. The midwife gives me a smile, nature doing its job. With each contraction, the more ready the body gets to push this life out.

"Let's get you into this, shall we?" She closes the door behind me. Dallas waits on the other side.

She helps me get undressed, putting the light blue gown on, tying me up in the back.

"Let's have you lay back." I do as I'm told because I know that she has to check me. Putting gloves on, she lubricates her fingers, and I thank the moon that Dallas and I never did what I want to this morning. That would be mortifying having her between my legs looking at some of Dallas coming out of me.

Thank the moon for the little things.

When she checks inside of me, I take a breath in. She has her hand on my lower abdomen. She smiles up at me.

"You're five centimeters and about seventy percent effaced. Rya, how long have you been in labor?" She asks her question as she takes off her glove and washes her hand.

"Last night I started to feel some contractions. They weren't regular and didn't last long until they finally went away. Then this morning the contractions started up again. My water broke, but they aren't regular yet, maybe every seven minutes, then one back to back, then another seven minutes might go by. The contraction itself only lasts a minute. I have a long way to go." I'm slightly nervous right now, and I kind of wish my mom was with me.

"Let's get you into our birthing rooms." She opens the door for Dallas to come in.

"I'm five centimeters and seventy percent effaced." I need to keep him informed about the progress.

"Well, this is a first for us." The doctor comes into the room.

"My mate and I have never had to deliver a doctor or midwife's pup before. We also never had to birth the next generation Alpha either, so this is exciting, to say the least." He gives Dallas a pat on the back. "We have done this many times. We have only had one female leave us, and Rya is in very good shape, extremely healthy, not the same case as that female."

I think the doctor just needs to try and settle Dallas's nerves down.

Another contraction slides in slowly at first, until it peaks and fades away.

"We have a shower here if you need it. I think maybe you should walk around inside here for a while. Get things progressing more. We're in for a long day." She walks away, going to talk with Luna Grace, who is nodding her head at her, the doctor talking to her as well. They probably are making a plan up if Dallas starts to unwind at the seams. He's a very strong male that would be a handful if he can't focus on the prize.

"We can do this." Dallas kisses my hand, then my cheek.

"We can do this." I'm a little scared when the next contraction slams into me. I do my best to breathe through it.

He's holding my hand, sweating.

Getting up, the walking starts, up and down the hallway stopping as the contractions start to become more regular, more focused in the education of pain.

Up and down for hours, we are walking, and Dallas is by my side the whole time. With the growing strength of the contractions, my lower back is starting to have an intense pressure pulse on it. I know I am switching from the active phase of labor to the transitional phase.

I'm a ball of sweat. Everything is sticking to me. Luna Grace has cool wet cloths on my forehead. I need to lay down now on my side. Dallas is pressing his palms into the base of my back; the pain is unrelenting. As soon as the contraction stops, the next one is there to take its place.

Another one is coming. The last one feels like it just ended. "No, not another one. It's coming again." Now my seams are coming undone, unraveling in mind-altering pain.

"I can't take another one." Shaking my head back and forth, preparing for it to peak, my whole abdomen is in a tight ball of hurt before it slowly loosens up.

"When the next one comes, Rya, remember to breathe. Don't hold it in. You need to breathe it out." This female is insane, easy for her say. She's not the one going through this. I'm losing my focus and giving in to the pain.

The next contraction has me grunting out, fingers clenched tight. My whole body seizes up to just focus on the pain. My eyes are even in pain.

"Dallas, I can't do this." I hold his gaze. "I can't do this." I'm starting to cry as the next one takes me on the pain train that's too fast to try to jump off. Over and over the contractions are fast and furious.

"Rya, you need to calm down. You need to focus. Let's practice that breathing." He starts to breathe. "Do what I do. That's right, in and out, that's all I want you to do when the next contraction starts." I focus on his voice that's in my ear now. In and out, the pain is so intense at this stage I feel as if I could vomit, and I do all over the floor.

This is grunting, teeth-gnashing, jaw-clenching pain. Sweat pours down my face as she checks me.

"It's time, Rya. We're going to start pushing." My eyes almost go in the back of my head. If I thought I went through pain before, this is going to be ten times worse.

Dallas angles me up in position, holding one of my legs while Luna Grace takes the other.

"Chin to chest, and I want you to bear down as if

you're going to have a bowel movement. We're going to count to ten. I want you to push the whole time with the next contraction." It's not a long wait until the contraction comes. Chin to chest, and I push for the ten count, resting only after ten.

"Good job, Rya." Dallas kisses my forehead. "I'm so proud of you. You're doing so good."

"You're doing so good, Rya, way better than I did my first time." Luna Grace gives me a much-needed compliment.

The doctor enters the room, sticking to the side.

Dallas starts to growl, low and threatening. He almost lets my leg go before we begin to count again.

This is repeated over and over again, me pushing, them counting, me collapsing down for a little rest before it's time to push again. I might have burst a blood vessel in my forehead with the exertion I'm putting forth. The midwife tries to ease his head out without ripping me.

This goes on for at least an hour before the midwife looks at the doctor.

"Would you like to check her?" Dallas immediately lets me go, coming to stand in front of my parted legs before the doctor has time to get there.

"What's the problem?" His voice is frigid, cold without emotion. He doesn't sound like my Dallas.

"I think maybe the head is too big for her. She might need his help to ease him out. I think he needs to just give her a little cut."

Another contraction grips me, and I push on my own without anyone telling me to; my body is taking over. It's telling me I need to push, some deep-seated instinct that you are just born with.

The body knows when it's time to push a pup out.

"Dallas, let the doctor do his job." Luna Grace is threatening, but she doesn't let my leg go. Instead, she encourages me to keep pushing my male out. She pushes my hair away from my forehead.

The doctor takes a step toward me, and Dallas crouches toward him with his teeth out. It's a threatening sight. His claws are descending.

The Luna puts a blanket on top of me before raising her voice. "We need you." In that second, the door opens, and Alpha Clinton comes inside.

"Your mate needs you now. Don't do this. Don't miss this the way I did with you. Never will you forgive yourself for it." The Silverback takes a step toward Dallas, whose eyes are the color of night. His female is at her weakest, and males are surrounding her. This is his natural born instincts; he's unable to control his need to protect.

The doctor takes another step toward me as I feel the thin layer of skin tear to make room for the head. Blood starts to pour on the floor in a steady stream. It's now saturating the room in a fine metallic taste.

The midwife lifts the cover that was hiding me from Dallas's father. She's between my legs, angling the bed so I'm in a squatting position. The need to push is so strong it's all I can think about.

"Dallas." It's all I can say, holding my hand out for him to take.

I can feel the head crowning. The ring of fire is

burning hot, like molten lava around the edges.

"I need you." My cries must be hitting his ears because his whole body starts to relax slightly. Turning away from his father, he snarls at the doctor before taking a position at my head. Holding my hand.

"Please, Dallas." Looking into his eyes, I feel hot tears drip down my cheeks.

"I can't do this without you." My hand is gripping his, turning the fingertips white. Another contraction ripples my flesh as I feel the head come out. Taking a quick breath in and out is a dizzying feeling.

"With the next contraction, I want you to push with everything you have," the midwife's stern, focused voice commands.

Bearing down with a long, teeth-mashing grunt, I push that big male out of my body the way all mothers must.

Instantly the pain stops to a level where I can see clearly. She puts the bloody blue-tinged body on my chest, wiping him off with a towel. She's rough with him, and I want to bite her hand with the way she's handling him. He pulls in a lungful of air before I hear that first sound of his cries.

It's the sound I will have imprinted on me until I go to the moon.

Dallas is crouched down, looking at his male. He's taking his smell in, listening to his cry. The midwife hands him a knife to cut the cord.

When Dallas cuts his cord of life that binds him to me, I feel the loss of him. The attachment is gone, only to be replaced with a much stronger, more deadly attachment.

I would kill for my little male.

I would protect him with my life.

This is my love, this tiny helpless crying male on my chest is my love, and I would never change my life, because then I would not have him.

I give thanks to the moon for this miracle.

CHAPTER 25

The Moon

White snow drifts fold as if they are frozen waves suspended just before they crest into themselves.

The tide of frozen snow.

Crisp air, biting cold, blue skies.

The sun seems to be shining brighter, making the sea of snow sparkle as if it were made of many tiny crystals reflecting the light, casting the world in glitter.

Snow can be beautiful and soft or unpredictable and harsh.

"I want to show you something." Dallas pulls off the main road onto a side road that seems to be recently plowed. The hard snow crunches under the tires of the car. Looking down at the tiny bundle securely strapped into his car seat, he's sleeping contentedly. I couldn't bring myself to ride in the front seat; I preferred to take the back with my male. This is his very first car ride, leaving the

369

clinic. After three days of just Dallas and me, it's time for him to meet the family for the first time.

Pulling up to a clear area of woods, he stops the car. Turning in his seat, Dallas regards me. "I just wanted to show you where, if you wanted, we could build our house." He looks at me, watching my face before he gets out of the car.

Opening the back door for me to get out, he takes my hand. I climb out gingerly, releasing a little hiss of pain from the change of movement. It's really not that bad as long as I take it slow and careful.

Little puffs of steam come out of our mouths as we breathe the arctic air.

"I thought that this is where we could build it, a big picture window here," he says, pointing with his hands. "A fireplace there. The kitchen in the back, with a deck off to the side." He's going on explaining in detail his dream house. I listen to him, looking on at the excitement of his descriptions.

It's lighting up his face. The future is shining out bright.

Taking in the scenery, I can picture the inside, fire crackling, hot chocolate and marshmallows, family dinners, barbecues in the summertime. Bonfires and guitars. Singing and playing. Young ones running around squealing in delight.

His words are giving me a picture of what our future could be like.

Looking out at the lake, it's starting to freeze almost to the middle. The stillness of the water says that another few degrees drop in temperature, the whole lake will be frozen solid.

"I don't want you to say anything. I just wanted

you to see what we could have here." His big body wraps me up in a hug. We stay like this for just a few minutes, he and I taking in the lake view while our little one is cozy warm in the car.

It's not the ocean with its deep pounding surf that vibrates my body in a rush. This lake has more of a promise to it, more of a homey feel, as if I could sip my tea on the deck and just enjoy the view without the saltiness of what the ocean can offer me.

"I need to be honest with you, completely honest. I don't know how much longer I can go without marking you. It's taking every ounce of control not to bite into your neck and claim you. I just want you to know this. I'm trying very hard to give you the time you need, but I'm having a hard time letting that happen." He's looking at the lake while he says this, hands in his pockets.

"I want you to mark me. I want to mark you when the time's right."

"Do you mean that?" He's watching my face.

"I do." Very gently he picks me up, kissing the spot on my neck as he twirls us around. Feeling his heart beating in his chest, the tingles begin to go up my spine. He's laughing and kissing my jawline, my neck every place my skin is exposed from the opening of the jacket.

Laughing with him, I twirl in the air as if I'm the lightest thing in the world to him. I won't forget this moment for as long as I live.

He's the ending to my fairytale.

"Let's go. My family is waiting to see him." No one was allowed to come into our birth den except the Luna, Alpha just barely, and the midwife. I couldn't tolerate anyone else interrupting the bonding that the three of us were having.

The imprinting of features, the time to get comfortable with him in my arms. The feel of him naked against my chest. I needed time alone away from any other wolves.

Dallas is so gentle with our little one. I could only sleep if I knew he had him in his arms tucked in safe. My hackles on full alert, every noise, every new scent had me in an uproar. Only Dallas could calm me down with him looking out the door, telling me that no one was there. That we're safe from harm. I made him sleep by the door just in case. No windows are in this room, just a door.

One way in, one way out.

They designed this room with mothers in mind.

A new mother with a just birthed young is delusionally fierce, almost borderline psychotic.

Getting into the backseat, making sure he's still sleeping, I can't help the smile that beams out of my face. He's wearing a light blue hat on his bald little head. Little tiny mitts on his hands keep him from scratching his face with nails that I can't cut yet.

He doesn't even squirm, just content in dreams.

It's still hard to believe that he was just inside me. I feel slightly sad with the loss of him kicking and stretching inside me. I had gotten so used to that, now he's not inside I feel slightly sad.

They grow so fast.

"Rya, everyone's going to be in the living room. We will walk in and introduce him. Remember, this is our family. No one will hurt him." He understands my nervousness. Letting others by him is nerve-racking. Even though I know they won't hurt him, it's hard to have others sniffing around something that's so fragile and is mine.

Walking into the house, it's calm, quiet, slightly darkened as the blinds have all been pulled down. The hair on the back of my neck raises as I take in the smells of the wolves I know. Stepping backward, I bump into Dallas's chest as he blocks the exit. He pushes me forward with his body, taking the first few steps inside. He has our male in his arms; he puffs himself up more. His whole body is rigid with a strength that new fathers possess, and he's only displaying it for my benefit.

New mothers are very skittish. I'm no exception.

Walking into the living room that's just off the side of the kitchen, I have never been in here before. It's hardly ever used. The kitchen table is where the family congregates.

The heart of the home.

Crane is on the couch, sitting beside Carson, who is looking at me with an easy, curious smile. Cash is on a chair regarding me with relief.

His experience bringing his twins home was not this. That was a totally different experience altogether.

Caleb's on the ground with both twins crawling all over him, his hair just beginning to grow out. He doesn't look at me as he continues to nip them on the neck, swat at their heads. They're pulling themselves up to standing positions, trying to bite his shoulders. They are a mass of arms and legs and squealing delight. You can tell that he is their absolute favorite.

Happiness is pouring out of them in waves of unfiltered bliss.

Belac is sitting on the couch, watching him, Treajure close by her side, still without glasses. Her head tilts up, taking in the new scent of a newborn life.

Alpha Clinton holds his position on the overstuffed chair. His body sinks into the cushions. He makes no move toward me. He holds himself still, bristling slightly. He just gives me a look, a hard stare, but he doesn't say anything.

Everyone is watching, waiting until I settle down in order to approach us.

"Come and sit here." After a few moments, Luna Grace pats the seat next to her on the couch.

Taking the seat, our arms are touching, as if she is providing me with her strength. She understands how hard this is for me.

"I remember when we brought Clayton home, I was so nervous having wolves around him. It gets easier. The first time is the hardest." She's trying to be reassuring.

Dallas gives him kisses on his head and cheek before giving him up to me. He takes a position at my feet on the floor. His arm resting on my leg, he gives a gentle squeeze as he looks up at me, smiling proudly.

Alpha Clinton is the first to start. He approaches slowly, trying to make himself as non-threatening as possible, which is impossible. The wolf in me gives a little warning growl but settles down instantly when he flashes his wolf's eyes at her for just a second.

He comes in sniffing deeply, touching and nuzzling the little one gently with his nose before he backs away for someone else to meet him.

Cash picks up Dee in his arms. He comes up to us walking softly. The little female in his arms looks at the newborn in wonder. Her little hand goes out before Cash holds it in his hands and gently shows her how to touch him.

"Nice touches, can you give Chance a kiss?" Her mouth opens big, as she touches her mouth *to* his head.

Cash then nuzzles my male gently with his nose, taking in his smell.

Caleb is the next to follow, bringing the little male with him. He's rough in the way he carries him almost sideways, but Ken looks like he loves it.

"Be nice, gentle." Caleb holds the male's hands as he strokes his face with gentle hands.

"Kisses." Both Caleb and Ken kiss the male I'm holding before backing away.

This is all repeated by the other brothers. All showing me how gentle they will be with him for now.

The twins crawl toward Dallas, pulling themselves up on his shirt. He grabs the male and tosses him high in the air before catching him; for the female, he tosses her not as high. He's gentler with her; with the male he's rougher. It's funny how they get treated the same but just a little different.

I wonder how they will like it when she grows up and wants to party in the basement? All fun and games when you have males in the house, but when a female is concerned, it all stops.

Different standards.

"Would you like to meet him?" I turn toward Belac and Treajure. Caleb doesn't even look their way. Instead he turns his back on them, pretending to be interested in the twins more than his own mate.

A tight tension is felt between them that wasn't there before.

"I'm not really good with pups," Belac states, as if she's somewhat afraid to approach. She's starting to put on a small amount of weight from her heat, along with Treajure, who is filling out her sharp corners nicely; her lips look fuller, redder. She's got beauty to her that is underlying. All you have to do is look at her to notice.

Too bad no one does.

She approaches, guiding Treajure along with her. Both bend down, taking his scent in before stepping away and going back to their spots on the couch. It's quick.

"He's beautiful," Belac remarks before sitting down.

"Thank you." I think he's the most beautiful pup I have ever seen, but that's just me.

"We have the nursery all set up when you feel comfortable putting him in there. Caleb gave up his room for your little one. For now, we have a crib set up in your room," The Luna states with eyes that shine.

"How's the house coming along?" Dallas questions Caleb.

"Good. They're all moved in. I put some boxes

in your room to go through. I couldn't bring myself to throw out some of the stuff." He gives Dallas a hard look before he looks away.

"I'll go through it," Dallas says, and everyone's eyes turn slightly sad over this.

"You need to come over and see what I did with the place." Caleb seems proud of himself. I'm not sure if I can go over there. The last time freaked me out.

"I will," Dallas says softly.

Looking around the room, seeing all the pictures showing family, a gallery of documented time. From little pups to big strong males. I notice Kennedy even has a place on the wall along with a picture of Maysa, bright green eyes framed by dark raven hair.

She's beautiful.

It's a picture of them holding each other. She looks so happy, and so does he. I feel slightly guilty sitting here with his male in my arms while she's holding their male inside her.

Looking at Dallas, his eyes are on me, watching where my eyes were. He says nothing to me as he looks at her, taking a deep breath before smiling at me, slightly. I know he said that he is over her, that he's ready to move on, but is he really?

Can he love me more? He says he can. I'm not sure where all these doubts are coming from. Maybe I'm just hormonal from the birth.

I still look at all the pictures. Not one of me hangs on their walls. It's an irrational thought, but it's still a thought. I'm not on the wall.

Luna Grace takes him from my arms, holding

him, nuzzling him, cooing her soft voice in his ear. She gets up, placing him in everyone's arms for just a short time. Getting me used to having others hold him. I wonder if her mother did the same thing when Dallas was born?

We sit this way for at least an hour as he's passed around to all the wolves here. Even Treajure takes a turn; she leans into his ear, a whispered word so soft it's lost even in the silence as we take her in. Belac watches her in silence.

Once Chance makes it back to me, I'm somewhat settled down. Dallas, the whole time, was rubbing my back, my leg, whispering in my ear, "It's okay, no one will hurt him, we're all family here."

Chance starts to grunt, rooting around for something to eat. His grunts start to turn into small whimpers until they are loud cries with real tears. He's putting on a good show for them.

"I think it's time for me to feed him." Getting up quickly from the couch, I take my pup from the family, thankful to get away.

"I'll come with you." Dallas starts to get up off the couch.

"No, you stay. I'm just going to feed him. I'll be back down soon." I'm slightly shaky at the moment, and I don't know why. My words come out harsh toward him; it's like a light switch is turning on and off.

My emotions sway back and forth.

They all give me looks of confusion as I leave but say nothing. Dallas gets up off the ground, getting ready to follow me, but I stop him with a look.

He does pause for a fraction of a second but doesn't listen as he follows me up to his room.

My chest is sore and swollen with the anticipation of his thirst. Chance fumbles around with lips that aren't parted enough. I take him off, only to place him better so his latch is open mouthed and wide.

He needs to learn to get it right or else he will hurt me with blisters and cracked nipples if he's not on me placed properly.

Finally, he settles in for a good feeding, his little body molding into mine, skin on skin, our bonding becoming stronger and stronger with each passing hour. He drains the first, only to move on to the second, his hunger nothing but pure greed. The little belly distended and firm as he fills himself up with mother's milk.

Once done, Dallas takes him from my arms, burping him, changing him, swaddling him in his blanket, before placing him in his crib. He's already asleep again. Brand new pups are so easy to care for. After the pup's needs are taken care of, Dallas turns to me.

"What's the matter, Rya? I can tell you're upset about seeing that picture. Talk to me. What's upsetting about it? Do you want me to take down her picture?"

"No, don't do that. It's nothing." I rock in the chair that's been placed in the corner of the room.

"Obviously it's something. Just talk to me. I can't read your mind yet, so tell me what's the matter." He goes between my legs, stopping the rocking motion with his knee.

"We need to talk about the things that make us upset." Pulling me off the chair, he sits down and positions me on his lap. He begins to rock us slowly, back and forth, as if we're on a boat that's lazily drifting on the waves in the noonday sun.

"Rya, she's part of my past, but like I said before, you're my now!"

"I know, sorry I'm emotional." He has my head on his shoulder as he rocks us both.

"Do you want me to take that picture down? I'll do it if you want." His fingers glide back and forth on the inside of my wrist.

"No, it's okay." I should not be jealous of the dead. It's not like they can come back and take him away from me.

"Are you sure? Just tell me if you're not. I will take it down, but I want you to know that she deserves to be up there. She has done nothing wrong. She is still part of the family, just like you are. She died, Rya, she died. She is no longer here, but I just can't pretend she never existed. We had a life together, we did, and now we have a life together." His voice is choking in his throat, clenching so tight it's hard for him to get his words out as his fingers fall onto my shoulders.

"No, it's okay." It's then I see the boxes piled high with memories of their life together.

We don't have boxes of memories, but we do have a living and breathing life that we made together who will give us our memories.

"I think I'm just tired. I haven't had a lot of sleep in the last few days. So I'll just take a nap until he wakes up. Is that okay with you?" Picking me up like a young one, he puts me in his bed, pulling the covers up under my chin.

"Get some sleep. I'll get you for dinner. Please don't worry, Rya, the past is the past. We need to concentrate on what's right in front of us." He gives another kiss before walking toward the boxes. Picking them up, he takes them out of the room, turning off the light before he closes the door.

I can't sleep. My mind won't calm down.

Vibrations on the bedside table alert me to a call. It's either my mother or him.

No one else calls me.

Looking at the screen, it's Clayton. I think it's time to tell him about my Chance.

"Hello."

"Rya, where have you been? I kept calling you, but you didn't answer. I was getting worried about you." His voice seems slightly relieved.

"I'm with Dallas, back in their pack."

"Oh." His voice has a downward angle to it, almost a disappointment in it.

"I have something to tell you." He doesn't deserve to know anything, but I should prepare him.

"What is it?" He doesn't sound like he wants to know.

"I'm going to let Dallas mark me. I just want you to know." I owe him nothing, yet I tell him anyway.

"Hello?" A long pause of silence. He says nothing back to me for a while.

"Rya—" He pulls the phone away. I can hear a quiet little intake of breath as if he's trying to hide his heartache from me.

"I had this hope inside me that you would come back here one day." His voice cracks again over the line. He takes a calming breath.

"We would start out as friends. Get to know each other as friends first. I have this dream about us that I think about constantly. It's the first thing I think about in the morning, the last thing I think about at night. I thought after some time away, years even, you might come back here for a visit. We would start out slow, but eventually, you and I would end up falling in love. It's a stupid dream, isn't it?" His voice is heartache.

"Clayton, you were the one to give me no chance in the first place."

"Rya, I understand everything I have done to you. I go over everything in my mind over and over again. Trust me. I understand completely what I have done to you, but I do have dreams about the future. I can still dream, can't I?" I pause because who am I to tell him he can't dream? He just can't dream about me anymore. He lost that chance to dream big.

"I just thought you should know to prepare yourself." He's sobbing quietly now.

"Before he marks you, I want you to ask him a question." His voice is trembling. I can picture giant tears coming down his face. I hear something breaking in the background, as if a glass is shattering against a wall.

"Before he marks you, ask him this one question. Who does he walk with when he goes to the moon, her or you? Ask him this question. If he says you, he lies." My throat tightens on his words.

"When I go to the moon, I will be there waiting for you, Rya. I will take your hand when he has hers in his. I have been doing so much thinking, and I realize that my only chance is when we go to the moon. I'll be there waiting for you to get there." He's crying, and I start crying too, because what he says is the truth. I'm Dallas's fraud in the now, but in eternity I'm just a fleeting thought that kept him company for just a brief amount of time until he is reclaimed by her.

Dallas comes inside, looking at me oddly.

"What's the matter, Rya?" He sits down on the edge of the beds.

"I have to go." I hang up before he says anything more to me.

"Rya, what's going on?" Dallas has my face in his hands, thumbs wiping away my tears.

"I have a question to ask you." The tears won't stop. How can I be so jealous of a female who's dead? Because deep down I understand in death she will have him again.

"When we go to the moon, who would you choose to walk with, her or me?"

"Where is this coming from? Is it because you saw her picture? Rya, don't do this."

"Answer my question, Dallas."

"That's not a fair question, is it, Rya?"

"Tell me please." The shaking increases throughout my body when he hesitates with his answer.

CHAPTER 26

What We Are Taught To Believe

A tidal wave is crashing down on my soul the more time goes by without him answering me.

My throat feels torn out; it's impossible to breathe.

Vocal cord sounds are hysterical sobs.

Dallas watches me, waits, and listens as I start to rant on and on, with waving hands.

Pacing back and forth, finger pointing, accusations thrown his way. He stands there, never wavering, taking everything I'm spitting his way, standing tall, strong, as if he can bear all the bricks that I'm hitting him with.

Lies.

Lies.

Lies.

"I am the lie in your life!" Another volley of words that seem to just spike out of my mouth, continuing to beat against his solid chest.

He's iron that will not bend.

Pointing at my heart, I cry, "I'm not a lie!" These are old wounds that are splitting apart. The fabric of my life is coming undone.

The unjust card has been dealt, fate's cruelest tricks.

I have been taught since I was a small pup that when you find your mate, you will walk hand in hand in this life and together in the moon's embrace for eternity, never to be alone.

For me, nothing is possible. I will constantly be rejected up there no matter who I choose. The only one to wait for me is Clayton, and I don't want him to be there waiting for me.

"Why me? All I ever wanted in life was to be loved, to be put first. Is that so much to ask for?"

He's listening to me come undone.

My currents of emotion are a tide flowing in, only to spew out a hurricane of fury that is jumbled together as he's holding onto the ship, riding out my waves.

He's a patient captain, knowing the storm can only last so long.

"I deserve to be first; I deserve to be loved! I won't do this with you. I can leave. I don't need you; I don't need anyone but him. He's what I need. I don't have to settle for second best. I would rather be alone than know that I'm just being used for company. To fill a void left by your dead mate." I smack my hand on the dresser, wishing it was his face. I know one thing: I am raging mad, tears of anger, sadness mixing themselves together as he watches me break down.

"What happens to me? What happens when I go

to the moon and no one is there for me? Is this fair to me? Is this how I have to live my life, knowing that when we part you will turn your back on me, forsake me? I'm good enough for this life and the next. I'm worthy to be someone's first." I wipe away my pain, my heartache, that just keeps pouring out of my eyes.

My ribcage feels brittle with the way it wants to collapse inside itself. A slight pain starts throughout my body. Is this real heartache?

I thought I knew heartache.

Taking deep breaths in, I try to calm myself down.

Once my pointing finger lays limply at my side, he comes to me.

Closer and closer. He doesn't hunch his shoulders; he keeps them straight with his head held high.

I've had my tantrum.

He's the casualty of what my words have left. Never can I take back what has been said. We can move on from words, but never can I take them back.

"Rya, I'm not sure what's going on here. When I left you to nap, you told me you were fine. When I come back in the door, I'm met with you accusing me of things that I have no control over." He's an even calm.

Facing me head on.

"Just answer my question."

"No matter what I say, it will be the wrong answer. No matter what I tell you, it will be wrong. Do I walk with her or you?" He sits on the edge of the bed, pulling me on his lap. I try to move away, create space between us.

"I listened to you; I let you talk and talk. My turn, Rya." His nose touches my neck before he pulls his face away to look at me in the eyes.

"Maysa was my mate, Rya; there is no changing that. I would never change that, ever. Just like I will never change the fact you are my mate now. You are what the moon has given to me as a second chance at happiness. She has gifted me with you; I'm not sure why. I have asked her this many times, but she doesn't answer me back. This question you ask seems as if the rest of our future depends on it. This question has no solution to what you seek." He's holding both my hands now, gripping them firmly in his.

"Maysa was my first; I thought she would be my last. I couldn't even imagine myself loving someone as much as her. Until you." He brings my hands to his lips, kissing the tops gently, looking me in the eyes the whole time.

"I like to think that what we have is so much more; there was no bond between us at first. I saw this female that I was drawn too, that I wanted to get to know more. Slowly over time, I wanted to spend more time with you because you were worth spending time with. I couldn't wait to go to the office in the morning to catch a glimpse of you. Just to see your smile, your face. Maybe get a chance to hold a conversation with you. Our story started out slow, with some difficulty, ups, and downs. But here we are now, together." He still holds both my hands, not letting them go.

"I love you. I want to spend the rest of my life with you, raise our pups together, grow old together, and when we go to the moon, we believe that there is no separation, that we can all walk together in the next life." A tear rolls down his cheek, just one.

Emotions are playing hard over his face.

"I want to see her again; I want to see my male that I never got the chance to look at. I picture her holding him in her arms welcoming me up. At the same time, I picture myself waiting for you up there to welcome you in my arms. If you go first, I think that Maysa would be waiting for you as well. She would welcome you with her arms open. I don't think jealousy up there exists; I think emotions transcend themselves into the purest form. Nothing but love exists up there, nothing but belonging. I think she's looking down from her view of us and she's happy for me, for us." He's not letting my hands go. He's like the water that washes me clean, wiping away my doubts and fears away.

He's proposing a fresh new way of seeing things that I never knew could be possible.

What we are taught, others are not. Every pack has different beliefs when you go to the moon.

The question is, who's right?

"She was my first love, but you're my last love. That's my answer to you, Rya. I can't choose between the two of you. I don't think it's a fair choice that you ask me. My true mate or my chosen mate, two different mates, but the same strong love. Unrelenting love." He kisses my cheeks, my forehead.

"I won't make a decision because when we meet again in the next life, we will be standing together, all of us, our friends, family, offspring, we will all stand with one another as one giant pack." He's looking at me now as if deciding something.

"Sometimes life has you making decisions. Right now I'm going to make a decision that I should have made a long time ago." He stands us both up so we're facing each other. Still, he holds my hands in his, except there is space between us.

"Our wolves have bonded to each other; we have a pup together. I love you with my soul. In my heart, you are my mate, Rya." He takes a small step toward me, bringing our bodies slightly closer.

"You are mine." He takes another small step toward me. The humming between our bodies is vibrating my skin.

"You are my hope." Another step my way, so now our chests are almost touching. Hummingbird wings flutter inside my stomach.

"My love." Now he brings us together, our chests touching. Still, he's holding my hands, not breaking contact.

"My light." His voice cracks slightly. Nothing but pure happiness is what I feel from his strong emotions that are radiating out of him. Emotions are of pure happiness that makes you want to cry from the beauty of it.

"My weakness." His head dips down to place a kiss just above the hollow in my neck.

Now he stills himself, taking a deep breath while smiling down at me with nothing but the purest love that's shining in his eyes that are becoming lighter and lighter, almost white in color.

"My strength." The last words flow slowly from his mouth. No space between us now, bodies pressed close together. His hands leave mine now. Taking my face in both his hands, he kisses my lips until I kiss him back. His mouth trails to my jawline, down my neck. His nose is taking in my scent as I take in his.

Pulling back, he lets me look at him and his wolf together in agreement. Canines descended, he's on my neck again. Sharpened teeth hover, barely puncturing flesh.

He holds himself for just a few seconds before I feel them sink into the skin.

A gasp escapes my mouth.

A rhythmic high pulsates in pleasure that I have never felt before. This is a whole new level of experience.

His quivering body moans out in pleasure. He continues to hold me with teeth that are binding me to him. He's in no rush to let go. An arm around my waist, trying to pull me in more, to create as little space as possible between us. I can feel his legs shaking with the effort of standing.

Something inside me opens up like a flower blooming for the first time. My petals that were held in tight are loosening up, as they start to unfold themselves. Releasing my inner essence to him.

Intertwining.

My world is disappearing for a fraction of a second as he's inside me; I can feel his presence, his soul pushing into me.

The energy of him weaving with mine.

Still, he holds me with his teeth; my legs weaken, giving out from the bombardment of sensations. He holds me up with strong arms that won't let me fall.

Electricity is now cracking and popping between us.

Our bond weaving into something so much more.

Spiritual ecstasy.

My spine curves, only to press my chest into his more.

We stay like this entwined, holding onto one another.

I feel his teeth retract from the marked skin, his tongue sealing the holes closed.

There is blood on his face as he regards me, seeing me really for the first time. He doesn't say a word, but I can tell his mind is active, pupils dilating then pinpointing. Is he flipping through the layers of my life?

Can he see who I am?

"I can see everything, Rya." He answers my thoughts back to me. My eyes go big in wonder.

"You marked me?" Putting my hand to my neck, I feel the way it will scar slightly. It's deep; nothing will be able to hide his love for me.

"I thought that this was a perfect time. I made an effort. Either you tap out, or you get knocked out. I wasn't going to tap out this time, and there was no way I was getting knocked out by your words." He seems happy with himself.

I'm still slightly shaky from the marking, and I can tell he's trying his best to look strong for me.

"I want to show you something." He takes my hand, leading me out the door into a room down the hall. Opening the door, it's the nursery for our Chance.

A deep blue on the walls, changing table to the side. It's small but perfect for a little one. No crib, I guess we will move it into here once he gets bigger, and I don't need to keep a vigil on him.

"Look on the walls. I came and checked the room out after you went down for a nap." He's behind me now; his body pressed up against mine.

Looking at the walls, I smile at the large picture of Dallas and me on a chair with my back against his chest. I remember Caleb taking this picture. I see other pictures mounted on the wall of the three of us, right after his birth, that Luna Grace took of us. Dallas is looking down at us while I look into the camera with the biggest smile I think I have ever worn on my face.

"My mother will put you up on the wall when it's time. It's her house, not mine. I can ask her to take Maysa's picture down, but she was a part of their lives just like she was mine. They loved her just like they love you. I can understand how you feel, and it's okay to feel that way." He's holding me while I take our male's room in. The love she invested into everything she has done for me gives me a rush of gratitude for a female who always has my back.

"We should have come in here before we went to our room. You could have seen this. You are important, you are supposed to be loved and cherished, and that's what I will spend the rest of

392

my life doing. It's my moon's promise to you. All you have to do is believe in me, in us." He kisses the back of my head before turning me around in his arms.

"Can you believe in us, Rya? Can you give us a chance?"

CHAPTER 27

Having Faith

Decisions.

"Rya, I can see it in your eyes you don't one hundred percent believe me. You have doubts." Dallas has my face in his hands, thumb pressed against my jawline.

Braille, that's what my skin reads like with the goosebumps that are rising from his touch. Almost as if I am a wanted mate to someone.

"I'm not a second, Dallas. I'm nobody's second, here or in the moon." I quietly whisper the words to myself, really not to him. I want to tell myself this, I am important to myself, and I need to be my number one, or else my Chance will grow up thinking it's all right his mother is always second to everyone else, even herself.

"Rya, please have faith in us. Give us a chance." Dallas's soft words are hitting the fibers that bind my soul to his. I can feel them being pulled tight and rigid with his unconditional belief in what we can be together now and in the moon.

Hearing Chance start to whimper in the next room has both of us going to him when he's just starting to stir himself awake with a hunger that rages through his system at this age. I pick him up, legs still pulled in tight as all newborns do until they stretch themselves out.

He nurses while I rock him in the chair that Luna Grace has put into the room for us to use. Dallas is sitting on the edge of the bed watching, not saying a word, but I can see a hint of anxiety rules his face. It's as if he's afraid this picture he's seeing will disappear at any moment.

"I'm afraid, Rya." Dallas admits with a truthful vulnerability. "I'm afraid that the one question you asked will always haunt you. In the back of your mind, it will always be there when you least expecting it to come up. All I can do is show you the mate I will be for you. I will show you how every day you are cherished and how much I give thanks to the moon that you have been put in my path when I needed someone the most. You have given everything, and I am going to give you so much in return. Give me a chance, Rya, just a chance to show you what I can be." Dallas stands, taking Chance from me, changing him, putting on a new outfit before placing him on his shoulder to rub his back. He's got his hand on the back of his head, rubbing it, pressing his cheek against the hair that's coming out.

"Today there is no need to make any decisions. We'll go down, have some dinner, come back here, and go to bed early. Tomorrow we will start a new day, then the day after that is our new day. We will get you through that question together. One day, hopefully, in the future you will come to understand and trust in my answer enough to mark me as yours, and I will be waiting here patiently for that day to happen." The purest sound of his truth speaks out of a body that is firm and unbending in his beliefs.

We are taught to believe things, and going against those beliefs is never easy.

Looking at Dallas, really looking at him, do I put my views in my teaching of the Moon and trust his teaching of the Moon?

As he says, no decision should be made on my part today. What I will do is watch, listen, and learn.

Getting up from the rocking chair, I go into the bathroom, wiping my eyes and face. Taking a deep breath, I follow Dallas out of the bedroom, walking down the stairs. All his family is there, and no one is speaking.

Caleb is sitting by one of the high chairs feeding a twin, while Cash is in the middle of the twins feeding the female. The little male, Ken, has the hair on his head clipped very short. Looking toward Chance, he will start to wear the hair that's growing out on his head short as well, just like this pack believes a male should wear it.

By the way, they are acting, but they probably heard every screamed word to Dallas, all my accusations flying out for their ears to grab onto.

Dallas sits on his father's left while I take the seat next to Dallas. During dinner there is an awkwardness, forks scraping loudly on plates. They are talking to each other with their eyes, but hardly anyone speaks.

Dallas holds Chance against his shoulder while he starts to eat. For some reason, I just can't put food into my mouth, so I sit there staring at my plate full of food.

"Little Moon, at our table all you have to do is eat, that's all." The Silverback speaks in a low tone but still vibrates outward profoundly.

"Rya, I'm sorry I have no pictures on the wall of you. It was just so soon. You arrived, then gave birth. I wasn't thinking correctly. For that, I am sorry. When you feel up to it, we can go through pictures of you and tell me what one you like the best and I'll have it mounted and put up."

"I don't want you to put it up just because you heard I was upset about it."

"Rya, I want to put it up. I just overlooked doing it. I wanted to get the nursery done first, so you didn't have to worry about things not being ready." Luna Grace's expression holds how upset she is with herself.

"This has to be difficult for you right now. I remember how after having my first male how upset I was that my mate missed the birth." Luna Grace gives the Silverback a scathing look; his shoulders flinch with just a solid look from her eyes.

"It took a long time to forgive him for that, to be all alone as I pushed him out with only my hands to catch him with while he was puffing and strutting out the doctor who was supposed to help me." A little gagging sound is coming from Crane.

"Mom, I'm eating dinner, no birth talk, especially from you." Crane's voice holds how his appetite is being ruined as he sets his fork down. Luna Grace is quick with her rebuttal to her youngest—a quick throw of her butter knife hits him dead center in his chest. No real damage was done, but enough to say you better shut your mouth, I'm telling a story, and I don't like to get interrupted.

"As I was saying, Rya." Luna Grace lifts up her lip at Crane, who's pulling the butter knife out of his chest; it didn't go in deep, just a minor flesh wound.

"After that episode, I didn't trust that he would be there for me. I had doubts that he couldn't be what I needed in my time of greatest need. I was very conflicted." Luna Grace is giving me a little piece to her past.

"With time, my mate did show me that he has mended his ways and I began to trust that he would never make the same mistake twice." The Silverback picks up Luna Grace's hand, kissing the top of it, putting it against his cheek before putting it down on the table, and continues to hold it firmly in his monster grasp.

"With your question about the Moon, who does my son walk with? That's debatable. We could gather multiple packs together, have discussions and great debates about this very thing, and when we all leave at the end of the day, the question still will hold no answer to it. I believe you are my son's mate now and in the Moon. My personal beliefs about who we walk within the Moon is this. My birth pack taught me that we are born many times over and over. Evolving and learning through our new births. We have many mates who have many mates that are all connected to the moon. I still believe in this teaching. That's my views. Now my mate will tell you different about his beliefs. It doesn't mean I am wrong or he is wrong; it just shows that there are so many possibilities about the Moon that no one knows for sure until they get there." Luna Grace's words hold truth; no one knows for sure until they are dead.

"I thought we would have to call the police on you, Rya. Not too many domestics happen here." Caleb has a light joking grin on his face while he's feeding Ken, who holds his food all over his face.

Belac regards Caleb; her eyes hold a look of disappointment in them, as if his joking revolts her, then makes her smile. Caleb closes his mouth tight, focusing on getting the food off the twin's face.

"His hair is too long." Cash is looking at Chance's head. He only has a little tuft of barely visible hair.

"I know." Dallas is saying this while rubbing my pup's head.

"I never thought I would ever get a chance to shave my male's head." Dallas's voice coughs slightly outwards to his family. Now Dallas's hand goes over the top of mine, giving it a quick squeeze, not letting go.

Picking up my fork, I begin to eat until the full plate is finished while listening to the talking of the room. Glancing at Treajure, she's eating as well, still pressed in close to Belac's side, sitting between her and Caleb, creating a space between mates.

Caleb now and then shifts his eyes to Belac, who

doesn't meet his. She keeps eating everything on her plate, taking seconds for her and Treajure. Their heat is in full swing by the way their bodies are curving outwards. More feminine features enhancing and tempting to any males' eyes to devour. Treajure would have held an unattainable beauty if silver's intimate touch never feasted on her flesh.

Once done, Caleb picks up Ken and Dee to play on the floor after he washes both their faces. Cash is looking on, as if it's their routine between the brothers. Cash is lucky to have a brother like Caleb.

Belac is getting up, thanking Luna Grace for dinner. Treajure gets up while holding the back of Belac's shirt. She's still not wearing glasses, and it's as if she is blind and needs the guidance of Belac.

Dallas is getting up, picking up both our plates and bringing them to the sink, whispering something into Crane's ear that has Carson laughing.

"I'm going to give him a bath," Dallas is telling me while walking up the stairs.

"Thanks for dinner." Luna Grace and the Silverback smile out toward me when I get up to follow Dallas up the stairs.

Dallas is filling the sink up with warm water. I sit back watching him bathe our male. Once done and dried, he takes the clippers out of a drawer and shaves Chance's head where the finest hair is growing out. The pup does not like the vibration or the sound of it and starts screaming his displeasure out for the wolf inside me to bristle up her displeasure toward Dallas.

Taking a few steps toward me, he hands me the fresh-smelling infant so I can feed once again and rock him to a calming, deep sleep until the next feeding is needed. He might be only eight pounds, but this male rules with his iron fist with his constant needs that have to be met.

"Why did you shave his head? There wasn't even hardly any hair there," I ask while rubbing the head of my pup.

"It's my responsibility to shave all my males' heads until they can do it themselves. It's how we do things here. It's always been done," Dallas explains.

Once Chance is put down next to me in his crib, the need to rest is overwhelming. Getting into bed, Dallas follows behind me. Holding me in his arms until it's time to feed the crying pup again, only two hours between feedings does things to your mind when all you want is a full night's sleep. Dallas is helping out, changing him, bringing him to me.

This routine is night after night. For Dallas's part, he doesn't look too phased by the lack of sleep, where any chance I get, I need a nap during the day. Asking him once, he said his medical residency was way more demanding than his little buddy.

By the end of the week, we get invited to Caleb's house for dinner.

Coming up the drive, no longer are there dead limbs of trees littering the driveway. Everything has been cleaned up and trimmed down. It must look the way it has always been supposed to look. A strongly built house that holds life inside its walls. All the cracks in the driveway's cement have had the growing trees pulled out. Nothing is living in those spaces anymore.

There are no spider webs in the window, no dust or grime covering the glass. This house has been cleaned to a sparkling new.

The three of us stand at the front door of Dallas's old home. He's got Chance in his arms. I can hear the echoing of laughter from inside; the place feels lively.

"Are you ready to go inside?" My words are spoken to Dallas with concern. I can't imagine how hard this must be for him. He hasn't been here since her death.

"I'm ready, Rya." Knocking on the door, Caleb answers with a big welcome smile on his face.

He takes Chance from Dallas's arms, cradling him carefully. My wolf now feels very comfortable with him handling him.

The walls are painted fresh, new pictures up. Dallas is handing Caleb a present for his walls. It's a blown-up picture of Caleb in fur form tied to a post looking utterly shameful. My eyes watered when Dallas showed me the gift; I brought him a plant. It's a money tree, a representation of good fortune for the future.

There holds no past presence that prickles my skin or raises the hair on my arms. Nothing remains inside this home but what is here now. Turning to Dallas, he's looking at every corner, every wall; there is no sadness in his eyes. He's just looking at what Caleb has done with the place, his old place.

Looking at Dallas, his eyes find mine, and what I'm seeing is that I am his new place now.

CHAPTER 28

A Choice

Six months later

A fairy tale ending is what I have always wanted since I was a little pup, the prince on his white horse sweeping me off my feet, riding off into the sunset, happily ever after.

I'm not the Cinderella of my stories past.

I'm not perfect, I'm not a princess, but I am loved like a fairytale ending. He is my ending. He's not perfect, but for me, he is.

We have created our own fairytale, our own personal hand-holding walk into the sunset.

He's not a prince on a white horse, no knight in shining armor, but he is my end of the story.

My final page.

The beginning of my story was about love and security in my pup years. It's my summer years filled with abundance.

A harvest of a promised life.

A bountiful future.

As my pages turned one after the other, a darkness starts to descend over who I thought I was.

From light, there will be darkness.

Anguish, heartache, unbearable pain that I thought would be the rest of my story.

It taught me how hard love is, how hard I was to be loved by someone made just for me. Someone who didn't want to take a chance on me.

It showed me I was not special. This was my Autumn years.

The thinning of a soul, the decay of a life. Slowly eroding who I was, until I was just a shell that was breathing, just barely breathing.

As with life, my pages keep flipping, moving forward, my winter years filled with gut-wrenching sorrow. There is no love. Never will I love or be loved. That's what my story was teaching me in my winter years.

Love is nothing but a barren wasteland.

It made me think that I was unlovable, that I was wrong in some way.

He destroyed my soul. Somewhere along the way, the Moon took pity on me for some unknown reason and granted me with a gift.

My gift was never used. How could I when all I have ever known was that I am not good enough?

That what I have to offer someone was nothing anyone wanted.

I'm defective in some way.

Again my fairytale story keeps turning, spring arriving filled with fresh growth, new beginnings, and I meet him, my prince, but he's disguised. I never really gave him a true chance because I was blinded by my own history to really consider myself worthy enough. All those years of thinking myself unworthy, that love is a terrible thing, really destroyed my perspective on how things should be.

Every step of the way, my prince challenged me, made me feel things that I have never felt before.

Good and bad.

He was able to give me my firsts, breathe life back into me.

Without him, I would never have my beautiful Chance.

As the final page glares blank in my face, it's my choice to start a life that has been given to me. I just need to take that chance that I am making the right decision.

In my heart, I know that this is what I want, this is what I need, and this is just the beginning to my happy ending.

I walk down the path on my own, looking into the guests' eyes. My family comes into view, my father, mother, sisters, and their mates all present.

"I love you, Rya." My father's whispers hit my ears as my steps slightly falter. My mother has her emotions dripping out of her eyes.

Those are tears of great happiness.

The little female pups are looking at me like I'm a princess dressed up in red, made up just for this day. I think in their minds they want to look like me on their special day.

"A real princess," a little one whispers to her mother, pointing at me in awe.

It's the last time I will wear red. No more will I

show my availability. I'm completely taken.

Luna Grace has outdone herself with the planning, the decorations, the music.

Everything is magical…the final scene in the romance movies.

The tiki torches light our path, casting soft dancing shadows in the tree line. The moon creates a soft glimmering glow of light from her full body.

Even she is watching on.

All eyes are on us. The whole pack is gathered, including my family; they said they wouldn't miss this for the world.

Dallas is standing there, eyes only for me. They blaze with the intensity of his love.

The corner of his mouth trembles slightly, but he tries not to show it, standing strong and proud.

My iron.

We decided to have our mating ceremony where we will build our home together. He will do the outside, and I get to have the inside, a combination of visions.

He gives me a look, and I know exactly what he's thinking, not because I can read his mind yet, but because I know who he is.

His hands reach out to mine as I clasp them, entwining our fingers together.

Since he has marked me, I am the one to do all the talking. I am the one to show everyone gathered here that this is my choice to make.

His family takes the front row. They will witness it all.

Looking into his eyes, I begin.

"You are mine." I am the one to take a step

toward him. His breath is coming out faster, eyes dilating.

"You are my hope." Another little step. I can feel the heat of his body saturating into me. His fingers brushing over my knuckles.

I think I hear Luna Grace crying softly. I don't look because all I can focus on is Dallas.

"My love." Chests press against each other. Visible shakes of his body with the contact. He can't hide that the bond strumming so strong in his system that every night he has to mark me over and over again as we make love like new lovers over and over again.

"My light." I smile. No truer words have I spoken.

"My weakness." He wraps his arms around my waist, picking me up so I am slightly taller than him in just this minute.

Can he feel my heartbeat pounding in his chest? Because I feel his.

"My strength." I pull my face away from his slightly so he can see my teeth that will mark him. A shiver so faint that I almost miss it shifts his spine.

Putting my mouth on his neck, I pick the spot that will bear my love. It's a quick strike that takes him off guard slightly. It's a deep mark, a growl rumbling from my whole body as I lay my claim to him.

Somewhere deep inside me, I feel it, the tide of him rushing inside me, pushing out the hold that Clayton had with extreme force.

I can now start to see his layers, deep and

complex. This male is everything I think he is.

The bond between us is finally completed. A gasp from his mouth, now my body is on fire.

Volts of highly charged electricity pulsates between us, jumping the gap into each other's body. It stirs a deep ache inside me that only he can fill.

Shock waves.

The energy is alive between our bodies.

Soul touching.

With no hesitation, he grabs my face in his hands and kisses me with a passion that romance stories are made from. It's deep, powerful, full of his need for me.

Clapping and shouts of encouragement are heard, but they sound far away because in this moment all I can feel is him.

We feel complete.

We are our truest selves.

I love you. That's what he's saying to me inside my head, and I say it back.

I love you.

Out loud, he says, "Go, I'll find you. Give me a good chase, because when I find you…" He doesn't have to say anything else because I know what he wants to do when he catches me.

With a leap into the air, fur replaces flesh, and I run into the night for him to come after me.

It excites me to have my male chase me into the night.

I won't make it easy, I'll give him a good chase, but eventually, he will find me because that's who he is.

So begins the first pages of our romance book.

Standing at the top of the stairs looking down, it's funny how at certain times in your life you can take the stairs fast and furious, slow and thoughtful, you can trip and stumble, but in all of us, you still climb up them to get to the top.

Conversations fills the air with smart, challenging banter, the sea of voices all friendly and loving to one another.

Voices getting weaker, dying down as we approach.

A breakfast morning greets me full of pancakes, French toast with pure maple syrup, bacon, eggs, oatmeal with brown sugar and milk. Orange juice, tea, and coffee.

This is the Luna's morning love for her family, a feast of food.

Everyone's sitting at the heart of the home, and two chairs are saved for us to take our places at the family table.

Acknowledgements

The International Wildflower Pack: without you holding my hands every step of the way I'm not sure this would have been possible. *presses my cheek to yours*

About the Author

Rachelle Mills lives in Canada with her family and two dogs. She's a lover of all things that have to do with Nature and Wildlife.

Mills has won acclaim from readers for her fantastically realized paranormal werewolf universes, where alpha males fight tooth and claw and society – more often than not – is determined to make the path of true love as rocky and uncomfortable as possible.

Her rich, paranormal universe is packed with characters that frustrate and enthrall readers with an expert grasp of the complexities of the primal fight that werewolves have; their human, controlled side, and the vicious, ugly, and virtually untamable were-side which can leave a trail of destruction in its wake.

Mills' writing style is charged with emotion and richly descriptive, bringing the universe of her often-gritty stories into vivid life.

Facebook:
https://www.facebook.com/Rachelle-Mills-298700590732805/?ref=bookmarks

Twitter:
https://twitter.com/whiskeyqueenn?lang=en

Goodreads:
https://www.goodreads.com/author/show/14827762.Rachelle_Mills

Instagram:
https://www.instagram.com/whiskeyqueenn/

Join our Reader Group on Facebook and don't miss out on meeting our authors and entering epic giveaways!

Limitless Reading

Where reading a book
is your first step to becoming

limitless...

LIMITLESS PUBLISHING *Reader Group*

Join today! *"Where reading a book is your first step to becoming limitless..."*

https://www.facebook.com/groups/LimitlessReading/